GIRL in SCARLET HIJAB

Suresh U. Kumar is a professor, serial entrepreneur, start-up mentor, author and non-profit leader. Born in Kochi, India, he began his journey as a student political leader before embarking on a global career in the United States. Suresh co-founded his first venture in 1999, igniting his passion for leadership and innovation. He now serves as the Founder and CEO of R-Factor.AI, and a professor and Director of Innovation and Entrepreneurship at the New Jersey Institute of Technology. He continues his activism as the Co-Founder of Indian Americans for Harris and as the President of The Indus Entrepreneurs (TiE)—New Jersey Chapter.

An avid reader of historical fiction, Suresh resides in New Jersey with his family.

Visit https://authorsureshkumar.com/books/ to learn more about Suresh and join his newsletter.

You can also connect with him on:
LinkedIn: https://www.linkedin.com/in/drskumar/
Facebook: https://www.facebook.com/people/Author-Suresh-Kumar/61560862713931
Instagram: https://www.instagram.com/authorsureshkumar/
TikTok: https://www.tiktok.com/@authorsureshkumar

GIRL in SCARLET HIJAB

SURESH U. KUMAR

Published by
Rupa Publications India Pvt. Ltd 2024
7/16, Ansari Road, Daryaganj
New Delhi 110002

Sales centres:
Bengaluru Chennai
Hyderabad Jaipur Kathmandu
Kolkata Mumbai Prayagraj

Copyright © Suresh U. Kumar 2024
Map by Martin Lubikowski, ML Design, London
Illustrations by Rajesh Chirappadu, Kerala

This is a work of fiction. All situations, incidents, dialogue and characters, with the exception of some well-known historical and public figures mentioned in this novel, are products of the author's imagination and are not to be construed as real. They are not intended to depict actual events or people or to change the entirely fictional nature of the work. In all other respects, any resemblance to persons living or dead is entirely coincidental.

All rights reserved.

No part of this publication may be reproduced, transmitted or stored in a retrieval system, in any form or by any means, electronic, mechanical, photocopying, recording or otherwise, without the prior permission of the publisher.

P-ISBN: 978-93-6156-671-4
E-ISBN: 978-93-6156-866-4

First impression 2024

10 9 8 7 6 5 4 3 2 1

The moral right of the author has been asserted.

Printed in India

This book is sold subject to the condition that it shall not, by way of trade or otherwise, be lent, resold, hired out or otherwise circulated, without the publisher's prior consent, in any form of binding or cover other than that in which it is published.

I dedicate this novel—my humble attempt at telling a story about heroism rooted in love, not hatred—to honour the memories of the unknown freedom fighters all over the world, especially those who, when the hard-fought hour of triumph arrived, instead of sharing the spoils of victory, walked away from its enticing embrace.

This book is also dedicated to my family, whose lives and lessons made this story possible, and to Kochi, the enchanting city of my youth, which will always hold a special place in my heart.

*'If you want to see the brave, look at those who can forgive.
If you want to see the heroic, look at those who can love
in return for hatred.'*

—Bhagavad Gita

*'When the will defies fear, when duty throws
the gauntlet down to fate, when honour scorns to
compromise with death—that is heroism.'*

—Robert Green Ingersoll

Contents

Cast of Characters xi
Prologue xv

1. A Revolver Called Kali 3
2. The Man Who Could Have Been the Chief Minister 11
3. Under the Bamboo Grove 15
4. Monsoon Musings 22
5. The Azad Dasta 27
6. Rebel with a Cause 39
7. Of Wristwatches and Walking Sticks 43
8. Enemies Unseen 49
9. History Lessons 54
10. Crossroads on the Highway 60
11. The Legend of Jayaprakash Narayan 65
12. A Son's Promise 69
13. Conspiracy in the Garden 72
14. The Return of Mahabali 79
15. Two Confessions 85
16. Sons of Sailors 88
17. The Girl in Scarlet Hijab 97
18. The Protégé 104
19. New Beginnings 111
20. When an Old Lion Roars 115
21. A Shooting and a Killing 125
22. Race Against Time 131
23. The Commissioner's Dilemma 136
24. A Call to Action 142
25. The Press Briefing 153
26. Murali's Bold Gambit 157

27.	The Secret Manuscript	164
28.	The Price of Resistance	171
29.	A Glimmer of Hope	173
30.	The Tapestry Unfolds	183
31.	The Renaissance Man	188
32.	The Dark Horse	191
33.	A Visitor at Night	194
34.	The Commander's Plan	198
35.	Gathering Storm	213
36.	Hope Stirs	217
37.	The Blockade	220
38.	The Vigil	227
39.	Old Lady with the Flag	230
40.	The Manuscript Mystery	236
41.	Victory in the Streets	239
42.	A New Dawn	250
43.	The Nurse from Kashmir	263
44.	The Home Minister's Waterloo	270
45.	Secrets Revealed	274
46.	Scarlet Bonds	280
47.	A Night to Remember	287
48.	Kiss on the Kerala Express	293
49.	Last Rites	301
50.	The Governor's Offer	305
51.	Young Revolutionaries	315

Acknowledgements   322
Glossary   325
Author's Note   329

Cast of Characters

Rukhsana Mirza: A young girl who relocates to Cochin from Abu Dhabi for college and joins the Young Democratic Socialists of Kerala (YDSK) political movement.

T.K. Karunakaran (also called Vaikom Karnan/Karnan): A freedom fighter who joined India's freedom struggle under the mentorship of Jayaprakash Narayan. Post-independence, as an activist, writer and professor, Karnan became a key figure in Kerala's socialist movement.

Muralidhar Panicker (also called Murali): Vasudev's son who idolizes Karnan and is the general secretary of the YDSK.

Vasudev Panicker: A former sailor of the Royal Indian Navy, he served as a soldier in the Azad Hind Fauj, later joining the Azad Dasta, where he befriended Karnan.

Shiva Kumar (also called Shibu): Muralidhar's best friend and an important leader of the YDSK.

U.A. Velayudhan: Shibu's father and a former sailor in the Royal Indian Navy and then the Indian Navy.

Ashraf Ali: Sub-inspector of police (Cochin City) and a former student of Karnan.

Alex Kuriakose: Karnan's neighbour and helper.

Geethanjali Menon: Rukhsana's best friend.

P. Shivan: Member of the Legislative Assembly of Kerala and the leader of the YDSK.

Baby Velayudhan: Wife of Velayudhan.

Mallika Sukumaran: A Malayalam poet and social activist, who is also Geethanjali's aunt.

Sreelekha Sriram: Police Commissioner, Cochin.

Sashi Kumar and Suresh Kumar: Shibu's brothers.

Abdul Navaz: Head of the Kerala Taxi Drivers' Union.

Dr Joseph: Head of the cardiothoracic unit at the Medical Trust Hospital, Cochin.

Dr Pulikkan Verghese: Founder and managing director of the Medical Trust Hospital.

Hippie Jayan and Prakash: Friends of Shibu and Sashi, and members of the Vellaiparambil gang.

Thomas Alexander: Deputy Superintendent and head of the Home Minister's security detail.

Johnson: Head of the Cochin Auto Rickshaw Drivers Union.

K. Ramachandran: Home Minister of Kerala.

Ramesh Babu and Shah Navaz: Student leaders of the YDSK.

Vijaya Patwardhan: Member of the Azad Dasta and Jayaprakash Narayan's personal secretary.

HISTORICAL FIGURES

Jayaprakash Narayan: Indian revolutionary and freedom fighter, and leader of the Congress Socialist Party and the Azad Dasta.

S.K. Pottekkatt: Famous writer from Kerala and winner of the 1980 Jnanpith Award.

E.K. Nayanar: Freedom fighter and leader of the Communist Party of India (Marxist), who was the chief minister of Kerala from 26 March 1980 to 20 October 1981.

Jothi Venkatachalam: The governor of Kerala from 14 October 1977 to 26 October 1982.

Ram Manohar Lohia: Indian freedom fighter and socialist leader.

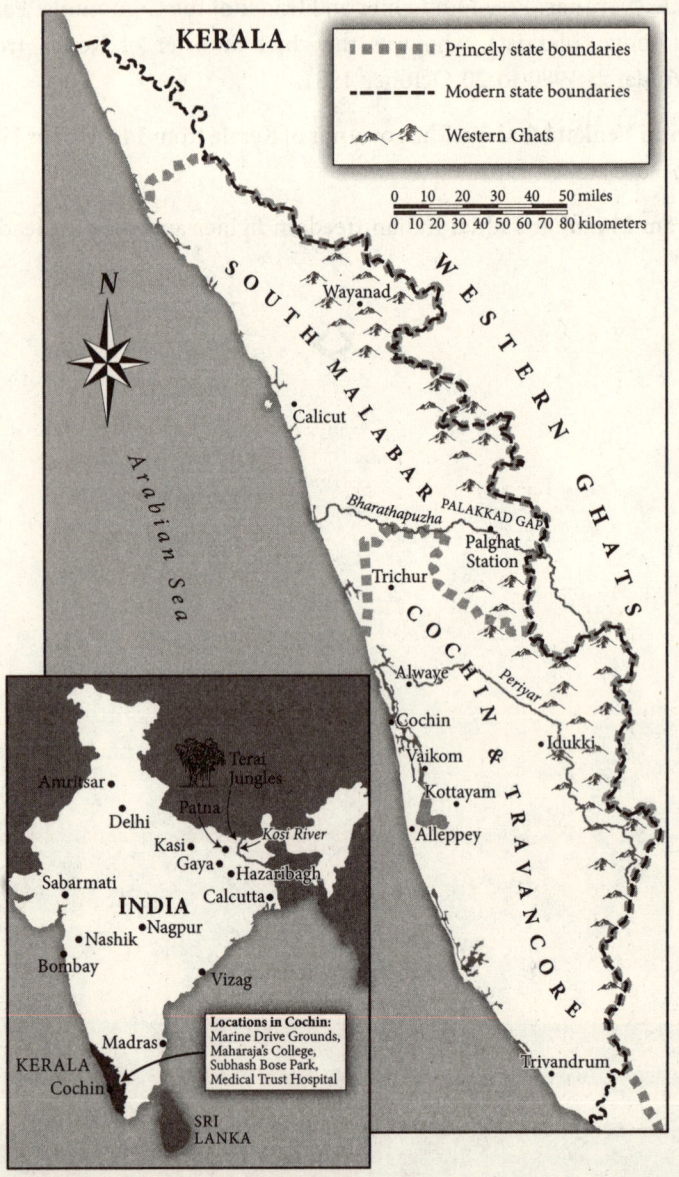

Prologue

Entry from Karnan's diary
10 November 1942, northern India

It has been five days since my last diary entry and a nerve-racking 48 hours since the jailbreak. Earlier today at the village tea shop, I was surprised to learn from a newspaper that the daring escape of Jayaprakash Narayan and five of his closest associates from the heavily guarded Hazaribagh Central Jail had made headlines, with the news spreading like wildfire all across India. It made me giddy because I consider Jayaprakash to be my elder brother (we address each other as 'bhai'). To avoid attracting attention, I had to hide my emotions.

Playing a small part in planning the jailbreak is the biggest blessing of my life. A blessing from whom, I wonder. After all, I have not prayed since leaving home almost 11 years ago in the middle of the night to join the Indian freedom struggle. Could it be my mother's daily prayers to Lord Shiva, our family deity, or the blessings of my late uncle T.K. Madhavan or those of his close friend and mentor, Mahatma Gandhi, whom I was fortunate to meet when I was 14?

Two days ago, as everyone celebrated Diwali, I took my assigned position in the shadows of the cluster of banyan trees behind the Hazaribagh Jail complex, disguised as a street-side fruit vendor. My task was to closely watch the jail gates and report any unusual activity by the police. Fortunately, other than the grinding sound of the wheels of the bullock carts ferrying people from their homes to the nearby temple and the occasional celebratory firecracker, the night was silent. I later learnt that our plan had gone exactly as we had hoped. My heart had skipped a beat when, at half past midnight, I saw a group of six people hurrying towards me. At the centre of the group, I spotted him. Unable to contain my excitement, I called out, 'Jayaprakash bhai,' and rushed forward to greet him. It had been a mistake.

Not knowing if I was a friend or foe, two of his men immediately tackled me. Thankfully, despite my disguise, Jayaprakash bhai had recognized my voice and ordered his men to set me free. 'Do not touch him. This is the young man from Travancore I told you about, the one who helped plan our escape. He has left everything behind—absolutely everything—to join our struggle,' bhai said.

One of the men, who I later learnt was the famous freedom fighter Suraj Narain Singh from Bihar, muttered 'Madrasi' under his breath. Apparently, he'd had a lot of pent-up anger stemming from long periods of solitary confinement. I felt the urge to correct his poor knowledge of the geography of South India. 'Did you not hear what bhai said? I am from Kerala, not Madras,' I told him. He smiled apologetically and released his hold on my arm.

Then, a miracle happened. Jayaprakash bhai extended his hand to help me stand up. He warmly embraced me, looked me in the eye and said, 'It feels so good to walk on the soil of my motherland as a free man. Thank you, little brother.' He turned to his comrades and told them, 'We are the leaders our people need in this hour of darkness. From this moment, our real work begins.'

My entire life's purpose had built up to this singular moment. I felt I had finally done something that mattered. I helped free six genuine heroes. Their leader, Jayaprakash Narayan, is as revered by the people of India as Mahatma Gandhi or Subhas Chandra Bose. A man who could help liberate India from the British. The 53 dhotis that I had helped get smuggled into the prison were tied together to form a long rope that the men used to scale the 17-foot prison walls. I was so overwhelmed by the gravity of the moment that tears poured down my face. The men seemed amused to see a grown man cry but bhai understood.

I quickly regained my composure and handed a local map with the escape routes marked to one of the men. After a brief huddle with the others, Suraj asked if I could scout the area and warn them of any lurking danger from the British collaborators. I was responsible for guiding them to the home of one of bhai's trusted Congress associates in the village of Gaya, in Bihar. The group was split into two, the one travelling with bhai moving at a slower pace due to his back pain.

I have constantly been on the move since then. I developed a simple routine: walk about five kilometres ahead of the group, scan the terrain and then turn back to report what I found. It is exhausting. No shelter. No rest. My sandals have holes in them, causing painful blisters on my feet. I have run out of money to buy food. All I have eaten for two days are the forest fruits I found on trees and a few mouthfuls of water from an abandoned village well.

Yet, I feel a sense of excitement, a strange exuberance I have not felt since the first time the British police arrested me. With the detention of all the senior leaders of the Indian National Congress (INC), including Mahatma Gandhi, Jawaharlal Nehru, Sarojini Naidu and thousands of freedom fighters across India on the eve of the Quit India movement, it had seemed like our fragile dream of independence from British rule was on its last legs. This jailbreak has completely restored my faith and confidence. Sometimes, facts can be stranger than fiction.

The day before I left my home, I sought the advice of my former schoolteacher, Balan master. He told me, 'Son, if you want to hear words of great wisdom, go to Mahatma Gandhi. If you want to see acts of great courage, meet Subhas Bose. If you want a combination of both, seek Jayaprakash Narayan. Whichever path you choose, you will be doing your duty for your motherland.' Good advice for sure, but how does a 21-year-old from a small village in Kerala choose from among three towering figures of the Indian freedom movement?

After several days of debate with my friend Muhammad Basheer, I chose Jayaprakash bhai. Young, bold, intelligent and unafraid to take a principled stand on complex issues, bhai represented the future of India. He had a clear vision for the social and economic upliftment of the common person. Bhai represented the middle ground between Gandhi's sometimes naive hope that the British would miraculously undergo a change of heart and Bose's rather hasty embrace of our enemy's enemies, Hitler's Germany and imperial Japan. I saw bhai for the first time in Bombay in the summer of 1932, speaking at a secret meeting of freedom fighters. A few months later, I befriended him when we were prisoners at the Nashik Central Jail. He became my mentor in a matter of hours and assumed the role of the elder brother I never had.

I wonder what the woman I love would have made of this development. I hope she will be proud when she learns about my involvement in bhai's escape. After years of toil, the jailbreak is the only reason I can show for leaving her without even a goodbye. I wish I could see her again, just one more time. But then, what would I tell her? Will she understand that my duty to my motherland had pulled me away? How can I explain that I had to answer bhai's summons in the middle of the night for a secret mission? So many questions, no good answers.

I love her just as much as I love my nation. This may not be good enough for her, but that does not alter the truth. Though I do find it hard to accept, my love for her might have been in conflict with my desire to live in a free country. What an impossible choice for a man to make! Perhaps I should ask bhai for personal advice, given that he has crossed the same bridge. But that will have to wait for another time. Right now, all I need is a few hours of rest. Who knows what new dangers the sunrise will bring.

I am lying on the cold, hard earth under the clear moonlit sky, keeping a watchful eye on the small shed about half a kilometre away where bhai and his comrades rest. With me are my constant companions—this old diary and a pen. To make up for the last few days, I have written a few extra pages tonight, using a smaller font to conserve the last few pages I have left.

Jayaprakash bhai could well be the last revolutionary walking free in India today. That alone is reason enough for hope. Even the stars above have a special glow tonight as if amused by the little games that mere mortals play here on earth. The future still looks uncertain, but I cannot help but think about the possibilities for my people. I am hungry, tired and lonely, but tonight, I shall dream once again. The fragrant dream of freedom!

PART ONE

PREMONITION AND CONSPIRACY

~1~
A Revolver Called Kali

8 October 1980
Kerala, India

'IS YOUR OLD REVOLVER, KALI, STILL WORKING? BRING HER with you, fully loaded.'

Vasu wondered if his friend had had a premonition. *Did he know that something terrible was going to happen? Or could it be that someone had threatened him? But then, who would dare to hurt a beloved freedom fighter—someone who had sacrificed all but his life for his country?*

The gusty winds blew raindrops into the half-open window of the car, splashing on Vasu's face and forcing him to squint as he bent to roll up the glass. Vasu sat in the passenger seat of the old white Ambassador. His son, Murali, who was driving, also rolled up his window. The heavy monsoon rains had drenched the roads, with the rainwater concealing the potholes that reappeared at the same time every year, as if on a fixed schedule.

The relentless raindrops created their own symphony on the car's roof as the tall coconut trees by the roadside, witnesses to countless monsoon rains, swayed playfully in the wind. Vasu's head bumped against the roof as the car hit a large pothole. *Thank God the road is familiar; else, driving in these conditions would be dangerous*, he thought. Vasu estimated it would take two hours to travel from their home in the coastal town of Alleppey in central Kerala to Vaikom, where his friend Karnan lived. The bad weather could add another hour.

Murali had been driving for about 25 minutes but had not

exchanged a single word with his father since leaving home. Vasu knew that Murali was unhappy with his parents' conservative views regarding his choice of life partner. The heated argument Murali had with his mother, Jalaja, that morning had all but guaranteed there would not be much of their usual small talk on politics during the drive.

Finally, Murali broke the silence. 'Could it be that Karnan *maamen* was just joking about the revolver?' he asked without looking at his father.

Vasu was pleased that his son, who had turned 24 a month ago, continued the childhood practice of addressing Karnan respectfully as 'maamen' or 'uncle', even though they were related neither by blood nor by marriage. It was no secret that Murali idolized Karnan and never missed an opportunity to discuss politics or history with him.

'Son, how long have I known your maamen?' Vasu asked.

'*Acha*, what kind of question is that?' Murali glanced at his father. 'Very long…I remember maamen always being around when I was a little boy.'

'That's right. I have known him since 1943—13 years before you were born,' Vasu replied. 'He does not joke about such matters. This is the first time he has asked me to carry my revolver. I was worried, so I made a few enquiries.'

'What did you find out?'

'What we already know. Your maamen is beloved by the people, but he has enemies in high places, even within his own party. The powerful party bosses hate him as much as the rank-and-file party workers love him. Some of them want to silence his voice of dissent. That is why he asked me to carry Kali.'

'Acha, do you really believe that they will try to hurt maamen tonight?' Murali's voice filled the car, cutting through the drumming rain. 'He shouldn't have let it come to this. He should have taken up the leadership of the Communist Party years ago when he had the chance. What good is it to have the support of the people when the real power rests with the party leaders?'

Vasu smiled at his son's off-the-cuff comment, which reflected their differing perspectives. The many heated conversations he and Karnan had had on this topic flashed through Vasu's mind. Maybe Murali had a valid argument; yet, as always, Vasu decided to stand by his friend.

'Son, you have the benefit of hindsight—something your maamen did not have,' he said calmly. 'Remember, Karnan is not your run-of-the-mill politician. At his very core, he remains a revolutionary. And revolutionaries, at least the true ones, never give up on the cause they hold dear, regardless of the temptations of power or who stands in their way. That is why they have powerful enemies.'

'You have always referred to maamen as a freedom fighter. Why did you call him a revolutionary now?' Murali was curious. Since receiving the call from Karnan to carry Kali to the rally, Vasu had been thinking about his friend's legacy. How would Karnan be remembered by the people of Kerala? 'Well, there are many good reasons,' Vasu explained. 'Let me ask you—do you understand the difference between a freedom fighter and a revolutionary?'

'I have not thought about that. But I think of revolutionaries as freedom fighters killed in action.'

Vasu smiled at the simplicity of his son's thoughts. He half-turned in his seat to face Murali. 'Son, do you think I am a freedom fighter?' he asked.

'Acha, that is the second strange question you have asked me today!' Murali replied, his voice raised. 'Yes, of course. That is why the government gives you a freedom fighter's pension. Why do you ask?'

Vasu shifted in his seat as if he had anticipated the response. 'Okay, let's assume the government is correct and I am indeed a freedom fighter. However, the fact remains that I am no revolutionary. You see, it is a lot easier to help free a nation from oppressive foreign rule, especially when the people are united. But to build a new social order and an economic structure seen by the people as just and fair, and doing that in the face of powerful conservative forces that oppose change, is an entirely different level of commitment and sacrifice.'

'By that measure, maamen certainly is a revolutionary.'

Vasu nodded and slapped his thigh with the open palm of his right hand in emphasis. 'Exactly!' he said. 'Where the freedom fighter's work ends, the work of the revolutionary starts. This makes a revolutionary—a good one like your maamen—a very rare, almost extinct, species.' Vasu was surprised by the clarity of his own words.

'Yes, that makes sense. You have told me about maamen's past. Years ago, I remember reading the diaries he gifted you.'

'Son, as you have read maamen's diaries, you know that his past and mine are intertwined. Given your interest in politics, I think it's the right time for you to learn more.'

Caught behind a slow-moving lorry overloaded with timber, Murali cursed softly under his breath and honked, but received no reaction from the lorry driver. He continued to follow at a slower pace.

'Acha, you said you first met maamen in 1943. How do you know so many details from before you met him?'

Despite their disagreement that morning, Vasu was pleased with Murali's eagerness to learn about Karnan. From the day they met, Karnan had been like an elder brother and mentor to Vasu, a bond that had only grown stronger with time and life's vicissitudes.

'Since our first meeting, we have been inseparable, like twins,' Vasu replied. 'You see, we were the only people from Kerala who had enrolled with the guerrilla fighters of the Azad Dasta. We lived and travelled together wherever our leader, Jayaprakash Narayan—you know him as JP—sent us. We had plenty of time to get to know each other.'

'What kinds of missions did JP send you on?'

'Oh, they were of all kinds, but primarily to organize and execute armed attacks on the trains carrying British weapons inland.'

'Armed attacks? Is that how you got your revolver?' Murali asked.

'No. Kali was a gift from Mohan saab, my commanding officer.'

'Do you mean General Mohan Singh, the leader of the Azad Hind Fauj?' Murali turned to his father, his mouth hanging wide open. 'Tell me about it.'

'Oh, yes, yes. After the Fauj disbanded in December 1942, Mohan saab came to see me at the harbour when I was leaving Malaya to return to India. The War had spread to Southeast Asia, and guards and spies were everywhere. He wore traditional clothes and a white turban, disguising himself as a member of a large Punjabi family. As I was getting ready to board the steamer, he found me and came up from behind—'

'I can't believe it! General Mohan Singh came to see you off!' Murali exclaimed. 'I don't recall you telling me you were close friends.'

'Mohan saab was fond of me because I had trained a large group of volunteers of the Fauj in the use of firearms, even some who had never held a gun before.' After a pause, Vasu continued, 'Coming back to that day—Mohan saab quietly slipped a heavy leather pouch into my backpack and whispered, "Vasudev bhai, we have had a fallout with the Japanese. They are looking all over for me. That's why the disguise. Inside this case is my service revolver. I call her Kali. She is as fierce as Durga Maa. Take her with you to India. She will protect you in times of grave danger. Never give up the fight to free our motherland. Jai Hind."' Vasu broke off as his voice cracked.

'What did you tell him?' Murali asked eagerly.

'I turned around, but before I could utter "Jai Hind", Mohan saab was gone. I could only see the tip of his white turban fluttering in the wind. That was the last I saw of him.'

Unable to contain his excitement, Murali pulled the car off the road. The brakes squealed as it came to an abrupt stop. He turned and looked at his father, his eyes wide.

'That is amazing! Kali—the fiercest form of the goddess Durga—a fitting name for a weapon that kills! What a priceless gift you received from one of the bravest sons of India. Kali is not just a gift; she is a memento!' Murali looked at his father with awe. 'No wonder you clean and polish her so often as if she is made of gold.'

'Kali is the only artefact I have kept from those days. I even taught your maamen how to use it, although I don't recall him ever hitting a target!' Vasu laughed. 'He always found refuge in the saying that the pen is mightier than the sword.'

The image of his uncle—whom he had known mainly as an author and an intellectual—wielding a gun brought a smile to Murali's face. Yet, he remained focused on what he'd just heard. 'Very interesting… So our old revolver belonged to a great hero. Did Kali protect you from danger?'

'Yes, on three different occasions, when I was on missions for the Azad Dasta. Each time, she helped us make a getaway following attacks on British weapons convoys.'

'Acha, you have evaded answering this question since the first time you showed me the revolver,' Murali said, a hint of anticipation in his voice. 'I want to know today—did you ever kill anyone with Kali?'

Their eyes met briefly as Vasu glanced at his son. *Murali is right. When he was a teenager, I avoided his repeated questions on the topic because, at that tender age, I did not want to expose him to my violent past. But he is all grown up, ready to handle the truth. Now, I owe him an honest answer.*

'When you are on the run, there is no time to find out. Let's just say that I never wasted a bullet. One of the men I shot was a young British police officer. Bang on his left knee,' Vasu said, a hint of pride in his voice.

'Oh, that must have hurt. Did you feel bad for him?'

'Yes. I confess I did,' Vasu replied with mock seriousness. After a brief pause, he added, 'But only for half a second.'

Murali leaned forward and burst out laughing, holding on to the steering wheel for support. 'I must tell this to *amma*. She thinks you cannot hurt a fly,' he said between fits of laughter. 'Oh, how I wish I were there with you and maamen.'

Vasu could sense a shift from the tense atmosphere that had hung in the car when they started the journey. *It is so good to hear my son laugh like he did as a little boy*. A year ago, Murali's mother had been worried that he would leave home, like a prodigal son, lost in the wilderness of politics. Thankfully, as the family astrologer had predicted, after the negative shadows cast by the movement of the planets passed, almost magically, Murali's fortunes had turned around.

Vasu mentally thanked his family deity, Lord Shiva. *Almost like a butterfly emerging from a caterpillar without going through the quiet pupa phase, Murali is now ready to bear the responsibilities and burdens of his family, friends and people*, he thought.

Murali reached down under his seat, grabbed the jute bag with the revolver wrapped in a towel and held it up. 'I am glad that we have Kali with us today. Who better to protect maamen tonight! All my fears are gone,' he said. 'Acha, can I keep Kali?'

Vasu smiled and nodded. 'Son, Kali has always been yours. She belongs to you just as she belongs to Mohan saab, or me, or, for that matter, anyone who fights injustice. I was merely her caretaker for a few years. I meant to hand her over to you when you were ready.'

'I am ready now.'

'I know you are. The fact is that you are a better marksman than I ever was.' Vasu paused. 'But not today, son. Not today. Too much is at stake.'

The smile left Murali's face. His knuckles turned pale as he tightly gripped the steering wheel. 'No, acha,' he shouted. 'I made a promise to amma that I would carry the revolver. You also agreed to it.'

Vasu spoke calmly. 'I know I did. But your amma is not aware of the danger we could face tonight. Son, I will have to carry Kali today, perhaps for one last time.'

Murali's voice further rose in frustration. 'Acha, you are no longer the carefree, gun-wielding young freedom fighter of the Azad Hind Fauj. You are 65. Your hands are not as steady and you have difficulty with your eyesight at night. Please let me carry Kali today,' he pleaded.

Vasu glared at his son. 'We can talk about this later. Keep your eyes on the road,' he said sternly. 'We have to get to maamen's home and take him to Cochin by 6.30 p.m.' Vasu paused for a few seconds, then added, 'The event tonight means a lot to him. He has a vital message for the youth of Kerala. We must make sure he delivers it and returns home safe.'

From the corner of his eye Vasu noticed Murali shake his head and wondered if his son was right. *Murali is a better marksman than me, but he has never been tested in a dangerous situation like this. Does he possess the calmness to handle an emergency without overreacting? Should I take a chance with him tonight?*

Vasu watched as Murali carefully placed the revolver back into the bag and slid it under the driver's seat. The uneasy silence that had accompanied them at the start of the journey returned to the confines of the car.

Girl in Scarlet Hijab

~2~

The Man Who Could Have Been the Chief Minister

INSIDE THE COCOON OF THE CAR, PAST AND PRESENT collided as Vasu and Murali, unable to suppress their anxiety, engaged each other in casual conversation. Facts and legends intertwined like the roots of an ancient banyan tree as they delved into Karnan's life and discussed its profound impact on theirs.

The rain had eased up considerably. Murali estimated that they were about 30 minutes from Karnan's home. Feeling drowsy, he slowed the car and stopped by a small roadside tea shop with a sign that read 'Murugan's Special Tea'. Father and son alighted from the car and walked into the shop for tea and some freshly cooked *pazham pori*.

Murali and Vasu sat on a wooden bench and watched as the tea maker poured boiling tea into a large metal jug and added hot milk. Lifting the metal jug over his head with a flourish, he poured the hot liquid from one vessel to the other a few times. He then transferred the bubbling hot tea into two small glass cups and served it with a plate of two pazham poris.

As they sipped tea, Vasu and Murali absorbed the echoes of political chatter from the table across from them, where two elderly men were engrossed in a lively discussion over the newspaper.

'Did you read what our home minister (HM) called Vaikom Karnan?' asked one man.

'Vaikom Karnan?' the other responded.

'I mean T.K. Karunakaran, the freedom fighter. Around here, we call him "Vaikom Karnan" as he was born in the nearby town of Vaikom,' the first man explained.

'Oh, I see. Of course, I have heard about Karnan. Who has not?' the second man said. 'The HM must have said something nasty; after all, they are old political rivals.'

'Well, the HM is a nasty son of a bitch for sure,' the first man replied, not bothering to hide his contempt. 'But he is no fool. The term he used for Karnan is "Lion in Winter", meaning someone with one foot in his grave. I must admit it was clever. He can wash his hands later, saying he had meant it as a compliment.'

The second man planted the palm of his right hand on his forehead. 'Oh Lord! It's a shame that the home minister of Kerala has nothing better to do than hurl curses at an old freedom fighter. It's shocking how low our politicians stoop,' he said.

'The HM is a street fighter, but I think this time he has picked a fight with the wrong man,' the first man said as he put down the newspaper. 'Did you know that if the dice had rolled a little differently, Vaikom Karnan would have been sitting in the chief minister's (CM) chair today?'

The second man shook his head. 'Just think about that! Had that happened, the HM would have been as obedient as a dog.'

The first man laughed. 'You have spoken the truth,' he said.

Sitting on the wooden bench beside each other, Vasu and Murali exchanged glances.

After paying the bill, father and son stepped out of the tea shop. The rain had stopped, providing the locals a much-needed reprieve to go about their daily chores.

Tension etched in the lines of his face, Vasu lit a cigarette, a silent signal of his disquiet. Curiosity about his father's thoughts on the tea shop conversation brimmed in Murali's eyes.

'Acha, is it true that maamen could have been the chief minister of Kerala?'

Vasu took a long drag of the cigarette and pursed his lips as he blew the smoke out. 'Well, it's a long story. If the choice was up to the people, I do not doubt that Karnan would have become the chief minister. However, in India, the chief ministers are not directly elected by the people but nominated by the party with the majority in the assembly. It is the party leaders who call the shots behind the scenes and Karnan had too many open disagreements with them.'

'Is that why the party leaders never considered maamen for the role of the chief minister?'

'It was one of several reasons,' Vasu said, glancing at his watch and taking a last puff of the cigarette. 'Let's go. We can talk in the car.'

Murali was quick to defend his idol. 'Maamen may be headstrong, but he is a saint compared to the politicians running the state today.'

'That is true,' Vasu said, crushing the cigarette stub with the tip of his sandal. 'What matters is that, to this day, he is idolized by the people whose lives he has changed for the better. To them, Karnan remains the quintessential rebel.'

'Murali, have you told maamen about your girl?' Vasu suddenly asked. The unexpected question shifted the focus and unlocked a door to personal matters again.

Murali threw up his hands. 'Acha, you keep forgetting! I have been wanting to tell him for a very long time. But amma told me not to. And you know why!' he said angrily, his loud voice startling a lady passing by.

'Calm down, Murali,' his father admonished. 'You don't have to raise your voice. Your amma's views have been influenced by her brother and his wife. Following tradition, they want to get their only daughter married to you,' Vasu said. 'Anyway, that was a few years ago. At that time, we thought your girl was just an infatuation that would pass.'

'Infatuation! I was the president of the college's Student Council. You should have trusted my judgement,' Murali complained. He looked around, leaned in and whispered, 'Acha, the truth is that amma feels Rukhsana is not *one of us*. Not good enough for her only son. That is what makes me angry!'

Vasu touched his son's shoulder. 'Murali, you are aware that your mother comes from a conservative Hindu family. This is not easy for her. I think you should discuss the matter with maamen today. I have known him for many years, and he is a man of great wisdom. I am sure he will give you good advice. Remember, if there is anyone who can change your mother's mind, it is your maamen.'

Murali thought for a few seconds before replying. 'Fine, I will do that today. But why did you bring this matter up now?'

'You know all about my friendship with Karnan. If he brings up the topic of your marriage today, which I think he might, I cannot hide anything,' Vasu explained.

After they got into the car, Vasu asked, 'By the way, you never told me when and how you first met Rukhsana.'

'Acha, you never asked,' Murali said. He turned the ignition and shifted the car to the first gear. 'It was on 15 August 1977… India's Independence Day.'

As Murali eased the car on to the highway, Vasu noticed a faint smile on his son's face.

Girl in Scarlet Hijab

~3~
Under the Bamboo Grove

August 1977
Maharaja's College, Cochin

THE EXCITEMENT ON THE COLLEGE CAMPUS HAD REMAINED high ever since the Student Council announced that Vaikom Karnan would be the keynote speaker for the annual student literary festival, which was held every year during the week following India's Independence Day. Although Murali, a final-year Bachelor of Arts (BA) student, was already popular due to his good looks and musical abilities, he could sense that the announcement had further elevated his status among students. Word spread quickly that he was related by blood to Vaikom Karnan. Murali, finding no harm in the rumour, chose not to correct it.

As the date of the event approached, Murali was invited to various student clubs and associations to speak or perform as part of the Independence Day celebrations. One was scheduled for 3.30 p.m. on 15 August—the 30th anniversary of India's independence from the British. Although a public holiday, as it fell on a Monday, the college's facilities manager granted the students special permission to have informal gatherings. The History and Political Science Club, a group of students interested in history and politics, had organized this particular event.

Murali was invited to sing the national anthem and deliver a speech to welcome nearly 200 new undergraduate students to the campus. The special guest for the event, Professor A.V. Polson, the well-liked former head of the History and Political Science department, spoke about the importance of studying history to understand and help shape contemporary politics.

Shiva Kumar, Murali's closest friend, who was called 'Shibu' by everyone, spoke next. The fiery leader of the Students' Federation of India (SFI) on campus, Shibu was the front-runner for the position of the president of the Student Council. Despite his quick temper and limited facility with Malayalam, he commanded a loyal following among the left-leaning students by virtue of his bold frontline leadership style. Wearing his trademark blue jeans and black T-shirt and speaking in halting Malayalam, Shibu reminded the attendees of the importance of keeping the country above politics. He lauded the role that the students of Maharaja's College had played in resisting the national Emergency imposed by the Government of India in 1975. He emphasized that the strength of a group was not merely in numbers but in the unity of its members.

Murali was the final speaker. Unlike Shibu, he was dressed in traditional clothes—a cream-coloured *mundu* with a red border and a white shirt with the sleeves rolled up. He spoke in flawless Malayalam, his speech laced with humour—light-hearted and effortless—an art he had learnt by watching his uncle speak at public events. Murali spoke of how his uncle, Vaikom Karnan, and Professor Polson had helped him gain deeper insights into India's history. Mentioning the names of his closest friends, Shibu and Geethanjali, Murali spoke movingly about the strong bond one could forge through shared personal experiences on a college campus.

To the surprise of the students gathered, instead of the current national anthem of India, Murali chose to sing the anthem of the Provisional Government of Free India that the Indian National Army (INA) had sung before India became independent. He told the audience that he had learnt the words of the song 'Subh, Sukh, Chain' from his father, who had served as a soldier in the INA. His soulful rendition received a standing ovation and requests for another song. Murali invited Geethanjali, a junior student who sang duets with him for campus events, to join him on stage. Together, they sang a romantic Hindi song, 'Kisi Raah Mein, Kisi Mod Par', from the film *Mere Humsafar*. Another round of rousing applause followed.

After the event, as Murali and Shibu walked to the bus stop, they were stopped by Geethanjali. She was with a group of six girls who had attended the event.

'Murali, my friends wanted me to tell you they loved your songs. Now that you have become the most wanted singer on the campus, we think you should run for the Student Council President,' Geethanjali said.

'Get out of here, Geetha,' Murali replied, smiling. 'I am not good at giving speeches. And besides, who has the time for politics?'

Geethanjali persisted. 'I am serious. You don't have to talk. Just sing and your voice will get all the votes of the girls in the college. Here, ask any of my friends.'

Shibu reacted first. 'I think you are just looking to butter Murali up to get more singing opportunities, Geetha.' He turned to the other girls. 'Do any of you agree with her?' he asked.

'Yes, yes, we do,' one girl chimed in. 'We pledge our votes to Murali.'

Shibu could not let the opportunity to embarrass his friend pass. 'Okay, let me ask it another way. Do any of you think Murali should NOT contest?'

There was a long silence.

'I do.' The soft yet confident voice came from a girl partially hidden behind Geethanjali. She had a serious expression on her face. Murali noticed that her large hazel eyes were framed by a scarlet-coloured hijab made of a soft cotton-like material, which was wrapped tightly around her head, covering her hair and neck. She was wearing a black salwar kameez, which covered her from neck to toe, exposing only her face, hands and feet, the deep red hue accentuating her pale skin. *Maybe she is a Muslim…but not all Muslim girls in Kerala wear a hijab. Perhaps she comes from a traditional family.* Murali felt strangely curious.

'Oh, I don't think you have met Rukhsana, my best friend,' Geethanjali introduced the girl. 'She's from Abu Dhabi and is a first-year BA student in History and Political Science. We live together at my aunt's house. She and my aunt Mallika talk about Indian history all night long; it puts me to sleep in seconds—no need for any sleeping pills!' she joked.

'Hello, Rukhsana. Welcome to the History and Political Science Club.' Murali masked his nervousness with a smile. 'I was not aware that history students can also foretell the future,' he said in an attempt to sound clever.

The girls giggled. Rukhsana looked down at her feet.

This is the first time any student has expressed the opinion that I should not contest in the college elections. 'Are you one of those bookworms who don't like mixing studies and politics?' Murali asked.

Rukhsana looked up, smiled, and spoke softly, 'I don't mean to sound negative, but I think that as students, we should focus on our education and not get distracted by politics. There is so much to learn and discover in our field of study.'

Though impressed by Rukhsana's words, Murali was unwilling to back off. 'Don't you think it's also important for students to be actively involved in shaping their future? As Professor Polson explained today, politics affects everyone, not just those who participate in it—'

Shibu interjected, 'Look, Rukhsana, let's stick to the main question of the day. Do you really think Murali will not make a good president of the Student Council?'

Rukhsana smiled shyly, aware that she had fallen into the trap laid by Shibu. She hesitated, adjusting her hijab nervously before replying. 'It's not that. When a man has many talents, I think he should do what his heart says,' she said, stepping out from behind

Geethanjali to face Murali. 'Tell me, Murali, does your heart say politics or music?'

'Oh. That is an easy question. It's been music for a very long time,' Murali replied. 'But Shibu has been after me to join his political party. What if my heart changes to politics in the future?'

'If that were to happen, you should follow your heart,' Rukhsana explained. 'It's not a good idea to resist your heart's desires.'

'I see. I love the idea of following one's heart. You have given me something to think about. Thank you, Rukhsana,' Murali said as their eyes met.

Murali and his friends walked with the girls to the bus stop outside the campus. Murali was intrigued by Rukhsana and the aura of mystery surrounding her, accentuated by her shy demeanour and hijab. Her slight accent while speaking Malayalam and her unique perspective on things captured Murali's attention, but he suppressed his natural desire to talk to her to avoid appearing too eager.

∞

The following day, Murali found Geethanjali alone and took the opportunity to ask her about Rukhsana. Geethanjali confirmed that although not a strictly practising Muslim, Rukhsana wore a hijab when attending college and public events. She had a love for history, books and literature. She also took credit for introducing Rukhsana to new interests—painting henna tattoos on her arms, and Malayalam films—things that neither of them had had the chance to explore when they lived in Abu Dhabi.

Geethanjali informed Murali that Rukhsana was eager to attend his uncle's upcoming talk. Since the event was already sold out, she asked if he could help secure a ticket for Rukhsana. The same day, Murali spoke to Shibu, who volunteered to give up his ticket. Murali knew it was a major sacrifice as Shibu was a big fan of Karnan. Tucking it into an envelope along with a handwritten note, Murali met Geethanjali after class at the bus stop to hand it over.

∞

On the day of the event, Rukhsana sat with Geethanjali and a group of Murali's friends. Torn between wanting to be with his uncle and sitting by Rukhsana's side, Murali finally chose the former. *Perhaps she will like that I am with maamen, someone she admires.* During the event, Murali frequently glanced at Rukhsana from the side of the stage, only to see her focused on scribbling on a notepad. He was a little disappointed that Rukhsana did not ask questions during the lengthy Q&A session.

The following day, Geethanjali handed Murali a sealed envelope. Inside was a handwritten 'thank you' note from Rukhsana—

Dear Murali,

I don't know how to express my heartfelt gratitude for arranging the ticket. Your uncle is a great man. I found his talk fascinating; it felt like he was directly speaking to me. I hope to meet him in person one day. Till then, please let me remain his secret admirer.

Warm regards,
Rukh

P.S: Do you think we can be friends? If you would like to meet during lunch break, I will be at Subhash Bose Park, under the largest grove of bamboo trees.

As soon as the lunch bell rang, Murali came up with an excuse to leave his friends and rushed across campus to the park. He saw several bamboo groves all over the park but found no one around. *Which bamboo grove?*

After a frantic search that felt like an eternity, Murali spotted the deep reddish colour of Rukhsana's hijab. She was sitting on a bench by herself, reading a book under a giant grove of bamboo trees. Upon seeing Murali, Rukhsana put down her book, tucked away a strand of hair that had escaped her hijab and smiled nervously. As he came closer, Murali noticed her hands, which had fading henna tattoos in a leaflike design, and the fine Indian artwork on her hijab. Heart beating fast, he sat down beside Rukhsana and nervously complimented the colour of her hijab. Rukhsana's cheeks turned pink as she thanked Murali and promised to tell him the story behind the non-traditional colour choice some day.

They talked for hours about college, books, family and friends, missing the rest of their classes for the day. Rukhsana laughed at Murali's comment that henceforth, 15 August, the Indian Independence Day, would have a new meaning for both of them. She reminded him of their different faiths and suggested that it would be best to remain friends. Not wanting to scare her away and feeling a strong desire to meet her again surging in his heart, Murali agreed.

~4~

Monsoon Musings

8 October 1980
Kerala, India

THE RAIN HAD PICKED UP AGAIN. WATER WAS EVERYWHERE, more in the line of sight than on the land, but Vasu had come to like the rainy season. Having grown up in different cities across northern India, where his father served in the British Indian Army, Vasu hadn't known much about Kerala's monsoons until he moved back to the state as an adult. It was after their marriage that his wife educated him on the topic.

Jalaja explained that Kerala had two monsoon seasons. The northeast monsoon, which was underway now, was less welcomed by the locals than the first, the southwest monsoon, which arrived in June, bringing immediate relief from the hot summer months of April and May. By the time the second monsoon, called *Thulavarsham* by locals, arrived in the Malayalam month of *Thulam*, October according to the English calendar, the people would have had enough of the rains. Regardless, the rains in Kerala were so predictable that one could set the calendar by the ebbs and flows of the monsoon seasons.

Earlier that day, Vasu had used his auto-mechanic skills to get the car's stalled engine running again. He loved few things more than driving in his faithful old car, but this time, he had been forced to let Murali take the wheel. The previous morning, Vasu had climbed into the attic to retrieve his old revolver from the wooden chest. When Jalaja saw him, she demanded to know why. Upon learning about Karnan's unusual request, she sensed danger and insisted that Murali accompany his father. She made Murali promise to drive the car and carry the revolver, wrapped in a towel and placed inside a jute bag, after ensuring that they would only use the weapon as a last resort. Murali had readily accepted the responsibility and changed his plans to fulfil his mother's request.

Today, the eighth day of October, was special for another reason—Karnan's 70th birthday. Vasu realized his friend might not even remember it since he lived alone. Due to the trip to Cochin, their usual birthday routine—a relaxing canoe ride along the backwaters of Alleppey followed by a quiet evening on the beach near Vasu's home, enjoying a bottle of rum while talking about their younger days—had to be postponed.

Even though Karnan might have forgotten his birthday, he had reminded Vasu during their call the previous day that 8 October was the death anniversary of their mentor, Jayaprakash Narayan. *Had Karnan accepted the invitation because Murali, the organization's general secretary, had made a personal request? Or did he want to use JP's first death anniversary as a call to action for the students?* Vasu wondered if Karnan had a plan brewing in his mind.

As they drove, Vasu couldn't shake off the feeling of unease. He couldn't help but wonder what awaited them at the conference. Despite the fear, he was determined to stand by Karnan, no matter the circumstances. It crossed his mind that Karnan had not accepted an invitation to speak at a public event for almost two years because of his failing health. Yet, he retained his influence, especially among the youth, farmers, and daily wage workers, through his monthly opinion column in the newspaper *Deshabhimani*.

The call from his friend kept replaying in Vasu's head. *Karnan asking for help is not unusual; he has often called on me for personal or confidential matters. I am happy that Karnan retains the trust he always had in me. However, this time, the nature of Karnan's request was highly unusual.*

Murali's voice interrupted Vasu's musings. 'Acha, I was thinking about the conversation we overheard at the tea shop. Was maamen upset about being denied the chief minister's position?'

Vasu smiled. 'No. Not at all. You see, just like his mentor, Jayaprakash Narayan, Karnan was never enamoured by position or power. Both men believed they could do more good by staying out of power and keeping a close watch on those who wielded it.'

'But that belief only played into the hands of the party leaders. Didn't it?' Murali asked, concerned. 'No wonder they continued to sideline him.'

'You are correct. Yet, because of the widespread support among the people, his name kept coming up as a candidate for the chief minister well into the 1960s and 1970s. Every time, the party leaders found a new excuse to deny him the most important role, even though they had no choice but to publicly acknowledge his courage and integrity.'

A smile appeared on Vasu's face as he recalled the many phone calls he had received over the years from political leaders to get Karnan to endorse their policy positions. Little did they know that Karnan had learnt from and taken to heart the style, substance and values of his mentor, Jayaprakash Narayan.

Murali turned to face his father. 'Acha, why did maamen allow the party bosses to decide his future?'

'What happened was that fate and the reality of communal politics intervened. The newly formed Left Front repeatedly voted to maintain the status quo. They backed the Communist Party stalwart, E.M.S. Namboodiripad, an older, mild-mannered man and perhaps a consummate insider, as the chief minister in 1957 and 1967, and then C. Achutha Menon in 1969 and 1970. By that time, Karnan had given up an active role in politics.'

'You said there were other reasons the party leaders were angry with maamen.'

'It's a little complicated. To people uninitiated in politics, the official party line—that Karnan lacked state-level governance experience—seemed reasonable enough. After all, he was just 46 years old then, young by political standards, and had lived outside Kerala for most of his adult life. But to those who knew the inner workings of things, the writing on the wall was as clear as daylight. Do you know why?'

'Was it his drinking?' Murali asked.

'No, no. Karnan's drinking became a habit many years later. You see, Karnan had multiple strikes against him. Unlike most politicians, he had not built a personal political network based on patronage or a vote bank. To make matters worse, perhaps because he had spent so many years fighting against powerful government systems, he was never afraid to speak the truth, often to his detriment. Many of the left-leaning leaders saw Karnan's public criticism of the human rights violations by the Soviet Union as a betrayal of their cause.'

'I can see why the party leaders considered maamen to be a troublemaker, something similar to MLA Shivan now,' Murali commented.

'Oh yes!' Vasu smiled. '"Troublemaker" is a fitting word to describe your uncle back then, maybe even now. However, and this is important for you to understand, the last nail in his coffin was that he belonged to the socially backward Ezhava community, which did not carry the political support of the affluent and powerful Nair community.'

Murali tilted his head and furrowed his eyebrows. 'Strange! I would have imagined that after the success of the Vaikom Satyagraha, things would have improved on the caste front.'

Vasu shook his head. 'Yes, I know it is hard to believe that in 1957, some 20 years after the temple entry proclamation by the maharaja of Travancore, which opened the doors of all temples to Hindus of all castes, the high-minded progressive politicians of Kerala were still not immune to the caste-based prejudices.'

'The words of the men at the tea shop now make sense. I can

see why maamen has powerful enemies,' Murali said after Vasu had finished speaking. After a pause, Murali added, 'Acha, I noticed something interesting in maamen's diary notes describing the first time he met you.'

'What is it?' Vasu asked.

'It is the longest entry for any single day in maamen's diary. Perhaps even with the brief meeting, he sensed a special friendship. Do you remember your first meeting with maamen?'

Surprised at the astute observation, Vasu glanced at his son. 'How can I forget! It was March 1943, at the camp JP had set up to train guerrilla fighters. It was called the Azad Dasta. It indeed was a very special day for both of us,' he said.

'Azad Dasta!' Murali repeated. 'The freedom brigade; quite an apt name.'

~5~
The Azad Dasta

March 1943
Terai jungles, India–Nepal border

'SAAB, IS YOUR NAME KARAN?' A SHORT, STOCKY MAN IN HIS 60s, wearing an ill-fitting green paramilitary uniform, asked in Hindi with a heavy Nepalese accent.

The question was directed at a man sitting on the rock bed by the riverbank, half-naked, preparing to enter the calm waters for a swim. He looked young, perhaps in his early 30s, with long black hair and a closely cropped beard. Squinting in the sun that was now directly over his head, he replied, 'It's Karnan, not Karan. What is the matter?'

'Sorry, saab. I am still learning how to say the names correctly. I am Hira Singh, the new security guard of the camp. Jayaprakash saab wants to meet you.'

'Okay. I am going to take a swim now. I will be there in about 30 minutes.'

The guard hesitated. 'Saab, he wants to meet you immediately. He instructed me to bring you into the meeting he is in now. It is most urgent.'

'Meeting with whom?'

'Ram Manohar Lohia saab and the madam who arrived yesterday.'

'At the headquarters?'

'Yes, saab. Please follow me.' The guard turned and started to walk briskly on the narrow footpath that led away from the river and into the thick jungles.

Karnan picked up his clothes and hurried after Hira. He had arrived at the camp a week ago and knew most of the people there, so he wondered who the new lady was. *Perhaps a journalist seeking to interview bhai? Not surprising.* Karnan's mind went over the recent developments in the Indian freedom struggle.

In an unprecedented move before and after the Quit India movement declared by Mahatma Gandhi in August 1942, the British arrested and jailed most senior leaders of the INC. With Subhas Chandra Bose leaving the country, the mantle of leadership had fallen on younger leaders like Jayaprakash bhai and Ram Manohar. Following Jayaprakash bhai's daring escape from Hazaribagh Central Jail, the revolutionary zeal of the nation had been reignited. Almost overnight, Jayaprakash and Ram had become the focus of the national media.

With a dozen long strides, Karnan caught up with the guard. He spoke in broken Hindi sprinkled with English words. 'Hira Singh, may I practise my Hindi with you? Everyone here speaks Hindi, so I need to learn fast. Tell me, are you from here? How did you hear about this camp?'

Hira took a few seconds to understand Karnan's mix of Hindi and English. 'No, saab, I am from Kathmandu. I retired from the Nepal Army a few years ago but had to take up this job due to financial trouble. My wife is from the nearby town of Hanuman Nagar. Where are you from?'

'Where am I from?' Karnan repeated, trying to find the right words in Hindi. 'I am confused myself, as I have been all over India for the past 12 years—Madras, Bombay, Nashik, Calcutta—I have lost count. I am originally from Kerala.'

'Oh, near Madras. That is so far away. That explains your difficulty with Hindi!' said Hira. 'Have you known Jayaprakash saab for a long time?'

'How long have I known Jayaprakash saab?' Karnan echoed, his mind perusing through his limited vocabulary of Hindi words.

'Long enough, and I'm close enough to call him bhai. I first met him inside Nashik Jail in 1932. The police had arrested me for organizing protests against the British—a minor offence—but I had a letter from my uncle addressed to bhai in my pocket, so they took me in for questioning and let me go after a few weeks. Bhai and Ram Manohar saab were the big fish the British wanted. Since then, I have been following him all over India.'

'Oh my! You met Jayaprakash saab in jail?' Hira exclaimed. 'I guess it is a good place to meet great leaders, as they have nowhere else to go.'

Karnan laughed. 'I guess you are right. Had it not been for Nashik Jail, I probably would never have met JP in person, and I would not be walking with you today.'

'It's destiny, saab,' Hira mused. 'You have a very close relationship with Jayaprakash saab. No wonder he always asks us if we have served you food on time. If you don't mind me asking, when did you first get involved with the Indian freedom struggle?'

'In March 1925, when Mahatma Gandhi visited my village to lead a Satyagraha. My uncle, a Congress leader in Kerala, took me to meet Gandhiji after his morning prayer session. That's when my journey began.'

'Good Lord! You met Mahatma Gandhi?' Hira shouted.

'Yes, Hira Singh. As you said, it's destiny. I just happened to be at the right place at the right time.'

The men emerged from the darkness of the forest to a clearing where the Kosi River curved, creating a large sandbank. They crossed the river, stepping carefully from rock to rock. As Karnan splashed the cool water on his face, Hira's question lingered in his mind. How did he get involved with the Indian freedom struggle? It had all happened so fast that the details were a blur. His maternal uncle, T.K. Madhavan, whom he called *ammavan*, had introduced him to political activism at a very early age. Karnan especially enjoyed stories about the famous Indian revolutionaries operating against the British in North India, like Bhagat Singh and Chandrashekhar Azad.

Karnan recalled that in 1924, when he turned 14, ammavan had taken him to protest against the rules that prohibited temple entry for lower-caste Hindus, despite Karnan's mother's objections. Ammavan led the protests, challenging temple authorities and the police by entering the restricted roads that led to the temple. The demonstrations continued for several months, giving Karnan ample opportunity to listen to the many arguments and counterarguments among the protest leaders. Karnan's young mind struggled to understand how squabbles between fellow Indians could help the fight against the British rulers.

The answer came in March 1925, when Mahatma Gandhi visited the sleepy town of Vaikom to show his support for the protests. By listening to the Mahatma's daily talks following morning prayers, Karnan understood a simple fact—for the fight for freedom against foreign rule to succeed, people across India had to be genuinely united, with equal rights and opportunities. His confusion dissipated when Mahatma Gandhi quoted the great American President Abraham Lincoln, stating, 'A house divided cannot stand.'

Hira's voice interrupted Karnan's musings. 'They must be waiting for us at the headquarters. Let's hurry,' Hira urged as they re-entered the forest on the other side of the river. 'Be careful. There are leeches in this forest. Let me walk ahead so you don't touch the plants.'

∞

The term 'headquarters' was somewhat of a misnomer; it referred to a hut made of wood and baked mud, larger and stronger than the other huts in the camp. Located on a hillock on the banks of the Kosi River, it provided a good view of people approaching from all sides. Despite its rather pedestrian looks, the recruits who had joined the Azad Dasta found the headquarters special because of the daredevils who occupied it.

Karnan saw Jayaprakash Narayan, Ram Manohar Lohia and a tall, slender woman with sharp features sitting on a carpet outside the hut, engrossed in conversation. As the two men approached, Jayaprakash waved to Karnan, gesturing for him to join them.

'Karnan, you already know Ram very well. I want you to meet Vijaya,' JP said. 'She is Achyut Patwardhan's sister and has come all the way from Bombay to join the Azad Dasta. She will work as my personal assistant from today.' Jayaprakash turned towards Vijaya. 'Vijaya, this is Karnan, an excellent thinker and writer who handles most of our communication requirements. We first met at Nashik Central Jail, where he proved to be the most eager learner at my daily book review meetings. He knows more about the way my mind works than I do myself. Isn't that right, Ram?'

'Very true,' Ram Manohar agreed. 'Karnan learnt a lot in the few weeks he spent with us in jail.'

'Yes, I did. Much more than in school and college combined, thanks to the both of you,' Karnan said. He then greeted Vijaya with folded hands and spoke in halting Hindi. 'Madam, welcome to our camp. I met your brother in Bombay. He is a great orator and an inspiration to all of us.'

The lady smiled, nodding in acknowledgement. 'Namaste. You can call me Vijaya. Jayaprakashji informed me that you helped organize his escape from Hazaribagh Jail. Looks like you have been very busy.' She paused and smiled, 'Karnan sounds like a North Indian name, but from your accent I gather you are from South India?'

'Yes. I am from Kerala. My real name is T.K. Karunakaran.'

'Oh, I see. Now that makes sense. Did you modify your name when you came to North India?'

'No, madam. The name change happened when I was a boy—'

'Oh, Vijaya, did JP tell you who changed Karnan's name? Can

you take a guess?' Ram Manohar Lohia interrupted.

'Well, must have been someone from the north'—Vijaya's face lit up with a gentle smile—'since we cannot properly pronounce most South Indian names.'

'Good guess, Vijaya!' Jayaprakash said. 'But actually, he hails from Sabarmati Ashram in Gujarat, technically in western India.'

'Oh my Lord! Mahatma Gandhi changed Karunakaran's name to Karnan?' Vijaya exclaimed, turning to Karnan. 'I would love to hear all about it.'

'Well, madam, it happened in 1925 when I was 14. On the personal request of my uncle, T.K. Madhavan, a Congress party leader, Bapuji visited Vaikom, my little village in Kerala. One day, my uncle took me to meet him in person. Madhav Desai, Bapuji's personal secretary, ushered me into the room to meet the great man.'

'Then what happened?' Vijaya asked, her curiosity evident.

'Bapuji put on his eyeglasses and peered at me over the rim.' Karnan lowered his head, looked up, and mimicked Gandhi's voice and facial expression. '"Young man, Madhav tells me you are TK's nephew and the youngest satyagrahi here. That makes you the most important person to me. What is your name?" When I answered with my full name, "Thekkanveetil Keshavan Karunakaran", a look of concern crossed Bapuji's face. He walked up to me, placed his hand on my head and said, "Beta, I know what the burden of having a long name is like for a young man. Let's change that today." Bapuji thought for a moment and then asked, "*Kya main aapko Karnan bulaoon?*" (Can I call you Karnan?)'

'What did you say?' Vijaya asked eagerly.

'Well, back then, I did not speak a single word of Hindi, so I was speechless. Fortunately, my uncle, who was standing right behind me, stepped forward and loudly proclaimed that henceforth, my name would be Karnan.' He paused to let Vijaya's laughter subside before continuing. 'Later, my uncle explained to me that when someone as great as Mahatma Gandhi gives you a name, you don't dare change it. And that's how, in just two seconds, T.K. Karunakaran became Karnan.'

'That's such a sweet story,' Vijaya said, clapping her hands. 'So, we have Gandhiji to thank for making our lives a little easier. Karnan, you are a natural storyteller. I would love to hear your Hazaribagh story some other time. Have you written about it?'

'Not yet. I have been on the move since then, but I document my experiences and thoughts in my personal diary every day. Some day, after all this is over and India is free, I will return to Vaikom and write the story of Hazaribagh—'

'That's wonderful, Karnan,' Jayaprakash interjected. 'Writing is a powerful tool for social change. We must continue to educate the masses, and your writings can play a big role in that. Make sure you don't lose that diary; it is an important historical document. I am curious, what will you title the story?'

'Yes, bhai. I always keep my diaries with me,' Karnan said with pride. 'I have not thought of a title yet, but what do you think about "Hazaribagh Jail Diaries", with the subtitle "53 Dhotis that Saved the Indian Freedom Struggle"?'

Jayaprakash laughed. 'That is indeed a very appropriate title, Karnan. I pray that day comes soon. I am glad you have not forgotten about the 53 dhotis. Without the strong double-layer dhotis you helped smuggle into the jail, we would not have been able to scale the tall prison walls and escape undetected.'

'Of course, bhai. Along with you and the five others who escaped with you, the dhotis will surely be important characters in the story.'

Jayaprakash laughed again and everyone joined in. After the laughter had subsided, Jayaprakash addressed the group.

'Now that the introductions are complete, let's focus on the tasks at hand.' Jayaprakash turned to Vijaya. 'Karnan has been helping Ram and I draft a manifesto for the Congress Socialist

Party. I want you to work with them to incorporate my views from my handwritten notes.'

Vijaya, who had been taking notes, looked up and nodded.

Jayaprakash then turned to Karnan. 'I'd like you to lead the planning for an all-India Congress Socialist Party conference in the next three or four months. We should invite one representative from each state to attend. Ram will introduce you to all the left-leaning Congress leaders at the state level. We should also coordinate with the leaders of the Congress. Any questions?'

'I will get started on this right away,' Karnan replied, trying to contain his excitement at the unexpected escalation of his responsibilities. 'Is there anything else you want me to do?'

JP leaned in towards Karnan. 'Yes, there is a rather sensitive matter that we need your help with.'

'What is it, bhai?'

As was his habit when discussing important matters with Karnan, Jayaprakash switched to English. 'We have a new volunteer trainer who reported to the camp last night. He briefly served with the British Indian Navy and then joined the Azad Hind Fauj. He says he reported directly to General Mohan Singh, the founder of the Fauj. He also boasts of expertise in firearms and making explosives from commonly available materials. He will be an excellent candidate to help train our recruits in guerrilla warfare tactics.'

'That is good news. What is the problem?' Karnan asked.

Ram Manohar, who had been silently listening, leaned forward. 'Karnan, we like this man, but we are suspicious of his background; it is too good to be true.'

'What makes you suspicious?'

'Think about it. What are the odds that someone with exactly the skills and experience we need just happens to walk into our camp? It is no secret that the British have been trying to infiltrate our ranks and are pressuring the Nepalese government. We need to be very cautious about whom we recruit. One mistake and we could end up in jail again.'

'I see,' Karnan said, rubbing his chin thoughtfully. 'Isn't Nityanand Singh, being a former member of the Azad Hind Fauj, the right person on our team to verify his background?'

'Good thinking, Karnan. We did talk to him,' Ram Manohar said. 'He informed us that with the World War spilling into Asia, the entire Fauj leadership has gone underground; we have not been able to contact General Mohan Singh or any other senior member of his team.'

'I am still unclear about how to help with this situation.' Karnan looked puzzled.

'Let me explain,' Jayaprakash said. 'The newcomer's name is Vasudev Panicker. Like you, he hails from Kerala and has family there. We feel the only viable option is for you to go to Kerala and conduct a background check on him.'

'But bhai, I am working on many time-sensitive projects—'

'Yes, we know. But this is a higher priority. We will arrange for your travel. If you agree, I would like you to meet Vasudev immediately. You can decide if you want him to accompany you to Kerala. I think meeting his parents under some pretext would be a good idea. I don't feel comfortable having him around the camp until we are sure about him.'

Jayaprakash waved to Hira Singh, who came running. 'Hira, can you ask Vasudev to come meet me immediately? He should be with Suraj.'

As Hira left, Jayaprakash stood up and tapped Karnan on the shoulder. 'Karnan, come walk with me.' Karnan followed JP as he walked towards the edge of the river.

In a low voice, Jayaprakash said, 'Listen, I have heard from my friends in Kerala that your mother had a stroke and is in hospital. Her condition is critical. That is mainly why I want you to travel to Kerala—to be with her for a few days.'

The Azad Dasta

Tears welled up in Karnan's eyes as a thousand thoughts flooded his mind. He knew his mother was unwell but had not been aware that she'd been hospitalized. Guilt washed over him for leaving home without bidding her goodbye. His heart pounded in his chest as a slow rage directed at himself began to build, suffocating him. His mother was a devotee of Lord Shiva—why had the Lord not protected her?

Karnan felt a comforting hand on his shoulder. 'Freedom fighters have mothers, too. Karnan bhai, what is her name?' Jayaprakash asked.

Wiping away his tears, Karnan muttered, 'Meenakshi...her name is Thalayolaprambil Meenakshi.'

'Meenakshi,' Jayaprakash repeated softly. 'Named after the queen of Madurai...such a beautiful name.'

Karnan wiped a tear from his face and composed himself. 'Bhai, I am very grateful for your understanding. If possible, can I leave this evening? I will return as soon as I can.'

'Yes, of course, Karnan bhai. Take your time. Spend a few days with your mother. Don't worry about us,' JP said gently. 'Many years ago, when my mother was sick, I couldn't care for her the way she deserved. Like you, I was caught up in the freedom struggle. It's a regret I carry to this day and I don't want you to feel the same way.'

'Thank you, bhai. I will never forget your kindness,' Karnan said.

'This is the least I can do for a brother,' Jayaprakash said. 'Karnan, I will be leaving camp shortly and returning late. If you have time before you leave, could you update Vijaya on the important tasks you are handling?'

'Sure, I will.' Karnan touched the feet of his mentor to seek his blessings.

Jayaprakash pulled him up by his arms and embraced him tightly. 'Your place is by my side. My thoughts and prayers are with you and your mother.'

The two men walked back to rejoin the others. Hira Singh returned with a short and well-built man with a dark complexion and closely cropped hair, dressed in military fatigues. *He looks very young, maybe in his mid-20s*, thought Karnan.

'Hello, Vasudev. Did you get a good night's rest?' Jayaprakash greeted the newcomer. 'I want you to meet Karnan, one of my closest advisers. He is from Kerala too.'

'Yes, sir. I am well rested and ready to start my work,' Vasudev replied in clear Hindi, betraying no sign that it was not his native language. He then looked at Karnan. 'I have been following your writings. It is an honour to meet you.'

'Likewise, Vasudev. I am glad to meet another person from Kerala here at the camp. Where in Kerala are you from?' Karnan asked.

'Please call me Vasu. My family is from Alleppey, near the Arabian Sea. My father, Mohana Panicker, is a local Congress activist. He knows your uncle well.'

'Is that so? It sure is a small world,' Karnan remarked. 'Vasu, I am travelling to Kerala on an important errand and could use your help. Would you like to join me?'

'Of course, if Sir permits,' Vasu replied, glancing at Jayaprakash.

'That is an excellent idea!' Jayaprakash said. 'While it is true that today we only have the two of you representing Kerala, we have many supporters there who believe in our cause. I want you to meet my good friends, E.M.S. Namboodiripad and A.K. Gopalan, two brilliant and committed young socialist leaders from your state. I will prepare letters of introduction.'

'We will be honoured to meet them in Kerala,' Karnan said.

Jayaprakash continued, 'Ram knows most of the union leaders in Kerala. With their help, I am confident we can enlist thousands, maybe even lakhs of supporters in Kerala for the Indian freedom struggle. In fact, I see Kerala as the spearhead that will pierce the British bubble just as Marthanda Varma, the maharaja of

Travancore, defeated the Dutch East India Company at the—'

'Battle of Colachel, 1741,' Karnan interjected.

Jayaprakash nodded. 'Shabash! Exactly. The first time an Asian kingdom defeated a European power.' Glancing at his watch, Jayaprakash said, 'It's time for me to leave. Vijaya will arrange your tickets so you can get to Calcutta by the late night train and continue to Kerala from there. Go and come back safely. Jai Hind.'

Karnan and Vasu stood tall and responded, 'Jai Hind.' With a wave, Jayaprakash turned and walked back to the headquarters.

~6~

Rebel with a Cause

8 October 1980
Kerala, India

VASU WAS TIRED FROM THE LONG AND BUMPY JOURNEY BUT forced himself to stay awake, worried that the silence might lull Murali into dozing off. He could sense Murali's eagerness to meet Karnan again, as it had been over three months since they last saw each other. Karnan had thoughtfully made a surprise early morning visit to their home to accompany Murali on the first day of his new job as the Director of Field Operations for MLA P. Shivan, the newly elected member of Kerala's Legislative Assembly. A rising political star, he was also the leader of the Young Democratic Socialists of Kerala (YDSK), which had won seven seats in the last State Legislative Assembly elections—a surprisingly strong performance for a new political party.

Vasu reflected on the positive changes in his son's life over the past few months. The prestige of being MLA Shivan's right-hand man, who was being groomed to run for office, coupled with the distinction of having Karnan as his uncle had boosted Murali's nascent political career. This had elevated him to a leadership position within the YDSK, with speculation in the media suggesting that Murali might contest the next State Assembly by-election from Vaikom, his famous uncle's home town.

'Murali, are you feeling sleepy? Do you want another cup of tea to keep you awake?'

'No. I am not sleepy at all, just a little tired.'

'Son, are you worried about today?'

'A little. I was thinking about the history you shared about maamen before India became independent. What happened after that?'

'We both moved to Bombay in January 1946. By then, the freedom struggle was winding down as talks had begun with the British for a political settlement. The INC, under the leadership of Nehru and Patel, largely ignored JP and his followers, leaving us to fend for ourselves.'

'This is the part I do not understand. After all their sacrifices, why didn't JP and his followers receive the recognition they deserved?'

'Good question, son. The truth is, we were simple people, unschooled in the world of politics. It was too late by the time we realized what was happening.'

'What happened to maamen and you?'

'Well, I wanted to settle down in Bombay. Despite my pleadings, Karnan returned to Kerala. I remember going with him to the Dadar train station on 16 August 1947, the day after Jawaharlal Nehru proclaimed India's independence. As we made our way to the station, people danced in the streets, bursting firecrackers and distributing laddoos. Did you know Karnan travelled by train with a third-class ticket? That's all the money we could scrape together.'

'Why did you stay back?'

'Because I loved Bombay. Even back then, it was the city where dreams came true. I got a job as a mechanic at an automobile workshop owned by one of JP's friends. The pay was good, and I could save enough to send money home every month.'

'How did you keep in touch?'

'Through letters. Every year, when I visited Kerala during Onam, we spent a few days together. Our friendship deepened, and he eventually convinced me to return to Kerala in 1952. In fact, I lived with him at his ancestral home in Vaikom until I married your mother the following year.'

'Amma told me that maamen became famous in Kerala in the mid-1950s. Were you with him at that time?' Murali asked.

'Well, the fame came a little later. It was in Kerala, in the decades following India's independence, that Karnan's talent blossomed in many new directions,' Vasu explained. 'Firstly as a grassroots political activist on a mission to create an egalitarian society, then as a journalist crusading for workers' rights, followed by several years as a popular author of widely acclaimed novels—and finally, as a visiting professor of political science at Maharaja's College in Cochin. These forays into public roles helped him build a sizeable following, especially among the youth and workers.'

'Yes, I remember reading maamen's novels with great excitement in high school. To this day, my favourite remains *The Mahatma and Me*. Amma told me the story was about maamen and his friend Muhammad Basheer. Is that true?'

'Karnan has never publicly confirmed it because the publishing company promoted the book as a work of fiction. However, I believe it is the true story of him and Basheer during and after the Vaikom Satyagraha.'

'Amma also told me that women were crazy about maamen,' Murali said, winking at his father. 'How come he did not get married?'

Vasu smiled. 'Well, he was indeed very popular with women, but it was not just for his looks. He was an intellectual and had a way with words. Women were drawn to his ideas and his passion for the betterment of society. He inspired many of them to become politically active.' Vasu paused. 'I did bring up the topic of marriage with him several times, but he was so focused on his political work that he felt he would not be able to do justice to family life.'

Vasu and Murali continued their conversation, discussing the battles Karnan had fought for the rights of workers and ordinary people, his impact on their lives and how they felt proud to have him as their mentor and friend. Murali joked that his friends were envious that he had a famous freedom fighter as an uncle, while he, in turn, envied his father's close friendship with Karnan.

Vasu smiled as he reflected on their friendship. 'Well, I feel lucky to have Karnan as a friend. It is his unwavering dedication to the ideals of the Indian freedom struggle, his refusal to back down to bullies and his ability to communicate from his heart that makes him a true rebel.' Vasu added with a sigh, 'A rebel with a cause.'

Murali grinned, his joy evident. 'I love the sound of that. Your best friend, my maamen, a "rebel with a cause".' The thought made Murali's chest swell up with pride.

~7~
Of Wristwatches and Walking Sticks

MURALI SLOWED DOWN THE CAR AS HE EXITED THE highway and entered the local road leading to Karnan's home. He was careful not to splash the rainwater collected in the muddy potholes on the road on to the uniforms of the children returning from school. As the road curved to the right and merged with another newly paved one, Vasu's eyes caught the new street sign: 'Lok Nayak Road'. He smiled, recalling the nearly 10-year-long struggle that Karnan had endured to get the municipal corporation to approve renaming the road to 'Lok Nayak', a title conferred upon Jayaprakash Narayan by the people of India.

It took mounting public pressure following the 1975 national Emergency and JP's passing in 1979 to convince the mayor and city council to act. There was little debate across India that Jayaprakash Narayan's moral force had been instrumental in uniting the fragmented opposition parties to overthrow the autocratic Congress party under Prime Minister Indira Gandhi.

Despite his monumental achievements, as JP had operated mainly in northern India, few in Kerala knew much about him. This was why Karnan was so determined to have the road named after him. He hoped that by doing so, the local people would be reminded of the great revolutionary. Vasu remembered Karnan's prophecy on days they felt dejected by the red tape and delays in getting approval from the town council. 'Mark my words, Vasu,' Karnan had said, 'one fine day, a little boy or girl, as old as your grandchildren, will look up and wonder who the road is named after. The child will walk into the local library and request a book about JP. On that day, all our efforts will be worthwhile, for who knows what fire JP's heroic deeds will light in the child's heart.'

∞

Murali brought the car to a stop in front of the gate. The house, a traditional single-storey structure with a red-tiled roof and a veranda in the front, stood in the middle of a small plot of land shaded by a large mango tree and about a dozen tall coconut trees. In front of it was a concrete pot with a large *tulsi* plant growing in it. The garden, with its plants of various hues, was in need of trimming.

Vasu stepped out of the car and stretched his back. Murali came around to join him.

'Murali, we have a long evening ahead of us. Why don't you get something to eat at the tea shop around the corner? I will go and get your maamen. I did not inform him you were coming. He is very protective of you, so I fear he may get upset with me. Join us when we are ready to leave. That way, we won't waste time.'

The rain had subsided to a drizzle, and the sun was peeking through the clouds. Vasu followed the gaze of people walking by and saw a faint rainbow in the sky. *A good omen for this auspicious day*, he thought as he walked through the open gates. Standing in the courtyard under the shade of the mango tree, reading a newspaper, was Alex, who lived next door and did odd jobs for Karnan.

'Vasu sir! I have been waiting to meet you.' Alex extinguished the bidi he had been smoking and unfolded his *mundu* as a sign of respect. 'Did you read the home minister's comment about Karnan sir?'

'Yes, I did. That is now old news,' Vasu said. 'They have a rivalry that goes back decades. Did Karnan see it?'

'The first thing he does every morning is to read the newspaper from front to back, so I am sure he must have seen it.' Alex paused, hesitating. 'Vasu sir, I want to tell you something else. In private.'

'What is it, Alex? All okay with your wife and children?' Vasu enquired, expecting to hear Alex's customary request for some money to pay his wife's medical expenses, as she was a cancer survivor.

'I am fine, but I am afraid Karnan sir is not,' Alex blurted out.

'What do you mean? Speak clearly.' Vasu demanded.

Alex looked conflicted. 'I know Karnan sir will not like me telling you this. He fell down twice last month. Once while tending his garden and then while taking a stroll in the backyard. I think it has something to do with his vertigo or the ear problem, which is affecting his hearing and balance. Fortunately, I was with him on both occasions, and as he fell on soft soil, he was not hurt. I am afraid if he falls again, and on hard ground, he may break a bone and become bedridden. He will only listen to you.'

'My God!' Vasu exclaimed, placing his right palm over his heart. 'He never gives me any health-related news because he knows I will insist he see a doctor. This is serious. Is he taking his blood pressure medications daily?'

'I remind him every day when I stop by to drop a pack of cigarettes or a drink for him,' Alex said apologetically, knowing that Vasu disapproved of this activity. 'But honestly, I don't know if he actually takes the medicine at night before bed. Vasu sir, there is another small matter...'

'What is it, Alex?'

'As you know, I have been a member of the local Communist Party trade union for 15 years. Yesterday, a group of new members threatened me, demanding I stop helping Karnan sir. I don't know why, but it felt strange.'

'What did you tell them?'

'I was so angry that my blood boiled,' Alex said, his voice edged with emotion. 'I reminded them that when my wife was sick with cancer, it was Karnan sir who sold his ancestral land to pay the hospital bills. Neither the Communist Party nor my comrades gave me a single rupee. When my *ammachi* passed away five years ago, Karnan sir paid for all the funeral expenses and even carried her coffin on his shoulders. None of my comrades showed up.

'Last year, Karnan sir helped my daughter get admission into Maharaja's College, giving her a chance for a bright future. Do they think I will forget all this just because they want me to?' Alex exclaimed, wiping the sweat from his forehead. 'Vasu sir, I might not be educated, but I am not an ungrateful fellow. I made it clear to those idiots that what I do for Karnan sir is none of their business.'

'If I were you, Alex, that is exactly what I would have said. It is good you told me this. You are a good man.' Vasu reached into his shirt pocket and fished out a 50-rupee note. 'Here, keep this. Please keep a close watch on Karnan sir. He only has you and me to depend on.'

'Don't worry, I will. Karnan sir has given me his house keys. I stop by almost every day after work to check on him. My wife comes to cook his meals and clean the house every day.' Alex paused, lowering his voice to a whisper. 'Vasu sir, please don't mention the fall today. I don't want him to think I am Judas.'

Vasu thanked Alex for the information and promised to take care of the matter. As he walked towards the front door of Karnan's house, he couldn't help but feel worried for his old friend. He had always known Karnan to be tough and independent, never one to complain about his health. But the news of him falling twice in a month was concerning. Vasu knew they needed to have a serious talk about getting a medical check-up, but now was not the right time.

At the other end of the veranda, Vasu noticed a newspaper spread out on the *charu kasera*, Karnan's reading chair that was made of polished teak wood with a well-worn cane seat. Removing his sandals near the doorstep, Vasu called out, 'Karnan *chetta*.' He had addressed Karnan as 'elder brother' from the very first day. 'Are you ready? We have a long drive ahead.'

Receiving no response, Vasu raised his voice, 'Karnan chetta?'

Karnan stepped into the veranda, holding on to a walking stick. 'Ah, Vasu. I have been waiting for you.' His deep voice had retained its youthful resonance. 'My old wristwatch stopped working, so I was trying to get it started again. No luck!'

Vasu noticed Karnan had his thick black-rimmed spectacles on. He wore his customary spotless white shirt and white mundu, like he always did for important events. His long hair and flowing beard, almost all white now, were neatly combed. Despite his advancing years and failing health, Karnan maintained his confident, upright posture, albeit with the aid of the walking stick.

'Don't worry about your watch. Here, wear mine.' Vasu quickly removed his watch and strapped it on Karnan's right wrist.

Karnan looked a little uncomfortable but did not object. 'Now your watch too? As if paying for my medicines and electricity bills is not enough. You do too much for me, Vasu.'

'Don't be silly,' Vasu replied. 'Thanks to God's mercy, my auto repair business is doing well, so I can afford it. We both know how meagre the government pension is for freedom fighters. Even a clerk in the village office gets a better pension these days. Anyway, we can discuss complaints another day—today is your big day—the youth of Kerala are honouring you today. I cannot even dream of getting such recognition when I turn 70.'

Karnan smiled. 'Be patient, Vasu. You still have many more years to get to 70.'

'Well, just five years, to be precise.'

'Five years, ten years! What does it matter? I will be long gone by then,' Karnan exclaimed dismissively.

The flippant manner in which Karnan sometimes spoke about death made Vasu uneasy. 'Let's not spoil this auspicious day by talking about death,' Vasu said sombrely, changing the topic. 'Before I forget, let me wish you a healthy and peaceful birthday. Murali and I will be staying here overnight. You and I can have our usual birthday celebration tomorrow.'

'Thank you, Vasu. That's a good idea,' Karnan agreed. 'We met decades ago as foot soldiers in the Indian freedom struggle, and all through these years, you have been there for me. It must be the result of some good deed I unknowingly did in my past life.'

~8~

Enemies Unseen

AFTER LOCKING THE FRONT DOOR, KARNAN SLIPPED INTO his sandals and followed Vasu out on to the narrow path leading to the main gate. The distinct dull thudding of a motorcycle filled the air and moments later, a Royal Enfield Bullet came into view and stopped in front of the house. A tall, well-built police officer in uniform dismounted the vehicle and walked directly towards Karnan and Vasu. Removing his helmet, the officer addressed Karnan. 'Professor, I don't know if you recognize me,' the officer said as he removed his sunglasses. 'I am Ashraf, your student at Maharaja's College from about 12 years ago.'

It was a few seconds before recognition dawned on Karnan. 'Oh, thank God! Based on my past experiences, whenever I see someone in police uniform, I assume they are coming to arrest me!' he said with a mock expression of fear. 'Ashraf Ali, how could I forget you! So happy to see you, my boy.'

'Sorry, I did not have time to change out of my uniform,' Ashraf said. 'I was posted to Cochin last month and had been waiting for an opportunity to meet you again.'

'Yes, I am aware. In fact, I read in the newspapers just last week—with great pride, I must add—that you have taken over as sub-inspector (SI) in Cochin. I remembered my words to your *umma* when you left college before completing your degree to join the Kerala Police. If you recall, I promised her you would become a sub-inspector before you turned 30. Looks like you made it even ahead of schedule. Are you just passing by?'

'Professor, it was your promise that convinced my parents to let me leave college. I am so grateful.' Ashraf then leaned forward and whispered into Karnan's ears, 'I rushed here today to meet you and discuss a sensitive matter. Can we step inside your home to talk?'

'I am running late for an important event in Cochin. If you don't mind, we can talk right here.' Karnan pointed to Vasu. 'This is my friend, Vasu. He is going to the event with me.'

Ashraf positioned himself between Karnan and Vasu, ensuring the curious onlookers gathered on the road could not overhear them. 'Professor, I came to personally inform you about a threat to disrupt the event where you will be speaking tonight. We received this information from a reliable source just an hour ago.' Ashraf paused, expecting a reaction. Seeing none, he continued, 'We suspect the threat comes from your so-called friends in the Communist Party leadership. Not directly, but through hired goons.'

Vasu was irate. 'Ashraf, we are aware of the threat. But hired goons? Are we living in a banana republic?' he asked.

Ashraf ignored the question and continued speaking with urgency. 'We received information that the Communist Party has engaged a group of thugs from the "Pigs Nest", one of the most crime-infested areas of the city. The problem is that they are mercenaries—well armed and ruthless. They often use people from other states—Tamil Nadu, Andhra, etc.—to execute their plans. And they will do the bidding of anyone who pays them. Since no party workers are involved, there will be no trace.'

'I have received several calls from friends and enemies to avoid this event,' Karnan said calmly. 'But why this one? Why would the party running the government want to disrupt the biggest conference of their own youth wing?'

'Look, Professor,' Ashraf said, 'here is what I know. Based on your interview published in the *Mathrubhumi* newspaper last week, the party leadership suspects you may use today's event to call for a student revolt. You don't need me to tell you that the Left Democratic Front (LDF) government needs the support of the YDSK members in the Legislative Assembly to stay in power.

'Besides, ever since the national Emergency and your role in exposing police atrocities in Kerala, some politicians—on both sides, I must add—and many senior police officers have been wary of your continued influence over students, labour unions and workers. Many powerful people see you as a threat to the survival of the fragile Left Front coalition government in the state.'

Karnan threw up his hands. 'I am a retired old man, minding my own business. I have the right to express my opinions. How could I be a threat to anyone, much less a powerful state government?'

'My sources tell me that the HM tried to pressure the organizers into inviting him as the chief guest today,' Ashraf said, 'but the YDSK executive committee led by MLA Shivan—your protégé—withdrew the invitation last week due to the corruption charges you helped expose. The HM is upset that you are replacing him at the event. It's the usual petty politics, but with a minister involved, our hands are tied.'

'Bastards! They make my blood boil!' Vasu exclaimed. 'Sub-Inspector, isn't it ironic that the Kerala Communist Marxist Party, an organization that Karnan has dedicated his life to for over two decades, now sees him as an enemy? And why? Because he has the guts to point out corruption and nepotism in the leadership. Last I checked, the party's flag still bore the same symbols—a sickle, hammer and star—representing hard-working people. But what has the party done to give them a better future?'

Karnan held up his hands to interrupt. 'Vasu, why are you so surprised? The problem is that none of the members of the politburo have ever held a sickle or a hammer or looked up to see a star in the sky. They are completely out of touch. That is why I am doing all I can to hold them accountable. You know that they have been issuing veiled threats ever since I formally resigned from the party. Now, they are just being more blatant about it. Do they really believe it will work?'

'Well, they have gone too far. They don't know who they are dealing with,' Vasu fumed.

Karnan turned to Ashraf. 'Look, I greatly appreciate you coming all the way from Cochin to inform me about this. However, I promised the young party workers that I will attend their conference as the chief guest today. Come what may, I must keep my word.'

'Professor, it could be a costly decision. I urge you to reconsider,' Ashraf pleaded.

'No, Ashraf. I will not be intimidated,' Karnan said firmly. 'If I give in to their threats, it will only encourage them to do it again. I will go to the event and deliver my speech as planned; they can't silence me. But thank you for your concern.'

Realizing the futility of any further attempts to change the minds of the two men, Ashraf shrugged wearily. 'Well, I respect your decision, Professor. I really do. Somehow, I had a feeling that a threat like this would only embolden you. I am told that a big crowd—over 25,000 people—is expected today, which will be very difficult to control. My advice is to keep your speech a little low-key to avoid trouble.'

'Low-key? What is that?' Karnan smiled. 'Don't worry, I will be fine.'

Ashraf shook hands with Karnan and then with Vasu. 'I will be at the venue tonight. I have requested for a few additional policemen to help but am not sure if it will be approved. Let's see what happens. Please be careful. See you there.' He then turned around and, with the agility of an athlete, got on his motorcycle and strapped on his helmet.

As Ashraf departed, Vasu moved closer to Karnan and touched his shoulder. 'I think you made the right decision. If JP were alive today, he would be very proud. Just before I left home, I received a call from MLA Shivan. He told me they invited you to send a clear message to the party leadership.' Vasu's voice betrayed a hint of concern for what lay ahead that day.

'Today is Jayaprakash Narayan's first death anniversary. I think it is a good day to share his message with the youth of Kerala.

What do you think, Vasu?'

'I couldn't agree more. And who better to deliver that message than JP's most devoted lieutenant?'

'We are no strangers to danger. I am convinced that the threat was deliberately leaked to scare me away from attending the event,' Karnan said.

'Seems like they have forgotten who you are,' Vasu commented.

After a long pause, Karnan looked Vasu in the eye. 'Vasu, you are aware of all my health-related issues. Perhaps this may be my last chance to get my message across to the youth of Kerala. All our dreams are at risk. The time that Martin Luther King warned us about—when silence is betrayal—has arrived.'

Vasu shook his head slowly. 'Until this morning, I was unsure whether you were doing the right thing by addressing this student rally. But after meeting Ashraf, I am convinced that you are.'

Karnan spoke hesitatingly. 'I really have no choice. And yet, I fear…if the threat is true…I cannot help but feel guilty about possibly endangering the lives of the innocent young students at the event. What do you think, Vasu?'

Vasu pondered the question for a second. 'Karnan chetta, do you remember the advice Jayaprakash bhai had if the enemy confronted us?'

'Don't think; just follow your heart and act.'

'Exactly! I think you should follow your heart today.'

Karnan turned to face Vasu. 'Thank you, Vasu. Oh, before I forget—I have left a few important documents in a sealed envelope with your name on it inside the drawer of my writing desk. I have instructed Alex to hand it to you if anything happens to me. He has the keys to the home—'

'Karnan chetta, you are worrying unnecessarily,' Vasu interrupted. 'Nothing will happen to you. I am with you.' He leaned close and whispered, 'Besides, we have Kali with us tonight. Remember, she has protected us during times of far greater peril.'

~9~
History Lessons

VASU FOLLOWED KARNAN AS HE WALKED TOWARDS THE gate. Seeing the police officer arrive, a small group of local people had gathered at the corner of the road, talking to Alex. Among them was a little girl in school uniform.

'Looks like the people have not yet forgotten their beloved freedom fighter Vaikom Karnan,' Vasu whispered. 'You are still a hero to them.'

Karnan stopped and looked up at the group of people. 'Maybe it is you they have come to see,' he responded softly, adding with a flourish, 'Vasudev Panicker, the brave soldier of the Azad Hind Fauj and the man behind the mutiny of the Royal Indian Navy.'

'Man behind the Royal Indian Navy Mutiny?' Vasu scoffed. 'You have unnecessarily glorified my role in your book. All I did was secure the flags for the real heroes to execute their plan. I will bet my last rupee that no one here has even heard of the Mutiny.'

'Are you saying no one in Vaikom has read my book?' Karnan smiled. 'Come, let's find out if, between the two of us, we still have a few followers left in this strange land of ours.'

As they stepped into the street, Alex approached Karnan. 'Karnan sir, some of the people here saw the police officer walk in and wanted to make sure you were okay,' Alex said, adding, 'some of them would like to talk to you but I told them you are going to an important meeting in Cochin.'

'Everything is okay, Alex. The police officer is a former student who was just passing by. Nothing to worry about.'

One of the men from the group stepped forward. '*Namaskaram*. I am Chandrashekhar, grandson of the late Balan master.'

'Namaskaram, Chandrashekhar. Of course I know who you are. Balan master was not only my favourite teacher but also a father figure. He inspired me to join the freedom struggle,' Karnan said warmly. 'I miss him every day.'

'Karnan sir, do you have a few minutes? My daughter wants to meet you.'

'Why not?' Karnan looked down as a little girl came to stand next to Chandrashekhar. 'So, you are Balan master's great-granddaughter. What is your name, young lady?'

'Vijayalakshmi Chandrashekhar,' the little girl responded in a shy voice. 'I like freedom fighters. My father told me you are the only one from Kerala still alive.'

Karnan threw his head back and laughed. 'Your father is half correct! I am certainly not the only freedom fighter alive in Kerala, but it is indeed true that I am alive,' he said with a hearty laugh. 'You know, Vijayalakshmi, there was a great American writer by the name of Mark Twain who once dismissed the news of his death with the famous understatement, "The reports of my death are greatly exaggerated."'

Some of the men in the group joined in the laughter. The little girl, not fully understanding the joke, looked a bit confused but, not wanting to be left out, joined in as well.

Karnan bent down and cupped the little girl's face in his hand. 'Vijayalakshmi Chandrashekhar…that is the most beautiful name I have ever heard. Do you know that it includes the names of three very famous Indian freedom fighters?'

The little girl raised her eyebrows curiously. 'Three? I did not know that. Who are they, uncle?'

'Vijaya, please address him as "*muthachan*". He would be the same age as your grandfather,' Chandrashekhar sternly corrected her.

'Let me tell you. "Vijaya" is for Vijaya Patwardhan, the brave assistant of Jayaprakash Narayan; "Lakshmi" is for Captain Lakshmi

Sahgal, the leader of the Rani of Jhansi Regiment of the INA. And of course, "Chandrashekhar" is for...' Karnan paused and looked quizzically at the little girl. 'I am sure you know—'

'Azad! Chandrashekhar Azad, the freedom fighter,' the little girl shouted, no longer shy.

'You are correct, Vijayalakshmi.'

'Muthachan, do you know that my grandfather named my father after Azad?'

'Is that so? I wish my father had thought of that!' Karnan was now thoroughly engrossed in the conversation, oblivious to the others standing around them. 'Tell me, Vijayalakshmi, do you know the name of the freedom fighter this road we are standing on is named after?'

'My father told me that "Lok Nayak" is Jayaprakash Narayan. Was he a freedom fighter too?'

'Absolutely correct! People called him "Lok Nayak" for a reason. Jayaprakash Narayan was tall and handsome—just like a film star... Who is your favourite?'

'Mammootty!' Vijayalakshmi shouted.

'Yes, just like Mammootty,' Karnan said with a smile. 'Women all over India fell in love with him. He was also fearless and brilliant, and he truly loved the common people of India. Do you know that the people in North India called Jayaprakash the "Second Gandhi"?'

Karnan could barely conceal his delight at the opportunity to do what he loved most—educate a curious child.

'Vijayalakshmi,' Karnan continued, 'you are the smartest little girl I have met. I want to give you a gift for answering this difficult question correctly—a book written by the great Ruskin Bond. Will you come by the day after tomorrow evening to pick it up?'

The little girl smiled shyly and nodded. Her father spoke softly, 'Vijaya, do you know that muthachan was a good friend of Jayaprakash Narayan?'

'Is that true? Did you fight the British too?'

'Vijayalakshmi, I am a simple writer, so instead of guns, my weapon was a pen,' Karnan replied. 'But I had the good fortune to have helped many great leaders fight the British and drive them out of India.' He pointed to Vasu, who was standing behind the little girl. 'Do you know that this uncle fought the British with real guns? He knows how to make bombs too. He can tell you many interesting stories of his adventures. Would you like to hear some of them?'

Vijayalakshmi's eyes lit up. 'Yes. I can tell my friends that I met two real freedom fighters. I am sure none of them ever have.'

Karnan smiled warmly at the little girl and ruffled her hair. 'That's great, my dear. Remembering the sacrifices and struggles of our freedom fighters is important. It keeps their spirits alive and inspires us to continue working towards a better future.'

Vijayalakshmi nodded eagerly. Vasu could see that she was already proud of her connection to freedom fighters.

Karnan looked at his watch and straightened up, sighing. 'Vijayalakshmi, I'm afraid I have to go now. But I promise we will meet again soon and have a long chat.'

Vijayalakshmi beamed, and Chandrashekhar thanked Karnan for taking the time to talk to his daughter. Chandrashekhar turned to his daughter. 'Vijaya, it's time for muthachan and his friend to leave. Now, seek their blessings.'

The little girl bent down and placed her tiny hands first on Karnan's and then Vasu's feet. Then, she stood up with her palms clasped together, her head bowed in respect for the elders. Visibly moved, Karnan and Vasu placed their hands on her head to bless her. Almost in unison, they whispered, 'May God bless you with a long and healthy life.'

The two men bade goodbye to the group, which had grown to about two dozen people. As they walked back to the car, Vasu couldn't help but feel a sense of pride and purpose. This encounter with Vijayalakshmi reminded him of why Karnan remained beloved by the people. Vasu was thankful for the opportunity to be with his friend today and was filled with renewed determination to face what lay ahead.

A man walked unsteadily to join the group. 'Comrade! Comrade Karnan!' he slurred. 'I have been waiting for your next book for 10 years. When can we expect it?'

Vasu glared at the man and kept walking. The other men in the group shushed the drunken man, who stumbled away and collided with Murali, who had just arrived at the scene.

Murali pushed the man aside. 'Get out of my way, you drunkard. Watch your dirty mouth and be careful of who you are talking to!' he shouted, glaring at the man. As the man quietly left, Murali walked over to open the car's passenger door for Karnan. Delighted to see him, Karnan gave him a warm embrace.

'How are you, son?' Karnan asked Murali as he held him tightly.

'Keeping busy with my new job, maamen. That is why I have not been able to visit you for so long,' Murali replied.

'I understand. With you being a young leader now, I thought I would only see you at the event tonight. But I am glad you are accompanying us. You are a far better driver than your father,' Karnan joked. 'Besides, it's been long since I heard you sing. Come, let's talk as we drive.'

Murali helped Karnan and Vasu settle in the back seat before getting into the driver's seat. He put the key in the ignition and heard a clicking sound. The engine did not start. He tried again, with the same result. *Not a good omen*, Vasu thought.

Alex stepped forward. 'Vasu sir, is there a problem with the car?'

'Just some trouble starting,' Vasu responded. 'This vehicle is old but runs well. I guess a little push will help.'

'Come on, everyone; let's give the car a push!' Alex gestured to the others in the group. They surrounded the car and pushed it in unison. As the car started to move, Murali turned the keys and shifted into gear while pressing the accelerator to the floor.

The car didn't budge. Undeterred, the men repeated the manoeuvre a few times. On the fourth attempt, the vehicle sputtered slowly, and after a few seconds, the engine came to life, letting out a thick plume of black smoke.

'There!' Vasu called to the men. 'I told you it is a good car. Thank you, all.'

Vasu watched as Karnan waved to the little girl, who waved back enthusiastically. Vasu was aware that Karnan was grateful for the small but significant encounter with Vijayalakshmi. He knew from personal experience that these little moments of connection and inspiration fuelled the rebellious flame in Karnan's heart.

~10~

Crossroads on the Highway

THE BOTTOM OF THE CAR SCRAPED THE GROUND AS THEY headed towards Cochin. The sun was still shining, making the air warm and moist. With the car's AC not working, Murali rolled down the window and asked the others to do the same. Karnan sat silent, deep in thought.

Vasu quickly updated Murali about the encounter with SI Ashraf. When he finished, Karnan asked Murali, 'How is it working for Shivan?'

'I love it,' Murali replied. 'I truly believe that public service is my calling. MLA Shivan is in politics for the right reasons—he genuinely believes he can help the working class through policymaking. He regards you as his guru and has a framed photo with you and his parents from when he was a young boy. That must be why he hired me based solely on your letter of recommendation.' Murali looked at Karnan through the rear-view mirror. 'I did not get a chance to thank you in person. Thank you, maamen.'

'I am delighted to hear that,' Karnan said. 'Shivan is lucky to have you on his team. He takes after his father, who was a well-known community leader. He is exactly the bold and dynamic leader, not bogged down by ideology, who we need to take Kerala forward. Working for him is a good way for you to transition from student politics to state-level politics. Now, I want to know when you plan to give me the big treat.'

'How about tomorrow? Let me also join in to celebrate your birthday.'

'Good idea! Let's do that. You and your father should stay with me tonight as it will be late by the time we return. We can all go to Alleppey tomorrow.' Karnan turned to Vasu. 'Vasu, now that our Murali has secured a good job and is of legal age to tie the knot, are you looking for a bride for him? What are we waiting for?'

'I don't think that will be necessary. It seems Murali has found a girl for himself. They met a few years ago at college. But Jalaja is not too happy about it.'

'Is that right, Murali? Why did you not tell me about this? Anyway, why is your amma unhappy?' Karnan asked.

'Because the girl is not a Hindu,' Murali said, glancing at Karnan through the mirror. 'She comes from a conservative Muslim family and wears a hijab.'

'Wears a hijab! So what?' Karnan leaned forward. 'Many Hindu women in North India cover their heads and faces. Different communities call it by different names—*niqab, ghoonghat, chadri*—but essentially, they are all the same,' he said. 'What is her name?'

'Her name is Rukhsana. She is in her final year of BA,' Murali said and paused. 'She wears a scarlet-coloured hijab.'

'Knowing you, Murali, I am sure that Rukhsana is smart and good-looking. Tell me, is she as passionate as you are about politics and social causes?'

Murali had already anticipated this question. 'Yes, she is smart and good-looking, but more importantly, she is a good person and passionate about history. I introduced her to politics.'

'Perfect, son. That is what really matters,' Karnan said. Smiling, he turned to Vasu. 'Our Murali has grown up so quickly. I wonder where he has learnt all these life lessons so fast. I doubt it is from either of us.'

Karnan and Vasu laughed.

Eager to tell his uncle more about Rukhsana, Murali ignored the comment and continued, 'Rukhsana is an authority on Kerala's history. I introduced her to MLA Shivan, who liked her and appointed her as joint secretary of the YDSK. She is the first and only woman to hold that position.'

'Is that right? Looks like you have found yourself a good match,' Karnan commented as he reached out to playfully squeeze Murali's shoulder.

Murali was happy to see his uncle being supportive. 'Oh, maamen, I forgot to tell you—Rukhsana is a huge fan of your novels. In fact, she knows more about your writings and speeches than I do. She will be at the event tonight. I would like you to meet her.'

'Oh, that explains why you were eager to drive us to the event,' Vasu quipped. 'I thought you wanted to spend quality time with your father and uncle.'

'Well, that too,' Murali said shyly.

'I am so excited!' Karnan said. 'Murali, I would love to meet my newest fan, Rukhsana. I would like to know which of my novels she liked the most and why. That will tell us something about her. Make sure you bring her to meet me at the reception before the event starts.'

'Sure, maamen. I was planning on doing that,' Murali said.

Karnan looked out of the window, lost in thought again. After a few minutes, he leaned forward and placed a hand on Murali's shoulder.

'Son, I am not sure whether your dad told you about this, but when I was around your age, I met a girl in Bombay. Her name was Nafeesa.'

'No, I was not aware of this. Nafeesa…a Muslim?' Murali guessed from the name.

'Yes. She was so beautiful that I could not think of anything else. It was love at first sight, at least for me. We met often at Juhu Beach. She loved pav bhaji from the food vendors. It gave me gas, but I had no choice.' Karnan laughed at the memory, then fell quiet. 'Those were the happiest days of my life…but my joy was short-lived.' His voice trailed off.

'Why? What happened, maamen?'

'Those were also the days of heightened tension between Hindus and Muslims all over India. Things didn't turn out as I had hoped. As soon as Nafeesa's family found out about us, they placed her under house arrest,' Karnan said, his voice breaking. 'To her parents, I was just one among millions of anti-British protesters without a proper job or future. While I was in Calcutta for several months on an important mission with Jayaprakash bhai, her parents forced her to marry a Muslim man who was much older.'

'How did you find out?'

'Through a letter her friend gave me the day after I returned to Bombay.'

'That must have been heartbreaking. Is that why you never married?'

'How could I? It was the first major failure in my life. But I could not do much in a place where I had few friends and no family. It hurts even today...' Karnan paused for a few seconds. 'Son, please don't let my experience discourage you. The fault was mine. The truth is, when I needed courage most, it deserted me.'

There was a heavy silence after Karnan stopped talking.

After a minute, Murali spoke. 'Maamen, you were very young then, so don't be hard on yourself. The little that I know about courage and character, I learnt from you.'

Getting no response from Karnan, Murali persisted. 'I would like to know if you have any words of wisdom for me based on your experiences.'

'Son, I am the last person who should dispense matrimonial advice—I have zero experience with marriage!' Karnan managed an awkward laugh. 'However, since you asked, I have one piece of insight: life is filled with ups and downs. Enjoy the good times, but do not expect them to last forever. Take your time with important decisions. Don't rush them.'

'Murali, did you hear your maamen?' Vasu asked. 'Marriage is a big decision. Take your time and do what feels right for you.

Whatever you choose, we are there for you.'

'Yes, I understand,' Murali replied. He felt relieved that he had told his uncle about Rukhsana. It was comforting to learn that his uncle had had a relationship with a Muslim woman during the tumultuous days before India's independence. Although the relationship did not come to fruition, Murali knew it took great courage in a time when Hindu–Muslim relations in India were strained.

~11~

The Legend of Jayaprakash Narayan

TRAFFIC HAD SLOWED DOWN TO A CRAWL. VASU NOTICED that the newly set up manual checkpoint for collecting toll on the new bridge had backed up the vehicles. The voices of men shouting could be heard in the distance. The young men operating the booth were busy trying to calm a drunk driver who refused to pay the toll, claiming he had already paid it in the morning.

A few more minutes passed before Murali stopped at a petrol station and got out to fill the tank.

Inside the car, Karnan turned to Vasu. 'Why did you bring Murali with you? He has his entire life ahead of him. Why expose him to danger?'

'It was his mother's idea,' Vasu explained. 'Murali was at the youth conference all day yesterday and would have been there anyway. He came home late last night to drive us to Cochin today.'

'So Jalaja knows? You should have spared the poor woman all the worry,' Karnan said. 'You heard Ashraf. This is serious stuff… A little too much even for seasoned veterans like us, don't you think?'

Vasu shook his head in disbelief. 'I am still in shock. I never thought I would live to see a day when the party leadership would turn against you. Disloyal cowards!'

Karnan smiled. 'A threat, that too from our old friends! And yet, the little girl we just met gives me hope for the future. Her name reminded me of our beloved Vijaya…' His voice trailed off.

'Yes, that is who I have also been thinking about,' Vasu said, half-turned in his seat to look at Karnan. 'Our old comrade-in-arms, the beautiful and fearless Vijaya Patwardhan.'

Both men went silent, lost in memories.

'Vasu, I have not told you this before...' Karnan spoke with uncharacteristic hesitation.

'What is it?' Vasu asked.

'After the disaster of my love affair with Nafeesa, Vijaya was the first person I confided in. She understood my anguish and provided me with great comfort. It was thanks to her that I was able to carry on as a freedom fighter. I almost fell in love all over again,' Karnan said.

If Karnan was expecting a reaction from Vasu, none was forthcoming.

'Well, you did not have to tell me,' Vasu said calmly. 'Everyone at the Azad Dasta camp knew about your feelings for her.'

'Everyone? How? I never told a soul,' Karnan asked, genuinely surprised.

'It was as clear as daylight, by the look in your eyes when you spoke about her, the many gifts you brought her from your visits to Kerala,' Vasu said. Then, sensing Karnan's discomfort, he added, 'Sorry to hurt your feelings, brother, but if it brings you some comfort, I want you to know that you were not alone.'

'What do you mean?'

'Half the men at the camp were in love with Vijaya, while the other half wanted to protect her like a sister.'

'Interesting...this is news to me,' Karnan said. 'Which camp were you in?'

Vasu smiled, casting a shy glance at Murali.

'Really, Vasu? This is unbelievable,' Karnan said, mock seriousness in his voice. 'Were you waiting for me to turn 70 to break this news?'

'Well, you didn't tell me either!' Vasu responded. Realizing that he may have overstepped, Vasu softened his voice and continued. 'And what's wrong with a man falling in love with a tall, charming, intelligent and brave young lady who also happened to be the sister of the great freedom fighter, the personal secretary of another great

Girl in Scarlet Hijab

freedom fighter and a skilled guerrilla fighter herself?'

Karnan laughed. 'I see absolutely nothing wrong with that, except in those days, Vijaya had her heart set on only one person—Jayaprakash Narayan. I realized that much later, after she had left the camp. She was completely dedicated to helping him carry the flag of revolution at a time when the British had jailed most other senior Indian political leaders.'

'I did not want to hurt your feelings back then, but it was no secret that Vijaya was completely in awe of Jayaprakash Narayan. She would have followed him to the ends of the earth. And who can blame her? He was one of a kind, a real daredevil!'

'No question about it. A daredevil with a sharp intellect and a big heart.'

'Karnan chetta, did I ever tell you that I first heard about JP's daring escape from Hazaribagh Central Jail when I was in Singapore? I immediately knew I had to return to India.' Vasu paused. 'It was later at the Azad Dasta that I learnt you had been involved in planning the jailbreak. Good Lord, that must have been a thrilling experience.'

'Although I played a very small part, I must say that it was the proudest moment of my life.'

As Murali opened the driver's door to get back inside the car, he caught the last part of the conversation. 'What was, maamen?' he asked.

Karnan leaned forward and patted Murali on the shoulder. '*Mone*, I was telling your father that helping Jayaprakash Narayan escape from jail was the proudest moment of my life. It helped me regain the courage that had deserted me just a few years earlier.'

'I read in your book that the jailbreak happened on the night of Diwali,' Murali said.

'That's correct. In 1942,' Karnan confirmed, pleased that Murali remembered. 'It was on that night that I decided to dedicate my life to the cause of Indian freedom. I remember thinking that if someone as great as Jayaprakash bhai was ready to risk his life, why not an insignificant person like me? The news of his escape lifted the sagging morale of every Indian. We all loved bhai because he kept our fragile dream of freedom alive.'

'Yes, maamen. I have heard this about a thousand times from my parents.' Murali smiled.

'Karnan chetta.' Vasu sounded nostalgic. 'Do you recall the day we met for the first time?'

'Oh yes,' Karnan sighed, 'as if it happened yesterday. It was the year following JP's jailbreak.'

'Yes. It was in 1943. That makes it 37 years ago,' Vasu said. 'I still find it hard to believe that none other than Jayaprakash Narayan introduced us.'

The two friends fell silent again, realizing that 37 of the best years of their lives had passed so quickly.

~12~

A Son's Promise

THEY HAD BEEN DRIVING FOR ALMOST 30 MINUTES SINCE leaving Karnan's house. The sun had disappeared behind the clouds, and the overcast sky carried the lingering threat of rainfall. Vasu could sense that Karnan's mind was preoccupied with memories of the past and anticipation of the evening's event.

Karnan leaned forward to address Murali. 'Son, it has been a long time since I heard you sing. Can you sing something for me? It will help me relax a little before we get to Cochin.'

'I have not sung in years, maamen,' Murali protested. 'Besides, I have forgotten the lyrics to the old *nadaga gananal* you like.'

'What? A university music award winner has forgotten lyrics?' Karnan teased. 'You can tell that to others, not to me. Okay, forget drama songs. How about the song sung by Jayachandran that is on the radio every day, "Hridayeswari"?'

'Oh, Murali sings that song very well,' Vasu said.

'All right, fine.' Murali smiled. 'At least I know the words.'

A few seconds passed before Murali's melodious voice filled the car.

'The one who reigns over my heart,
In your sigh I heard a sweet music…
The music of love…'

∞

As they approached the Vaikom Sree Mahadeva Temple, Vasu instructed Murali to stop near the entrance. He stepped out of the car and stood outside the front gate to say a silent prayer to the supreme deity.

O Lord Shiva, please accept the gratitude of this humble devotee. I thank you for all the blessings you have bestowed on my family and me. Today, I humbly ask for one more favour. Please extend your protection to my dear friend Karnan.

Before returning to the car, Vasu glanced around at the old shops with red-tiled roofs that surrounded the temple. Not much had changed from the early 1950s when he had stayed in Vaikom. A flood of memories rushed into his mind as he recalled the stories he had heard during his brief stay. The small town was made famous by Mahatma Gandhi's visit in March 1925, in a show of solidarity with the lower-caste Hindus demanding their right to enter the temple.

Vasu recalled the townspeople telling him it was here that Karnan, then just a 14-year-old boy, was the youngest protester in the Vaikom Satyagraha, which went on to become an important chapter in the Indian freedom struggle. It was on the unpaved roads leading to the temple that Karnan first cut his teeth into the rapidly unfolding saga of the Indian freedom movement, setting off a chain of events that would eventually lead to their paths crossing in a distant land.

'Karnan chetta, I just remembered the phrase you often used: truth is stranger than fiction,' Vasu said as he got back inside the car. When there was no response, he turned to look at Karnan and found him fast asleep, head slumped over his left shoulder.

Vasu's thoughts shifted to the event that lay ahead. He raised his wrist to check the time, only to realize that he had given Karnan his watch. Reaching forward under the driver's seat, he grabbed the jute bag and removed the revolver with caution, unwrapping the cloth around it. The cool, hard metal of the weapon felt reassuring.

Vasu carefully opened the revolver and then the pouch containing the bullets. One by one, he placed five bullets into the magazine, leaving the chamber for the first bullet empty—a safety precaution he had learnt from General Mohan Singh. As Vasu placed the revolver back in the bag and slid it under the seat, he noticed Murali watching him through the rear-view mirror.

'Son, I think I should carry the revolver today.'

Murali slapped his palm against the steering wheel. 'There you go again!'

Karnan stirred, but did not wake up.

'Shhh…let maamen get some rest,' Vasu admonished.

Father and son were silent for several minutes, after which Vasu put his hand on Murali's shoulder. 'Son, I have made my decision. From this moment, Kali is yours. However, remember the promise you made to your mother…'

Murali glanced at his father, his face lighting up with a grin. 'Yes, I know. I will not use the revolver unless there is no other choice.'

'Yes, and remember to stay close to maamen tonight,' Vasu added after a brief pause. 'And never forget that Kali carries the burden of history. Promise me that you will always take care of her, just as I did. Do you hear me?'

'Yes, I promise. Thank you, acha,' Murali replied.

The dark clouds had returned to the sky, blocking the evening sun. A light rain fell again.

~13~

Conspiracy in the Garden

8 October 1980
Trivandrum, Kerala

THE GLEAMING WHITE CAR WITH A SMALL FLAG OF INDIA fluttering on its bonnet came to a screeching halt in front of a large bungalow that served as the official residence of Kerala's home minister. Instead of number plates, the vehicle bore the words 'Director General of Police, Kerala' (DGP). One of the armed guards opened the passenger door, stood back and saluted. The DGP stepped out, ceremonial staff in his hand, returned the salute and hurried up the steps. Another guard opened the front door, also saluting. Inside, a lady dressed in a sari received him.

'Good evening, sir. I am Padmaja Srinivasan, new secretary to Home Minister Ramachandran. He is with a few of his party colleagues in the garden and would like to meet you there.'

'If he is busy, I can wait,' the DGP offered.

'No sir, this is the best time. He has a meeting with the chief minister in 15 minutes. Please follow me.'

DGP V. Subramanian followed the lady through a long hallway, past a well-furnished living area, to the glass doors opening into the garden. Home Minister K. Ramachandran was seated with five other men, each holding a glass of whisky. The DGP recognized three of them: Mr Anirudhan, an MLA from the ruling Communist Party, and Mr Shanmugam, the minister in charge of community development and sports. The third person was a journalist known for his closeness to the home minister. The other two men, dressed like businessmen, were unfamiliar to him.

The police chief approached the group and saluted the home minister. 'Good evening, sir.'

'Good, you are on time,' the HM replied, glancing at his watch. 'I have to leave for a meeting soon, but I wanted an update on the law and order situation in Cochin—the YDSK event tonight. Is everything going as planned?'

'Yes, sir. I conveyed your decision to withdraw police security for the event to the commissioner of Cochin. She initially disagreed, so I had to apply a little pressure.'

'I know Sreelekha well. She is not someone we can count on,' Ramachandran said, squinting over the top of his glasses. 'I hope you did not mention my name.'

'Of course not, sir. I devised a VIP duty for the men who had been assigned the event's security. However, one of the junior officers wanted to get the order in writing, claiming he had clear evidence of potential violence at the event.'

'Who is this junior officer causing trouble?' The home minister stood up.

'Sir, Sub-Inspector Ashraf Ali. He solved the Kannur murder case last year. He is a former student of Vaikom Karnan and is well respected by his subordinates.'

MLA Anirudhan interjected, 'DGP sir, what's the big deal? Just transfer him to Idukki or some other godforsaken place.'

Subramanian fidgeted with his staff. 'Unfortunately, that will not be possible in this case; he was promoted and posted to Cochin just last month. Another transfer now, in the middle of major news events, would raise many questions in the media, especially since he is a Muslim. I don't recommend it.'

'Okay, just deal with him,' Home Minister Ramachandran said, sitting down and checking his watch again. 'Mr Kurian, the MLA from Angamaly, has made—let's call them special arrangements—for the event. I am told there will be fireworks in Cochin tonight.' He smiled and looked at the men seated around him.

Conspiracy in the Garden

Anirudhan stood up and raised his glass. 'Let the fireworks begin,' he proposed. Except for the home minister, all the men laughed as they stood and clinked their glasses.

Ramachandran raised a hand to stop them and looked at the DGP. 'We just want the Cochin Police to keep their hands off and let things happen. This is a political squabble that does not concern the police. No arrests. Am I clear?'

'Sir, if there is violence, the commissioner of Cochin will make the decision. She is a capable officer and has a good track record. But I will convey the message.'

'Let me clarify, Mr Subramanian. The stakes are very high; you must step up,' the home minister said sternly. 'If Karnan convinces the seven MLAs affiliated with the YDSK to withdraw their support from the Left Front government, and if some of the MLAs from A.K. Antony's group join them, the government could fall.' Ramachandran paused and looked around. 'It is no secret that the governor is ready to declare president's rule in Kerala again. It's like a game for those sitting in Delhi. If our government falls, there will be widespread violence and thousands could die. And remember, none of us will retain our positions or privileges.' The home minister paused, before adding, 'Neither I, nor you.'

A brief silence followed.

The journalist piped up. 'DGP sir, why is a 70-year-old washed-out man, who has one foot in the grave, so beloved by the YDSK members? I have been following Kerala politics for over 30 years, and I just don't get it. When will these young ungrateful fools learn not to bite the hands that feed them?'

'Politics is not my forte,' Subramanian replied, before looking at the home minister. 'Is there anything else, sir?'

'I want you to monitor the venue closely and keep me updated.'

'Certainly, sir.' DGP Subramanian saluted and turned to leave.

'Oh, I forgot to mention one more thing,' the home minister called out.

Subramanian stopped mid-stride and turned. 'Yes, sir?'

'I know you brief the chief minister every week. The CM does not need to know about this conversation. Remember, the Cochin police commissioner started her career as the head of the CM's security detail. They are still very close.'

'I will keep that in mind, sir.' He saluted again and turned around to walk out.

'Fireworks!' Minister Shanmugam exclaimed after the DGP had left. 'I don't know about the rest of you, but I love fireworks. Anyone wants to go to Cochin tonight?'

PART TWO

A LION IN WINTER

~14~

The Return of Mahabali

8 October 1980
Marine Drive Ground, Cochin, Kerala

THE COOL EVENING BREEZE DRIFTING IN FROM THE Vembanad Lake felt soothing against Murali's skin. The fresh air, cleansed by the rainfall and mixed with the scents of salt water and seaweed, breezed through the car's open windows, invigorating him and stirring memories of his college days. As they approached the makeshift wooden arches that led to the Marine Drive grounds, Murali slowed the car.

After parking, he stepped out and held the door open for Karnan. He then reached under the driver's seat to retrieve the bag containing Kali and slung it over his left shoulder. The three men stood silently, surveying the bustling activity before them.

Several hundred young volunteers worked in small groups, arranging chairs within an area marked with a yellow ribbon in front of the stage. Another group was frantically working on the stage, which featured a large red banner with the words 'Young Democratic Socialists of Kerala Welcomes Shri T.K. "Vaikom" Karunakaran' printed in large white letters.

Murali noticed the loudspeakers were playing a popular song from a Kerala People's Arts Club drama, based on one of Karnan's novels. Even though it was a political event, the atmosphere felt festive, just like the many university arts and music festivals Murali had attended as a student. The setting sun cast a crimson hue across the backwaters, creating a beautiful backdrop.

Just the right atmosphere for maamen to feel welcome, Murali thought.

∞

Murali's best friend Shibu, who was directing the volunteers, was the first to recognize Karnan. He turned and hollered at his colleagues, 'Look, Vaikom Karnan sir has arrived. Come, let us receive him. Can one of you run backstage and get MLA Shivan?'

A hurried scramble ensued. About two dozen volunteers stopped what they were doing and ran towards Karnan. A female volunteer, carrying a copper plate with fresh flowers and a lighted lamp, applied tilak on the foreheads of Karnan, Vasu and Murali. Seeing the commotion, more onlookers joined the volunteers.

Shibu raised his clenched fist and cried out with a booming voice, 'Long live Vaikom Karnan!'

The other volunteers echoed the chant.

'Freedom fighter Vaikom Karnan, zindabad!' Shibu bellowed, and the crowd repeated.

Shibu turned to face his followers and asked, 'Friends, say out loud. Who is our leader?'

The volunteers around him responded in unison, 'Karnan, Karnan, Vaikom Karnan. Now and forever, Karnan is our leader!'

Pleased with the response, Shibu raised his clenched fist again and bellowed, 'Friends, say aloud. Who is our modern-day King Mahabali?'

'Karnan, Karnan, Vaikom Karnan. Now and forever, Karnan is our Mahabali!'

Murali glanced at his father and received a smile and nod of approval. The fact that Karnan was compared to Mahabali, the mythical king of Kerala, was something he had learnt from his father and subsequently shared with Shibu. The comparison was initially made famous by the slogans of striking workers of Cochin Port in the 1960s, who had lionized Karnan.

The group of students had now grown to a long procession of several hundred people and still more rushed to join in. Somewhere in the crowd, another group started beating a drum as the chants grew louder and louder.

Murali saw Karnan remove his spectacles to wipe a tear. *All this must be too much for maamen.* He also felt happy that, after a very long time, his maamen could experience the love of the youth—his most loyal group of supporters. Murali looked around, marvelling at the display of affection Kerala's youth had for his maamen.

Isn't it ironic that the youth is more enamoured with a 70-year-old man, someone who has never held a position of political power, over hundreds of other powerful politicians trying to win them over? Could it be that young people, who do not carry the baggage of ideology, religion and caste, are better at judging the true character of men? Murali's reflections were interrupted when he felt someone tug at his right arm.

'Murali, this is Sub-Inspector Ashraf, a former student of maamen,' Vasu introduced. 'He came earlier today to warn us about a plot to disrupt this event. He is here off duty and wants to speak with you urgently.'

Ashraf pulled Murali aside. 'I was told you are the general secretary of the YDSK. We must get Karnan sir away from the crowd immediately. Come with me.' He sounded upset.

'You go with him,' Vasu instructed his son. 'Ashraf is our man. Let me hold on to the bag until you are back.'

Murali pulled the bag away. 'No, acha. I will hold it. I will be back soon.'

As Murali hurried after Ashraf, Vasu stepped up to take Murali's spot behind Karnan as the procession inched towards the stage.

Murali slung the bag over his left shoulder and quickly caught up with Ashraf, who turned to talk to him. 'You need to make an announcement to stop the procession and disperse the crowd. Can you get hold of a microphone or a bullhorn?'

Murali immediately leapt up the steps leading to the stage and walked over to the student volunteers setting up the sound systems, who recognized him right away. Grabbing a microphone from one of them, he stepped forward to the front of the stage.

'May I have your attention, please? I am Murali Vasudev, general secretary of the YDSK. This is an urgent announcement.' Murali paused for the noise to die down. 'To ensure the event goes smoothly, we request all audience members crowding around our chief guest, Shri T.K. Karunakaran, to please step aside so he can make his way to the stage. Kindly find a spot to sit down. I promise that all of you will hear him very soon.'

A loud buzz arose from the crowd. As the procession slowed and came to a halt, the crowd started to disperse, leaving Karnan, Vasu and Shibu standing by themselves in the centre. They slowly walked towards the stage together as a tall, thin man sporting a black beard and wearing spotless white khadi clothes emerged, flanked by two volunteers.

'Maamen, MLA Shivan is here to welcome you,' Murali whispered, joining them. He waved to Shivan, who returned the gesture.

Volunteers closed in to form a protective outer ring around the VIPs. One of the volunteers handed a large garland of fresh flowers to MLA Shivan, who placed it carefully around Karnan's neck, felicitating him. He then asked the volunteer for a second garland, which he placed around Vasu's neck.

'Namaskaram, Karnan sir and Vasu sir,' MLA Shivan said, his palms clasped in welcome. 'It's a real honour to have both of you blessing us with your presence. As you can see, our young members are very excited. We have been waiting for this moment for a very long time.'

'Namaskaram, Shivan. The honour is ours. To tell you the truth, there is no other place we would rather be right now.' Karnan placed his right hand on the MLA's shoulder. 'I must say you are doing vital work organizing and awakening the youth of Kerala. I had started the work but left it unfinished...' Karnan paused briefly before continuing, 'and now that Murali, who is like a son to me, works for you, that makes you a member of our family. Isn't that right, Vasu?'

'Absolutely,' Vasu replied and looked at MLA Shivan. 'We did not want Murali to get into politics for a long time but it has given Murali the two brothers he always wanted. He considers you his elder brother and Shibu his twin.'

MLA Shivan smiled and playfully slapped Murali on his back. 'This young man just found his true calling. He has proved that he is a natural at leading people. Trust me on this—some day, in the not-too-distant future, Murali will make a great MLA, maybe even the chief minister of Kerala. And I have no doubt that Shibu will be there by his side.'

'That's very kind of you, MLA Shivan,' Vasu said. 'We are proud of Murali and want him to be a happy and responsible young man. Anything more than that will be up to the Almighty.'

As the men reached the bottom of the steps that led to the stage, Vasu held Karnan's hand and helped him climb up, with MLA Shivan and Murali following closely behind. Vasu, Ashraf and Shibu stayed close to the bottom, guarding the only access to the stage.

'Come, Karnan sir,' MLA Shivan said and offered his hand. 'Let's go to the waiting room at the back of the stage. I would like to introduce you to the YDSK's leadership team. They are the leaders of tomorrow.'

'No, not of tomorrow, Shivan,' Karnan said. 'We should be careful not to repeat the mistakes of the past. We should regard the youth as leaders of today. I would love to meet them.'

'You are right as usual,' Shivan smiled.

Murali interrupted the conversation. 'The crowd is getting a little impatient. Can you both turn around and wave at the audience?'

Karnan and MLA Shivan turned around, held their clasped hands up, and waved with the other. Seeing the two leaders—one ageing and the other young—the members of the audience stood up and cheered wildly. Shivan reached out to Murali and pulled him in. The cheers grew louder.

Ramesh Babu, a student leader from Trivandrum, had gathered a group of 15 YDSK volunteers in the area close to the stage. He raised his fist and shouted:

'Long live Vaikom Karnan!'

'Long live MLA Shivan!'

'Victory to Leader Murali!'

'Victory to Leader Shibu!'

'Long live our revolution!'

'Glory to YDSK!'

On cue, the crowd joined the chant.

As Karnan and Murali followed MLA Shivan to the rear of the stage, Murali glanced back and noticed that the ground was packed with people; some were even perched on the trees that fringed the grounds.

It's sure going to be a hell of an evening, Murali thought.

~15~

Two Confessions

THE STAGE WAS EMPTY, AND THE CROWD WAS GETTING restless. It had been 20 minutes since Karnan, Murali and MLA Shivan had gone backstage. Vasu and Ashraf remained at the bottom of the steps that led up to the stage. Shibu had stepped away to investigate a commotion at the far end of the grounds.

Vasu turned to Ashraf. 'I am glad you are here. The crowd is much bigger than we had anticipated. Where are the other policemen who came with you?'

'The other policemen?' Ashraf repeated, a hint of sarcasm in his voice.

Ashraf lit a cigarette and offered it to Vasu, who took a quick puff and handed it back.

'So, it's just you? What happened?' Vasu asked.

'You really want to know what happened?' Ashraf took a long drag and exhaled the smoke slowly. 'Just as I was getting ready to leave the police station in a van with 10 armed policemen, we received orders from the higher-ups to stand down. I was told my unit was urgently needed for some VIP protection duty.'

'Did the orders come from Cochin or Trivandrum?'

'I have no doubt that the orders came from the home minister! That dirty son of a bitch is playing with people's lives. The Cochin police commissioner is honest; she is not aware of the politics involved. I got her to approve a small patrol of three unarmed constables. If things get serious, they are on standby in an unmarked car outside the main gates. I am not on duty. I came here on my own.'

Vasu looked at Ashraf. 'So that means the threat is real.'

'Yes, it is. I am not surprised. The HM is not the kind of person who will spare old political foes. He will do anything to crush Karnan sir just to score a political victory. The only part of my job I hate is taking orders from scoundrels like him!'

'What can we do now?'

'Nothing much, I am afraid. Let's hope that nothing bad happens.'

Vasu looked at Ashraf. 'Ashraf, you are just a few years older than my son. Can I tell you something in complete confidence?'

'Sure, Vasu sir. You can trust me.'

'Murali is carrying my old revolver with him. We were not confident about the arrangement for police protection today, so we decided to bring it just in case.'

'What? A loaded revolver? Is that what is in the bag on Murali's shoulder?'

'Yes. It is old—a gift given to me by an old friend, way back in 1942.'

'In 1942!' Ashraf was surprised. 'Does it work? Does Murali know how to use it?'

'Oh, it works just fine. Murali is a natural; I did not have to train him more than a few times. Just like Ekalavya, he practised on his own to hone his skills,' Vasu said. 'A few months ago, he shot a betel nut placed on top of a bottle without breaking the bottle.'

'Really? I don't think I can do that.'

'My only worry is about his temperament to use a weapon in a high-tension situation, especially one that involves protecting a person he loves dearly,' Vasu said. 'I hope we don't have to find out today.'

'Let's hope so. Even as a police officer, I am not allowed to carry a gun when I am off duty.' Ashraf lowered his voice. 'Vasu sir, now that you have told me your secret, I also have a confession to make. Today, for the first time ever, I decided to break the rules. I am carrying my official handgun even though I am not on duty. It is right here. Loaded and ready.' Ashraf smiled and patted the area near his lower back, along the waistband of his pants.

'Two guns are better than one. I do not have a good feeling about today. Perhaps for the first time in my life, I feel fear. Not for myself, but for my dear friend and my son.'

'Don't worry, Vasu sir. I will be right here until the event is over. If a situation arises, I will deal with it. When the programme begins, I suggest you watch the crowd. If anything catches your eye, just point to the location, and I will get there as soon as possible. Ensure that Murali does not use the gun unless I use mine first. Do you get it?'

'Yes. I don't know how to thank you, Ashraf. I admire your love for your former teacher.' Vasu took a deep breath and placed his right hand on Ashraf's shoulder. 'An upright young police officer, who happens to be a Muslim, with his entire future ahead of him, going out of his way to risk his own life for the safety of his ageing teacher, who happens to be a Hindu. Why? Because it is the right thing to do!'

Vasu turned to face the crowd, but his mind was elsewhere. 'Ashraf, I am a believer in God. Karnan chetta is an atheist. Yet, this is exactly the secular India that we had dreamt about during the darkest days of our freedom struggle,' he said, turning to face Ashraf again. 'You give me hope. May God bless you.'

~16~

Sons of Sailors

AS KARNAN AND MURALI FOLLOWED MLA SHIVAN DOWN A narrow corridor behind the stage, the chants of the crowd echoed through the walls, growing louder and louder. The corridor opened into a dimly lit room. When they walked in, the 10 people inside stopped what they were doing, all eyes shifting towards the newcomers.

MLA Shivan raised his hands and summoned everyone to the centre table.

'I want all of you, the executive team of the YDSK, to be the first to meet our chief guest for tonight—freedom fighter, author and my political mentor, Shri T.K. Karunakaran. Of course, he needs no introduction to all of you. In many ways, the YDSK, a new political organization to promote socialism using democratic means, is the result of decades of his hard work. The crowd gathered outside, like us, is fed up with the usual politics and wants real and lasting change. This is our moment. Let's seize it!'

Shivan paused and looked at the volunteers gathered around him as a round of applause broke out in the room.

He continued, 'Thanks mainly to Karnan sir, today the young socialists of Kerala have a seat at the government table, where historically only old men of privilege sat. He is here with his closest confidant, Vasudev Panicker, also a freedom fighter and the father of one of our own, Murali.

'I would like to invite you to meet Karnan sir in person. Please keep it brief so he has time to take a break before he gets on the stage.'

Another round of applause arose, which Karnan acknowledged

with folded hands. A volunteer served hot tea in tiny cups to Karnan and Murali as the members of the YDSK team formed a line.

Murali summoned Shibu and the latter walked over to meet Karnan. 'Maamen, this is my best friend, Shibu. We studied at Maharaja's College together. He is the son of retired Commander U.A. Velayudhan, who served with achan in the Navy.'

'Commander Velayudhan's son!' Karnan raised both his arms in genuine surprise. 'Shibu, did you know that in 1946, your father was a young sailor onboard a British India naval ship anchored at Bombay Harbour? I believe it was named HMIS (His Majesty's Indian Ship) *Talwar*.'

Shibu looked flabbergasted. 'No, I was not aware.'

Karnan clasped Shibu's shoulders. 'Son, are you aware that your father was involved in the famous mutiny of the Royal Indian Navy?'

Shibu was speechless. After a few seconds, he managed to utter, 'My father does not talk about his past, but I have heard about the Mutiny from Vasu uncle.'

'Well, Shibu, I suggest you read my book, *The Rebel Sailors*. It is the true story of how a band of humble Indian sailors revolted against the British empire.'

'What did they do?' Shibu asked.

Karnan smiled. 'Well, son, the more appropriate question would be "what did they not do?" Your father was a member of a group of Indian sailors led by K.K. Nair. Both were influenced by the Red Fort trials of INA officers and Subhas Chandra Bose's call for armed struggle against the British.'

Leaning forward, Karnan said, 'Here is something you will find interesting. At night, when the British officers left the ship and returned to the comforts of their bungalows, your father and his friends gathered in the sailors' mess, raising a popular slogan in support of the INA soldiers.' Karnan paused and said, '"*Lal Qiley se aayi awaaz: Sahgal, Dhillon, Shah Nawaz*." Do you understand what that means?'

'Yes. It means, "The voices from the Red Fort are calling for Sahgal, Dhillon and Shah Nawaz",' Shibu translated easily, adding, 'I grew up on naval bases speaking Hindi.'

'Exactly right, son!' Karnan's face was aglow with childlike excitement. 'Prem Sahgal, a Hindu, Gurbaksh Singh Dhillon, a Sikh, and Shah Nawaz Khan, a Muslim. Those were the names of the brave INA officers on trial. The British handpicked three men from the major religions of India to send a message to the people. Your father and his friends did not stop with just slogans; they painted "Jai Hind" and "Quit India" on the walls of the ship. Can you believe that?'

Shibu's face was flushed. He had thought of his father as an ordinary sailor who had retired from the Indian Navy after serving for 35 years. Hearing Karnan's praise, he glanced at Murali, who also seemed surprised.

Murali recovered first. 'Maamen, I do recall achan telling me that he and Shibu's father were both in the same batch of sailors who had joined the Royal Indian Navy during the early days of the Second World War. But I was under the impression that they went their separate ways after acha left to join the Azad Hind Fauj.'

'Yes, they indeed parted ways, but they kept in touch through letters. On 1 January 1946, Vasu and I had a visitor at our hotel room in Bombay. At the door stood a handsome sailor in a sparkling white uniform. It was Shibu's father, Velayudhan.'

'Really? You met my father in 1946?' Shibu could hardly believe what he was hearing.

'Yes, son. Back then, he looked exactly like you do today. Dark skin…curly hair…like the Malayalam film star Ummer.' Karnan smiled. 'Having heard that his old friend Vasu was in town, he had come to meet him with a bizarre request.'

'What kind of request?' Shibu was curious.

'He wanted 60 flags each of the Congress, the Muslim League and the Communist Party of India.'

'Sixty flags! Why?' Shibu asked.

'That is exactly what we asked him!' Karnan laughed. 'Your father told us how the sailors had planned to lower the Union Jack and hoist the flags of the three major national political parties on the mast of each of the Royal Indian Navy's 60 ships that were stationed in the Bombay harbour.' Karnan paused. 'Difficult to believe, isn't it?'

'No, Karnan sir,' Shibu said. 'I can see my father getting involved in something like this. It was the right thing to do. So, it was really a rebellion against British rule!'

Karnan continued, 'It is a common misconception that the Navy's mutiny was only about the poor working conditions and the racist behaviour of the British officers. The truth was that even the tall walls of the naval barracks were not high enough to contain the surging tide of nationalism. To tell you the truth, Vasu and I were blown away by the sheer audacity of the plan.'

'Did you get the flags to the sailors?' Shibu asked.

'Of course! We worked hard for the next 10 days to raise money and purchase the flags. With the help of Achyut Patwardhan, the Bombay-based Congress leader, Velayudhan and Vasu hatched a plan to smuggle the flags one by one into each ship. The day after the last flag was on board, the mutiny of the Royal Indian Navy started. If my memory serves me, it was on 18 February 1946.'

'Did the plan work?' Shibu asked eagerly.

'Did it work?' Karnan mused. 'By early the next morning, the flags of the Indian parties were fluttering on the masts of all 60 ships! We were told that the British officers went crazy, like chickens with their heads cut off. They could not even conceive of something so audacious happening under their very noses.'

Shibu shook his head. 'Unbelievable!'

'Indeed. It was almost unbelievable,' Karnan agreed. 'If we did not have first-hand information on the developments, we would not have believed it either. The next day, the mutiny spread to other naval stations like Calcutta, Karachi, Madras, Visakhapatnam, and our own little Cochin. Vasu and I celebrated with a full bottle of Hercules 3X that your father had gifted us. That was the best rum we'd had in our lives. I remember Vasu praying for your father's safety before he poured a very large drink.'

'Maamen, that's incredible! But why is the mutiny of the Royal Indian Navy not so well known?' Murali asked.

'Good question, Murali. The British and their allies had just won the Second World War and seemed invincible. My theory is that they did not want the world to know that a ragtag group of Indian sailors had humiliated them. As India was in the midst of a political settlement, most of the Muslim League and Congress leaders did not support the mutiny. Our brave sailors were labelled as "misguided hotheads" by a senior Congress leader. Unfortunately, this glorious chapter of the Indian freedom struggle has almost been forgotten.'

'I can't believe there was not even a single political leader who extended support,' Shibu said.

'Well, there were a handful of leaders from the Congress Socialist Party and the Communist Party of India who did. Jayaprakash Narayan saw the mutiny as a landmark event that challenged the imperial might of the British. In fact, he was the one who encouraged me to write *The Rebel Sailors*. He wanted the truth about the sacrifices of Indian sailors to be recorded for posterity.'

'Does the book mention my father by name?' Shibu asked.

'You see, Shibu, there were some complications. The investigation into the mutiny and the sailors involved lasted well past India's independence. As your father decided to remain with the Indian Navy and was promoted to an officer, we changed his name in the book. That is why very few civilians know about his involvement. But people in the Navy knew who the rebel sailors were.'

'Where can I get a copy of the book?' Shibu asked.

'I must have a couple at home. I will be surprised if your father does not have a copy hidden somewhere. After all, he was my main source for the story. It was my first book and took me about six months to write. JP helped edit the manuscript and introduced me to my publisher,' said Karnan.

'Karnan sir, thank you for this valuable lesson in Indian history. I now understand better what my father went through when he was a young man,' Shibu said.

Karnan placed his hand on Shibu's shoulder again. 'Son, I want you to know that the little-known mutiny, in which your father played a small but important role, rattled the British government and paved the way for a political settlement.' After a brief pause, Karnan continued, 'Anyway, all this may seem like ancient history. Where is your father these days? How is his health?'

'We live in my mother's ancestral home in Pallimukku, near the new Medical Trust Hospital. Father has high blood pressure. He keeps to himself most of the time; I guess he is not yet used to civilian life and misses his friends from the Navy.'

Karnan looked down at the floor, his voice a whisper, as if a heavy weight was bearing down on his shoulders. 'I understand. Many sailors involved in the mutiny were court-martialled and jailed. A few, like your dad, escaped jail only because the British were forced to leave India before they could get to them. Perhaps he feels guilty that many of his friends were killed or jailed. That has been the fate of many freedom fighters,' he said.

After a brief moment of silence, Karnan looked back at Shibu. 'What a pleasant surprise to meet the son of one of the brave rebel sailors. Son, are you Velayudhan's only child?'

'No, sir. I have three siblings. Shashikala, the oldest, is a teacher. My older brother Sashi Kumar—we call him Kumar—is doing his master's degree at Sacred Heart College. I also have a little brother, Suresh Kumar, who is studying at Central School, Naval Base, Cochin.'

'I notice that you and your siblings do not have the typical caste-based last names used by the people of Kerala. I can see your father is living by his values.'

'The credit for that goes to my mummy, Baby Velayudhan.'

'Oh! Interesting that you call your amma "mummy"... I guess that comes from your English-medium education and having grown up in North India. Well then, let's give your mummy all the credit she deserves. I am so happy to have met you today.'

'No, Karnan sir, the honour is mine,' Shibu mumbled.

'Shibu, I want you to know that the courage of young leaders like you has helped the YDSK grow. And thank you for your steadfast support to Murali.'

'Karnan sir, Murali is my best friend. I will die for him,' Shibu said.

Murali walked up to Shibu and embraced him.

'*Makkalae*, seeing the two of you together, I just realized why your bond of friendship will remain strong forever,' Karnan said, smiling.

'Why is that, maamen?' Murali asked.

'Though you have different family backgrounds, education, and how you think, talk and dress, you both have something significant in common, which is the basis of your friendship,' Karnan said. Seeing the puzzled look on the faces of Murali and Shibu, he added, 'You are both sons of sailors. Brave sailors!'

Murali and Shibu looked at each other and smiled. Indeed, they were sons of sailors and had just learnt that their fathers had a friendship that went back several decades—one forged under the fire of freedom.

Karnan waved at Shibu. 'Convey my regards to your parents. I will meet them the next time I visit Cochin.'

With arms on each other's shoulders, Murali and Shibu stepped aside and made way for the next YDSK volunteer waiting in line to meet Karnan.

Seeing Karnan sip his tea, the next student in line hesitated. He was wearing a white shirt and a matching traditional mundu.

'Come on. What are you waiting for? I can have tea and talk at the same time,' Karnan said. 'You and I are dressed alike, but you look much better than me. I wish I was 20 years old again. What is your name, son?'

'My name is Shah Navaz. My *uppa* knows you. He is Abdul Navaz, head of the Kerala Taxi Drivers' Union. You are our hero,' the young man said nervously.

'Of course, I know Abdul very well. I am happy to see that you are following in his footsteps.'

Murali was pleased to see Karnan smiling and enjoying himself while talking to the YDSK executive team members. Karnan asked each volunteer their name, their roles in the organization, which part of Kerala they were from and about their parents and siblings. Finally, he thanked them for their service and reminded them that their political activism mattered.

When it was time for the last person to step forth, Murali stepped up to Karnan and whispered, 'Maamen, this is her.'

Karnan saw a petite girl wearing a white salwar kameez approach him. A scarlet hijab covered her hair, neck and upper body. Her face was half hidden by the shadows created by the dim lights in the room.

'You must be Rukhsana,' Karnan said. 'I was looking forward to meeting you.'

'Yes. Did Murali tell you about me?'

'Just your name. Nothing else, I promise,' Karnan assured her with a smile. 'But I would certainly like to get to know you. Where are you from?'

'I was born and brought up in the Gulf. I came to Cochin in 1977 to study.'

'Oh, I see. What are your subjects?'

'The ones you used to teach,' Rukhsana said shyly. 'History and Political Science.'

'Good combination,' Karnan said. 'They go well together and also complement your political activism. I was told that you are the first female joint secretary of the YDSK. That is a significant achievement for someone as young as you. I am sure you must be very busy.'

'Thank you, Karnan sir. I also volunteer as a nursing assistant.'

'That's wonderful. It looks like you have many interests.'

'History and literature are my twin passions. Nursing sick patients is dear to my heart. Also, it helps me get some work experience and pay for my expenses,' Rukhsana explained.

'That's truly remarkable,' Karnan said. '*Molay*, you speak good Malayalam for a girl born and raised in the Gulf.'

Surprised at the use of the endearment, Rukhsana looked up timidly. 'Oh, my grandmother deserves credit for that.' Her teeth flashed briefly in the dim light as she tried to suppress a smile. '*Ummama* insisted I learn Hindi and Malayalam when I was a little girl. Besides, I have lived here for a few years so my Malayalam has improved.'

'Your ummama indeed did you a big favour. But you deserve full credit for listening to her and reconnecting with your Indian roots,' Karnan said.

~17~

The Girl in Scarlet Hijab

BY THE TIME KARNAN FINISHED TALKING TO THE LAST volunteer, it was well past the scheduled start time of the event. The crowd's chatter was getting louder and over the din, the sound of the drum could be heard.

MLA Shivan entered the room and quickly approached Karnan. 'Karnan sir, we are all set to start the programme,' he said. 'Given the security situation, I will take the stage to introduce you and then invite you up. Murali will lead you to the podium. Our volunteers are stationed around the stage perimeter to deal with any troublemakers. So don't worry.'

'I have no fear for my personal safety. My only worry is for the students gathered here and for my friend Vasu, who is here because I asked him to join me. Can you ensure your team gives Vasu full protection in case of trouble?'

'I have already taken care of that.' He paused and raised a finger to his ear. 'Can you hear the noise from the crowd? They are all fired up.'

'Good. I am eager to share whatever little wisdom I have,' Karnan said. 'My ailing health has not let me take part in public events for the past year, but I feel the time is just right to pick up the gauntlet thrown at us by our own party leaders.'

'The young students of Kerala are excited to hear from you and so am I.'

'Shivan, I must thank you for this opportunity. To be honest, I don't know if I will ever get another chance like this to talk directly to the youth of Kerala. I have tried in the past and failed to get my message through. Now, I feel that the youth is ready.'

MLA Shivan nodded, then turned and returned to the stage with Shibu, leaving Karnan with Murali and Rukhsana.

Rukhsana looked at Murali and took half a step to get closer to Karnan. 'Karnan sir, I want you to know that we are all eager to hear your advice on the way forward. Not just the YDSK members but everyone. We believe in you.'

Surprised by her boldness, Karnan looked at Rukhsana. 'I hear you. I am here to entrust my vision to the youth of Kerala,' Karnan said.

Rukhsana reached for the empty cup in Karnan's hands. 'Would you like some more tea?'

'At this time of the day, I'd prefer another kind of drink,' Karnan said with a smile. 'But I guess I will have to make do with tea tonight. No sugar, please.'

As Rukhsana walked away, Karnan turned to Murali. 'I can see why you fell for her. She is a person with poise and confidence. She spoke to me as if she has known me for years! After we get back, I need to talk to your mother.'

'Thank you, maamen,' Murali said. 'Right now, I am more concerned about your safety. Do you mind if Shibu and I stand on either side of you on the podium? Just in case anyone in the crowd has any wrong ideas.'

'Relax, Murali. The threats are empty.' Karnan reached out to hold Murali's arms. 'The bag on your shoulder…are you carrying Kali?'

'Yes. Amma did not want achan to carry it. His hands are not as steady as they used to be.'

'It is my fault. I should not have asked Vasu.' Karnan shook his head slowly. 'Promise me, Murali, that you will not use Kali unless I tell you to.'

'Maamen, you know I cannot do that. You will be too busy with your speech to notice what is happening in the crowd. Leave that to Shibu and me. Please trust me on this one.'

'Son, you know I trust you as much as your father.' Karnan looked into Murali's eyes. 'Just remember that your life is more precious and valuable to people than mine.'

'Are you joking? Do you not see how many people have come from all over Kerala to hear you speak?' Murali responded. 'Maamen, why don't you sit down and relax for a few minutes? Let me quickly check if everything is all right on stage.'

As Murali walked up to the stage, Rukhsana arrived with a cup of tea and handed it to Karnan.

Karnan took a sip and looked at Rukhsana. 'I heard that you have been reading a few interesting books of late.'

'So, Murali told you... Yes, I love to read and write. I have read your novels multiple times and all your newspaper articles. I find your ideas and thoughts fascinating.'

'Is that so? Fascinating in what way?'

'I admire your unshakeable belief in, and tireless quest for, an egalitarian social order that is fair and just for everyone. And yet...' Rukhsana hesitated.

'And yet what? Molay, tell me. I want to hear your thoughts.'

'After living in Kerala and closely following political developments over the last two years...I often wonder if that is possible.'

'Is it possible?' Karnan repeated. 'I believe so. It may not happen in my lifetime, but I am 100 per cent certain it will in yours. We just need to convince enough middle-class people who are relatively well-off to join our fight against those with a vested interest in maintaining the status quo. It's just a matter of organizing and educating the people, and executing our plans with patience and discipline.'

'I remember you saying the exact same words at the Kerala Press Club event last year, and also at the Ernakulam Law College the year before. But not much has changed, except you now have new enemies who hate you more than the British ever did.'

Karnan threw back his head and laughed. 'You are absolutely right. As the great Greek philosopher Plato said, "No one is more hated than he who speaks the truth." If my words and actions have upset powerful people, that is evidence that I am speaking some inconvenient truths.' Karnan paused and looked at Rukhsana. 'It seems that you have been keeping close track of what I say at various events.'

'Yes. I have attended most of your talks since moving here.'

'Is that right? I do not remember seeing you at my events. Maybe you did not ask me any questions; I usually remember the faces of those I have engaged in conversations with.'

'Well, in my case, that would have been rather difficult because I used to be very shy at public events, so my friend Geethanjali used to ask them on my behalf. You will surely recognize her when you see her.'

'Hmm…interesting…You have been observing me from a distance without being noticed. You may know more about me than most people.'

'Maybe… But I have a question I always wanted to ask you.'

'What is it?'

'Do you have any regrets in life?'

'Oh, that is a rather difficult question as I have many regrets—private and public. Let's keep the private regrets aside for another discussion and focus on the public ones. It has to be that I was naive in assuming that after independence, our people would make good decisions while choosing their leaders, and those elected leaders would act responsibly. I was wrong. Very wrong. And…'

'And?'

'I wish I had done more to use my influence and experiences to make change happen when I had the chance. Now, at my age, all I can do is write articles and educate people on the constant vigilance that is required to safeguard our freedom from enemies—external as well as internal.'

'Have you considered writing a book on this topic?' Rukhsana asked.

Karnan sighed and looked down. 'I wish I had done that 20 years ago when I was active in politics. Now, I am afraid the time for me to write another book may have passed.'

'Well, your fans would not agree with your assessment,' Rukhsana said.

Karnan smiled. 'Rukhsana, the truth is that I am living on borrowed time. I can't focus on anything for more than 30 minutes. Books need time, focus and attention—none of which I possess today. Moreover, my journalist friends tell me that very few people have the time to read books these days. Perhaps this event could be my final opportunity to get the word out.'

'Well, I hope that this is just the starting point, not the end. Since I asked you a question, do you have one for me?' asked Rukhsana.

'Yes, I do. I hope you don't mind my asking the most obvious question…about your hijab?' Karnan was hesitant, unsure whether Rukhsana was open to discussing the topic. 'Most Muslim girls in Kerala don't wear one. Is it your choice or a religious requirement imposed by your family?'

'No, I don't mind at all,' Rukhsana smiled as she replied. 'Just now, when I was backstage, I overheard a volunteer refer to me as "the girl in the scarlet hijab". That is how most people have known me since I arrived in Cochin. When I turned 13, my uppa insisted that I wear a hijab—a traditional black one.'

'Your hijab has been a constant companion. I don't think I have seen a girl wearing a scarlet-coloured one. Does the colour have a special significance in Islam?' Karnan asked.

'No. Not to my knowledge. Scarlet was my grandmother's favourite colour. She said it is associated with strength, passion and love. I was raised by her after my parents passed away in a car accident. She is the one who advised me to pursue higher education in Kerala. After arriving in Cochin, I started wearing this scarlet hijab in her honour,' Rukhsana said.

Karnan nodded. 'I am sorry about your parents,' Karnan said. After a brief pause, he continued, 'I am glad to see the respect you have for your grandmother and that you take pride in your tradition. These days, not many young people do. Your ummama is right. For soldiers and freedom fighters, the colour scarlet holds a different meaning. It is the colour of blood and represents courage, sacrifice and revolution.'

'To be honest, Karnan sir, I did not want to wear a hijab when I came to Cochin, as I was told most Muslim girls in Kerala do not. But my ummama insisted I continue to wear it—not for religious reasons. She felt that most boys would be intimidated by its bold colour and leave me alone,' Rukhsana explained, adding with a smile, 'I must confess that it was an easy way to add a dash of colour to my identity without breaking my tradition.'

'Very interesting,' Karnan said with a smile, feeling intrigued. 'Your ummama is a wise woman. But it looks like one young man was not intimidated.'

Rukhsana's white teeth flashed again. 'Well, ummama said "most boys". Murali is different. So, in a way, she was right. She always was. May Allah bless her soul.'

The realization that Rukhsana had lost her parents and grandmother triggered Karnan's compassion. 'I am so sorry to hear that. When did your ummama pass?' he asked softly.

'In 1976. It was her wish that I live and study in Kerala. She had also saved some money to meet my expenses.'

'Molay, I have no doubt she is watching over you from heaven and is very proud,' Karnan said gently. 'I enjoyed meeting you, Rukhsana. I hope to see you again very soon—with Murali.'

'Inshallah,' Rukhsana said softly, surprised by the warmth in Karnan's voice. 'Karnan sir, you must be exhausted. Please rest for a few minutes.'

'Yes, some rest would be good for my old heart. However, I insist you stop adding "sir" to my name. It sounds too formal.'

Rukhsana's heart raced as she reached out to take the empty teacup from Karnan. A fleeting thought crossed her mind—her relationship with Murali had brought her to this moment, sharing a casual conversation with his uncle.

From the stage, Murali's voice rang out, announcing that the event would begin soon.

~18~
The Protégé

BY THE TIME THE CURTAINS WERE LIFTED, IT WAS PAST 7 p.m. and the sun had set, casting a dark shadow over the backwaters. The rain had stopped, but the smell of the breeze drifting in carried hints of impending rainfall. *I hope the rain gods hold off until the event ends*, Murali thought.

The large floodlights at the four corners of the grounds illuminated the area, revealing that every inch of space within the bamboo-fenced area was packed with people. Except for those seated in the first 10 rows, the rest were standing. MLA Shivan, standing on the podium, gestured for the crowd to settle down.

'Friends, let me begin by thanking everyone who has come from all over the state to attend the concluding session of the first YDSK state conference, our biggest event to date,' MLA Shivan said, speaking into the microphone. 'Thanks to your support and the dedication of our executive team and volunteers, we have seven members in the Kerala Legislative Assembly today. While, as socialists, we support the LDF government, I want to clarify that our first allegiance is to the working people of Kerala. The LDF should not take our support for granted. We did not accept a position in the E.K. Nayanar ministry because we are waiting and watching to see whether the government will keep its promises to the working class.'

Shivan's speech gained momentum. 'Today, I have the great honour of introducing our chief guest for the evening. Most know him for the critical role he played in mobilizing the opposition in Kerala against the national Emergency imposed by Prime Minister Indira Gandhi in 1975 and for exposing the police brutality in the

Rajan murder case. I was by his side as an aide when he got the phone call from his mentor, Lok Nayak Jayaprakash Narayan, asking him to lead the charge against the Emergency. Despite hailing from different corners of our great nation, Jayaprakash Narayan and Karnan sir seem to be cut from the same cloth. Today, I would like to tell you something not many people of Kerala know—Karnan sir's long saga of courage and sacrifice as a freedom fighter at the epicentre of India's fight for independence.'

A loud cheer erupted from the back of the audience, where students from local colleges stood. The slogans rang out again:

'Who's our hero? In whom do we trust?'

'Karnan, Karnan, Vaikom Karnan!'

'Now and forever, Karnan is our hero. In him we trust!'

MLA Shivan raised his hands to quiet the chanting before continuing.

'Friends, our chief guest, Shri Vaikom Karunakaran, is no ordinary person. Under the loving care of his uncle, T.K. Madhavan, Karnan sir became the youngest protester at the Vaikom Satyagraha. The father of our nation, Mahatma Gandhi, gave him the nickname "Karnan" at Vaikom. Perhaps the great soul had the foresight to know that one day the young boy—like his namesake, the great warrior from the *Mahabharatam*—would grow up to wear the *kavach*, the impenetrable armour made of courage and steadfast devotion to the freedom of our motherland.' MLA Shivan paused to catch his breath and look around the grounds. The voices had died down.

'I met Karnan sir when I was 18 to get some advice on community service. It did not take me long to realize that he was a great revolutionary and a true leader—not one of the pseudo-intellectuals without an original thought or the armchair pundits who never risked life or limb, or one of the politicians secretly lusting for power. Karnan sir walked with—as my father put it—half a step behind—the giants on the national stage during the two decades that culminated in India's hard-fought independence from the British.

'As if his sacrifices for the nation before independence were not enough, soon after India became free, as hundreds of politicians rushed to Delhi to partake in the spoils of power, Karnan sir quietly returned home. Drawing on the lessons he had learnt by working closely with great leaders like Jayaprakash Narayan, Aruna Asaf Ali and Ram Manohar Lohia, Karnan sir built a grassroots movement that soon engulfed the entire state, leading to the first democratically elected socialist government in India. He walked alongside the people he loved the most—the poor, the dispossessed and the daily wage workers—showing them the path towards claiming their rightful place in a young, fragile and fractious democracy.

'In the years that followed, Karnan sir, a prisoner of his own conscience, repeatedly shunned offers to run for political office and courageously stood up to the hypocrisy and nepotism of the governing elite in Kerala, many of whom were his former party colleagues.

'After Kerala attained statehood in 1956, buoyed by the steadfast support of the students and workers of the state, it seemed almost certain—even if only for a few tantalizing months—that Karnan sir was the people's choice for the highly coveted position of the chief minister. They believed that Kerala needed a young, dynamic and visionary leader to usher the state into a new era.

'To the great misfortune of our beautiful land, our narrow-minded political dealmakers, trying to appease various communal forces, squandered this opportunity, and our history took a familiar turn. This was repeated in the 1960s. As an elected official, I cannot help but wonder where Kerala would be today had Karnan sir taken his rightful role as the chief minister.

'Friends, if you indulge my imagination for a few seconds, I can tell you that Kerala would have become a model socialist democracy, not just in name but in practice. I can envision every worker enjoying good living standards, every child having free access to education and healthcare and our people governed by a system free of corruption. Karnan sir would have harnessed our immense human capital within the state and our talented expatriate community overseas. Instead of endless hartals, Kerala might have competed with megacities like Bombay and Bangalore as one of the leading business capitals of the nation.'

Shivan leaned forward on the podium, holding on to the microphone. Murali noticed Shivan's voice getting louder. 'Friends, if the people of Kerala had had their say back then, it is possible that today, our chief guest would have been our chief minister and our dream of the return of King Mahabali would have been a reality, not just a slogan. Think about that!'

Shivan continued, 'But we cannot live in the past. We must confront the reality before us today. We need to answer pressing questions: do we owe allegiance to a political ideology or the common man who elected us? Despite Kerala electing several so-called socialist governments, why does the gap between the rich and poor continue to widen? Why is our economy in such a bad condition that we must keep borrowing from the World Bank? Why are there no jobs in the state for our youth? What role should the youth play in politics and policymaking? The people of Kerala deserve honest answers to these questions.'

Shivan paused to take a sip of water before continuing, 'Friends, I only know this much—there is one person in Kerala today who has the experience, wisdom, integrity and courage to guide us through these challenging times.' Shivan stopped speaking, scanning the crowd. 'He is a son of our soil. He has served great leaders of India like Jayaprakash Narayan, as well as the poor daily wage and plantation workers of Kerala with the same devotion.

'What astounds me is that in between all this, Karnan sir managed to become a successful author and teacher. Recently, I learnt from reliable sources that, if not for the sabotage by the elite political class in our state due to his caste, Karnan sir might have won not only Kerala's highest literary award but possibly even India's.' Shivan paused, momentarily distracted by a commotion in the crowd. To drown out the noise, he raised his voice and continued. 'Dare I say the raw truth? Had his last name been Nair or Namboodiri, I have no doubt that he would have been the CM today.'

A hushed silence fell over the audience.

'Karnan sir is a guru not only to me but also to an entire generation of student leaders from the 1950s, '60s and '70s, across the political spectrum,' MLA Shivan thundered. 'The YDSK is his brainchild. You must have heard the YDSK members respectfully referring to Karnan sir as "Mahabali", after the greatest king of Kerala; so it is only fitting that he has graced us during the month of the Onam festival.

'I know he will not like me disclosing this, but today is Karnan sir's 70th birthday. And what glorious 70 years they've been! Friends, please join me in thanking him for his selfless devotion and service to India and Kerala. It is the highest honour of my life to invite him to the podium.'

∞

Mesmerized by MLA Shivan's rousing speech, Murali was jolted back to reality by a loud roar from the middle of the crowd. Peering into the distance, he saw a fistfight had broken out between two groups in the audience. *Are some people anxious to push forward for a better view of Karnan maamen? Or has the trouble that Ashraf warned about begun?* Murali felt the weight of Kali in the bag slung over his shoulder. The promise he had made to his parents flashed through his mind.

He glanced towards where his father was standing and saw him waving wildly, shouting, 'Don't bring maamen out now. Let the crowd settle down.' Murali nodded and rushed to the waiting room where his uncle was resting, oblivious to the commotion outside. *Perhaps it is good that his hearing has diminished with age.*

Karnan looked up. 'Son, is it my turn to speak?'

Murali decided not to burden him with the truth. 'Not yet, maamen. Shivan sir is still talking,' Murali lied, pulling up a chair beside Karnan. 'We have some more time. Please relax. I will let you know when we need to go.'

Karnan took Murali's hand. 'Son, I am glad you are with me today. You asked if you and Shibu could stand near me on the podium. Yes, I would like that. I want the people of Kerala to see two fine young men who will lead them one day.'

'Maamen, it's not about us, but about your safety.'

'I know, son. But make sure you put the bag away. I don't think we will need Kali today.' Karnan's face broke into a mischievous grin. 'And besides, you don't want a photo of yourself with a bag hanging from your shoulder on the front page of all the newspapers tomorrow, do you? That would be enough for Rukhsana to tease you for the rest of your life.'

Murali smiled at his uncle's clumsy attempt at humour and gently squeezed his hand.

'Murali, I am glad I met Rukhsana. She has a strong character. Since we have some time, tell me how you won her heart,' Karnan said. 'Hold on, let me guess—did it involve you singing?'

'Yes, maamen. I remember you advising me to use my voice like a *Brahmastra*,' said Murali, referring to the ultimate weapon of the Hindu god Brahma, 'to be used only as a last resort when everything else fails. That's exactly what I did.'

Murali heard the familiar sound of his uncle's hearty laugh. From a distance, he could also hear the slow beat of the drums played by a group of local college students and the faint sounds of the slogans in praise of Karnan.

'All right, then tell me all about how a Hindu boy from Alleppey, who got elected as the president of Maharaja's College Student Council, fell in love with a mysterious Muslim girl who wears a hijab…a scarlet hijab!' Karnan's smile failed to mask the seriousness in his voice. 'I want the unvarnished story, not the version you must have told your parents.'

Murali's gaze met Karnan's. 'Maamen, you will be surprised to learn that, unknowingly, you played an important part in bringing us together.'

'Is that right? Tell me all about it!'

Murali tried to focus, grappling to block out the din surrounding him. After a few seconds, his mind drifted to a quieter place. All he could hear was the soft rustling sound of the wind passing through the lush green leaves of bamboo trees.

~19~
New Beginnings

September 1977–April 1978
Maharaja's College, Cochin

AFTER THEIR FIRST MEETING AT SUBHASH BOSE PARK, Murali and Rukhsana began quietly slipping away from the college campus to meet under the shade of the bamboo grove two to three times every week. Rukhsana insisted they limit their meetings to the lunch hour. She brought lunch for two, making sure they made the most of their time together. Murali liked the way she made decisions on his behalf and the practical logic she used: 'Neither of us is born rich; we must graduate and get jobs to survive.'

Murali admired Rukhsana's boldness and pragmatism, especially when she questioned some of his preconceived left-leaning views. He was drawn to her confidence and deep understanding of Kerala history—a topic he became increasingly interested in due to his growing involvement in campus politics. He marvelled at how organized she was with her studies, meticulously making handwritten notes in her journal every day. But what he loved most was her deep interest in his uncle's past. Murali was happy to share what he knew about Karnan with her, and even happier when Rukhsana bonded easily with his closest friend, Shibu.

On 19 November 1977, Rukhsana's 19th birthday, Murali met her at their now familiar meeting place under the bamboo groves in the park. He came bearing a gift wrapped in red paper. Playfully, he gave her three chances to guess what was inside. Judging by its book-like shape, Rukhsana guessed three different novels on her reading list that she knew Murali was aware of. She was wrong each time. With a smile, Murali handed her the package. Rukhsana opened it to find several old, worn-out diaries. Her curiosity piqued, Rukhsana opened the cover of the first one. It took her a few seconds, but when she realized she was holding the personal handwritten diaries of Vaikom Karnan, she jumped up, grasped Murali's hand and looked deep into his eyes.

After the initial rush of excitement, Rukhsana hesitated. She told Murali that she did not deserve to read these personal diaries. Murali assured her that it was all right, explaining that the diaries had been gifted to his father on his 60th birthday by Karnan. She could treat them like any other book from the library—read and return them. Touched by Murali's thoughtfulness, Rukhsana accepted the special gift. They decided to skip college that day. Later, they went to Bharat Tourist Home, a popular vegetarian restaurant just a short walk from the park. They feasted on freshly made masala dosa, which was served with coconut chutney, and hot filter coffee. Hours slipped by as they talked, sitting on the lawn of the restaurant. Murali then treated Rukhsana to her favourite ice cream from Dasaprakash. As the sun began to set, they walked to the nearby Rajendra Maidan and watched the tugboats push large cargo ships inland.

Murali walked Rukhsana to the bus stop to see her off and then went to meet Shibu. On the bus ride home, Rukhsana replayed the conversation she had had with Murali. It occurred to her that since she had arrived in Cochin, this was the first time someone other than Geethanjali and Mallika aunty had treated her with so much kindness. A warm feeling enveloped her as she thought about the next day. Pulling her hijab tightly over her head, she closed her eyes and silently prayed for her grandmother, thanking her for planting the idea of pursuing higher education in Kerala.

∞

News of the unlikely romance between the handsome, bearded Hindu boy with the golden voice and the bold, mysterious Muslim girl in the scarlet hijab spread like wildfire across the sprawling campus of Maharaja's College.

Two months after Murali and Rukhsana's first meeting, Shibu invited them for a private conversation. In a candid moment, Shibu confessed to Rukhsana something only Murali knew—that he was struggling to overcome a drinking problem. His efforts to stay away from alcohol led to mood swings, which he believed made him unfit to be the party leader on campus. Shibu expressed his desire to see Murali become the president of the Student Council, explaining that Murali possessed many qualities—calmness, likeability and powerful communication skills in Malayalam—that could help him win the elections and perhaps propel him into higher political office. Shibu also pointed out areas where Murali needed to improve, such as his knowledge of Kerala's political history and his debating skills, suggesting that Rukhsana could help him in these areas. Rukhsana readily offered her assistance.

With Murali's and Rukhsana's consent, Shibu drafted a petition to the district leadership of the SFI—the student wing of the Communist Party—demanding an end to the nomination of student leaders by the district party committee. The petition called for internal elections within each college to determine the student representatives. It was signed by over 5,000 students, leaving the district leadership no choice but to allow internal elections.

With Shibu spearheading his political outreach, Murali was easily elected as the leader of the SFI's unit at his college. The victory set the stage for him to contest the Student Council presidential elections, a position previously held by many ambitious young student leaders who later rose to state-level and national-level prominence. Before filing his nomination, Murali persuaded Shibu to run for general secretary, the second most powerful position in the Council. The news was met with jubilation, with students loyal to Shibu bursting firecrackers in celebration.

A few weeks later, encouraged by Geethanjali, Rukhsana

dipped her toes into campus politics. She formed a group called 'Girls Who Vote' to encourage female students to participate in college elections. The group quickly gained popularity, with an enrolment of 1,000 female students within a month, making Rukhsana a well-known figure on campus. Riding the waves of her new-found popularity, Rukhsana set aside her initial apprehensions about politics and threw her support behind Murali's candidacy. At Geethanjali's insistence, she enrolled in dance lessons and performed at the college's annual arts festival, marking the first time anyone saw her without her trademark scarlet hijab.

The unlikely quartet of Murali, Shibu, Rukhsana and Geethanjali—each with very different backgrounds, talents and physical appearances—soon gained a sizeable following on campus. They handed out election flyers during lunch breaks and organized informal sessions at various locations across the campus. Between them, they had something interesting to offer everyone. Female students flocked to hear Murali sing a few lines of their favourite songs; the older, more politically active students enjoyed listening to Shibu's fiery rhetoric; juniors were drawn to Geethanjali, the chatty girl who seemed to know everyone on campus; and young girls were eager to catch a glimpse of Rukhsana, the student-turned-political activist with henna tattoos on her hands and a scarlet hijab.

Campaigning tirelessly across the campus, riding a tidal wave of popularity, Murali and Shibu won the general election by record margins. Murali secured 75 per cent while Shibu garnered 69 per cent, the widest margins in the college's history. Local newspapers reported the election results, with *Mathrubhumi*'s front-page headline reading: 'Vaikom Karnan's Nephew Murali Smashes Electoral Records'. Although the headline was biologically incorrect, Murali's connection to the famous freedom fighter caught the attention of local political leaders, including P. Shivan, the newly elected and youngest MLA of Kerala, and a protégé of Vaikom Karnan.

~20~

When an Old Lion Roars

8 October 1980
Marine Drive Ground, Cochin

THE LIGHT BREEZE CARRIED A FAINT SMELL OF RAIN, MAKING Vasu restless as he nervously paced near the steps that led to the stage. It had taken 20 intense minutes for the YDSK volunteers to break up the fight between the two groups in the audience. One consisted of students who were YDSK supporters, while the identity of the other group, which consisted of older men, was unclear.

With Ashraf's help, the volunteers detained one man from the older group. A search revealed that he was carrying a knife. Vasu's mind raced; *some of the others involved in the fight will certainly have dispersed all over the grounds.*

During the chaos, Shibu had quickly organized a group of students to form a human circle around the stage, instructing them to keep the intruders out. Vasu climbed the steps to the stage, lifted the curtain and called out to his son, 'Murali, you can bring maamen out now. Stay with him on the stage. I will be waiting near by the steps.'

The crowd was abuzz with anticipation as Murali lifted the curtain and held it aside for Karnan. MLA Shivan approached, clasped Karnan's hand and led him to the front. The crowd broke into a rapturous standing ovation, while the beating of the drum and slogan chanting started again.

Vasu noticed Murali, standing behind Karnan, had placed his bag on the shelf under the speaker's podium. *Will Murali be able to reach the revolver fast enough if the need arises?*

Karnan reached the podium, adjusted the microphone and surveyed the packed ground. He raised his clenched fists high above his head, a gesture that was greeted by loud applause. As he began to speak, a hush fell over the audience.

'My dear friends, namaskaram,' Karnan began in a subdued tone. 'I was told that following MLA Shivan as a speaker is not a good idea, for few people can articulate progressive ideas as clearly as he does, and there is almost no one in Kerala who has fought to bring these ideas to life like him. The credit for the YDSK holding seats in the Assembly almost entirely goes to MLA Shivan and his leadership.'

Karnan paused for a few seconds, pondering on his next words. 'Today is a difficult day for me and my good friend Vasu, who is here with me. It is the first anniversary of the death of our guru, friend, elder brother and source of inspiration—one of the greatest leaders of the Indian independence movement, Jayaprakash Narayan—"JP" to most of you. It was at the feet of this giant of a man that Vasu and I learnt almost everything we hold dear: honour, loyalty to our country, unwavering commitment to a cause, love for the people we serve, and above all, courage.'

Vasu had heard Karnan speak hundreds of times, but there was an added emotional intensity in his voice this time. *Is the threat still on his mind? Is Karnan aware of the fights that took place earlier? I pray he finishes the speech quickly so we can leave.*

Karnan continued, 'Back in the 1940s and 1950s, long before he earned the title of "Lok Nayak", JP was called the "Second Gandhi" by the people of Bihar, Orissa and Uttar Pradesh. How many of you know that, if he had wanted, JP could have been Nehru's successor when he passed away in 1964? Or that he was the consensus candidate for the president of India in 1967 and again in 1977?

'But JP had learnt from Mahatma Gandhi that he could serve the people of India better by holding those in power accountable for their actions. He was the voice of the voiceless masses of India.

He always put our motherland above everything else, including his family and party. That, my friends, is the purest, deepest, most selfless form of love I have ever witnessed.'

Karnan paused briefly, his voice now more emotional than ever, before continuing. 'Friends, I must admit I took a tiny sip from JP's heady cup of love. Perhaps that is the reason why I was sad this morning. It is unfortunate that, even 33 years after driving the British out of India, we have a government acting more imperial than they ever did. Our officials behave like an entitled class, superior to the ordinary people. They travel around in their fancy cars with armed guards as if they are afraid of the very people who entrusted them with power.

'I remember JP's prophetic words from 1948, warning us against what he aptly called "the tyranny of the state". As a naive young man back then, I thought tyranny would naturally end with the British Raj. I was completely wrong. The only difference now is that the tyrants have brown skin, just like us. That, my friends, is the reason for my sorrow.'

An eerie silence gripped the crowd. Karnan's message of gloom was unexpected from a man known for his humour and optimism.

'But today, after setting foot on the Marine Drive grounds and witnessing your resolve, your fierce determination, and the quiet courage of your dynamic leaders—MLA Shivan, Murali, Shibu—and the young members of the YDSK executive team I met backstage, all my worries have melted away. All I saw was love. Love for your friends, family, Kerala and India. Love for the country above the party—that is what I witnessed today. It is the same love I saw in JP's eyes when I first met him at Nashik Central Jail in 1932.

'Friends, now I am reassured and at peace, knowing that our state and nation are in strong and caring hands. I do not doubt that you are ready to take on the tyrants and make real, lasting change in the state. It is with this confidence that I share my thoughts on the way forward for the youth of Kerala.'

The crowd broke into loud applause. Vasu noticed that Murali's attention was fixed on his uncle and not the crowd. He tried in vain to catch Murali's eye.

'But before I do that, allow me to share an amusing bit of information I read in the newspaper today. The home minister of Kerala called me a "lion in the winter", meaning I do not have much fight left and will be gone soon.'

The crowd booed in disapproval. Vasu noticed the shift in Karnan's voice as it took on a relaxed, almost playful tone. *Here comes the sarcasm.*

Karnan held up his right hand. 'No, no. I hate to admit it, but this one time, the HM is right. It is no secret that I am old. I turned 70 today. My health is in bad shape. My doctor told me that among all his patients, I am number one. What he meant was that I have the most ailments—blocked arteries in my heart, high blood pressure, vertigo, hearing loss, back pain…the list is endless.'

The crowd went silent, hanging on his every word.

'For over a decade, literary circles in Kerala have been abuzz with rumours that I have lost my ability to write. Some armchair doctors diagnosed me with writer's block. Truth be told, I have not written much in the past 10 years. It is also true that there is nothing I love more than writing. However, creative writing needs tranquillity of the mind and peaceful sounds, like the waves of the Arabian Sea. How can I write when all I hear are the cries of anguish from the poor, the hungry and the unemployed? How can I focus when peace and tranquillity have long bid my land and my people *alvida*?

'Friends, the home minister is right. I am indeed in the winter of my life. The only good news is that he called me a "lion", not a cow or a sheep. I guess I owe him a thank you.'

Laughter rippled through the crowd.

Karnan's voice grew grave. 'But there is something the HM did not consider. A lion in the winter of his life may not be able to hunt or feed his family, but as surely as the monsoon rains of Kerala arrive in June, an old lion will do one thing till his last breath: he will fight. When hyenas attack an old lion, he fights back. The lions in his pride hear his deafening roar, and they come to his rescue.'

Karnan's pause was met with pin-drop silence.

'Yes, I am a lion in winter, but I belong to the YDSK pride. I will fight and keep roaring till my last breath. Together, we will roar so loud that the home minister of Kerala, sipping fine whiskey with his cronies in the comforts of his mansion in Trivandrum, will hear us loud and clear. Tell me, my young friends, are you ready to fight?'

The crowd roared in response. Drums beat in the middle of the grounds, and slogans rang out, leaving no doubt that they loved Karnan's combative tone and the challenge he posed. Vasu's mind flashed back to the mid-1960s. *Back then, the Cochin dock workers' response to Karnan's speeches had been similar, but today's crowd is much larger. History has a way of repeating itself.*

'Yes, I thought so too!' Karnan's voice was now animated. 'Friends, my guru, the great revolutionary Jayaprakash Narayan, once told me, "The revolutionary will die some day, but the revolution must live on." I have five simple messages and one action plan to make his vision come alive. Can I have five minutes of your undivided attention?'

The crowd shouted their consent. Karnan raised his right hand, and silence enveloped the grounds.

'First, our loyalty must be to the ordinary people of Kerala, not to a political party or a cabal of unelected people sitting in an ivory tower—which is what the politburo of the Communist Party has become—or to an elected government that does not keep its promises. This must be a cardinal rule that should never, ever be broken.

'Second, while we believe in our chosen path of democratic socialism, blind allegiance to a political ideology is not the solution. An ideology must be flexible enough to address our problems. As

MLA Shivan has shown us through his many legislative wins, we must remove rigid attachment to ideology. When an idea no longer works, we should be willing to look at new solutions with an open mind.

'Third, communalization of politics has poisoned the body politic of our state. I am afraid we have not made much progress since 1892, when Swami Vivekananda called Kerala a "lunatic asylum of casteism". To fight poverty, hunger, disease and unemployment, and move Kerala towards a state of equal rights and opportunities, we must kill the beast of communalism. That cannot be done by old men carrying age-old prejudices. Only the youth of Kerala can undertake this important and arduous task.

'Fourth, there can be no socialism—or, for that matter, even capitalism—without democracy. Many of our Marxist colleagues running the government secretly believe that a Soviet-style dictatorship is necessary for a socialist state. Nothing can be farther from the truth. I don't have to remind you of the systemic human rights abuse that is taking place in the Soviet Union. My vision of Kerala is of a socialist state—a political and economic democracy—where people are not slaves to a party or the state.

'Fifth, after driving the British out of the country, the people of India handed power over to the conservative and communal forces that dominated the Congress. They assumed that these leaders had the nation's best interests in mind. That was a big mistake. I am guilty of not doing enough to warn them of the harm that people of ill will did in just 33 years. We should never let that happen again. We must be vigilant and, if needed, be willing to fight and die for what we believe in.'

Karnan paused, his eyes scanning the grounds. The silence was palpable.

Vasu could sense the anticipation building up. *Here comes the call for action. I wonder how far Karnan will go tonight.*

'I believe in the five principles I outlined,' Karnan thundered. 'But these principles are not my ideas. Jayaprakash Narayan uttered these words during the 1940s and 1950s—words that the leaders of the Congress largely ignored. Words that have come back to haunt us. Here is my question: this time around, what are we willing to do? What sacrifices are we willing to make?'

A loud voice pierced the silence. 'Karnan sir, just tell us what should be done!' Vasu recognized it as Shibu's.

Karnan looked in the direction of the voice. 'That is a very logical question. Of course, I don't have all the answers but let me share my thoughts shaped by my experiences. The youth, each of you here today, are the future of our party, state and nation. If you stand united, no force on earth can stop you from realizing the destiny of Kerala—not five or ten years later, but today!'

Karnan bellowed, 'Friends, there is no easy path to make our dreams come true. We must make sacrifices, each and every one of us. I call upon the youth of Kerala to put their education on hold for the next 100 days. Get out of the classrooms and organize protests, root out corruption and demand that political leaders keep their election promises.

'Friends, today I am calling on the YDSK to lead a total revolution across Kerala. This is the same clarion call that the great Jayaprakash Narayan gave to the young students of India in 1974 when authoritarianism started to take root in New Delhi. They rose up as one to face the challenge, and, in a few years, they used democratic means to defeat the tyrants. Today, Kerala needs the same total revolution. Nothing short of that should be acceptable.

'I must warn you that those in power will try to maintain the status quo. The establishment will try to bribe you with money or the illusion of power. If that does not work, they will try to intimidate you with threats. They will let their attack dogs loose if you do not give in. Never, ever give in. Stay united behind the YDSK. Be disciplined, be peaceful and, above all, be patient.

'Remember, we believe in democracy, so we must win the trust of the common people of Kerala. Sure, it will be hard work, but it is not impossible. I promise you, although I may not be able to walk as fast as you, I will be there with you every step of the way.'

Vasu looked up at the sky as a flash of lightning illuminated the night, followed by a deep rumble of thunder. He felt a few drops of rain on his face.

Karnan waited for the rumble to fade, and then calmly continued, 'I think we should start right here in Cochin. I have heard of a great college with a storied history, located a few kilometres from here, called Maharaja's—'

The crowd erupted in cheers, especially the section with students from Maharaja's College, who voiced their approval with full-throated enthusiasm. Karnan paused, turning to Murali for a glass of water. Murali stepped forward, reached under the podium to pour water from a jug into a small cup, and handed it to his uncle. Vasu noticed Karnan was sweating profusely, his hands unsteady. Unable to take a sip, Karnan handed the cup back to Murali.

As Murali bent down to place the cup under the podium, a loud cracking sound, like a firecracker, shattered the air. Pandemonium broke out among the crowd as people near the stage leapt from their chairs, trying to escape. Loud shrieks echoed across the grounds.

Shibu instantly understood what had happened and rushed to the front of the podium to shield Karnan. He pointed towards the noise and shouted, 'Catch the bastard!' When no one followed his instructions, Shibu jumped off the stage and ran towards the sound.

Vasu looked at the stage. He saw Karnan slumped against the podium, Murali holding him by his right arm. Rukhsana, who had rushed in from backstage, placed Karnan's left arm on her shoulders. Vasu noticed that Karnan's face was flushed, yet he tried to wave to the crowd with one arm, as if trying to convey that he wanted to finish his speech. A large red stain was spreading across his white shirt.

Vasu felt his heart racing wildly. Suddenly, the horrifying realization dawned on him. *Oh my God, was that the sound of a gunshot?*

PART THREE

THE INCIDENT AT MARINE DRIVE GROUND

~21~
A Shooting and a Killing

8 October 1980
Marine Drive Ground, Cochin

THE SOUND OF WHAT SEEMED LIKE A FIREARM CAME FROM about 25 metres from where Ashraf stood. Wild screams erupted in the VIP section as people ran helter-skelter, crashing chairs in all directions as they attempted to get away from the stage. Murali and Rukhsana helped Vasu carefully lower Karnan's limp body to the floor of the stage.

Ashraf, positioned on the ground in front of the main stage, frantically scanned the crowd but was pushed back by the wave of panicked people fleeing the scene. He saw Shibu leap ahead of him and reached out, grabbing his arm.

'Stay back. Let me deal with this.'

Shibu stopped in his tracks and slowly backed away. Ashraf crouched, moving forward, his gun pointed at a tall, bearded man in a black T-shirt. The man was wrestling with two youngsters, who he guessed were the YDSK volunteers. It appeared that they were trying to snatch an object from the man's hands. Ashraf's line of sight was blocked by a young girl who stood frozen, confused about what to do.

Desperately looking for an opening to shoot, Ashraf heard another shot ring out from the direction of the stage. He turned around to see Murali standing at the edge of the dimly lit stage, holding a revolver. Ashraf quickly refocused and found his line of sight clear. He aimed at the chest of the man in the black T-shirt and pulled the trigger once. Then again.

The man slumped to the ground, his face covered in blood. His outstretched arms revealed a long firearm—possibly a rifle. Shocked by what they had just witnessed, the young volunteers stepped back. Ashraf gestured for them to move away from the body.

'Get down from there,' Ashraf shouted to Murali. 'There could be other gunmen in the crowd.'

Murali leapt off the stage, rolling to break his fall, and came to stand next to Ashraf, who was crouching down, gun still in hand.

'How many shots did you fire?'

'Just one. I aimed for his head,' Murali replied, drenched in sweat.

'You got him. The son of a bitch must have died before he hit the ground. I fired two more shots into his body just to be sure.'

'Anyone else?'

'I am sure there are a few of them in the crowd. They always move in packs but scatter when there's trouble—that's why we call these bastards "pigs". They have likely dispersed by now.'

Murali was breathing hard as he said, 'I am going back to maamen.'

Ashraf grabbed Murali's arm. 'Wait! Your father is already with Karnan sir. You come with me.'

Murali followed as Ashraf sprinted towards the waterfront, about 50 metres away from the stage. The area was dark and deserted.

'Give me your revolver!' Ashraf demanded. 'Quickly!'

Murali reluctantly handed over his weapon.

Ashraf inspected the gun, pulling back the hammer, rotating the cylinder that held the bullets and ejecting the cartridges.

'There are only four bullets. Did you fire two?'

'Acha loaded five. He always leaves the first chamber empty.'

Suddenly, the realization of what Ashraf was about to do hit Murali. 'Please don't throw Kali away. She belongs to my father… she has a lot of history. I beg you!' he pleaded, stepping forward to retrieve the revolver from Ashraf.

'Kali? You gave the damn gun a name?' Ashraf asked, surprised. 'Murali, I know your father's had it a long time but there could be witnesses. We cannot risk someone identifying you with a weapon in your possession. Your father would have done exactly what I am about to do.'

With a swift motion, Ashraf flung the revolver far into the backwaters. The splash was muffled by the waves. He repeated the action with each bullet. Then, he took out his own gun, opened it, removed one bullet and slipped it into the back pocket of his pants.

He turned to look at Murali. 'The water here is not deep, but the clay will hide the gun. I promise to retrieve it for you once things settle down. Remember—if the police ask, tell them I fired all three shots. Do you understand?'

'Yes.'

Ashraf's tone was urgent. 'Now, I want you to run to the front gate. Look for a black car under the big Bombay Dyeing billboard; there will be three policemen inside. Ask for Head Constable Jacob and tell him SI Ashraf sent you and that we have one person with gunshot wounds to take to the General Hospital. Ask him to get the car as close to the stage as possible. Then you follow him in your car. I will bring Karnan sir down.'

Murali hesitated. 'But I must be with maamen—'

'Don't worry about him. I am going to him now. Hurry!'

Ashraf rushed to the stage where he found Karnan lying flat on the floor, his head cradled in Vasu's lap. A girl wearing a scarlet hijab was on her knees, gently pressing her palms against Karnan's chest as he exhaled. MLA Shivan was on the other side of the stage, directing the YDSK volunteers to secure the area.

Vasu looked up. 'Where is Murali? Did he use the revolver?'

'He is all right. Nothing to worry about,' Ashraf reassured him. 'I sent him to get the police to rush Karnan sir to the hospital. Is he breathing?'

A Shooting and a Killing

'Barely,' the girl in the hijab replied without looking up. 'We need to get him to a hospital right away. The next 30 minutes are critical.'

'I see the car coming,' Ashraf said. 'Let's move Karnan sir down.'

The girl looked up at Ashraf. 'We need to keep his head elevated so he does not choke. I'll get some volunteers to help. Officer, can you take my place?'

She stood, turned and waved to a group of the YDSK volunteers gathered by the steps, directing them to clear the path to where the black police car was screeching to a stop. The car doors flew open and three plain-clothes policemen jumped out. A white car pulled up next to them, and Murali stepped out, following the police up the steps. They were joined by Shibu, who was out of breath from all the back-and-forth running.

Ashraf stood up to speak with the burly policeman wearing a head constable's badge. 'Jacob, I witnessed the shooting. I had my gun with me and shot the assailant three times. I believe he is dead. Karnan sir is breathing but we need to get him to the hospital right now.'

'Yes, sir,' Jacob replied. 'We were in the process of apprehending one of the pigs who was carrying a knife. He was being chased by the students. Amidst the chaos, we did not hear the gunshot.' Jacob then turned to his men. 'Lift him up and be careful.'

As the policemen bent down to lift Karnan, Jacob pulled Ashraf aside. 'Sir, with a shooting and a dead man, I have to register an FIR. Who do you believe triggered the shootings?'

Ashraf spoke quickly. 'A few fights had broken out after the event started, but the trigger, I believe, was Karnan's call for total revolution. He was shot right after he said it. That must have been the pigs' orders from their handlers.'

'I am sure we can get the captured accomplice to corroborate this. I think I should stay and talk to the event organizers and eyewitnesses. What do you think?'

'Yes, that is the protocol. MLA Shivan was on stage during the shooting—talk to him. I will drive the car to the hospital.'

'Sir, I thought you were off duty. Will that be an issue?'

'In an emergency, the police commissioner can place me back on duty at any time. I will take care of that.'

'In that case, here are the car keys. There's a transmitter in this vehicle, which connects directly with the commissioner's office and home.' Jacob stepped back and saluted Ashraf, who returned the gesture.

Ashraf rushed over to where Karnan lay. 'Hurry up. Let's move,' he instructed.

Murali and Vasu held Karnan's head and upper body while Ashraf and Shibu lifted his legs. Rukhsana directed them down the steps towards the black car. The two policemen who had accompanied Jacob opened the passenger doors and sat in the back seat, allowing Karnan's body to be placed across their laps.

Ashraf walked over to Murali. 'I am driving the police car. I want you and your father to drive as fast as you can to the General Hospital and let the emergency room know that the police are bringing a VIP with gunshot wounds in critical condition. Tell them to be ready.'

Murali quickly got into his car and gestured to Shibu, who jumped into the passenger seat. Vasu climbed into the back seat and looked out of the window. He saw Rukhsana standing nearby with a few YDSK volunteers, her hands stained with Karnan's blood. *She must be distraught by the events; yet, she acted with an unusual calmness for someone so young.*

Vasu rolled down the window. 'What are you waiting for?' he asked her. 'Come, get in.'

'You want me to come?' Rukhsana asked, unsure.

'Yes, of course,' Vasu replied. 'We need all the help and prayers we can get.'

Ashraf watched as Rukhsana carefully removed her hijab,

revealing long, curly black hair. She folded the cloth and used it to wipe the blood from her hands, the scarlet fabric matching the deep red stains of blood on her hands. She then took a few long strides and got into the back seat of the car, which took off even before the door was fully shut. Ashraf remembered seeing the girl on stage and wondered how she knew so much about treating gunshot wounds. He made a mental note to check with Murali about her later.

MLA Shivan's emotional voice could be heard over the loudspeakers, making a public appeal to the crowd still gathered on the grounds. 'There has been a violent attack on a peaceful and lawful gathering…an unprovoked assassination attempt on our leader, Vaikom Karnan. I promise I will not rest until we find those behind the attack and bring them to justice.'

Ashraf jumped into the driver's seat of the black police car, placing the emergency flashlight on the roof of the car and switching it on. Thousands of people had lined both sides of the road to catch a glimpse of what was happening; they parted as the police car with the flashing lights headed for the gates.

~22~

Race Against Time

PEOPLE CLEARED OUT OF THE GROUNDS, GATHERING IN large groups all along Marine Drive. Ashraf could hear them shouting, their anger palpable. About half a kilometre ahead, a group of students had stopped a Kerala State Road Transport Corporation bus, forcing the driver and passengers out. As Ashraf's car approached the bus, he noticed another group waving a large YDSK flag and blocking the path. Some of them were shouting anti-government and anti-police slogans, armed with sticks and stones.

'Oh no! Not now!' Ashraf muttered under his breath. 'This is not the time to grow a spine.' He leaned forward to remove his handgun from his waist and handed it to one of his men in the back seat. 'Anthony, take my gun. It has three bullets left. Keep it hidden and use it only if they attack us.'

Ashraf braked, bringing the car to a stop.

'This car has flashing lights. It must be a police car,' said one of the students in a red shirt. 'Let's find out what the heck they were doing when the shooting took place.'

A dozen students surrounded the car, taunting Ashraf to step out.

'We know who you are, even though you are not in uniform. Get out of the car, now!' demanded another, brandishing a stick.

Ashraf turned on the lights inside the car and placed his hands outside the window in a gesture of surrender.

'I am Ashraf, a sub-inspector with the city police. I am a former student of Vaikom Karnan and I know exactly what happened. We have an emergency here—please let us go.'

'What emergency?' the student in the red shirt shot back angrily. 'The emergency is over. We did not see a single cop at the event. Now you show up after Vaikom Karnan is shot?'

Ashraf kept his voice calm. 'I am going to get out of the car. I want two of you to step forward. I need to show you something. Are you okay with that?'

'Get out first, then we'll talk. Any other policemen in the car?'

Ashraf opened the door and slowly stepped out, his hands raised.

A young student volunteer rushed to the scene. 'Wait! Wait!' he shouted. 'I saw this man talking to Murali's father. I think he is on our side.'

The man in the red shirt turned to Ashraf. 'Okay, step aside so we can see who else is in the car. Are you carrying any weapons?'

He walked up to Ashraf and patted him down. 'He's clean,' he announced to his friends. He then peered through the front windows and saw the men in the back holding Karnan's body.

'OH MY GOD!' he exclaimed, recoiling. 'It looks like Karnan sir is in the back seat. There is blood on his shirt.' The man turned and grabbed Ashraf by the collar. 'Tell me, is he alive?'

'Yes, he is still breathing, but we must get him to a hospital immediately. If you delay us, it could cost him his life.'

The man turned back to the crowd. 'Step aside, everyone!' he screamed. 'Make way for the car. Karnan sir is still alive.'

A loud cheer rose from the group, and they quickly cleared the path for the car to pass.

Ashraf let out a loud sigh of relief. He jumped back into the driver's seat and sped away.

'Thank God, Ashraf sir, that you decided to drive the car!' said one of the policemen sitting in the back. 'If it were Jacob sir, we would be dead by now.'

The other policeman laughed nervously.

As they drove past the dispersing crowd, the transmitter in

the centre console lit up, and an operator's voice crackled through. 'This is from the commissioner's residence. Is it Head Constable Jacob? Over.'

'This is SI Ashraf Ali. Jacob is still on-site, making an FIR. I am driving the car to the General Hospital with Anthony and Babu. We have a person with gunshot wounds. Inform the commissioner. Over.'

There was a brief delay before a woman's voice came on. 'SI Ashraf, this is Commissioner Sreelekha. I just received word about the shooting. The situation across the city is getting dangerous. How is Mr T.K. Karunakaran? Over.'

'Barely alive, madam. He took a bullet in his chest and has lost a lot of blood. He is unconscious. We are headed to the General Hospital. Over.'

'Okay. Get there as fast as you can.' The commissioner sounded upset. 'I should have listened to you. The politicians who give orders are never around when things go wrong. If Mr Karunakaran does not make it, we will have a major problem on our hands. It could get serious. We must be ready. Over.'

'Yes, madam, I understand. I am praying for the best. We are just five minutes away. Over.'

'I am sending a van with armed guards to secure the hospital. I want you in charge there. I am on my way to an event at Fort Cochin, but I'll meet you at the hospital in a few hours. Over and out.'

'Understood, madam. I will wait outside the emergency room. Over and out.'

It was now past 9 p.m., and with the traffic clearing up, Ashraf drove faster. The police car passed Subhash Bose Park and turned left on to Maharaja's College Road. Within a few seconds, they entered the front gate of the Ernakulam General Hospital. Ashraf pulled up at the entrance of the emergency ward and quickly stepped out to open the back doors.

Ashraf saw Vasu and Murali with the girl from the scene of the shooting directing a group of hospital attendants, who were pushing a wheeled stretcher. A nurse carrying an oxygen mask accompanied them towards the police car. Carefully, the hospital attendants took out Karnan from the vehicle and slid him on to the stretcher.

The nurse walked up to Vasu. 'Sir, the hospital allows only two family members to accompany patients into the emergency room. Who are the patient's closest relatives?' she asked.

Vasu and Murali exchanged glances before the latter piped up.

Murali pointed to Vasu and Rukhsana. 'Nurse, the two people accompanying the patient are Vasudev, his brother, and Rukhsana, his son's fiancée.' He turned to Vasu. 'I will wait here in case you need anything.'

Rukhsana felt a surge of blood flush her face and looked down. It was the first time Murali had referred to her as his fiancée, and a warm sensation spread through her body.

Vasu spoke to the nurse. 'Excuse me, in case you are not aware, the patient is T.K. Karunakaran, the writer. He was shot in the chest and has lost a lot of blood.'

'Vaikom Karnan sir?' The nurse looked at Vasu, wide-eyed. She quickly bent down to place the oxygen mask on Karnan's face and gestured to the attendants to push the stretcher.

'Yes. Please do all you can to save him,' Vasu pleaded.

'Don't worry. We always do our best.'

Ashraf watched as four attendants wheeled Karnan into the emergency ward, Vasu and Rukhsana following closely behind. He pulled Murali aside and fished out a crushed cigarette from his pocket. Lighting it, he leaned against the car and looked at Murali.

'Who is the young man with you?' Ashraf asked under his breath.

'He is my best friend, Shibu. Why? Is there a problem?' Murali replied.

'No, I am just thinking ahead. In case someone witnessed you with the revolver—what did you call it—Kali? I was wondering if

Shibu would be willing to take responsibility for carrying it. It will likely be a minor offence with a fine and no jail time.'

'Are you serious? Do you think I will let my best friend take the rap for my actions? No way. If it comes to that, I will accept full responsibility.'

'Murali, I know how the system works. I do not think that is a good idea,' Ashraf said. 'You are a public figure. If anyone identifies you as the one carrying a revolver, the home minister will try to frame you. What is usually a minor offence could escalate into a major investigation. That will tarnish your image and ruin your political aspirations. Think about it.' He took a long drag and then offered the cigarette to Murali.

Murali took it and leaned against the car. 'Can we deal with this later? But just so you know, Shibu will gladly accept the responsibility to protect me. He is one person I trust with my life.'

'Good to know. I am a police officer, but I can't say that about any of my friends,' Ashraf said. 'By the way, did I hear you right? Rukhsana, a Muslim girl, is your fiancée?'

'Yes, Sub-Inspector. Nothing wrong with your hearing,' Murali said, taking a drag on the cigarette.

Ashraf was not satisfied with the response. 'How long have you known her?'

'Long enough,' Murali responded.

'I see. But you are a Nair. Per tradition, aren't you supposed to marry your uncle's daughter? Your *murappennu*?' Ashraf pressed.

Murali took another drag and handed the cigarette back to Ashraf. 'Rukhsana may not be my murappennu, but I have no doubt that she is the girl I will marry.' After a brief pause, he added, 'She shares your religion, but don't you dare try to steal her from me.'

Both men looked at each other and smiled.

~23~

The Commissioner's Dilemma

9 October 1980
General Hospital, Cochin

IT HAD BEEN ALMOST THREE HOURS SINCE ASHRAF HAD arrived with Karnan, and by midnight, the usually deserted area outside the General Hospital's emergency ward was packed with over 200 people. Ashraf's trained eyes noted that those who kept pouring in were mainly young college students affiliated with the YDSK and members of the press. They all sought the same information—an update on Karnan's condition.

The lobby was cordoned off by the hospital's security staff with the help of the armed policemen who had arrived in a van. A senior officer from the armed police unit walked up to Ashraf, the stars on his shoulders indicating that he was a circle inspector (CI)—a rank above that of an SI. He was there on the police commissioner's instructions to assist Ashraf. Just as the CI was about to speak, the sound of police sirens echoed from a short distance away. Soon, two police vehicles—a jeep escorting an officer's car—came into view.

'The commissioner is here,' Ashraf said to the CI. 'We can talk later.'

Officers jumped out of the jeep to open the rear door of the other car. The police commissioner stepped out, her diminutive frame neatly draped in a blue sari with a white blouse. She immediately noticed Ashraf saluting her and nodded.

'Sub-Inspector, come with me,' she told Ashraf. 'Any updates from the doctors?'

'None so far, madam. I have tried asking a few times; they

said they were short-staffed, with only one doctor working in the emergency ward.'

The armed policemen guarding the entrance saluted and stepped aside to let the commissioner and Ashraf pass through.

'Take me to where Mr T.K. Karunakaran is being treated,' the commissioner said to the lady at the reception. 'I would like to meet the doctor treating him.'

Ashraf followed the commissioner as she hurried after the receptionist. At the end of the long corridor was a set of double doors with the words 'Operating Theatre—Only Staff Beyond This Point' written on them. There, seated on a bench, were Vasu and Rukhsana.

'Madam, they are close friends of Karnan sir's,' Ashraf informed the commissioner. 'He does not have children.'

The commissioner nodded at Vasu and Rukhsana.

Just then, the door opened and a doctor came out. She looked visibly tired, and her loose-fitting gown was stained with blood. Vasu and Rukhsana quickly stood up and approached her.

'I am Dr Mary Eapen, the surgeon on duty. The good news is that the bullet narrowly missed his heart. It was deflected by the sternum, which is a thick bone right here.' The doctor pointed to the centre of her chest. 'We have removed the bullet, which was lodged against the back of a rib. The bad news is that the impact nearly stopped his heart. I believe the lack of oxygen is why the patient lost consciousness, but it also could be due to the heavy blood loss.'

'Doctor, will he survive?' Vasu asked in a shaky voice.

'Honestly, it is impossible to make any determination at this time,' Dr Eapen said, turning to Vasu. 'I understand your concern, but I don't want to sugar-coat things. The patient is in a very serious condition. There is blood in his lungs, which makes breathing difficult, so we have put him on a ventilator. My best guess is that he will need multiple operations, but we can only perform those after he stabilizes. That could take several days, if not weeks.'

There was a brief silence, and then Commissioner Sreelekha spoke up. 'Doctor, the patient is a VIP. Hundreds of people and members of the press are waiting outside for an update. Can you speak to them?'

'I do not have the authority to talk to the press. That will have to wait until the chief medical officer (CMO) arrives in the morning.'

'That's fine. Due to security concerns, the hospital entrance is cordoned off by police. They will allow only hospital staff and patients through. Hope that is all right?'

'I don't see a problem with that.'

'Thank you, doctor.' The commissioner then pointed to Ashraf. 'This is SI Ashraf Ali. He is in charge of the emergency ward's security. Let him know if you have any updates on the patient.'

'I need to go back to the operation theatre now,' said Dr Eapen. 'Can you inform the hospital security officer about this arrangement?'

As the doctor headed back inside, the commissioner looked around at the people gathered around her. 'This is the first shooting in Cochin since I took charge. Let's pray that everything turns out well.' She turned and walked out the way she had come, with Ashraf following closely behind.

'Ashraf, this is your most important assignment to date. I trust you to ensure that the patient is protected at all costs. No accidents. No excuses. Is that clear?'

'I will take care of it, madam,' Ashraf assured her.

As they reached the lobby area, the armed guards shuffled to make way for the commissioner to exit the building. Before she could leave, Ashraf whispered, 'Madam, before you go, there is something I need your help with...'

'What is it?' the commissioner enquired. 'Hold on, it's too noisy here. Come, let's go to the room behind the reception counter.'

Once inside the room, Ashraf spoke nervously. 'Madam, I was

off duty this evening and attended the event as a private citizen. But when the shooting happened, my training kicked in, and I pulled out my gun and shot the assailant twice, killing him instantly.'

'Are you sure your shots killed the person? In that case there will be a departmental investigation,' the commissioner said.

'Yes, madam, I know there will be an investigation. It would help if you can officially reassign me on duty from 5 p.m. onwards. That way, I will not have to explain why I was at the event. Otherwise, I could face suspension. I know it is asking too much—'

The commissioner held up her hand to stop Ashraf. 'Don't worry about it. Upon hearing that you were on location, I assigned you to duty around 8.30 p.m. However, I did not think about making the assignment effective from 5 p.m. I will take care of that.'

'Thank you, madam.'

'Since you used your service gun, did you turn it in for a ballistics test?'

'No, madam. I have it in the car. There was too much going on.'

'I understand. But you know the protocol; you need to turn it in. Since the shots that killed the assailant came from you, there should not be a problem.'

Ashraf hesitated before speaking. 'Madam, there is a complication. There was a third bullet that hit the assailant, and it was fired by Murali, the young man you met inside. He is like a son to Karnan sir. He used an old revolver that belonged to his father and I doubt it is licensed. I can vouch that he fired in self-defence after the assailant shot Karnan sir.'

'In that case, we must detain him for questioning.'

'I know, madam, but is there any way to avoid it? I am willing to say I fired all three bullets. Murali is a young man with a bright future, and works for MLA P. Shivan. I do not want to spoil his future by dragging him into this. Please, madam, I need your help with the internal inquiry.'

'What about eyewitnesses? Ashraf, I may be the police

The Commissioner's Dilemma

commissioner, but even I have limits.' She paused and looked away. 'Bring your gun to my office tomorrow. You said three bullets hit the assailant, so make sure your gun has three empty chambers and three unused bullets. I will talk to the ballistics officer, but I cannot promise anything.'

'Thank you, madam. I am very grateful.'

'I am doing this because you are the only person on my team who warned me about this incident. I wish I had listened to you and sent more policemen. We could have avoided this tragedy.'

'You did, madam. You decided to send three men in an unmarked car. Karnan sir's life may well depend on that single decision.'

'I suspected something was wrong when I got the call from the DGP. I must thank you for convincing me to act.' The commissioner paused. 'I am curious to know—why do you call him "Karnan sir"?'

'It is an old habit, madam. He was my professor at Maharaja's College. I learnt so much from him. I even owe my job to him. He is like a father figure to me.'

'I see,' the commissioner said, and then added, 'it may surprise you to know that I am also a fan of your Karnan sir—his literary side, not the political. When I was the head of the CM's security detail a few years ago, he gifted me one of Karnan's novels, *The Mahatma and Me*. I only got around to reading it recently; it is one of the best books I have read. No wonder he has such a large following.'

'Karnan sir is not only a great writer, but a man of immense courage and integrity.'

'Indeed,' the commissioner said. 'We can use some of that in our department. It is rife with spineless men, with a few exceptions.'

Ashraf was not sure if he made the commissioner's list. 'Madam, forgive me for asking these favours. As a police officer, I know I should not be breaking the law myself.'

The police commissioner looked Ashraf in the eye. 'I want

you to remember this, Ashraf. Sometimes, to uphold justice, you may have to break the law. You just need to judge when it is the right thing to do.' The commissioner wrapped the end of her sari around her body and moved towards the door. 'Think about that. I will see you in my office at 8.30 a.m.'

Ashraf saluted as the commissioner strode out of the lobby. He watched as she smiled at the reporters, who hurled questions about the shooting. Her guards opened the back door of her car, quickly whisking her away, with the jeep leading the way.

The CI walked up to Ashraf. 'Tell me what is going on. This is the first time I have seen the commissioner in person. She is tiny—much smaller than I had imagined.'

'Yes, small in size but big in stature,' Ashraf replied, his gaze fixed on the departing car.

~24~

A Call to Action

MURALI WAS AWAKENED BY THE CHATTER OF PEOPLE gathered around the police barricades at the hospital. Though the sun was out, the chill from the previous day's rains remained in the air. His watch read 6.45 a.m. It had been almost 10 hours since the shooting, and Murali had barely caught a brief nap in his car. He was surprised to see that the crowd in front of the emergency ward had swelled.

Murali's heart raced when he noticed Ashraf in uniform, deep in conversation with MLA Shivan. *Is there any update on maamen?* He attempted to straighten his crumpled shirt, ran his fingers through his hair and walked over to them.

'Any update from the doctor?' Murali asked.

'None yet, which in a way is good news,' MLA Shivan responded. 'However, things are looking bad outside. The district collector stopped by to inform us.'

'Why? What happened?'

'Our worst fears have come true. Overnight, there were three separate incidents of students burning buses owned by the Kerala government,' Ashraf explained. 'In one instance, the police had to use tear gas to disperse a large mob heading towards the Cochin police station. You were fast asleep, so we asked Shibu to meet the protesters and try to calm things down.'

Murali gasped. 'You should have woken me up. Don't you think a formal announcement on maamen's condition by the hospital will help?'

'I agree,' Ashraf said. 'I suggest you and MLA Shivan meet with the CMO. If they can hold a press briefing around 10.30 a.m., I will find out if the commissioner can also attend. I have a meeting with her at 8.30 a.m. Now, follow me.'

Murali and MLA Shivan followed Ashraf to the front desk, where he introduced them to the receptionist. She quickly wrote down their request to meet with the CMO and asked them to wait while she spoke to her supervisor. Ashraf waved to Murali and exited the building.

Murali turned to MLA Shivan and asked, 'I am going to quickly check on my father and Rukhsana. Would you like to join me?'

'Of course,' Shivan replied.

Murali found his father asleep on the bench outside the operating theatre. On seeing him, Rukhsana jumped up from her chair and rushed towards him. Murali noticed that Rukhsana's hijab was back in place, draped over her head and around her neck.

'I have been thinking about you,' Rukhsana whispered to Murali, her voice trembling. 'It's been very tense waiting here, not knowing anything about you or Karnan sir. Murali, the shooting... are you in trouble?'

'Rukhsana, relax. Everything is fine. SI Ashraf is doing what he can to help. Don't worry about me. If you have doubts, you can ask MLA Shivan.'

Rukhsana looked at MLA Shivan for reassurance.

MLA Shivan's tone was measured. 'Look, Rukhsana. It has been less than 12 hours since the incident. We still don't know what the police's next step will be. Thankfully, we have an honest police officer in Commissioner Sreelekha. I trust she will do the right thing.' He added, 'I am just thankful Karnan sir is alive. Did you hear from the doctor?'

'Thank you, Shivan sir. We are very grateful.' Rukhsana used the end of her hijab to wipe away her tears. 'The doctor met us around 5 a.m. to inform Karnan sir remains critical and needs to be moved to the ICU for closer monitoring. She said the medical team will be meeting at 9 a.m. to review the reports. I am worried.'

'I am too,' Murali admitted. 'I can't help but think I should have done more to save him.'

'Why do you think like that, Murali?' Rukhsana scolded softly. 'You did all you could. You even got the assailant!'

The conversation woke Vasu, who stood up and looked around, disoriented. The sudden movement caused him to stumble and Murali rushed forward to steady his father. As he helped Vasu sit down, it struck Murali how much older and frailer his father looked—no longer the strong soldier turned freedom fighter he had known all these years. *Is it his age? Or is it the awareness of mortality brought on by the unexpected injury to his closest friend?* Murali felt a pang of guilt for the way he had spoken to his parents the day before.

MLA Shivan and Rukhsana gathered around the bench where Vasu was seated.

'Don't worry, I am fine. Just a little tired from lack of sleep,' Vasu said, his voice unsteady. 'I was not sure whether I heard actual voices or was dreaming. Any updates?'

'We have not heard from the doctors again,' Rukhsana said.

'Vasu sir, we just got word that there have been a few violent protests led by students,' MLA Shivan said. 'It looks like some of them have taken Karnan sir's call for total revolution as a call for an armed rebellion—'

Murali interjected. 'Who can blame the students? They just witnessed the shooting of a great leader—someone they admire—so they are blaming the government. In the event of bad news, things could get out of control very soon.'

'Oh God!' Vasu exclaimed, covering his mouth with his hands.

'What a difference a day makes,' Murali said, shaking his head in disbelief. 'If maamen could speak to us now, I wonder what his advice would be. Acha, no one knows him as well as you do. What do you think he would have said?'

A heavy silence settled over them as Vasu pondered Murali's

question. After a few minutes, he took a deep breath and said, 'You are correct, son. Karnan is my brother. No one knows him like I do. Yet, I don't have his depth of knowledge or his way with words. All I can do is share what I know of his deepest desires for you and the land he loves.'

'Please tell us, acha,' Murali pleaded.

Vasu spoke in a slow, deliberate tone. 'Karnan chetta often said that most people live their lives on earth dreaming of one day reaching heaven, but the wise know that the real heaven is right here—on earth, within our grasp. Guided by this belief, he lived a full and eventful life in service of the less fortunate among us.

'He believed it was our—his and my—good fortune to have been born when our motherland was in chains... A time when life had but one singular purpose...when we had leaders of the stature of Bapuji, Netaji and Lok Nayak to show us the way forward. Then, all of a sudden, soon after independence, their voices were silenced. Opportunists stepped in to fill the void. Within a few years, the dreams of millions of Indians were shattered...orphans—that's what we felt like.' Vasu paused, searching for the right words.

'Karnan had no choice but to get back into the arena, this time to hold our own leaders accountable. Time flew by, and our hair turned grey, and our bodies weakened. Now, rather abruptly but not unexpectedly, it seems that his time on this beautiful land is coming to an end.' Vasu's voice faltered and he stopped for a few seconds to collect his thoughts.

Vasu looked at Murali, Rukhsana and MLA Shivan before continuing. 'Karnan's last desire would be for all of you, whom he regards as his own children, to work to unite the people of our beloved land, help them rise above the man-made divisions of party, ideology, caste and religion, and to defeat corruption, nepotism and communal politics. Unfortunately, he can no longer lead us, but his life is our best guide.'

'Undoubtedly,' MLA Shivan said. 'Karnan sir has shown us

how to do that through his own example.'

'Yes, Shivan,' Vasu agreed. 'He has, and you have learnt your lessons well. But I know his desire was to see lasting change. The outcome of this epic struggle should be no less than total freedom and justice for every man, woman and child in Kerala. I have no doubt that this is the final battle he was preparing us for.'

A profound silence fell over the group as the gravity of the task ahead, implied by Vasu's words sank in. Murali whispered to his father, 'Acha, I know this is very difficult for you, but it's important that we hear your advice.'

Vasu wiped away a tear with his palm. After a few seconds, he began to speak again.

'My advice would be exactly the same as his. He would love to see a new generation of young political leaders—like MLA Shivan and the young leaders of the YDSK—step into the arena. He would say, "Makkalae, the stage is set, and the curtain has risen. Step into the limelight; it's your time for glory."' Vasu paused and looked around.

'Exactly! Those would be his words!' Murali said softly. 'But where do we begin? How do we find our way in the darkness?'

The others nodded in agreement.

Vasu looked at Murali. 'Yes, it is true that all this is easier said than done. As Karnan said in his speech last night, there will be times when all seems lost, when the night is the darkest. During those periods of trial, just remember that we—my brother Karnan and I—are there with you, always.'

Vasu fell silent as tears ran down his face. The shroud of silence descended again. Murali embraced his father as MLA Shivan and Rukhsana moved closer, interlocking arms until there was hardly any space between them.

Murali spoke. 'I can feel that the baton has been passed to us. It's our responsibility now to carry on the fight,' he said. 'Shivan sir, you are our leader—lead, and we will follow.'

'I appreciate your confidence in me,' Shivan replied, 'but Karnan sir warned us about the dangers of personality politics that arise from having one supreme leader. From today, we will lead the YDSK together. Let's show the people of Kerala that we can build a progressive and compassionate socialist movement—one that includes everyone with goodwill.'

Rukhsana spoke up, her voice now upbeat. 'Shivan sir, I really love the idea of a compassionate socialist movement. To begin, we need to agree on a plan of action. May I suggest the first step?'

As all eyes turned to Rukhsana, Murali felt a surge of pride, happy to see her speaking confidently to people with more political experience.

'Go ahead, Rukhsana,' said Vasu.

Rukhsana's voice grew stronger. 'From his speech, it was clear that Karnan sir wanted the youth of Kerala to lead a total revolution to overthrow the current government. Since he can't speak now, our primary responsibility should be to mobilize the youth towards this singular goal. Are we all aligned on this?'

MLA Shivan stroked his chin thoughtfully; as a sitting MLA, his views carried significant weight. 'In principle, yes. However, I don't see a path forward without an alliance with the ruling Left Democratic Front or the opposition United Democratic Front. The political math simply does not work in Kerala. What do you think, Murali?'

Murali hesitated before answering, torn between the differing views of Rukhsana and MLA Shivan. 'Shivan sir is correct. The prospect of a third political front in Kerala is very bleak. But that was in the past. Should we continue to let the past define us?' he asked in a raised voice.

'That is the right question to ask, Murali,' Vasu encouraged. 'What do Shibu and the other YDSK leaders feel?'

'Shibu is with me on this. We both believe it's time to try changing the status quo of Kerala politics. I am confident that most YDSK members will follow our lead.'

Vasu turned to Rukhsana. 'What do you think?'

Rukhsana did not hesitate. 'It is understandable that we each have slightly different views on how to make Karnan sir's vision come true. But I feel it is best to take our orders from what he actually said in his last speech—his words were "*total revolution*",' she emphasized, gesturing with her hands, 'that is, an overthrow of the current order—not just political, but also social and economic. That is the message thousands of the YDSK supporters heard from their leader's mouth minutes before he was shot. They will demand nothing less from us.' Rukhsana paused before adding, 'We should also want nothing less from our supporters.'

Silence followed as the men absorbed the significance of Rukhsana's words.

Murali looked at her, trying hard to suppress his awe. He had rarely seen her speak with such conviction about politics. He could sense a revolutionary cadence in Rukhsana's voice; her determination and clarity of words felt radically new.

Vasu smiled. 'Excellent! Rukhsana, you just articulated a call for action that will galvanize the youth.'

'You make a good case, Rukhsana. And with Karnan unconscious, we have a strong reason to launch this total revolution,' said MLA Shivan.

Encouraged by their approval, Rukhsana pressed on. 'So the most important question now is: what specific actions should we take to remove the government from power?'

All eyes turned back to MLA Shivan. 'Currently, we only have seven members in the State Legislative Assembly. The government can survive even without us. But if we are able to build more public pressure, I am confident we can get the MLAs from the Antony and Mani groups of the ruling coalition to join us. If we can get 15 more MLAs to withdraw support from the Left Front, it will spell doom for the government.'

'What would be the outcome of that?' Rukhsana enquired.

'Well, going by history, the governor would have no option but to declare president's rule in Kerala,' MLA Shivan replied.

Rukhsana smiled and said, 'I meant how will this help us fulfil Karnan sir's vision.'

Murali chimed in, 'The way I see it, if president's rule is imposed, it will buy us some time to build our movement by attracting the best talent and organizing a grassroots campaign for the next election.' He looked at MLA Shivan and smiled. 'Between us, we know a thing or two about winning elections.'

'All this sounds promising, but we must proceed cautiously,' Vasu said. 'We will be taking on powerful forces, so we must prepare for a long battle. This is a noble endeavour, one worth trying. I believe this is exactly what Karnan chetta had in mind.'

'Vasu sir, what do you suggest our call to action for the YDSK should be?' Rukhsana asked.

Vasu thought for a few seconds before responding. 'I suggest that the YDSK immediately release a call to action addressed to the student and labour leaders across the state. Murali, Shibu and you should lead the protests.' Vasu looked into the eyes of each person around him. 'As you embark on this journey, please don't worry about Karnan. Rest assured that while you fight the good fight, I will be right here by my brother's side until he recovers. I pray that one day, before his last breath, he will be able to see the fruits of your actions.'

Just then, the receptionist approached the group and informed MLA Shivan that the CMO had arranged a press briefing in an hour. She requested his assistance in inviting the police commissioner and the district collector of Cochin.

MLA Shivan excused himself and headed back to the lobby.

Vasu turned to Murali with urgency. 'Son, your amma must be worried. You should go home and get some rest. I will manage things here.'

'Yes, acha. I will leave as soon as the press briefing is over.'

'Oh, before I forget—remember to stop by maamen's home on your way and pick up his prescription and some fresh clothes. Just knock on Alex's door; he has the keys and knows where the medicines are kept.'

'Okay, I will take care of it,' Murali said before asking, 'Acha, how reliable is Alex?'

'Alex's *appachan* was a close childhood buddy of maamen's. After he passed, Karnan took care of the family. That is why Alex regards him as his own father.' Vasu yawned and rubbed his eyes. 'I am feeling tired; I need a nap,' he said, closing his eyes.

Murali turned to Rukhsana and commented, 'You look exhausted. Are you worried?'

Rukhsana leaned forward and looked into Murali's eyes. 'I am feeling strange. I am the odd person in this group. I should be anxious, or even afraid. But I am not. My only emotion is to do something that will make you proud of me.'

'Why do you think of yourself as the odd person in the group? Just because you are a woman and wear a hijab? I know maamen wanted you to be more involved. He thinks very highly of you.'

Rukhsana looked up, tilting her head. 'How do you know?' she asked. 'He just met me for the first time last night.'

'Well, he told me when I met him backstage just before his speech. I am not joking. And he is a good judge of people.'

'I am flattered that someone as great as your maamen thinks highly of me. But I think it is more of a reflection of his love for you; I want to earn his respect.'

'You are already doing more than anyone I know.'

'Murali, I would like to go to my hostel to bathe and change my clothes. I will also cook and bring fresh food for you and your father.'

'You heard him. I must visit my amma to see how she is doing and stop by maamen's home.' Murali paused, and then asked,

'Rukhsana, why don't you come with me?'

Rukhsana hesitated. 'Are you sure your amma will be okay with me coming along? There is enough trouble already; I don't want to cause more.'

'Well, let's find out!' Murali replied. 'I know today is not the best day for you to meet my mother, but we have to do it sooner or later. As a bonus, you will also get to visit your favourite writer's home.'

Rukhsana smiled and relented. 'All right. I will go with you.'

Murali glanced at his father, who was now stretched out on the bench, fast asleep.

'I must go meet Ashraf now. Please keep a close watch on acha. I will bring some food for both of you as soon as the canteen opens.' Murali held Rukhsana's hand and looked into her eyes. 'I noticed that you removed your hijab in public for the first time yesterday.'

'I did not realize I did that. I was in a trance, sleepwalking through what seemed like a bad dream. It wasn't until your father asked me to get into the car that I noticed my hands were stained with Karnan sir's blood. My hijab was the only way to wipe them clean,' Rukhsana said. She leaned in and said, almost in a whisper, 'Murali, when I did that, I noticed something—'

'What?'

'The colour of Karnan sir's blood is exactly the same as my hijab's. I could not tell the difference. Here, take a look,' Rukhsana said, pointing to the lower part of the garment.

Murali examined it and nodded. 'You are right, Rukhsana. I am surprised that amidst all the confusion, you had the presence of mind to notice this,' Murali said. 'I know that covering your hair in public is important to you…that is why I asked.'

'You are so thoughtful,' Rukhsana replied as she reached out to touch Murali's hand. After a brief pause, she whispered, 'Murali, there is something you said last night that has been on my mind. Can we move over to a corner?'

Murali followed Rukhsana to a corner that was dimly lit and out of view from the main corridor.

Murali was curious. 'What is it, Rukhsana?'

'Last night you referred to me as your fiancée for the first time... Did you really mean it?'

Murali pulled Rukhsana closer to him. 'It was not a slip of the tongue. I have never been more serious. Don't you believe me?'

Rukhsana looked up at Murali and said, 'I believe you, Murali. And I also believe in you. I always have.'

They held hands in silence.

After a few seconds, Rukhsana whispered, 'Murali, I am very tired. I must also be looking and smelling terrible.'

Murali slowly pulled away, his gaze steadily on hers. 'Yes, you do look tired, but you are the most beautiful woman I have ever seen.'

~25~

The Press Briefing

BY THE TIME MURALI WALKED OUT OF THE EMERGENCY ward lobby, it had started raining again. The microphones and speakers that had been set up to brief the press had to be moved from the open area to under the covered portico just outside the lobby. The murmur of the crowd indicated their growing impatience. Judging by the number of people who had either a notepad or a recording device, Murali estimated that there were about 50 press reporters present. The rest of the crowd consisted of young students from nearby colleges, most of whom were active members of the YDSK.

After a few minutes, the lobby doors opened and five people approached the microphone. Murali recognized MLA Shivan, Commissioner Sreelekha Sriram, District Collector Krishna Kumar and SI Ashraf. The fifth person, whom Murali could not identify, stepped up to the mic and introduced himself.

'I am Balachandran Nair, the chief medical officer of Ernakulam General Hospital,' he began nervously. 'I will give a brief medical update, after which the police commissioner, the district collector and the MLA will inform you about the law and order situation. We will not be taking questions today.

'Last night, freedom fighter Mr T.K. Karunakaran, more commonly known as Vaikom Karnan, was admitted to the emergency ward around 9.20 p.m.' Dr Nair paused as a reporter shouted a question, followed by murmurs among the onlookers.

'Please allow me to speak,' Dr Nair said. 'The patient was unconscious when he was admitted. We believe this could be due to the impact of the bullet that pierced his chest, narrowly missing his heart. His ECG reading suggests that he may have suffered a heart attack either just before or shortly after the shooting.' He glanced up again as another reporter shouted a question. The police commissioner glanced at SI Ashraf, who stepped forward, raising his hands to calm the crowd.

Dr Nair hesitated before continuing, 'It appears he was on blood thinner medication for a prior heart condition, which caused more blood loss than usual. As a result, he is showing early signs of oxygen deprivation in his vital organs. His condition remains critical. He is in the ICU, breathing with the help of a ventilator. He is receiving food through a tube that has been inserted through his nose.

'It is a miracle that Mr Karunakaran is alive. We believe he survived thanks to the quick actions of those who brought him here.' Dr Nair referred to his notes. After a few seconds, he continued, 'Now, I will give you an update on certain important decisions the medical team made about 30 minutes ago. The patient will need additional surgeries to extract broken bones from his lungs. However, the General Hospital does not have the facility or equipment for advanced procedures. Therefore, we recommend that the patient be moved to Medical Trust Hospital. I have spoken to Dr Pulikkan Verghese, the managing director at Medical Trust, and he has agreed to take over the case as soon as the patient's condition stabilizes, which we expect will take a few days. The police will make the necessary arrangements for transportation. I now request Commissioner Sreelekha to speak. Thank you.'

The reporters shouted questions at the CMO, but he quickly stepped aside, ignoring them, to make way for the commissioner. Dressed in uniform, her hair neatly tucked under her cap, she carried a shiny leather holster on her hip, the pistol's handle visible. True to her reputation as a no-nonsense police officer, she got straight to the point.

'Since the time of the incident, there have been seven instances of destruction of government property, including the burning of three Kerala State Road Transport Corporation buses. Some people have blamed the Kerala Police for the lack of adequate security at the event. Contrary to the rumours that are circulating, some of which are being carried by the press, my officers, led by SI Ashraf Ali, were present at the Marine Drive grounds when the incident happened. Thanks to the quick action taken by SI Ashraf and his team, the shooter was killed on the spot. The weapon used was found on his body.

'Our team also apprehended one of his accomplices, who is currently in police custody, undergoing interrogation at the Kasba Station. We cannot disclose their identities until the investigation is concluded. We have arranged for a medical examination and blood test to check for alcohol and drugs. We suspect there could be other collaborators who may be involved in planning this incident.' As the commissioner paused, the reporters shouted questions at her.

'Hold on!' she shouted back. 'Didn't the CMO say no questions? Please respect the policy of the hospital. I also wanted to mention that the police will arrange to move Mr Karunakaran to Medical Trust Hospital. Due to security concerns, we will not announce the date and time in advance. I have proposed that the collector impose a curfew in Cochin after 11 p.m. for the next five days, starting tonight. I urge all protesters to exercise their rights peacefully. I assure you that the police will get to the bottom of this case very soon. We should have an update within the next few days. Till then, I ask for your patience. Thank you.'

As she stepped back from the mic, one of the reporters in the front row shouted, 'Are the reports that there was another shooter up on the stage true?'

The feisty police commissioner could not resist breaking the no-questions rule. 'Do you have any witnesses?' she retorted. 'The FIR prepared by the police after interviewing over 15 eyewitnesses immediately following the incident indicates that there was a single shooter involved, and he was taken down. As per policy, we are conducting an internal inquiry and will submit all the findings as soon as it is complete. Please be patient.'

The district collector then provided additional details about the curfew and requested the journalists to carry the news the same day. MLA Shivan followed, demanding that the home minister of Kerala immediately hand over the investigation to the Central Bureau of Investigation (CBI). He made an emotional appeal to the students and youth to use peaceful means of protest and pray for Karnan. He added that the YDSK would be issuing a statement on the next steps for the organization in a few days.

In under 25 minutes, the briefing was over. As members of the press started to pack up and leave, Murali followed the signs to the canteen and placed an order for some breakfast and tea. As he waited for the food, his mind drifted back to the unexpected news about moving his uncle to Medical Trust Hospital. He had heard good things about the hospital from Rukhsana, who volunteered there as a nursing assistant.

Murali was glad the move would happen after a few days, as it would give him enough time to go home to check on his mother, stop by his uncle's home, and return to Cochin the next day. *The next few days will be hectic.* At least I will be able to see amma and get a few hours of sleep in my bed. *But what about Rukhsana? Where will she sleep tonight? Well, I'll let amma figure that out.*

~26~

Murali's Bold Gambit

IMMEDIATELY AFTER BREAKFAST, MURALI ARRANGED FOR a hurried meeting with MLA Shivan, Rukhsana and Shibu to discuss media communication and the messaging to the YDSK members. They agreed to proceed cautiously, with discipline and firmness, avoiding actions that might inflame tensions. Given his sensitive role as an MLA supporting the governing Left Front coalition, Shivan stepped down as the president of the YDSK, assigning the role to Murali. Rukhsana was assigned as the party's general secretary, while Shibu was appointed the joint secretary in charge of coordinating student protests.

Later that afternoon, Murali received his father's consent to bring Rukhsana with him to check on his mother and grandmother. Shortly afterwards, they left the hospital through the back exit, avoiding the press who were eager for updates on the incident. As he drove through Cochin, Murali noticed that Rukhsana was silent, perhaps absorbed by the enormity of the events that had occurred during the past 24 hours.

Murali felt a bond with Rukhsana that he had not experienced before. He hoped that after the day's events, his mother would warm up to her. *Perhaps maamen and acha's open-minded approach towards Rukhsana will help Amma realize her concerns are unfounded. Or maybe seeing the seriousness and calmness that Rukhsana has been exhibiting since the shooting will help. In any case, what is there to not like about her? She has acted just like a close family member would.*

At Rukhsana's request, their first stop was at a mosque in the nearby town of Kaloor, which she visited on important occasions. To avoid attracting attention from those gathered for the afternoon prayer, Murali waited in the car while Rukhsana wrapped her hijab tightly and went inside to pray. The second stop was Geethanjali's aunt, Mallika Sukumaran's home located at Vytilla, on the outskirts of Cochin. Mallika was a well-known poet and former professor of Malayalam literature at St Teresa's College, Cochin. The girls stayed with her, and she had taken on the role of a foster mother to them.

Murali waited in the car for about 40 minutes—just enough time for Rukhsana to shower, change and pack fresh clothes, toiletries, a novel and her personal journal for the next few days.

When Murali saw Geethanjali and Mallika accompanying Rukhsana, he stepped out of the car. Sensing their concerns, he assured them things would be all right and that he had arranged for Rukhsana to stay with his mother that night. He informed them that Rukhsana would be back in a few days. Although Mallika knew the girls trusted Murali, she insisted that he write down his home address and phone number for her.

Back in the car, Murali could sense Rukhsana's nervousness from her silence and the way she had clasped her hands. He decided to give her space to process her emotions. But Rukhsana, unable to contain her anxiety, turned to Murali and requested him to stop the car so they could talk. He pulled into a small side road, stopping at a clearing that bordered a large lake.

Rukhsana looked into Murali's eyes, holding his gaze briefly. 'I am worried, Murali,' she said, her eyes welling up with tears. 'So much has happened since last evening…things beyond my wildest imagination. I can't breathe. What if the police find out you pulled the trigger?'

Murali reached out to hold her hand. 'Rukhsana, I understand your worries. Yes, we have been through a lot in the past 24 hours. But we did what we had to. We have no control over the outcome,' he said softly.

'Are you taking me home with you just to make me feel better?' she asked.

'All this is new to me too. I think some time away from the hospital will be good for you. To tell you the truth, I need your company as much as you need mine,' Murali replied.

Rukhsana looked down. 'But what if your mother does not like the idea?'

'I know my plan is risky. But I am praying that amma will understand our situation and welcome you. That is my hope.'

'Then that is my hope too, Murali. And I pray that your uncle's recovery will soon follow.'

They spent about 30 more minutes talking through their concerns, and Rukhsana gradually felt reassured, choosing to set aside her fears. When they resumed their journey, the sun had dipped into the horizon and dusk was setting in. Without her asking, Murali started singing 'Utharaswayamvaram', a Malayalam film song originally performed by her favourite singer, K.J. Yesudas. Touched, Rukhsana held Murali's left hand, releasing it when he needed to shift gears and then holding it again. As Murali's voice filled her heart, Rukhsana's mind soared among the lush green fields outside. She was drawn to the lyrics of the song—

'The dawn when a thousand dreams became a chariot…
I became Arjuna, and she, Uthara…'

Rukhsana's fears slowly melted away as Murali finished the song. She found comfort in the togetherness they shared within the small confines of the car.

∽

Twilight was setting in when Murali and Rukhsana reached their third stop, Karnan's home in Vaikom. At the gate, they encountered a little girl named Vijayalakshmi Chandrashekhar, who had come with her father to meet Karnan. Vijayalakshmi explained that she had come to pick up the children's book that Karnan had promised her. It seemed her father had not informed her of the shooting.

Murali asked Rukhsana to stay with Vijayalakshmi while he walked over to Alex's home to get the keys. After understanding the details of Vijayalakshmi's meeting with Karnan, Rukhsana gently informed her that Karnan was unwell and could not come, so he had asked her to meet Vijayalakshmi instead.

On seeing Murali, Alex burst out sobbing. He had heard about the incident and wanted to rush to Cochin but his responsibilities at home had prevented him from doing so. Murali consoled Alex, reassuring him that Karnan was alive and had a fighting chance. Alex grabbed the keys and accompanied Murali to Karnan's home.

Alex opened the front door to let Murali, Rukhsana and Vijayalakshmi in before leaving to fetch milk to make tea. Rukhsana held Vijayalakshmi's hand and walked into Karnan's library. After carefully examining the many books on his writing desk, she selected two: *Panther's Moon* by Ruskin Bond, and Karnan's own book, *The Mahatma and Me*. With Murali's approval, Rukhsana gifted the two books to a delighted Vijayalakshmi.

After Vijayalakshmi and her father left, Murali showed Rukhsana the extensive library containing his uncle's favourite books. The collection included works by famous Indian writers such as Rabindranath Tagore, Mahatma Gandhi, Jawaharlal Nehru, Jayaprakash Narayan, as well as international authors like Charles Dickens, Mark Twain, Karl Marx, Leo Tolstoy, Martin Luther King, Jr, and Ernest Hemingway. Rukhsana marvelled at the eclectic book collection.

She noticed the handwritten letters from Jayaprakash Narayan, in which he had addressed Karnan as 'bhai'. The letters were framed on the wall next to an inscription of a quote by Socrates on a block of wood, which read: 'The unexamined life is not worth living.'

When Murali went to the kitchen to speak to Alex, Rukhsana

took a closer look at Karnan's writing desk, made of rustic teakwood. She could not resist the urge to sit in the chair and place her hands on the desk. It was precisely how she had imagined it to be. The dark wood was strong but in need of care, and the oversized leather chair had a few holes but was still sturdy and comfortable. To the right of the table was an old Remington typewriter, the same as the one used by Mallika.

Alex served Murali and Rukhsana biscuits and hot tea sweetened with jaggery. They took turns telling Alex the details of what had transpired, taking care to frame Karnan's condition in a positive light. Alex packed all the medication that Karnan had been taking. As they prepared to depart, he disclosed his plans of taking the early morning train to Cochin to see Karnan. Murali tried to convince him to wait till noon so they could travel together, but Alex had already purchased the train tickets.

∽

A street dog barked as Murali stopped the car in front of his home. Shooing it away, Murali stepped out, opened the gate and parked the vehicle inside. Leaving Rukhsana inside the car, Murali knocked on the front door. Relieved to see Murali back home, Jalaja embraced her son. After a brief update on his maamen and father, Murali told his mother he had a special guest waiting in the car. To Murali's surprise, she knew exactly who he was talking about, but was not pleased with the news.

'Did you have to bring her home at this late hour? What will our neighbours think? Wait till I tell your father,' Jalaja admonished.

'Amma, I already discussed it with acha. Besides, I am sure our neighbours have better things to do than spy on us,' Murali replied, annoyed.

Despite being upset, Jalaja rushed outside to open the car door, bringing Rukhsana inside and apologizing for keeping her waiting. They were joined by Jalaja's 76-year-old mother, who was staying with them. Rukhsana lowered her hijab down to her shoulders and greeted her with a namaste.

'Oh, you both have been through so much and must be hungry,' Jalaja said. 'Why don't you wash up and have something to eat? Let me heat up the food and fry some *pappadams*.'

'Forget the pappadams. I am famished.' Murali turned to his grandmother. '*Amumma*, did you make my favourite *karimeen* fry today?'

'Yes, son, but we have only one fish left,' his grandmother replied, a look of concern spreading across her face. 'Should I make an omelette?'

'Don't worry, I will share it with Rukhsana.'

'Murali, come with me to the prayer room. Let's pray for your acha and maamen before you eat,' his grandmother said, leading him to the small prayer area in the corner of the living room. Rukhsana stood behind Murali, watching as his grandmother lit a traditional oil lamp and recited a prayer, which Jalaja and Murali repeated.

Over a simple dinner, which consisted of sambar, brown rice and fried fish, and ripe home-grown papayas for dessert, they discussed the unexpected events that had engulfed them. Jalaja insisted that Murali recount every minute detail from when he left home the previous day.

Finally, after almost 90 minutes of questions and answers, Jalaja decided it was time for them to get some sleep. She arranged for Rukhsana to sleep in her bedroom, on the side of the bed where Murali's father usually slept.

Murali spent 15 minutes talking with his grandmother, assuring her that Vasu and Karnan were okay. It was past midnight when Murali, weary from the weight and intensity of the past 24 hours, crawled into his bed. He could hear his mother asking Rukhsana questions and prayed it would not make her uncomfortable.

Murali knew that the unexpected developments had made it

possible for him to bring Rukhsana home to meet his mother. Under normal circumstances, *amma would not have agreed to meet Rukhsana. But today is different. Her visit has been overshadowed by events of far greater significance. I wonder what amma's first impression of her is. I hope they get to know each other, even if just a little bit.*

Murali lay in bed, staring at the lone garden lizard that crawled across the ceiling above him in pursuit of a mosquito. He wondered if it was the same lizard he had seen the last time he slept there. The lizard was lucky to have a simple, peaceful life—no enemies, no guns, no fear of getting shot, no one to follow, no one to lead. Just the lizard and its meal for the night.

Murali tossed and turned in his bed, unable to fall asleep. Images of him grabbing the revolver, aiming at the shooter's head and pulling the trigger swirled in his mind in slow motion. The face of the man he had killed came into sharp focus. *I wonder who he was. What had compelled him to take such drastic action? Did he have parents? Children? Was there a lover waiting for his return?*

Despite his exhaustion, sleep eluded him that night.

~27~

The Secret Manuscript

10 October 1980
Ernakulam General Hospital, Cochin

VASU WAS WOKEN BY A GENTLE PAT ON HIS SHOULDER. HE jolted upright, his heart pounding, expecting to see the doctor who had performed Karnan's surgeries.

'Is he okay?' Vasu asked.

'Sir, I am from the hospital security staff,' said a young man in a light blue shirt and navy pants. 'Someone named Alex is here to meet you. He says it's important. The police are not allowing anyone except staff and patients inside. Would you like to meet him outside?'

'Oh yes. I will meet him. What time is it?'

'It is almost 6 a.m.'

Vasu followed the man to the front lobby, where the police guarding the front entrance let him out. He saw Alex standing near a pillar in the front portico, dressed in a white mundu and grey shirt and holding a large packet in his left hand.

'Alex? Why did you come all this way? They are not letting anyone in, and Karnan is in the ICU.'

'Vasu sir, I had to come,' said Alex. 'Murali visited last night with his friend and warned me that I would not be able to see Karnan sir. But I have been very worried since hearing the news, and I could not just sit at home doing nothing. I am going to St Anthony's Shrine to pray for his recovery. Whoever did this will meet an untimely end.'

Vasu placed a reassuring hand on Alex's shoulders. 'I share your sorrow,' he said. 'I had also prayed to Lord Shiva at the Vaikom temple. Perhaps that is why he survived. Karnan is not a believer, but in times like this, even non-believers need divine mercy.'

'There is something else, sir,' Alex said, holding out two sealed envelopes, one small and the other much larger and thicker. 'Karnan sir entrusted these to me to give to you in person. That is why I had to come.' Alex handed both over to Vasu.

'Yes, Karnan mentioned the documents on our way to Cochin. Did he tell you what they are?'

'I know the small envelope contains his will, power of attorney and other legal papers. He has named you the executor. He got them notarized just a few days ago; I had accompanied him to the village office.'

'I see. Karnan chetta did tell me about the legal papers,' said Vasu. 'Maybe he sensed something bad was going to happen. Else, why would he make all these arrangements?'

'Now that you mention it, it does seem like he knew.'

'What is in the larger envelope?'

'Murali noticed it on Karnan sir's desk and asked me to bring it to you. I'm not sure what is inside.'

Vasu opened the larger envelope, carefully pulling out a tightly packed bundle of papers and reviewing them. 'This looks like a manuscript typed in Malayalam,' he said. Then the realization hit him. 'Oh my God, did Karnan chetta start writing again?'

'His house is visible from mine. Most nights, the lights in his library were on well past midnight. Maybe he was writing,' Alex suggested.

'Alex, do you know if Sheela visited him recently?' Vasu asked, referring to Karnan's former assistant at Maharaja's College, who often helped type his manuscripts.

'I have not seen Sheela madam in a very long time. Last I heard, she had moved to Madras to be with her youngest son about two years ago. Karnan sir might have sent her his drafts by post. I have taken many of his letters to the post office.'

'This is very interesting. He never mentioned getting back to writing again. Still, I hope you are right,' Vasu said, putting the papers back inside the envelope. 'I need my glasses to read everything these days. I'm glad you brought these documents; I have plenty of time to review them. Thanks for taking the trouble, Alex.'

'What trouble? Whatever little I do is nothing compared to the love and affection Karnan sir has bestowed on me and my family.'

The two men stood in silence for a few seconds. 'Vasu sir, you go inside,' Alex said. 'I have to get to St Anthony's before it gets crowded so I can return home by afternoon.'

'Go ahead, Alex. Do you have money for your fare?' Vasu reached into his shirt pocket, pulling out a handful of notes and stuffing them into Alex's hand without waiting for a response. 'I will see you in a few days, hopefully with better news.'

Vasu waited for Alex to leave before heading back to the hospital lobby, the envelopes clutched in his hands.

∞

It was half past noon when Murali returned to the hospital. Vasu was relieved to see him. Murali explained that Rukhsana was running a temperature, so his mother insisted that she rest at their home for a couple of days. Jalaja and Rukhsana would come to Cochin by bus after Karnan was transferred to Medical Trust Hospital.

'You took a bold step bringing Rukhsana to meet your amma,' Vasu said to his son. 'But remember, it is in our culture to be kind to strangers. I know your amma a little better than you…do not assume she will approve of you marrying a non-Hindu. I don't want you to be disappointed.'

'Thanks for bursting my bubble.' Murali smiled. 'But I understand and am in no rush. I know if maamen says a good word about Rukhsana, amma will come around.'

Vasu nodded in agreement, impressed by his son's maturity.

He then moved on to the topic weighing on his mind.

'Alex visited early this morning. He brought two envelopes that maamen had entrusted to him.'

'What was in them?'

'One had maamen's last will.' Vasu paused. 'Murali, he has left his home and the nine cents of land it is on to you.'

'Oh my God. But he has two brothers who are still alive.'

'Yes, but they do not share a good relationship. Maamen has spent a fortune on them. Most of the money he earned from his book sales went to paying off their debts. Besides, Karnan always thought of you as his own child. That is why he has left his home to you.'

Vasu continued, 'His share of some ancestral farmland in Vaikom is distributed between Alex and the YDSK in his will. I am amazed he got all this done in the last week. I am convinced that he knew what was coming... Yet, he still went to the rally. That, my son, is the definition of courage!'

'Acha, I don't know what to say. This is completely unexpected. But this is not important right now. His recovery is all that I really care about.'

'You are right.' Vasu nodded and then said, 'Son, you will be shocked to see the second document Alex handed me.'

'Why? What is it?'

'It's a secret manuscript!' Vasu exclaimed, a boyish smile lighting up his face. 'Your maamen has written a memoir titled *The Last Revolutionary*—a 300-page manuscript about his experiences during the Indian freedom struggle and his later years in Kerala.'

'That is unbelievable!' gasped Murali.

'That's what I would have said too, had Alex not handed me the papers. Unlike most memoirs, it is written in the third person... maybe he wanted to maintain some distance from the characters. I have not finished it yet, but from what I have read, I believe this could be his best work. Here, take a look,' Vasu said, handing

Murali the manuscript. 'Other than maamen and me, very few people would know these details.'

'Acha, just imagine how important his story will be to our cause. Maamen may not be able to speak now, but his words will resonate louder than ever.'

'That is exactly what I was thinking. As soon as I found out, I called Mr Vijay Gupta, the managing editor at Rupa & Co., which published maamen's other books. He was so excited that he wanted me to send him the manuscript by speed post. He promised to get it edited, translated into English and ready for publication in two to three months.'

'Let's do that. Give me the document. The post office is nearby. I will go there now and post it. Do you have Mr Gupta's address?'

'Yes, I do. But before you do that, make a photocopy of the entire manuscript. After I finish reading, I want you to read it.'

Murali followed Vasu to the front desk, where the latter wrote Mr Vijay Gupta's address on the envelope, placed the manuscript inside and handed it to Murali. 'Don't forget to take a photocopy,' he reminded Murali again.

Vasu watched as Murali walked away with the envelope held tightly in his right hand. All the worries he and Jalaja had harboured for their only son suddenly seemed trivial. *Karnan chetta was right. Adversity does not build character; it just reveals it.*

Vasu closed his eyes and whispered a prayer to Lord Shiva: *O Lord, please keep my boy safe and guide his footsteps so that he does not falter or waver on the difficult road ahead. May he be as resolute and courageous as his maamen, the great man he admires.*

PART FOUR

THE RENAISSANCE MAN

~28~
The Price of Resistance

11–12 October 1980
Kerala, India

WITHIN DAYS OF THE INCIDENT, NEWS OF VAIKOM KARNAN'S shooting spread like wildfire across Kerala and major cities of India, fuelled by radio and newspaper reports. On 11 October, college students organized coordinated mass protests in the districts of Ernakulam, Trichur, Alleppey, Kottayam, Trivandrum, Calicut and Kannur. These protests, led by students affiliated with the YDSK, were supported by various workers' associations and followers of Karnan. Reports of violence and destruction of government property flooded the news. In Kottayam, protesters even seized a police station, holding it for three hours before being overpowered by police reinforcements.

In Trivandrum, the mounting pressure from both the public and the press forced the home minister of Kerala to hold a press conference on 12 October. With the police chief by his side, the HM delivered a stern warning to the protesters and announced a strict ban on the assembly of groups larger than five people after 10 p.m. He also issued shoot-at-sight orders for anyone violating the curfew effective immediately in the cities of Cochin, Trivandrum and Calicut.

Later that night in Cochin, less than an hour into the curfew, a police convoy came across a group of about a dozen protesters outside the Thevara Police Station, near the main entrance of the Cochin Shipyard. After several verbal warnings, the police deployed tear gas but were unsuccessful in their attempt to disperse the group.

One protester warned, 'We have guns. Leave, or we will shoot.'

After a tense standoff that lasted almost 90 minutes, the police opened fire. The first to fall was Shah Navaz, the 19-year-old rising youth leader from Sacred Heart College and one of the YDSK volunteers who had met Karnan backstage on the day of the shooting. Struck in the chest, he collapsed. By the time his father, Abdul Navaz, arrived at the scene, Shah Navaz had fallen unconscious.

A crowd of taxi drivers gathered around Abdul, forcing the police to retreat into the safety of the police station. Someone in the crowd shouted that Shah Navaz had stopped breathing. A distraught Abdul lifted his son's limp body and walked over to the front gate of the police station. He laid the body down, cradled his son's head and sobbed uncontrollably. The group of furious taxi drivers began hurling stones, shattering the glass windows of the station. It took 20 minutes for police reinforcements to arrive and disperse the crowd.

~29~
A Glimmer of Hope

18 October 1980
Medical Trust Hospital, Cochin

IT HAD BEEN THREE DAYS SINCE KARNAN WAS MOVED FROM the General Hospital to the Medical Trust Hospital. The transfer, conducted under the cover of night, was heavily guarded by police, with the commissioner herself overseeing the operation. Karnan was admitted to the ICU under the care of Dr P.J. Joseph, the head of the cardiothoracic unit. Only one relative was allowed to visit per day, between 5 and 6 p.m.

The intense media scrutiny made it difficult for Vasu and Murali to move in and out of the hospital. To alleviate this, the hospital management allocated a private room for the family. Jalaja arrived with Rukhsana the same day Karnan was transferred. After accompanying Jalaja to the hospital, Rukhsana left to attend college, promising to visit the hospital every day on her way back home.

At 11.20 a.m., there was a knock on the door. Vasu, exhausted and sleep-deprived, was fast asleep on the sofa in the corner of the room, while Jalaja read the newspaper. Murali opened the door to find a young woman who informed him that Dr Pulikkan Verghese wanted to meet Vasu. Murali asked her to wait while he went to wake his father. Vasu quickly put on a clean shirt, and Jalaja asked Murali to accompany him.

Murali and Vasu followed the woman up two flights of stairs to the top floor. When they had arrived with Karnan, Dr Joseph and a few resident trainees had met with them. The doctor, a man of few words, had informed them that Karnan remained in critical condition and would stay in the ICU until he could breathe without a ventilator.

Dr Joseph had asked Vasu questions about Karnan's health conditions, noting details about his family history, medication and the shooting incident. The hospital staff had collected blood samples and taken X-rays of Karnan's upper body. The doctor had advised caution, explaining that he wanted to gather more data and consult his colleagues before recommending a treatment plan. Murali appreciated this approach, though his mother felt the doctor was too slow.

They stopped before a large door and the woman knocked. The door opened and they were ushered into a glass-panelled meeting room with an expansive wooden table surrounded by eight chairs. The room had a large glass window with curtains drawn shut. After informing Murali and Vasu that Dr Verghese would arrive shortly, the woman left.

About 10 minutes later, Dr Pulikkan Verghese walked into the room, accompanied by Dr Joseph.

'I am Dr Verghese. You have already met Dr Joseph. Mr Karnan is our most important patient right now,' he began, looking at Vasu and Murali. 'Everyone, from the chief minister to autorickshaw drivers, seems interested in his case. Tell me, how are you two related to him?'

'My name is Murali Vasudev. This is my father, Vasudev Panicker. He and Karnan sir have been close friends for a very long time—'

'Sorry, I forgot to ask! Would you both like to have tea?' Dr Verghese interrupted Murali. Without waiting for a response, he reached below the table to press a buzzer. One of the attendants came running in, and Dr Verghese requested four cups of tea with sugar on the side. He then turned back to Murali.

'Yes, I know all about both of you,' the doctor continued. 'Your father and I share a mutual friend, retired Naval Commander

U.A. Velayudhan. I play cards with him almost every night at Santosh Club across the street. He is very good at playing rummy; in fact, he takes away a good chunk of what I earn every month.' Dr Verghese laughed at his own joke. 'For the past few days, Velayudhan has been insisting I meet both of you.'

Vasu leaned forward, smiling. 'Oh, Commander Velayudhan is an old friend. We joined the Royal Indian Navy on the same day. We have a bit of history together—'

'I know, I know,' Dr Verghese said with a wave of his hand. 'A bit of history? That sure is an understatement. The commander told me that you both were involved in the naval mutiny of 1946, helping him and his friends from the outside. That is a huge deal. Velayudhan also told me that his son is a close friend of Murali's. I promised him I would meet you.'

'We are very grateful.' Vasu paused for a few seconds, concern clouding his eyes. 'Tell us honestly, doctor, how is Karnan's condition?'

Dr Verghese turned to Dr Joseph, who responded, 'I wish I could say he is recovering, but to be candid, Karnan's case is the most complicated one I have encountered in my 23 years of practice. Let's remember he is here because no other hospital in Kerala can handle such a complex case.'

Murali leaned on the table. 'That's why we came here, doctor. Do you have an update?'

'Yes, I do. We have reviewed the reports from General Hospital and the data we have gathered here, and we believe that Karnan fell into a coma due to a condition called anoxic encephalopathy. It occurs when the brain doesn't receive enough oxygen for an extended period.'

'Is it because of the gunshot injury?' Vasu asked.

'It is very likely, but we cannot say for sure. It could be a combination of the gunshot injury, cardiac arrest or respiratory failure. When the brain doesn't receive enough oxygen, the cells begin to die, leading to permanent damage that can result in coma or even death.'

'Is there anything that can be done about it?' Murali asked, his voice betraying his impatience.

'We do not recommend surgery for anyone over 70, especially someone with a serious heart condition,' Dr Joseph explained. 'Additionally, he is in a coma. We decided against an operation to remove the broken rib bones that are embedded in his lungs and making it difficult for him to breathe. We also had to postpone inserting a gastrostomy tube to make it easier to feed him. Unless his condition stabilizes, there is not much we can do.'

Murali's frustration grew. 'What are the chances of that happening? I mean—'

Dr Verghese interjected. 'You are asking questions for which there are no easy answers. Look, Murali, I don't want to raise your hopes, but there have been cases of patients with anoxic encephalopathy coming out of a coma after several months. Let's pray that it happens to Karnan, too. Until then, we will not sit idle but continue all the supportive treatments. What he needs most is rest and good nutrition.'

'In addition to us, hundreds of his supporters are standing outside the hospital praying for his recovery every day,' Vasu said.

Dr Joseph nodded. 'Look, Vasu, there are limits to what medicine can do. But as doctors, we are always hopeful. The human body has a remarkable ability to recover, adapt and heal. Recovery from anoxic encephalopathy can be a long and challenging process, depending on the severity of the damage to the brain. With the right treatment and support, some recover fully, while others may have long-term memory loss or cognitive impairment.'

Silence followed Dr Joseph's comments.

'Please do all you can,' Vasu pleaded.

Dr Verghese looked at Vasu. 'Vasu, I promise we will do our best.'

Vasu nodded. 'That's all we can ask for at this time. The rest is up to the mercy of God.'

Dr Verghese added, 'Yes, we need help from the Almighty, but do not forget that your friend is not some ordinary being. He is a freedom fighter. If anyone can get through this, it is him.'

'We are praying he pulls through. Too much is at stake. Many people will be affected.'

'Yes, I heard about the students' agitation,' Dr Verghese said, first looking at Vasu and then at Murali. 'We need your help with a situation we are facing. I am told that you are the best people to help.'

'How can we be of help, doctor?' Murali leaned forward.

'Let me show you something. Follow me.' Dr Verghese walked to the large window and pulled back the curtains. The afternoon sun streamed in, momentarily blinding them. 'You don't have this view from your room. Look at what is happening on M.G. Road,' he said, pointing to the main road.

Murali and Vasu leaned forward to get a glimpse. Thousands of people crowded the streets below, blocking traffic. In the inner circle of the crowd, a group of about a hundred well-organized individuals held large signs. Murali recognized them as members of the YDSK.

Dr Verghese walked back to the table. 'We don't mind the protests. There is one or another here almost every day. In fact, the city centre has shifted from Jos Junction to here; people now refer to it as the "Medical Trust Junction",' he said with a hint of pride.

'We are not very familiar with Cochin. We live in Alleppey,' Vasu said apologetically.

Dr Verghese acknowledged the comment with a nod and continued. 'I don't mind the protest, but the protesters are stopping vehicles and staff from entering the hospital. Now that is a big problem. Last night, they stopped one of my doctors as he was coming out of the hospital after his shift. They warned him that if anything happens to Karnan, they will burn down the hospital.'

Murali jumped up, pounding his fist on the table. 'But the protesters are mostly students. I know each one of them. They would not do such a thing.'

Vasu reached out to grasp Murali's hand.

'Calm down, young man,' Dr Verghese said to Murali. 'You are right. They are mostly students, but not everyone. I also do not believe that the student protesters did this. My best guess is that a few rowdy elements have infiltrated the protesters. Regardless, we cannot operate with threats to our employees.'

Murali sat back down. 'Did you inform the police?' he asked.

'Yes, I spoke to Commissioner Sreelekha. You would expect that with her reputation as a tough cop, she would send armed policemen and disperse the crowd. But she is very wise. She explained that given the sensitive nature of the relationship between the police and protesters in the city, direct action by the police would only make things worse. She suggested that I talk to both of you first.'

'Did she say what we could do to help?' Vasu enquired.

'Yes, she thinks you might be able to influence the protesters. She suggested that you both meet the leaders of the protesters today and explain that we are only trying to help. If they leave our staff alone, we can do our job.'

Vasu readily agreed. 'We are happy to do that,' he said, looking at Murali for confirmation.

Murali nodded. 'Under one condition. Dr Joseph gives them a medical update at the meeting. That will clearly establish the role of Medical Trust Hospital. Keep it positive.'

'Of course. Dr Joseph will be there to represent the hospital. I will arrange a meeting room on the first floor. Let's keep it at 4 p.m. Thank you for your cooperation on this matter.'

An attendant knocked on the door and walked in with a tray containing four cups of tea and some biscuits, which he placed on the table.

Vasu addressed Dr Verghese. 'Doctor, we have a favour to ask of you.'

'What is it, Mr Panicker?'

'By now, all of Kerala knows what we have known for a long time. Karnan has a lot of political enemies, some of whom would like to see him dead.'

'That is no longer hearsay. We have clear evidence of that,' interjected Dr Verghese.

'We want to make a humble request to verify that all the doctors, nurses and staff attending to Karnan are completely trustworthy. Not that I doubt their integrity.'

'The safety and security of our patients has never been a problem here. But we have never had a patient as famous as Vaikom Karnan. I understand your concern and will take care of it. I will ensure we screen the doctors and nurses attending to him.'

Pleased with Dr Verghese's response, Vasu further requested, 'Is it possible to have an armed security guard outside the ICU at night?'

'Security guard, yes. But not armed. Only the police can deploy them. Since the commissioner thinks so highly of you, why not ask her? In the meantime, we will monitor the ICU more carefully.'

'Thank you, Doctor.'

Dr Verghese finished his tea, stood up and took Vasu's hands in his. 'It's a partnership...patients, doctors, family, community, police... We should all work together.' He drew a cross with his right hand on his chest. 'Let's pray for the blessings of the Almighty. Today, we have a good reason to believe Jesus is on our side.'

'What do you mean?' Murali asked.

'This morning, someone called to pay Karnan's medical bills. And here is the best part: the person offered to cover all of Karnan's future medical expenses,' Dr Verghese said with a smile. 'I see it as a sign from Jesus, a tiny glimmer of hope!'

Vasu gasped, 'Who would that kind-hearted person be?'

'Well, he told me not to tell anyone,' Dr Verghese said, glancing at Vasu. 'But how can I keep this a secret? It was one Mr Gupta from Rupa & Co.; he mentioned that he and Karnan are old friends.'

Vasu shook his head in disbelief. 'He is the agent who helped publish all three of Karnan's books. Yes, they are very close friends. Karnan's books really lifted Mr Gupta's fortunes at the beginning of his career. He is now the managing editor.'

'This is certainly a good omen,' Murali said with a smile.

Dr Joseph spoke to Vasu. 'Do you have a power of attorney for Karnan?'

'Yes, Doctor. He prepared all the documents a few weeks ago, as if he knew what would unfold.' Vasu pressed his hands together in gratitude. 'I thank you both for your kindness. We will take your leave now.'

As they headed towards the door, Dr Joseph addressed them. 'Look, Dr Verghese is an optimist; that is how he built this institution. But I am a realist,' he said almost apologetically. 'I must remind you that Karnan is still not out of the woods. Even if Jesus shows his mercy, it will be a long road to recovery. I think it is a good idea to inform relatives. While we hope for the best, we should also be prepared for bad news.'

Dr Joseph bid them farewell at the door with some final advice. 'If you decide to inform people, please request them to keep the information confidential.'

Murali followed Vasu back to their room.

'Acha, don't you think it is time we updated close friends and family?' Murali asked. 'I will try to call them; there is an STD phone booth outside the hospital.'

'Yes. We should inform MLA Shivan, Alex, Ashraf and Mr Gupta. Do you have anyone else in mind?'

'Yes. Rukhsana and Shibu.'

'Oh, yes. I forgot. Please let them know. Do you have money for the calls?'

'Yes, I do. You go and talk to amma. But don't tell her everything. I will call the others and invite a few leaders of the protesters to meet us and Dr Joseph at 4 p.m. today.'

∽

Murali finished making the calls by 2.35 p.m. He had spoken to everyone except Shibu, whom he planned to inform in person later that night, and Alex, who did not have a phone. The ones he had shared the news with promised to keep it confidential. As he stepped out of the phone booth, the conversation with Rukhsana lingered in his mind. She had mostly been silent, and Murali sensed that she was likely in shock. Rukhsana mentioned feeling unwell and said she might not be able to visit the hospital for a few days. A pang of guilt washed over Murali; he wished he could be there for her, to hold her in his arms.

At 2.45 p.m., Murali approached the protesters, much to their surprise. Exhausted after days in the sun, the YDSK members mobbed him with cries of 'YDSK Leader Murali Vasudev zindabad! Long live Youth Leader Murali!' Quieting down the excited crowd, Murali quickly summoned the YDSK leaders and asked them to identify leaders of the other known organizations present.

Within 30 minutes, 12 leaders were identified and invited to accompany Murali to the hospital for the meeting. Dr Verghese, Dr Joseph and a few hospital staff members arrived at 3.50 p.m. while Murali went to get his father. As Vasu entered the meeting room at 4.05 p.m., all the leaders stood up as a sign of respect.

Urging them to sit down, Vasu started the meeting by thanking the protesters for their efforts and requesting cooperation to ensure the protest remained peaceful. Dr Joseph followed up with an update on Karnan's medical condition, keeping his message positive and hopeful.

Murali spoke last, emphasizing the need for greater discipline and vigilance to weed out external elements infiltrating their ranks.

He said that the protests had garnered national media attention and placed the responsibility of ensuring the safety of the hospital staff squarely on the protest leaders. After Murali had finished speaking, the leaders asked about operational matters and how they should report suspicious people or activity.

Murali thought that the meeting went well. In fact, it went so well that Dr Verghese did not need to utter a word.

∞

Early the next day, MLA Shivan arrived at the hospital to pick up Vasu for their meeting with the police commissioner, which got over in two minutes. She did not even bother reading Vasu's letter; instead, she picked up the phone to call SI Ashraf and assigned him to Karnan's security, reporting directly to her. She also approved Ashraf's request to have Head Constable Jacob assist him.

Late that night, as Murali reflected on the day's developments, he was pleasantly surprised by how quickly everything had unfolded. He was impressed by the seamless collaboration between his father and Dr Verghese—two very different men united by a common objective. They had discussed important matters and agreed on a joint action plan. *If people with credibility make an earnest effort to listen and trust each other, have good intentions and communicate honestly, things can get done quickly.* He wondered why this simple principle was not deployed more often in politics and policymaking. If it were, quick action could be taken to benefit large numbers of people.

~30~
The Tapestry Unfolds

November 1980–April 1981
Medical Trust Hospital, Cochin

THE IMAGE OF THE AGEING FREEDOM FIGHTER BATTLING for his life resonated deeply with the people of Kerala. At 70, Karnan's heroic struggle seemed like a remnant of a bygone era, yet his spirit continued to inspire the youth. The media trickled out pieces of his storied past, fuelling public fascination. Soon, those around him—Vasu, Murali, MLA Shivan, Rukhsana, Shibu, Ashraf, Alex and other YDSK activists—were caught in the growing tide, their lives unexpectedly thrust into the spotlight.

Among them, Rukhsana drew the most attention. Reporters took note of her quiet, steadfast presence at the hospital, arriving each afternoon and staying until dusk. While the press speculated about her connection to Karnan, Rukhsana was occupied with more practical concerns. She helped Jalaja clean the hospital room and collaborated with Murali and the YDSK leadership to manage finances and coordinate activities. As the sun dipped below the horizon, Murali would walk her to the bus stop, where they lingered in conversation, savouring their time together before she boarded the bus home.

Their closeness did not go unnoticed. *Vanitha*, a popular women's magazine, painted their relationship as a 'forbidden love story' between a Hindu boy and a Muslim girl. The story struck a chord with young readers, prompting the magazine to release a special edition for college students. In the feature, Shibu defended their relationship, stating, 'It's strange for people to label their love "forbidden" without knowing them. As their friend, I can say their love is genuine, and the youth of Kerala embraces it.'

Poet Mallika Sukumaran, writing in *Kerala Kaumudi*, added, 'Rukhsana is like a daughter to me. She and Murali have fought for justice side by side. Their love is as pure as the waters of the Periyar River, built on mutual respect and trust, not divided by religion or caste. I hope their bond breaks the shackles of caste orthodoxy in Kerala.'

Several newspapers also began to unearth forgotten stories and little-known exploits of Karnan and Vasu during the freedom struggle, bringing to light Vasu's role in the Azad Hind Fauj. His former mentor, General Mohan Singh, now 71 and retired from active political and military life, was quoted in *The Hindu*, saying, 'I share the sorrow of my friend Vasudev Panicker and pray for the recovery of T.K. Karunakaran. The Fauj was built on the blood and sweat of brave soldiers like Vasudev. Today, it's our time to stand with him.'

Jalaja, arriving at the hospital the same day Karnan was transferred, quickly transformed the sterile room into a sanctuary. In one corner, she set up a small altar adorned with idols of Shiva and Krishna. Every evening at 6.30 p.m., she would light a lamp and whisper prayers, her devotion serving as a beacon of hope amidst the uncertainty. As Karnan remained in the ICU, unconscious and on a liquid diet, Jalaja found no reason to cook. Instead, she, Vasu and Murali relied on the daily meals sent by Shibu's mother, Baby. Shibu personally delivered the food each day, while Murali fetched tea from Anand Bhavan, a nearby restaurant. Each evening, Mr Balajee, owner of the nearby Kamala Stores, generously sent snacks to their hospital room.

Jalaja learnt of the *Vanitha* article during a brief visit home. Her conservative sister-in-law, eager to stir trouble, added her own venom to the gossip. Jalaja returned to the hospital, her eyes brimming with tears. She reminded Murali of their Nair family tradition where men married their murappennu. Murali, realizing his aunt had poisoned his mother's mind, felt a surge of anger. He stormed out of the room, heading for a telephone booth on the street. Grabbing the receiver, he dialled his uncle. 'Stay out of my affairs!' he shouted, slamming the phone down before his uncle could respond. Later, he reassured Rukhsana, who had been shaken by the sudden invasion of their privacy. They agreed to avoid public outings for a while, hoping to let the gossip die down.

Meanwhile, Shibu's loyalty to Karnan and Murali caught the media's attention. *Deshabhimani*, a daily newspaper, hailed him as the backbone of the YDSK movement. Drawing parallels between his father's role in the 1946 Royal Indian Navy mutiny and Shibu's leadership in the ongoing protests, the paper dubbed him and Murali the 'Emerging Leaders of a New Kerala'.

SI Ashraf Ali also found himself celebrated in both *Mathrubhumi* and *The Indian Express*. *Mathrubhumi* highlighted how Karnan had helped Ashraf secure his first job as a constable, while *The Indian Express* focused on Ashraf's courage, which had fuelled his swift rise through the ranks.

Even the ever-humble Alex was thrust into the spotlight. A journalist from *Janayugam* noticed his constant presence in the ICU, quietly caring for Karnan, and followed him home to Vaikom for an interview. An emotional Alex spoke of Karnan's kindness to his family and openly hinted at who he thought was responsible for the attack. Every Sunday, Alex brought a large tiffin box filled with his wife Leela's cooking. Her mutton biryani became a sensation, and many suggested they could quickly find success if they opened a restaurant in Cochin.

Amid all this attention, Ashraf and Jacob continued their tireless vigil over Karnan's ICU room, taking turns guarding it round the clock. Jalaja, ever gracious, would offer them tea and snacks during their breaks, sharing stories of old films starring her favourite actor, Sathyan, and fondly recalling the dramas she had seen at the temple festivals as a young girl.

Almost oblivious to the storm brewing outside, life at the hospital continued to revolve around Karnan's bedside—a tapestry of hope, love and despair woven by the press and the people who refused to leave his side.

∞

On 20 January, the police commissioner visited the hospital. After briefly checking on the security arrangements with Ashraf and Jacob, she stopped by the ICU to check on the famous patient under her protection. Dr Verghese gave her an update on Karnan's status, explaining that while the hospital staff was offering the best care possible, Karnan's survival seemed driven by mysterious forces modern medicine could not fully explain.

As the commissioner was leaving, she met Vasu and Murali. In confidence, she shared an unexpected development that had come to her attention a few hours earlier. The assailant's accomplice, who had been captured, confessed to receiving instructions and advance payment from Mr Kurian, the MLA from Angamaly. Kurian, a member of the ruling Communist Party, was a close confidant of the home minister.

True to his reputation as an unreliable ally, the home minister denied any knowledge of MLA Kurian's actions. Leaders of the LDF government unitedly called for Kurian's resignation. After a frantic attempt to secure the chief minister's support, which did not materialize, Kurian had no choice but to resign.

∞

By February, student protests led by Murali, Shibu and Rukhsana had spread all across Kerala. The protesters had powerful allies, including the Cochin Port Labour Union, the Kerala Taxi Drivers Organization and fans of Karnan's literary works. These groups organized donation drives and set up stations to provide food, financial help and logistical support for the student protesters.

Karnan's cause found a strong ally in Mrs K.R. Gouri Amma, the well-respected Agriculture and Social Welfare minister. As the only female Cabinet member in the state government, her unannounced visit to see Karnan at the hospital, followed by a private meeting with Vasu, Murali, Rukhsana and Shibu, was seen as a public acknowledgement of the monumental role Karnan had played in shaping the socialist movement in Kerala. Her sentiments were supported by Mr V.S. Achuthanandan, the powerful secretary of the Communist Party of India (Marxist), Kerala State Committee.

Meanwhile, a group of young left-leaning MLAs, led by Shivan and P. Vijayan, staged a sit-in at the Kerala Assembly in solidarity with Vaikom Karnan. Citing the widespread student protests, MLA Shivan demanded a daily update on the status of both the police investigation and Karnan's condition. Mr Vijayan, who had been imprisoned along with Karnan during the national Emergency of 1975, called for the immediate resignation of the home minister until the investigation into the shooting was complete.

As the scorching summer months of March and April arrived, the student protests showed no signs of slowing. The demands of the protesters, reflecting those of the YDSK, included the immediate resignation of Kerala's home minister and the transfer of the investigation to the CBI.

The repeated strikes and hartals declared by student groups began to take a toll on Kerala's economy. A tourism advisory issued by France and the United Kingdom to their citizens travelling to Kerala, warning of unrest, was soon followed by similar advisories from other European nations. A week later, the United States and Canada also issued such warnings. For the first time in a decade, Kerala saw a significant drop in the number of foreign tourists, dealing a severe blow to thousands of small businesses dependent on tourism across the state.

~31~

The Renaissance Man

SINCE THE END OF THE NATIONAL EMERGENCY IN 1977, without any major national news events, many of Kerala's news organizations had become stuck in the rut of mundane political reporting. However, after the initial confusion and blame-shifting following the shooting of Vaikom Karnan, the media found a renewed sense of purpose. The story of the forgotten freedom fighter fighting for his life in a desolate ICU ward, with his loyal friend standing vigil, captivated millions across India, young and old alike. In Karnan, they found a hero worth admiring—and in his shooting, a scandal began to loom.

Speculation swirled in the press almost daily: who was behind the attack on Karnan? The story of this ageing freedom fighter who refused to yield, even after being shot, ignited the imagination of the people of Kerala. In the months that followed, the YDSK recruited thousands of students, many of them teenagers new to the political scene. A surprising number of recruits were Muslim girls, inspired by Rukhsana's story. They formed a women's unit called the Youth Mahila Sangam.

At an event in New Delhi on 23 March 1981, marking the death anniversary of the revolutionaries Bhagat Singh, Shivaram Rajguru and Sukhdev Thapar, the president of India, Neelam Sanjiva Reddy, spoke of Vaikom Karnan as embodying the same virtues as the heroes of the freedom struggle. Reddy, himself a former freedom fighter and disciple of the late socialist leader Jayaprakash Narayan, described Karnan's shooting as 'a shameful betrayal of our core values' and urged the nation to pray for his recovery. Breaking with protocol, the president voiced support for the students' demand to transfer the investigation to the CBI.

In a similar vein, Balram Jakhar, the speaker of the Lok Sabha, began a new parliamentary session with a prayer for Karnan's health. Even Kerala's chief minister, E.K. Nayanar, despite the tense relationship his party had with Karnan, wished for Karnan's recovery and for his old comrade to 'come back home' to the Communist Party. In an interview with *Mathrubhumi*, Nayanar emphasized that their differences were never personal. He nostalgically recalled fleeting moments from their days as fugitives during the British rule, including a rainy Onam day in Wayanad when, with police dogs barking in the distance, they had hastily shared a meal served on a single banana leaf before going their separate ways.

However, not all coverage was sympathetic. An influential journalist with known ties to the Communist Party suggested that the assassination attempt was an inside job by senior Kerala Police officers, retaliating against Karnan for exposing police brutality during the 1975 national Emergency. He argued that the immediate killing of the assassin by the police was a deliberate move to suppress the truth.

In the Kerala Legislative Assembly, Mr Shanmugam, minister for Community Development, dismissed Karnan as a 'false prophet' and accused him of using his provocative speech on 8 October 1980 as a ploy to overthrow a democratically elected government. He called for strict action against the student protesters, whom he derisively described as 'thugs roaming the streets of Kerala like wild elephants in heat'.

Amid these conflicting narratives, the portrait of Vaikom Karnan began to take shape: a man of immense character and courage, yet fraught with contradictions. He had left home at a young age to serve his nation during its darkest hour, but had quietly returned when freedom finally dawned. A staunch believer in socialist ideals, yet often measuring progress by the standards of the capitalist Western nations. A man who had spent his prime years elevating great national leaders, only to be undone by cunning local politicians. A celebrated writer who had yet to fulfil his potential, a lonely elder cast aside by communal politics yet cherished by the youth. A man who could have claimed the role of Kerala's chief minister but never did.

Reflecting the public sentiment, M. Mapilla, chief editor of *Malayala Manorama*, posed a provocative question in a special column: 'How is it possible that in a highly literate state, so many people never realized that a hero like Vaikom Karnan lived among us all these years?' He lamented, 'If it takes the near death of a man who walked in the footsteps of giants like Jayaprakash Narayan to reveal our moral failings, then it is indeed a sad day for us. It is time to reflect on where our values have gone astray.'

S.K. Pottekkatt, a celebrated Malayalam writer known for his deep admiration of Karnan, voiced a sentiment that resonated with many when he rephrased a famous Second World War quote by Winston Churchill: 'If we were to search for a single individual alive in India today who embodies the riddles of human virtues and flaws, wrapped in the mystery of Kerala's socialist movement and within the enigma of India's monumental struggle for freedom, I am certain my dear friend Vaikom would be the one holding the key. He is, perhaps, the only true "Renaissance Man" alive in Kerala today.'

As the days passed, the narrative around Vaikom Karnan continued to evolve, deepening the intrigue and cementing his place as a complex and unforgettable figure in Kerala's political landscape.

~32~
The Dark Horse

FOR RUPA & CO. BEING GRANTED THE PUBLICATION RIGHTS to one of its most successful authors, who was the centre of national media attention, was an unexpected windfall. As a result, Mr Vijay Gupta was promoted from managing editor to executive editor. He took it as a sign from the gods and went all out to bring Karnan's book to the market, not only in its original Malayalam version but also in English and Hindi translations.

Mr Gupta boarded a flight to Cochin to visit his friend and was received at the Cochin Airport by Murali, who brought him to the hospital. Upon seeing Karnan in the ICU, his slow breathing and pulse the only signs of life, Mr Gupta became emotional. Vasu and Dr Joseph provided him with an update on Karnan's condition.

Later, he joined Vasu, Murali, Shibu and Rukhsana for dinner, where he lifted their spirits by sharing interesting anecdotes about his experiences with Karnan and Jayaprakash Narayan. After dinner, Mr Gupta discussed the publishing contract terms with Vasu, securing a copy of the power of attorney authorizing Vasu to execute legal documents on Karnan's behalf.

By the time Mr Gupta returned to Delhi, his in-house editor had drafted a publishing schedule for the manuscript. And as he had anticipated, there were hardly any edits required. Within a record time of 10 weeks, he personally oversaw the entire publishing process, from editing and translation to the page layout, cover design and book description for the back cover.

Mr Gupta sent advance copies of the manuscript to several prominent writers across India, requesting reviews from each of them. The overwhelming majority of reviews hailed *The Last*

Revolutionary as a modern classic. The noted poet Harivansh Rai Bachchan, a former member of the Rajya Sabha and recipient of the Padma Bhushan award, went as far as recommending it as a history textbook for high school students across India. In Mr Bachchan's words, 'Karnan's memoir tells the history of India's freedom struggle with a rare authenticity and searing emotional intensity. I cannot think of a better way for our children to learn the true story of the Indian struggle for freedom. I can write flowery poetry, but very few people can reach down into the deep wells of personal experiences that Mr T.K. Karunakaran has drawn upon for this literary masterpiece.' Mr Bachchan also recommended that the book be nominated for the Bharatiya Jnanpith Award.

Buoyed by the positive reviews, in April 1981, Mr Gupta ordered the first print run of 10,000 copies in Malayalam, almost 10 times the normal output. He anticipated it would sell out in a few months. He was wrong. The first consignment of 5,000 books sent to Cochin sold out in three days. The entire first print run sold out in just one week.

The demand for the book among students in Kerala was so high that some resorted to making and distributing photocopies of the pages. As Murali had predicted, the book further enhanced the YDSK's image among students and the general public as a credible political organization led by a new generation of young leaders. Due to the buzz generated by relentless media coverage, the book also fared well outside Kerala in major cities like Bombay, Delhi, Calcutta and Madras. Elated by the results, Mr Gupta convinced the board of Rupa & Co. to do something unprecedented—a second print run of 1,00,000 copies of the book, half in English and half in Malayalam. These were printed and ready to be shipped in a record time of six weeks.

In June 1981, just days before the second print run was set to hit the market, news of a confession made by MLA Kurian—while in a drunken state to a journalist posing as a fan—arrived. The

MLA revealed that the home minister of Kerala had been aware of the assassination plan. Sensing an opportunity for free publicity, Mr Gupta contacted major TV stations and press editors across India; multiple media outlets gladly took ownership of Mr Gupta's idea and carried the story, further fuelling the controversy surrounding the book.

It took just three weeks for the second run of the book to sell out. Mr Gupta was hailed as the man with the Midas touch, credited with single-handedly reviving the company's fortunes. To meet the surging demand, the publishing house enthusiastically endorsed a third print run of 5,00,000 copies, including 1,00,000 in Hindi—another record.

By early July 1981, booksellers in countries with a large expatriate Indian population, such as the United Arab Emirates, the United Kingdom, the United States and Singapore, were clamouring for rights to sell the book. The Bharatiya Jnanpith organization took notice of the unprecedented sales of the book. The committee had previously received S.K. Pottekkatt's nomination for his seminal work *Oru Desathinte Katha* in Malayalam for the 1980 award. Citing extraordinary circumstances, the committee waived the policy of one book per official Indian language and unanimously voted to add *The Last Revolutionary* to the list of books being considered for the 1980 Jnanpith Award.

After an intensive month-long internal review of the nominees, for the first time ever, two nominees from Kerala, S.K. Pottekkatt and T.K. Karunakaran, were among the final five authors shortlisted for the 1980 Jnanpith Award. In early August 1981, the chairman of the Bharatiya Jnanpith organization, responding to reporters' questions, said that in keeping with past precedent, a member of the award committee would personally meet with each of the finalists.

~33~

A Visitor at Night

7 September 1981
Medical Trust Hospital, Cochin

SEATED IN A CHAIR WITH A CLEAR VIEW OF THE ICU entrance, SI Ashraf Ali heard soft footsteps coming down the hall and looked up from the newspaper he was reading. He saw the shadowy figure of a woman clad in white overalls trying to open the ICU door. After a second attempt, she looked around, spotted Ashraf and immediately walked away, disappearing around the corner towards the elevator. Ashraf relaxed when he noticed a stethoscope hanging from her coat pocket.

He glanced at his watch and noted the time was 10.25 p.m. *Must be a new medical resident who lost her way*, he thought, returning to his newspaper. *Nothing interesting is going on in the world outside. Since the day of the shooting, more exciting events have been happening in my little world.*

In recent months, Ashraf had undergone an internal investigation by the Crime Investigation Department of the Kerala Police. The investigator, Superintendent of Police Anurag Mishra, a batchmate of Commissioner Sreelekha, had asked him to explain the circumstances surrounding the use of his weapon and why he had been at the Marine Drive grounds with his police-issued pistol. Fortunately, Mishra had understood and even respected Ashraf's relationship with Karnan.

In his report, the superintendent cleared Ashraf of any intentional wrongdoing and commended him for his quick action of shooting and killing the assassin with three bullets—two of which were recovered from the body. Ashraf wondered what had happened to the third bullet, the one from Murali's revolver. *Did Commissioner Sreelekha use her connections to make the bullet disappear? Would it be appropriate for me to thank her?*

After a few minutes, the ICU door opened. Nurse Jasmine stepped out and walked towards Ashraf.

Ashraf put the newspaper down and looked up. 'Taking a break, nurse?'

'No. I had a terrible headache and fell asleep. The resident doctor was supposed to do his rounds. Did you see him?' Jasmine replied.

'I have been here for two hours and only saw a lady doctor about 10 minutes ago...'

'Lady doctor? We don't have a lady doctor on duty tonight.'

'I swear I saw a woman wearing white overalls. I could not see her face clearly. She tried to open the ICU door. When it did not open, she went away, towards the elevator. Are you telling me there is no lady doctor or resident on duty tonight?'

'That is correct. No lady doctors are on duty in the ICU today,' Jasmine said emphatically.

Ashraf jumped up from his chair. 'Oh my God! I need to find out who that was. Can you go inside and find out if Karnan sir is okay?'

'He is fine,' Jasmine said. 'I was inside with him.'

Ashraf ran to the elevator. Finding it engaged, he dashed down the stairs and raced to the ground floor. Seeing the empty lobby, he walked up to the security guard seated at the desk and asked if he had seen anyone leave in the last 15 minutes. The security guard confirmed that a few minutes ago, he had seen someone in white overalls leave the building and get into a waiting car.

Ashraf stepped out into the street and found it deserted. He turned back into the hospital and went up to the ICU ward, where Vasu stood waiting, his face flushed.

'Nurse Jasmine has updated me,' Vasu said. 'Any sign of that person?'

'No. I should have acted sooner,' Ashraf said, out of breath from the exertion.

Vasu shook his head. 'Ashraf, this is what I had feared all along! I had a feeling that there would be another attempt on his life.'

'Damn it! It's my fault. I wish I had stopped her and asked,' Ashraf exclaimed. He paced back and forth. 'Whoever is behind this must have an informant inside the hospital.'

'We have to be careful. This person knew exactly where Karnan was.'

'Vasu sir, who is in your private room right now?'

'Only Jalaja. Murali left to check on his grandmother.'

'What about Rukhsana?'

'She did not show up today. She was not feeling well last night and had commented she might not come today.'

'Hmm… That is interesting,' Ashraf said.

There was a brief silence.

Vasu placed a hand over his heart. 'Ashraf, do you really believe that…?'

'I do not know, Vasu sir. All we know is that she did not come today. Was she aware of something that we were not? That is for us to find out.'

There was silence again.

'Listen, Ashraf. This is a highly sensitive matter. You know Murali—'

'Vasu sir, you don't have to tell me,' he said. 'I know about the relationship between Murali and Rukhsana. Also, Rukhsana is now the most visible leader of the YDSK. That complicates everything.'

'Yes, it does,' Vasu said. 'Ashraf, just keep in mind that we are making assumptions. We do not have any evidence of her involvement. I want to give her the benefit of the doubt. Perhaps there is an innocent explanation for what happened today. Do you understand?'

'Yes, Vasu sir. I do,' Ashraf said. 'Maybe it is my police training, but from the moment I saw her, I have felt Rukhsana is hiding something. I just can't put my finger on it.'

'What do we do now?' Vasu asked, perplexed.

'I think we should place her under surveillance for a few weeks. I want to know who else she has been meeting.'

Vasu shook his head in disbelief and placed his hand on Ashraf's shoulder. 'Ashraf, this is a big shock for me. I trust you. Do what you think is appropriate. But promise me that you will keep this matter strictly between us. Murali should not know about it. Not even Jalaja.'

'Yes, Vasu sir. I promise. I will not report this incident for now. Given the high interest from the press, if I report it, it will get leaked. That will alert the enemies, whoever they are.'

~34~

The Commander's Plan

8–9 October 1981
Cochin, Kerala

ON THE EIGHTH DAY OF OCTOBER 1981, THE FIRST anniversary of the shooting, public interest in Vaikom Karnan and the outcome of the investigation reached its peak. Every major newspaper in Kerala, along with several national and regional news organizations, carried editorials and op-eds marking the occasion. Most of the reports criticized the Kerala Police, under the charge of the home minister, for their inability to bring the investigation to a conclusion and for the deteriorating law and order in the state.

In an attempt to appear in control of the situation in Kerala, the home minister blamed DGP Subramanian and dismissed him from his post. At a press conference, he announced his plans to visit Karnan in the hospital. In response to a reporter's question, the minister swallowed his pride and clarified that, almost a year ago, he had been misquoted as calling Karnan a 'lion in winter'. He insisted that he meant to call Karnan the 'lion of Kerala'. This sudden reversal was met with derision by the student protesters outside Medical Trust Hospital, who expressed their anger by burning effigies of the minister.

MLA Shivan got wind of the date and time of the home minister's planned visit and entrusted Murali and Shibu with organizing a protest to block his entry to the hospital. After discussing the matter with his father, Murali arranged a visit to Shibu's home. Vasu also wanted to meet his old friend, Shibu's father, who was now an influential leader in the local community surrounding the hospital. He also wanted to thank Shibu's mother for the daily home-cooked lunches she sent for them.

Early the next day, Vasu and Murali went to Shibu's home, which was about a short 10-minute walk from the hospital. As they neared the front gate, Shibu's mother, Baby, and his little brother, Suresh, greeted them. Both were busy scrubbing green moss from the brick wall that fenced their home. When Suresh spotted Murali, he let out a shriek of delight and ran up to him, calling out, 'Murali chetta! Murali chetta!' Murali handed Suresh the two chocolate éclairs he had brought for him.

As a sign of their mutual affection, Murali called Shibu's mother 'Baby amma', and she called him 'mone'. Murali bent down to touch Baby's feet, as he always did when they met, and she placed a hand on Murali's head and blessed him. Murali then introduced his father to her.

Baby held Murali's hands. 'Mone, how is your maamen? We were planning to visit the hospital today.'

'Amma, thanks to your prayers, maamen is still alive. He is in the ICU and will take time to recover,' Murali said as he lifted Suresh into the air.

'We have been getting daily updates from Shibu and the newspapers. You and your maamen have been in our thoughts and prayers every day,' Baby said.

Baby invited Murali and Vasu into her modest home, explaining that it belonged to her parents and was occupied, like most Hindu joint family homes, by her parents, her brother's family, and her own.

After they were seated under the fan in the veranda, Baby went inside to get her husband and older boys, who were still asleep.

The curtain separating the veranda from the inside of the home parted, and Velayudhan walked out, followed by a still-sleepy Shibu. Although retired, Velayudhan, a few years older than Vasu, carried himself with the serious air of a naval officer still in uniform. He was clean-shaven, with his short silver hair neatly combed back. He wore a white half-sleeved shirt with thin grey stripes and a white mundu. Upon seeing Vasu, his normally stern face broke into a wide smile. Ignoring Vasu's extended hand, Velayudhan wrapped his old friend in a bear hug.

'Ah, Vasu! My old friend. This is a surprise. It's been a long time. Last we met was almost two years ago—at the Naval Base canteen—waiting in line to collect our quota of alcohol,' Velayudhan said, still holding his friend in an embrace.

'Commander, your memory is sharp. Good to meet you again,' Vasu said as the two men sat down.

'Uncle, my amma says that going to the Naval Base to get his quota of alcohol is the one appointment for which acha reaches well ahead of time,' Murali quipped.

'Well, that is the discipline we learnt in the Navy,' Velayudhan said. The smile on his face vanished as he continued, 'We were so shocked to hear about Karnan. I hope he is showing some signs of improvement.'

'It is hard to tell. Fortunately, he is under the care of the best doctors in Kerala, so we are hopeful,' Vasu replied.

'Dr Verghese is a good man. We play cards every Thursday night. He assured me he would do all he can,' Velayudhan said. 'We must accept the reality and leave the rest to the doctors.'

Vasu nodded in agreement. 'Commander, I have wanted to arrange a get-together with Karnan chetta for a very long time. You have not met since his book on the naval mutiny was published. But it just never happened.'

'Shibu told me that he met Karnan for the first time on the night of the shooting. I was surprised to hear that Karnan remembered the details of the mutiny. You see, I never told my children about what happened in the past.'

'Yes, that was almost 34 years ago,' Vasu responded wearily. 'Most Indians have forgotten about it.'

'No, Vasu! Not those who have worn the uniform,' Velayudhan said, his voice rising with conviction. 'To us, the mutiny was a sacred moment—a time when we showed the British where our true loyalty lay. This may not surprise you, but the British pressured the Indian leaders to whitewash the mutiny. The incident remained largely unknown for years, until after Karnan's book was published.'

'Karnan changed your name in the book to protect your identity. I wonder how people in the services learnt about your involvement.'

Velayudhan leaned forward. 'My good friend Rear Admiral Gandhi once mentioned my name during a speech at the National Defence Academy. Of course, he made the remark as a compliment, to emphasize that cadets have a higher duty to the nation. The news spread fast. After that, men and women, young and old, from the Army, Navy and Air Force—wherever I have been posted—always stopped to thank me. They never forgot the rebel sailors who brought down the Union Jack.'

'And rightfully so, Commander. I will never forget the joy we felt when we heard that the mutiny was successful.'

'I will never forget your help with the planning and getting us the flags on time. I remember you even gave me an extra flag to keep.'

'I must be getting old; I do not recall the extra flag.'

'I still have it with me,' Velayudhan exclaimed. 'You know, when Shibu shared the story of the naval mutiny with his brothers, my youngest, Suresh, came into my room and demanded to see proof of my involvement. I was forced to take out the extra flag and show it to him. Would you like to see it?'

Velayudhan ducked through a low doorway into another room. After a few seconds, he came out with a neatly folded flag. Standing before Vasu, he slowly unfurled the flag and held it up. The flag had broad white-, green- and saffron-coloured stripes with the image of Gandhi's cotton spinning wheel, the *charkha*, at its centre. Visibly emotional, Vasu stood up in reverence to the pre-independence flag of the INC.

Velayudhan looked at Murali and Shibu. 'You see, children, without the symbolism of the flags, there would never have been the mutiny of the Royal Indian Navy.'

'Well, Commander, getting the flags was the easy part. You and your friends did all the hard work and put yourselves in harm's way,' Vasu said.

'We thought of it as our duty,' Velayudhan said. 'Recent estimates state that about 20,000 people were involved, including those in uniform and civilians. That is why we were able to almost take over Bombay. Had the Congress and the Muslim League not withdrawn their support, we would not have surrendered.'

Shibu turned to his father. 'When Karnan sir told me about the mutiny, I could hardly believe you had been involved in such a historic event. Why did you not mention it to us before?'

'Well, son, that is the ethos of sailors,' Velayudhan explained. 'We do not boast about doing what we think is our duty. I wanted you to hear the story from someone else. I am glad that it was from Karnan.'

As Velayudhan carefully folded the flag, Baby walked in with a tray containing three cups of tea. She offered Vasu, Murali and her husband a cup each, whispering to him that his tea was without sugar.

'Mild diabetes,' Velayudhan offered as an explanation to Vasu.

Murali stood up as Shibu's older brother, Sashi Kumar, whom he called 'Kumar chetta', entered the room and greeted everyone. Vasu enquired about how Sashi Kumar was doing following the open heart surgery he had recently undergone to fix a valve problem. Kumar assured him that he had fully recovered.

'I am yet to meet your daughter. Has she completed her college?' Vasu asked Baby.

'Yes. Shashikala completed her BA last year and is now a teacher at Toc-H Public School. She has gone to attend her friend's wedding in Fort Cochin. She says she doesn't want to marry until she is 30. Girls these days…'

'That is understandable. For today's generation, 30 is like what 20 was when we were young,' Vasu said.

Carrying a broken cricket bat, Suresh walked into the veranda and gestured to Murali, who bent down to listen.

'I know what happened to your uncle,' the little boy whispered.

'How do you know?' Murali asked, pretending to be surprised.

'Shibu chetta told me.'

'Did he? What do you think we should do?' Murali encouraged him.

'Catch the bad guys and shoot them in the same place,' the little boy said, pointing to his heart.

Baby was not amused. 'Suresh, enough of your grown-up talk. This discussion is not for children. Go inside and finish your homework.' The men looked at each other as silence descended.

Finally, Vasu spoke up. 'Commander Velayudhan, we came to seek your guidance on something important and confidential.'

'Tell me, Vasu.'

'We have learnt that the home minister is planning a visit to Medical Trust Hospital later this week. He is doing this for a photo opportunity because of the public outcry over the incident. We all know that he still harbours grudges of the past, and we have reasons to suspect he may be behind the shooting.'

'Unbelievable! We should stop that idiot,' Shibu shouted.

'Shut up!' Velayudhan glared at Shibu, presumably for using inappropriate language in front of elders. 'First, listen to what Vasu uncle has to say. Anger is not a plan.'

'Shibu is right!' Sashi backed his brother. 'We have the people to stop him from entering the hospital. We should start mobilizing them right away.'

'And then do what? Give the police advance notice of our plans?

What good would that do?' Velayudhan said angrily. 'Remember, as the home minister, he is in charge of the Kerala Police.' He stood up and paced back and forth, lost in thought. 'No, that is certainly a foolish idea.'

'Commander, I came to get your opinion as you have been in similar situations during your service. How should we handle this matter?' Vasu asked.

'Let's review the cards we have been dealt,' Velayudhan said, a hint of frustration in his voice. 'Our goal is clear—prevent the minister from getting inside the hospital. We want to protest but lawfully. That means our boys cannot carry weapons. Are we in agreement?'

Vasu nodded. 'Yes, no weapons, Commander.'

Velayudhan continued, 'However, the police are aware of the ongoing protests at the site, so they will come prepared. I will not be surprised if they arrive with a unit of the Armed Reserve Police. It is a classic case of what we call an asymmetric battlefield. In this situation, our only hope of snatching a victory is to effectively use the element of surprise to our advantage.' Velayudhan looked up and noticed the blank expressions on the others' faces.

'Let me break it down. If the HM's security team gets wind of our plan to block his entry into the hospital, they will have the local police clear the area well in advance. Our approach needs to be divided into smaller, separate actions. Each small group will have a specific task, but no one, NO ONE, outside the five of us should know the full plan. That is how we'll use the element of surprise to our advantage.'

'Daddy, I heard you. It is six people now,' Suresh chimed in, peeking into the room from behind the curtains, his head barely visible. The men laughed.

'Mummy, can you get this nosy boy out of here?' Shibu said.

'No, let him stay. It's time he learns how this world operates,' Velayudhan said.

'What is the plan you have in mind, Commander?' Vasu asked.

Velayudhan paused, thinking for a moment before speaking decisively. 'We'll mobilize students from nearby colleges and from the surrounding villages. Two hours before the minister arrives, our people will quietly enter the city using public transportation. No busloads, no processions, nothing that would attract attention.

'Instead of blocking the streets immediately, they will hide in shops, buildings and alleys near the hospital. Only when the HM's motorcade is close to the hospital entrance will Murali and Shibu give the signal. That's when everyone will come out and flood the streets. If we can execute this within a few minutes, it will create the element of surprise that the police will not be prepared for.' Velayudhan said, looking up at Vasu. 'This is our best bet.'

A moment of silence followed, with each man deep in thought. Vasu finally spoke up, his voice filled with admiration. 'Brilliant plan! This is exactly why we came to you, Commander. It's perfect.'

'But there are steps we need to take to ensure its success,' Velayudhan added.

'Just tell us, uncle,' Murali urged eagerly.

'The Cochin Police aren't my main concern. I have met Police Commissioner Sreelekha Sriram—she is a fair officer. My concern is about the home minister's security detail.'

'Why, uncle?' Murali asked.

'Think about it. When the motorcade is blocked, his security team will spring into action. They might initiate a lathi charge or use tear gas to disperse the crowd. That is their job. We need brave men as the first line of defence—men like you and Shibu. But we also need a large crowd who will back them. Can we organize that?'

Sashi, who was leaning against the wall, straightened up. 'The best way to gather a large crowd is to mobilize students from local colleges. We should organize a student strike and shut down the colleges.'

'I agree, Kumar chetta,' Murali added. 'The YDSK has strong

support in Maharaja's, Sacred Heart and St Albert's. We can easily mobilize thousands of student volunteers.'

Velayudhan nodded. 'Students will definitely help create a large crowd, but they lack experience in handling such a volatile situation. We need a few seasoned fighters who will stand their ground and not back down when the police come at them with batons and, if needed, fight with bare hands.'

'How about we enlist Hippie Jayan and Prakash?' Sashi suggested, referring to two local toughs known for their street fighting prowess.

'Who is Hippie Jayan?' Vasu asked Sashi.

'We call him "Hippie" Jayan because he has long hair,' Sashi explained. 'He is skilled in kung fu and *kalaripayattu,* and is the leader of the *Vellaiparambil* gang. Tough as nails. A few months ago, he rescued Suresh from child snatchers at the Ernakulam Shiva Temple festival. By the time I arrived at the scene, one of the men was lying on the ground, blood dripping from his nose. The other two had fled.'

Velayudhan looked at Sashi. 'Jayan and Prakash may not have the cleanest police records, but they are exactly the kind of men we need alongside Murali and Shibu on the frontline,' he said. 'It will help to have a few women too. The police will not dare to touch them.'

'We only have one female leader in the YDSK's executive committee. Her name is Rukhsana,' Murali said.

'I know—the girl in the scarlet hijab. I have seen the press reports.' Velayudhan said, a rare smile playing on his lips. 'I hate to put a woman in danger, but I think it will help if Rukhsana brings a few of her friends. They can form the core of the frontline. That would be our second surprise for the police.'

Vasu pursed his lips. 'It's a good idea, but the memory of police violence during the Emergency is still fresh. What if they decide to use force anyway?'

'That is definitely a risk.' Velayudhan paused for a second. 'There is a simple way to ensure this does not happen—invite the press. When the minister sees the cameras rolling, he'll wet his pants.'

The laughter of the three young men filled the room, but Velayudhan remained serious. 'From what I've heard, the minister is a bully and bullies are cowards at heart. When he sees the protesters standing strong, he will turn tail and run.'

'I hope you are right, Commander. I was right when I told Murali we must seek your advice,' Vasu said, standing up and addressing the others. 'Children, now we have a clear plan. Let's execute it.'

'Daddy, can I come too?' Suresh asked from behind the curtains.

Without turning around, Velayudhan replied, 'You can watch from a safe distance, but only if you promise to complete your homework on time every day. I will come with you. Deal?'

'Yes, daddy! I will do my homework every day,' said the delighted boy, just as his mother led him away.

Velayudhan turned to Vasu. 'Keep me updated on the plan.' Leaning closer, he whispered, 'Let's find out the colour of the blood inside the veins of these fine young men.'

'We will, Commander. We sure will,' Vasu said. 'Remember, in 1946, we too were unaware whether we had the courage to challenge the British. Maybe our ignorance of the magnitude of the odds helped us move forward. We simply did what had to be done. I see no reason why our children will come up short.'

Velayudhan nodded in agreement. 'That is my belief too. Adversity reveals character.'

Vasu shook hands with Velayudhan. 'Commander, I will see you again soon. Hopefully right here and not at the Naval Base canteen,' he joked. Velayudhan grunted in approval.

Vasu politely declined Baby's offer to stay for breakfast, explaining that he needed to visit his astrologer to seek blessings for the plan. Vasu and Murali said their goodbyes and headed out. Meanwhile, Shibu quickly went inside to put on a fresh shirt.

After they left, Baby turned to her husband. 'You just put Murali and our boys at risk with this plan. I have a bad feeling about this,' she said as she picked up the teacups. 'Remember that you are no longer a naval officer but the father of three boys and a girl.'

'My plan will protect them, but life is not just about safe choices. It's time the boys took some risks,' Velayudhan replied, his voice betraying his impatience. 'I may be retired, but I cannot turn a blind eye to injustice. Not when our own boys are involved. And what can those potbellied Kerala policemen do? Not a damn thing!'

'Why make fun of others when you are not as fit as you used to be,' Baby shot back. 'I think you should stay out of this.'

'Once a Navy officer, always a Navy officer. I have no choice but to be there myself. I cannot promise the safety of our boys, but I promise to do all I can to help them.'

Velayudhan then turned to Sashi. 'Kumar, you are still recovering from your heart surgery, I don't want you to get involved in the protest. You and Suresh can watch from a safe distance. I will arrange for Santosh Club to be opened. You can observe from there.'

'What health issues? Father, I am fine. Let me go find Jayan and Prakash right now.'

His parents exchanged glances but said nothing.

∞

Shibu was preoccupied with the important task Murali had entrusted to him the day before: mobilizing thousands of students to gather around Medical Trust Hospital during the home minister's visit. Shibu found the task complicated due to the lack of time and the fact that it had to be done entirely by word of mouth.

Shibu and Sashi walked the short distance to the hospital, carrying lunch boxes for Murali's parents. As they approached, the student volunteers affiliated with the YDSK huddled around them. They strategized sending one volunteer to each college campus in Ernakulam district. Shibu, known for his fearlessness and hot-headedness, laid down the objectives and message to be shared with the student leaders. On the other hand, Sashi, respected for his quick wit and calm demeanour, emphasized the importance of avoiding violence and maintaining secrecy to prevent alerting college authorities or the local police.

The brothers took turns answering the protesters' questions. The plan was to convince the local colleges to issue a call for a flash strike around 11 a.m. on the day of the home minister's visit. This move would close all local colleges and allow them to mobilize and direct as many student volunteers as possible towards the city centre, where Medical Trust Hospital was located. Sashi knew that most students, including those affiliated with the left-leaning SFI, loathed the home minister. This factor alone would boost participation.

Ignoring the onlookers who had gathered nearby, Shibu declared that come what may, he and Murali would remain at the frontline of the protest, holding the YDSK flag. He expressed confidence that, together, they would be able to prevent the home minister from entering the hospital. The one question that remained in Shibu's mind was whether students would hold their ground if the police attacked with batons. He felt reassured by his father's approval to bring in Jayan and Prakash. Satisfied with the arrangements, Shibu and Sashi went inside the hospital.

On their way home, the brothers stopped by Vijayan's petty shop to pick up a packet of Charminar cigarettes as instructed by their father, using the change to buy a peanut brittle for Suresh. As they turned on to Mills Lane, where they lived, they ran into Jayan and Prakash, who were sitting on the low wall of the local primary school. Jayan, tall and lanky with shoulder-length hair, worked as a helper and sound technician for the famous English music band '13AD'. Prakash, short and muscular, was training to be an electrician. Both men were high school dropouts who often played football and cricket with the brothers. These 20-something locals were fond of the three brothers and deeply respected their father's military service.

Shibu and Sashi conferred with Jayan and Prakash, reviewing the plans and securing their support. Sashi declined Jayan's request to carry handheld weapons but agreed he could bring steel knuckle guards in case the police resorted to violence.

PART FIVE

A MOTHER'S FIERCE COURAGE

~35~
Gathering Storm

15 October 1981
M.G. Road, Cochin

SHIBU ESTIMATED THAT ABOUT TWO DOZEN PEOPLE HAD crowded into the small sweet shop called Swastik. The store was tucked into the ground floor of the Medical Trust Hospital building on M.G. Road. As he scanned the room, Shibu noticed that very few were there to buy sweets. Most of the people gathered had been carefully selected by Murali and him to serve as the frontline protesters—battle-hardened men and women who, as his father had advised, would stand their ground no matter what.

Murali stood to Shibu's right, holding a large YDSK flag on a pole, giving last-minute instructions to Rukhsana, Geethanjali and Mallika. Rukhsana was dressed in a white half-sari and a long-sleeved white blouse with green cuffs. Her hijab, a slightly lighter shade of her usual scarlet, was loosely draped over her head and shoulders, almost like a headscarf. Shibu could not recall ever seeing Rukhsana in anything other than a salwar kameez. *If she has chosen this moment to dress like the other women, it is the perfect occasion.*

On Shibu's left stood Abdul Navaz, and beside him were Jayan and Prakash, both of whom exuded the quiet intensity of martial artists preparing for a fight. Ramesh Babu, the youngest student leader in the group, had come all the way from Trivandrum and stood next to Prakash. This group of six men and three women, forming the core of the frontline of protesters, would be backed by a second line of the seasoned YDSK activists. Behind them would stand around 200 students and Karnan's supporters.

Shibu looked across the street at the three-storey office building. On the third floor was a sign that read 'Santosh Club'. He spotted his father on the balcony, surveying the scene below, flanked by Sashi and Suresh. Suresh waved when he saw Shibu, who smiled and waved back. Shibu wondered how Sashi was dealing with their father's decision to exclude him from the protest due to his health.

Returning his gaze to the street, Shibu noticed students steadily streaming out of public buses, directed by the YDSK volunteers into bylanes and nearby buildings. Traffic was flowing smoothly. A glance at his watch showed it was 1.30 p.m. The home minister was scheduled to arrive in an hour. A police jeep passed by without stopping, a sign that everything appeared normal—*a good sign,* Shibu thought.

As minutes ticked by, thousands of students continued to arrive, guided into position by the YDSK volunteers. Their call for the strike had been effective, and most local colleges had closed for the day. At 2.55 p.m., Shibu felt a sharp nudge from Murali. 'Look at your father; he is signalling something,' Murali said.

Shibu looked up to see his father gesture with the hand signs they had practised the previous night—the home minister's motorcade was approaching from the south side of M.G. Road.

Gripping Murali's arm, Shibu said, 'Murali, it's time. We have five minutes.'

They exchanged a nod and, with arms interlocked, stepped out of the store on to the road. The other frontline leaders fell in line behind them, bringing traffic to a halt. At the centre of the road, they formed a solid human barrier, blocking the minister's path. Shibu glanced up again and saw his father pointing towards the upper floor of Medical Trust Hospital. Shibu turned to see Vasu watching the action unfold from the hospital's fifth floor.

Murali and Shibu looked at each other. Without speaking a word, Shibu knew that this moment was the pinnacle of their friendship. *The first real test of our courage—perhaps a smaller version of the mutiny that tested the mettle of our fathers.*

Together, they raised the YDSK flag. As it fluttered in the breeze, the two friends pumped their free fists into the air and stepped forward. The crowd erupted in cheers.

'INQUILAB ZINDABAD!' they shouted in unison, just like they had done countless times before.

All eyes shifted to Murali and Shibu as their defiant cry filled the air. The space between the hospital complex and the office buildings across the street suddenly seemed to shrink. The shout was the signal the YDSK volunteers had been waiting for. They sprang into action, directing students from the shops and bylanes to take their places behind the frontline leaders. A cheer went up as press photographers rushed towards Murali and Shibu, who were both smiling, enjoying the attention.

Shibu was pleased to see that what had been a nearly empty road just 30 minutes ago was now packed with thousands of protesters, with more still arriving. *Father was right. Surprise, indeed, is a significant advantage in an unequal battle.*

'Zindabad, zindabad. Vaikom Karnan, zindabad!' Murali shouted. The slogan echoed off the narrow walls between the two buildings, magnified by the thousands of voices joining in.

'Zindabad, zindabad. Vaikom Karnan, zindabad!' the crowd repeated.

'Home minister, go back! Go back!' Shibu bellowed.

This time, even more protesters joined in. 'Home minister, go back! Go back!'

A few minutes later, the first vehicle in the HM's motorcade appeared and stopped about 20 metres from the frontline protesters. It was a police jeep serving as an escort. Behind it was an armoured van, followed by the minister's car—a gleaming white Ambassador with tinted windows.

After a moment, a broad-shouldered police officer in a khaki uniform stepped out of the jeep. Shibu noted the extra star on his shoulder, identifying him as a deputy superintendent of police. The officer adjusted his cap, gripped his baton and slowly walked towards the protesters. Murali and Shibu ignored him, continuing to shout slogans, their voices now a powerful force that the crowd echoed back with growing fervour.

The officer raised his baton. 'Stop!' he commanded. The crowd fell silent. 'Do you have a permit for this rally?'

'What permit?' Murali shot back. 'Go ask the Cochin Corporation!'

'Put down the flag, you rascal,' the officer demanded, the veins in his neck bulging with anger.

Shibu stepped forward, his eyes scanning the name tag on the officer's chest. 'Look who we have here! Alexander the Great!' he taunted, his voice dripping with defiance. 'Want this flag, Alexander? THEN, COME GET IT!' he thundered.

Taken aback, Officer Alexander stood frozen, his hostile gaze fixed on Shibu. Jayan and Prakash moved to flank Shibu and Murali, their sleeves rolled up in preparation. The steel knuckle guard on Jayan's fist glinted in the sunlight.

A murmur rippled through the crowd, only to be replaced by an expectant silence. Thousands of eyes were on the officer, waiting for his next move in response to Shibu's open challenge.

Time seemed to stretch. Then, with a sudden turn, Alexander strode back towards the minister's car. The crowd jeered loudly. Murali and Shibu lifted the flag again and resumed shouting slogans.

A shiver of exhilaration ran through Shibu's spine. *The stage is set for the showdown, and this time, we are ready!* He glanced up at the third floor of the office building. His brothers waved and gave him a thumbs-up. Shibu noticed what seemed like a faint smile on his father's face—a rare expression of approval that filled him with pride.

~36~
Hope Stirs

15 October 1981
Medical Trust Hospital, Cochin

VASU AND ALEX WALKED SINGLE FILE BEHIND SI ASHRAF, who had just informed them that Dr Joseph urgently wanted to meet them in his office. Vasu's mind raced. *What could be the reason for this urgent summons? Has Karnan's condition taken a turn for the worse?*

As they reached Dr Joseph's office, an attendant ushered them inside. Dr Joseph greeted them. 'Vasu, we have some good news and some bad news. I know Murali is outside the hospital. Where is your wife?'

'She had to go home this morning to check on her mother. She will be away for a few days. Doctor, is Karnan okay?' Vasu asked.

'No, he is not just okay,' Dr Joseph said, allowing a rare smile to cross his face. 'He has shown signs of consciousness. Just 15 minutes ago, when the nurse turned him over, he tried to speak. It was not clear what he wanted to say, but the nurse thought she heard him ask for you.'

Vasu placed his hand over his heart, a wave of relief washing over him. 'May I speak to him now?'

'No. That is the bad news. After about five minutes, he fell back asleep— hopefully not into a coma again. By the time I reached his bedside, he was fast asleep. Well, this isn't entirely bad news; it's common for patients coming out of a long coma to experience brief moments of consciousness. It leads to major stress on the nervous system, so the patient cannot handle it for long. But it's a positive sign, and we can hope for more.'

'Anything we should do now, doctor?'

'Nothing more than being patient and continuing to pray for his recovery, just as you've been doing so faithfully.'

Vasu clasped his hands together in a gesture of gratitude. 'I am so thankful that Lord Shiva heard our prayers. Do you think he will regain consciousness again soon?'

'I wish I could give you a definite answer. Medical research does not give a clear verdict on this. It varies from person to person. However, there is something that you can do.'

'Anything, doctor. Just tell us.'

'For the next 24 hours, I want you to stay by his bedside. If he regains consciousness, there is something that I want you to ask him.'

'What is that, doctor?'

'I would like to know what his last memory is. Ask him if he remembers arriving at the event or anything that happened at home that day. His responses could provide important clues about the state of his memory, which will help us determine the best course of treatment.'

'Of course, doctor, I will stay with him tonight. Can we see him now?'

'Yes. To better monitor Karnan's progress, I suggest we move him into the new ICU ward. It is equipped with the latest technology and he will be the only patient there for several months until we fully open it to the public. This will give you some privacy. I suggest you and Alex take shifts of three to four hours each.'

'That should not be a problem, doctor. We are grateful to be of help.'

'If you notice any signs of movement, report it to the nurse immediately.'

'Doctor, are you aware of the protest outside? The protesters do not want to let the home minister enter the hospital and exploit

Karnan's condition for political gain.'

'Yes, we are aware. Talk about timing!' Dr Joseph shook his head. 'Dr Verghese received a call from the home minister a few days ago. Frankly, we don't care about the minister's visit. From a medical standpoint, the timing is terrible. I hope they don't let him in.'

'I had planned to go outside to support my son and his friends. But with this development in Karnan's condition...'

'I would recommend you stay with Karnan tonight. Your son will be fine. He has thousands of supporters outside and a few hundred inside the hospital.' Dr Joseph leaned closer and added in a whisper, 'Count Dr Verghese and me among them.'

~37~

The Blockade

15 October 1981
M.G. Road, Cochin

THE SUN HAD GIVEN WAY TO CLOUDS OVERHEAD. SASHI knew from experience that in October, it was impossible to predict when it would rain or how long it would last. Glancing at his watch, he noted the time was 3.50 p.m. An hour had passed, and the stand-off showed no signs of resolution.

From the balcony where he stood with his father and brother, Sashi had a clear view of the scene unfolding on the road below. From their hurried movements, it seemed the home minister and Alexander were growing impatient. *They must know that by 5 p.m., it will be rush hour. It won't look good for the home minister to be seen sitting helplessly in his car, confronted by a group of defiant students.* It crossed Sashi's mind that this impasse would only end if the minister left. He knew that as long as Murali and Shibu led the protests, the question of the protesters standing down would not arise.

Sashi noticed that Murali and Shibu had walked over to the area reserved for journalists, which was packed to capacity. The press had been alerted by Abdul Navaz, whose political clout as the head of the Kerala Taxi Drivers' Union ensured that editors sent their senior journalists. Sashi's heart raced as he remembered Abdul's son, Shah Navaz, who had been killed by the police. He had first met Shah at Sacred Heart College three years ago. Although Shah was two years his junior, they had bonded over their shared admiration for the Tamil actor Kamal Haasan. Shah Navaz's death had come as a shock and was the tipping point that pushed Sashi into political activism.

At 4.10 p.m., the home minister stepped out of his car and summoned Alexander. They conferred for about 10 minutes before the officer saluted the minister and walked over to the police van. He spoke with a junior officer sitting inside, who promptly stepped out to open the doors at the back. One by one, 18 policemen emerged, all wearing metal helmets and carrying long wooden canes and plastic shields. The policemen lined up behind the junior officer in three rows of six. A few onlookers opened their umbrellas as a light rain began to fall. Alexander looked up and cursed the rain gods before picking up a megaphone.

'This announcement is a warning by the police. The protesters have illegally blocked access to the hospital premises. We request all the protesters to disperse right now. We will give you five minutes.'

The announcement had a chilling effect on the crowd, but it only seemed to embolden Murali and Shibu. They raised the flagpole high over their heads.

'Zindabad, zindabad. Vaikom Karnan, zindabad!' Shibu shouted.

'Zindabad, zindabad. Vaikom Karnan, zindabad!' the crowd repeated, energized by his voice.

Rukhsana, Geethanjali and Mallika looked at each other and interlocked their hands. Together, they shouted, 'Home minister, go back! Go back!'

'Home minister. Go back! Go back!' the crowd continued repeating.

After five minutes, Alexander raised the megaphone again. 'This is the final warning. Leave now, or the police will clear the area in one minute.'

Murali and Shibu intensified their chants, and the frontline protesters stood firm. Alexander barked an order to his junior officer, who removed his hat, put on his helmet and slowly advanced towards the protesters, with the 18 policemen following closely behind. Sashi noticed the home minister's car inching forward.

The junior officer, now just a few metres away from Murali and Shibu, stopped and gestured with his cane for them to step back. Instead, they stepped forward, their faces inches from the officer's. After a tense stand-off, Alexander barked, 'Go ahead. Remove these rascals!'

The junior officer lunged at Murali, raising his cane high in the air. But before he could strike, Rukhsana stepped in front of Murali and the cane came down hard on her head, knocking her backwards into Murali's arms. As Rukhsana fell, her hijab came loose, floating briefly in the air before landing on the ground. A trickle of blood oozed from her forehead on to Murali's shirt.

Seeing Rukhsana injured, Murali panicked. He had never seen her so vulnerable and felt a deep sense of guilt for failing to protect her. His relief was palpable when Rukhsana whispered that she was okay but needed to sit down. Murali carefully lowered her to the ground, cradling her head against his chest.

Mallika and Geethanjali rushed to Rukhsana's side, tears streaming down their faces. Mallika pressed her handkerchief against Rukhsana's wound, trying to stop the bleeding. Shibu picked up the fallen hijab and handed it to Mallika, who folded it into a makeshift bandage, tying it around Rukhsana's head while keeping the handkerchief in place over the wound.

Seeing the consequences of his actions unfold, the junior officer hesitated. Sensing the moment, Shibu handed the flagpole to Abdul and let out a fierce scream, jumping up and delivering a powerful kick to the officer's groin. Almost simultaneously, Jayan stepped forward, smashing his steel-knuckled fist into the junior officer's face. The officer grunted and crashed to the ground, his helmet clattering loudly on the road.

Two policemen rushed over to help their fallen colleague, but Jayan stepped forward, raising his right fist so that everyone could see the steel knuckle guards. The policemen stepped back, fear evident in their eyes, as the crowd cheered.

'What are you waiting for? Beat up these *gundas*!' Alexander screamed at his men, gripping his baton tightly as he advanced menacingly towards Shibu.

Shibu did not back down. As Alexander swung his baton, Shibu ducked, causing the blow to miss and graze his left shoulder instead. Wincing slightly, Shibu regained his stance, while the deputy superintendent, thrown off balance, cursed and spat in frustration.

'You dog!' Alexander seethed with rage. 'Do you have the guts to fight the police?'

'OH YES!' Shibu shouted back, crouching in anticipation of the next attack. 'I have been waiting for this auspicious day. I dare you to put your baton down and fight like a man. Show me what you've got!'

The crowd taunted the deputy superintendent, chanting, 'Put down the baton!' His pride on the line, Alexander cast aside his baton. The two men began to circle each other slowly, first in one direction, then in the opposite, their arms raised defensively as they silently sized each other up. As the crowd cheered, Shibu smiled but kept his eyes focused on Alexander's feet, watching for any sudden movements.

Meanwhile, a group of policemen pushed through the crowd, their shields up and canes swinging as they tried to disperse the protesters. But Jayan and Prakash blocked their path. One of the policemen swung his cane at Jayan, who took the blow on his shoulder. In a swift motion, he twisted around, wrested the cane from the officer's hands and drove the end into the man's stomach, causing him to fall, clutching his abdomen. Holding the cane high, Jayan stared down the other two policemen, who quickly backed off, panic visible in their eyes.

Seeing his men retreat, Alexander spat on the ground in disgust. 'You fucking cowards. Get back here and fight these boys!' he shouted. The retreating policemen hesitated and turned to face Jayan and Prakash again.

Sensing his chance, Shibu stepped forward and delivered a powerful punch to Alexander's face, followed by another to his stomach, knocking him back a few steps. Lowering his head, Alexander charged at Shibu. The two men tumbled into the crowd, crashing into a pool of rainwater collected at the roadside. Finding his footing first, Alexander kicked Shibu as he tried to stand up, sending him sprawling into a bicycle parked nearby. Sensing victory, Alexander smiled as he stood tall, rainwater dripping from his soiled uniform.

After ensuring Rukhsana was safe with Mallika and Geethanjali, Murali rushed to Shibu's aid. But Alexander was quicker, stepping behind Murali and shoving him forcefully into the crowd. Abdul stepped in, helping Shibu up and handing him the YDSK flag. The crowd closed in and started chanting Shibu's name.

'Police, don't play with fire! If you touch one of us, we will take down 10 of you!' Ramesh Babu chanted, and the crowd echoed, their voices growing louder with each repetition.

'Fight, Shibu! Fight! Johnson and his men are here. We have got your back!' Abdul roared, placing a hand on the shoulder of Johnson, a man clad in a khaki shirt and black lungi, wielding an iron pipe.

'Fight, Shibu! Fight! We have got your back!' Johnson's group of about 20 men, similarly dressed, chanted in unison.

Hearing the commotion behind him, Shibu glanced at Abdul and the men surrounding him. *Are all these men autorickshaw drivers?* Shibu felt a rush of excitement as he turned and raised the flag high over his head, his eyes steely with resolve. *This is the moment of reckoning.* The words 'Sons of Sailors', which Karnan had uttered backstage on the day he was shot, flashed through Shibu's mind. *I cannot let my people down. I have to find a way to turn the tables on this son of a bitch. After all, I am the son of a sailor!*

The sound of heavy boots thudding on the ground brought Shibu back to the present. The junior officer reappeared, this time flanked by 18 armed policemen. Shibu's eyes widened as he noticed the junior officer carrying what looked like a sawed-off shotgun. The junior officer stopped next to Alexander, and the two men spoke in hushed tones, their eyes never leaving Shibu.

'They have a gun!' a protester shouted, triggering a wave of panic. The crowd rumbled with fear, and the sound of stampeding feet echoed through the air.

Shibu snatched the flagpole from Abdul. 'Stay where you are. Don't move!' he shouted, his voice cutting through the chaos. 'This is just a ploy. They don't have the guts to shoot innocent protesters. Not with the press watching.'

Alexander laughed and took the shotgun from the junior officer.

'This is my final warning!' he bellowed at the crowd. 'This gun has tear gas canisters. It is very painful to the eyes. Leave NOW!'

'Don't shoot. We are leaving,' someone from the back of the crowd shouted. People in the rear began to scatter.

Sensing the shift in the crowd's mood, Shibu and Murali moved closer towards the deputy superintendent.

'I dare you to shoot,' Shibu challenged, wiping the raindrops from his face with his left hand.

'Long live Vaikom Karnan. Long live the revolution!' Murali shouted, but only a few dozen protesters near the frontline repeated the slogan this time.

Alexander glanced towards the minister's car. Sashi noticed the minister's short frame leaning against his car, perhaps to get a better view of the drama. *Is the minister smiling?* Sashi wondered, before dismissing the thought with a curse in Malayalam. Suresh, standing beside him, giggled nervously.

Suddenly, Alexander turned back to face Murali and Shibu and pulled the trigger. A tear gas canister landed just a few feet in front of them and smoke began to fill the air. Alexander laughed as he reloaded the shotgun, this time deliberately aiming deeper into the crowd. The second canister landed amid the protesters, triggering a frantic scramble as they tried to escape the choking fumes.

From his perch above, Sashi watched in shock. The wind carried the tear gas smoke towards Murali and Shibu. As the smoke cleared, he saw them standing, coughing and rubbing their eyes, clinging to the YDSK flagpole for support. Behind them, Rukhsana slowly stood up, aided by Geethanjali and Mallika, all three coughing as well. The protester ranks had thinned considerably, with many retreating to avoid the gas.

After a few agonizing seconds, unable to bear the searing pain in his eyes, Shibu bent down in pain. Murali tried to hold him up, but it was clear that he was also suffering from the tear gas. Shibu went down on one knee, one hand rubbing his eyes, the other clutching the YDSK flagpole, ensuring the flag did not touch the ground.

Murali turned towards the remaining protesters. 'Someone bring water!' he shouted.

With a predatory smile on his face, Alexander slowly unbuckled his thick leather belt. Wrapping the free end around his palm, he let the heavy metal buckle dangle, making a loud, ominous sound as he approached Shibu with deliberate, measured steps.

The rain began to fall harder, driving more onlookers to seek shelter in the buildings nearby.

~38~

The Vigil

15 October 1981
Medical Trust Hospital, Cochin

IT HAD BEEN TWO HOURS SINCE VASU BEGAN HIS VIGIL BY Karnan's bedside. Unable to sit still for more than 10 minutes, he paced the room, torn between concern for Karnan and anxiety about the events outside. *How are Murali and Shibu managing the protests? This is their biggest test yet. They certainly do not lack courage. Please grant them wisdom and protection*, Vasu silently prayed to Lord Shiva.

Vasu was not surprised by the massive turnout supporting the protesters. After his meeting with Commander Velayudhan, he knew the plan was sound. Seeing Velayudhan and his two sons at the office building across the street from the hospital had reassured him. Vasu knew from experience that courage flowed like a river in Velayudhan's veins. *Should the need arise, Velayudhan would not hesitate to step in to protect the boys, just as he had bravely refused to name his co-conspirators during the mutiny.*

Nurse Jasmine and two male attendants entered the room to check on Karnan and prepared to feed him, clean him and turn him over—a routine they followed every eight hours. The nurse checked Karnan's blood pressure and pulse before removing the ventilator. She placed an oxygen mask over his mouth. As the male attendants lifted Karnan carefully, the nurse changed the bed sheets. When they set him back down, they heard a faint groan.

Jasmine looked at Vasu. 'Did you hear that?'

'I did. Was it Karnan chetta?'

'Let's find out,' Jasmine said, peering into Karnan's face. 'His eyes are open. Sir, can you hear us? Shake your head if you can.'

Karnan's eyes stared at the ceiling above. The nurse repeated the question and slowly, Karnan's eyes focused on her.

'Karnan sir, there are thousands of people on the street outside waiting for you to wake up,' Jasmine said slowly, as if speaking to a child.

Karnan's gaze remained on the nurse. 'Do you know who this is?' Jasmine asked, pointing to Vasu.

'Karnan chetta, it's me, your Vasu.'

A faint smile appeared on Karnan's face. He pursed his lips and whispered, 'Vasu…' He made an effort to move his hand towards Vasu.

Vasu wiped away the tears welling in his eyes with his hand. 'Karnan chetta, I have been praying for this moment. I have a lot to tell you.'

Karnan used his hands to gesture for Vasu to come closer. As Vasu leaned in, he could barely hear Karnan whisper, 'How long have I been in the hospital?'

'Not very long,' Vasu replied, deliberately vague. 'Do you know what happened to you?'

Karnan shook his head. 'I was on the stage…speaking…Murali by my side…'

'Correct. You were hurt, so we had to rush you to General Hospital. Now you are at Medical Trust Hospital. I am so happy to hear your voice,' Vasu said, choking up with emotion. He was overjoyed to finally hear the voice of his dear friend, something he had been praying for every day since the shooting. Vasu gave a silent thanks to Lord Shiva.

Karnan smiled again and squeezed Vasu's hand.

'Murali and Shibu?' he asked.

'They are fine. Right now, they are leading a large protest outside to prevent the home minister from entering the hospital.'

A look of concern crossed Karnan's face.

'Karnan chetta, I will tell you everything, but gradually. We are in no hurry.'

Karnan frowned and stared at Vasu.

Vasu relented. 'Okay. I will tell you now. But first, we have to inform Dr Joseph.'

'I will take care of that,' Nurse Jasmine said. 'Please ensure that he does not sit up or move. You can continue to talk to him.'

'Thank you, nurse,' Vasu said, looking at Karnan and placing his palm on the latter's forehead. 'Okay, let me start when you were on the stage with Murali…'

~39~

Old Lady with the Flag

15 October 1981
M.G. Road, Cochin

SASHI KUMAR HELD HIS BREATH. THE MOMENT HE HAD feared all along had arrived. With his brother locked in a direct confrontation with the minister's security forces, the stakes had escalated, just as his father had predicted. He watched as the protesters dispersed while Alexander approached Shibu, twirling his belt in his hands. Abdul came forward to hold the flag and helped Shibu to stand.

Suddenly, out of nowhere, the stout figure of a silver-haired woman appeared between Alexander and Shibu. Dressed in an ill-fitting, light green chiffon sari, a mismatched blue blouse and hawai slippers, the lady held an open umbrella in one hand and a shopping bag filled with vegetables in the other. She walked unhurriedly, ignoring the deputy superintendent as she headed straight towards Shibu. Alexander moved to stop her but Mallika quickly stepped between them, halting him in his tracks.

The lady stopped just inches away from Shibu. 'Mone, give me the flag!' she demanded.

With difficulty, Shibu opened one eye. 'Mummy, what are you doing here? Please step aside. You will get hurt,' he pleaded.

The lady would have none of it. 'Shibu, didn't you hear me? I SAID I WANT TO HOLD THE FLAG!' she repeated, handing Shibu her bag and umbrella. She looked at Abdul, who hesitated. The boldness of Baby's action reassured the protesters who had been sitting on the fence, and they began to reassemble, cheering her on.

Still rubbing his eyes, Murali took a few steps forward to stand beside Baby, Rukhsana following close behind. 'The lady seems lost. She will get into trouble. Let us get her out of the way,' she said to Murali.

Overhearing Rukhsana, the lady turned and said, 'Molay, I am Shibu's mother, Baby Velayudhan. Don't worry, everything will be fine. I want to hold the flag and shout out Shibu's slogan.' A faint smile lit up her face. 'Now he is all grown up, but you know, when Shibu was a child, he learnt to shout the slogans in rhythm from my father, his muthachan,' she said.

Baby wiped the raindrops off her forehead with the edge of her sari, glanced at Shibu and reached out to grab the flagpole from Abdul's hands. Her jaw tightened as she turned to face Alexander and slowly raised the flag. Even in the rain, the letters on the flag—**YDSK**—were clearly visible. The protesters cheered and resumed chanting slogans, but the smile left Baby's face as she locked eyes with Alexander.

Sashi was transfixed by the scene unfolding below, his mother's small frame suddenly looming large. Glancing around, he noticed that his father was nowhere to be seen.

'STEP BACK, OLD LADY!' Alexander shouted.

'OVER MY DEAD BODY!' Baby shouted back, defiant.

She raised the flag higher and called out, 'Inquilab zindabad!' her voice carrying to the farthest ranks of the protesters.

The crowd roared back, 'INQUILAB ZINDABAD!'

Baby raised her voice. 'Zindabad! Zindabad! Vaikom Karnan zindabad!' she shouted, her free fist punching the air.

'ZINDABAD! ZINDABAD! VAIKOM KARNAN ZINDABAD!' the crowd chanted.

Unsure of what to say next, Baby looked around at the others.

Rukhsana stepped forward to stand next to Baby. 'Police, follow the law. Leave peaceful protesters alone!' she shouted, her clenched fist raised above her head.

'Police, follow the law. Leave peaceful protesters alone.' The crowd's collective voice grew louder.

'Get out of here, you filthy dogs, before we lose our patience!' Ramesh shouted.

'Leave the lady alone. Go arrest the thief hiding inside the car!' Abdul yelled, and the protesters cheered, their disdain for the home minister on full display.

As the chanting intensified, Alexander looked at the crowd around him, surprised by the turn of events. He retreated a few steps as Murali and Shibu stepped forward.

∞

Sashi spotted his father talking to Hippie Jayan and Prakash on the street below. He desperately wanted to join his brother and parents but was bound by the responsibility of ensuring the safety of his youngest brother. A dull pain in his chest, still healing from his recent open-heart surgery, reminded him of his limitations. He turned to his brother, who had a worried look in his eyes.

'Suresh, it's time for me to go down and help mummy and Shibu. I need you to stay right here. Can you promise to do that?' Sashi asked.

'Chetta, that is not fair! I want to come with you. Everyone else is down there. Why not me?' the little boy demanded.

Sashi let out a deep sigh. The sadness in Suresh's eyes forced him to rethink. *How can I blame him? After all, his mother and brother are on the frontline of the protest.* He reached out and took Suresh's hand. 'Come, let's go down. But remember, you must always stay close to me.' Hand in hand, the brothers hurried down the stairs.

By the time they reached the street, Sashi was out of breath and had to stop. He watched helplessly as Suresh searched the crowd for someone who could help. Seeing no one, Suresh tried to assist his brother to sit down on the steps of a building. Sashi's heart pounded as he watched his little brother disappear into the throng of people, and he tried to shout after him to come back, but the effort was too much. His vision blurred, and Sashi blacked out.

When he regained consciousness, Sashi saw Suresh returning with Prakash and Hippie Jayan. The two men helped him stand up, and together they slowly walked towards the crowd, Suresh following behind. Jayan and Prakash pushed through the gathering to reach the front, where Baby stood. Alexander was standing in the same spot, belt in hand, unsure what to do next. Sashi noticed that his face had turned red as the restless crowd began chanting slogans in support of Baby. After a few tense minutes, Alexander let go of the belt and reached for the baton, stepping forward.

'STOP! STOP!' he shouted at Baby. 'I see this has turned into a drama. I don't care how old you are, lady. Put down the flag and step back. NOW!'

Baby did not flinch. 'Inquilab zindabad!' she called out again, her voice loud and clear. Murali and Rukhsana moved aside as Sashi and Suresh walked up to stand beside their mother.

'I have had enough of this nonsense!' Alexander took a few steps forward and raised his baton over Baby's head, his face contorted with anger. The clicking of cameras from the press box area echoed above the din of the crowd.

'DON'T YOU DARE!'

The voice, louder than a thunderclap, froze Alexander's arm in mid-air. All heads turned towards the source.

A dignified elderly man with grey hair stepped forward, walking steadily towards Alexander, flanked by Jayan and Prakash. He was dressed in a spotless white full-sleeved shirt and dark grey trousers, his leather sandals secured with buckles. In his left hand, he held a walking stick. Sashi recognized the voice even before he could fully see the man. It was his father!

Shaken by the unusual authority in the voice, Alexander took a step back. 'Who the hell are you, old man?' he demanded.

'Just an ordinary citizen,' Velayudhan responded calmly, his voice steady and demeanour composed. He continued walking towards Alexander. 'An ordinary citizen, like the thousands gathered here today. But not too long ago, I wore the uniform of this nation. Pure white, not your dirty khaki,' he hissed.

Taken aback by the old man's audacity, Alexander took a few steps back. 'Stop right there,' he ordered, his voice now shaky.

Velayudhan ignored the order and stopped just inches from Alexander. 'If you don't mind my asking, officer, why don't you pick a fight with someone your equal?' Velayudhan thrust his clenched fist close to the officer's face. 'Tell me, how was it fighting my son? Had it not been for the tear gas, he would have torn you to shreds, you coward!' he snarled.

Alexander stepped back further, his eyes nervously scanning for an escape route. Just then, a man in a police uniform pushed through the crowd and came running. Sashi felt a wave of relief when he recognized SI Ashraf Ali.

'Hold on, Deputy Superintendent sir! Let me tell you who this man is,' Ashraf shouted, breathing heavily. 'He is retired Navy Commander Velayudhan, a respected elder in this area. The lady holding the flag is his wife, Baby. They are the parents of Shibu, the young man with curly hair.'

In a feeble attempt to look like he was still in command of the situation, Alexander put both hands on his hips. 'What the hell is going on here? Is this a family drama?' he sneered.

Ashraf stepped closer. 'Sir, may I have a word with you?'

'Now?' Alexander looked surprised. 'Who the hell are you?'

'Yes, sir, now. It is very important. I am Ashraf Ali, a sub-inspector with the Cochin Police. The police commissioner put me in charge of the security here at the hospital. She is on her way here. I suggest you hold off any action until she arrives.'

Alexander scratched his head and took a few seconds to consider Ashraf's suggestion. After a brief hesitation, he and Ashraf moved away from the frontline and conferred for several minutes.

Alexander looked back at the crowd, which was growing more agitated. Unsure of what to do next, he slowly approached the minister's car.

Sashi watched as the short, stocky minister stepped out, slamming the car door shut behind him. As Alexander drew near, the minister began scolding him loudly. Sashi heard a string of curses coming from the minister's mouth, and the once-dominant officer now looked docile, his head hung low in shame.

~40~

The Manuscript Mystery

15 October 1981
Medical Trust Hospital, Cochin

VASU SPRANG UP FROM HIS CHAIR. 'DID I HEAR YOU correctly? *The Last Revolutionary* is not yours?' he asked, perplexed.

He had been talking to Karnan for about 40 minutes, recounting the significant developments that had taken place since Karnan had been shot. After Nurse Jasmine had placed a spoonful of water in his mouth, Karnan's feeble voice became more audible. He had stopped Vasu a few times to ask questions, and everything seemed to be going well until Vasu mentioned the manuscript he had received from Alex.

Karnan gestured for Vasu to sit down. 'From what've you told me, Vasu, it sounds like my memoir. But I can tell you conclusively that I am not the author,' Karnan said. 'You should have known that I would be the last person to write my own story.'

'Yes, I know that. But I assumed you had changed your mind.'

Karnan's voice grew louder. 'And you should have known that I would certainly not give myself the pompous title of the "last revolutionary". First, the tag of "revolutionary" should be reserved for the likes of Bhagat, Bose, Azad and Jayaprakash bhai. What have I done to deserve it? And second, does the title imply there will be no other revolutionaries to take India forward?'

'You know, it did cross my mind that you had never mentioned such a major project to me, but Alex told me that he saw the lights of your study on late into the night for several months—'

Karnan interjected sternly, 'Did you do it, Vasu?'

'What?' Vasu's shocked expression resonated in his voice. 'No. I swear on my mother's life, I did not.'

'Then who could it be, Vasu? Other than you, who else would know all the little details of my life?'

'I assumed you had written it, so I did not bother to think about it...'

'I understand. But let's calm down and think objectively. Who could be the mystery author?' Karnan said. 'Vasu, you told me the manuscript was written in Malayalam and handed over to you by Alex.'

'Yes, that is correct.'

'Alex is the only person besides you with whom I have shared most, if not all, of our old stories. Whenever I invited him to share drinks with me, he insisted that I tell him a story from the pre-independence days; however, he did not finish the fifth standard. We both know that he cannot write two lines of prose.'

'I agree. If Alex is involved, he likely has a collaborator. Could it be Murali?' Vasu guessed. 'I remember telling him many of our stories. Besides, you are his hero.'

'Yes. The only logical conclusion is that Alex and Murali must have worked on this together. But you told me that the writing style is similar to mine, which leads me to wonder if a third person was involved—someone who is an expert writer in Malayalam and familiar with my writing style.' Karnan paused. 'Vasu, could it be S.K. Pottekkatt? He is the best writer in Kerala today, far better than me. And he has read all my books and articles.'

'It is certainly possible, but that seems like a bit of a stretch,' Vasu replied. 'But I can see why Murali and Alex would want to give you credit. You have been the most important influence in their lives.'

'I appreciate their intentions, but I wish they had discussed something as significant as this with me. I could have guided Murali, maybe even written a foreword for the book. Let's talk to Alex and Murali separately. I want to know why they used my name as the author.'

Karnan paused, rubbing the stubble on his chin with the back of his hand. 'Vasu, can you get me a copy of this book? Let me try to figure out who our mystery author is.'

~41~
Victory in the Streets

15 October 1981
M.G. Road, Cochin

THE RAIN HAD STOPPED, AND A FEW RAYS OF SUN EMERGED from behind the clouds. The home minister and Deputy Superintendent Alexander had been in conversation for over 25 minutes. They also conferred briefly with SI Ashraf. Sashi noticed the minister glancing at his watch a couple of times. *Does the minister have a time constraint? Or is he just upset that a group of students derailed his plans?* Sashi wondered.

A few minutes later, another police car pulled up. Ashraf walked to the car, opened the door and saluted as Commissioner Sreelekha Sriram stepped out. She exchanged a few words with Ashraf, surveyed the scene and then approached the minister, offering him a sharp salute.

The minister, however, did not acknowledge the salute. 'Commissioner, what took you so long? What the hell is going on with law and order in your city?' he asked curtly.

The commissioner remained calm. 'Sir, I apologize for the delay. I had a previously scheduled meeting with the DGP regarding the protests across the state.'

The minister raised his voice. 'These students have wasted 90 minutes of my valuable time. I want them cleared out right now,' he demanded, not caring that the onlookers could hear him.

'Excuse me, sir. Have you looked around to see the crowd? There must be about 5,000 people watching. If you look carefully, you'll see that the vast majority are not students.'

'Not students? What do you mean? Who the hell are these people?'

'Mostly local people, sir. Look at the frontline of the protesters—an elderly couple, four women and one little boy.' The commissioner removed her cap and stepped closer to the minister. 'Sir, I speak from personal experience. With protests happening all over the state, this is not the right time to crack down on a peaceful one.'

'Do I hear sympathy for the protesters, commissioner?'

'No, sir,' the commissioner replied firmly. 'It is not sympathy; it is empathy. I know some of the people here. You see the old man with the walking stick on the frontline? He is Commander Velayudhan, a decorated Navy officer, a battle-hardened veteran of the Second World War and the Indo-Pakistan wars. He is a man who has stared death in the face more than once and survived.'

'Maybe the opposition is using him to discredit me,' the minister suggested.

'Impossible, sir,' the commissioner said with conviction. 'To my knowledge, Commander Velayudhan does not have any political leanings. He has but one affiliation—India. He has nothing to gain by being here today.'

'Then what the hell is he doing here?'

'Sir, I believe he came because he feels the students have a right to protest peacefully. He would gladly give his life to defend that right. From what I have been told, this crowd will do anything he tells them to.'

'Anything?'

'Yes, anything. Believe me, sir, you do not want him as an enemy. Not today. Not here.'

'Commissioner, I am the home minister of Kerala. Why don't you look at it from my point of view? Do you think it is a good idea for them to prevent me from entering the hospital?'

'I did not say that, sir. The blockade is misguided. However, these are good people. They are upset and are just voicing their concern for a man they respect—a man who is lying unconscious just 50 feet from here.' The commissioner leaned in and whispered, 'I know it is not what you want to hear, but can I give you my honest opinion, sir?'

'What is it?' The home minister sounded irritated.

'Sir, the best course of action for you right now is to show grace. Show the people you listened to their voices and respected their sentiments.'

'Show grace?' he looked incredulous. 'Commissioner, can you be clear? What do you mean?'

'Sir, you should cancel your plans to visit Vaikom Karnan today. It will put you in a good light with the people and the press. They are all watching how you handle this situation. People have been sensitive after the shooting last year, so we must be cautious.'

The minister looked at the crowd, his expression unreadable as he weighed the commissioner's advice.

'What if I want you to bring in more local police to clear the crowd?' the minister asked.

The commissioner threw her hands up in the air. 'Sir, you are the home minister. It is your decision to make. But as you would be going against my professional advice, I must insist that the order come from you directly.'

Deep furrows appeared on the minister's forehead. 'All right, commissioner. At least I know where you stand. I will let you have it your way for now,' he said begrudgingly.

After a few seconds of silence, the minister spoke again. 'Commissioner, I want you to personally inform the press that it was my decision to withdraw out of respect for the people's sentiments. I don't want this to be seen as a slap in my face.'

'Of course, sir. I will take care of that. You have made the right decision, sir.'

The minister, still calculating his next move, added, 'Commissioner, since you know Commander Velayudhan, can you ask him to meet me in my car? The press is here. I would like to be seen publicly giving him a handshake to settle this matter.'

'Sure, sir. I will ask him right away.'

She gestured for her officers to stand down and step back. Cap in hand, she slowly walked up to the frontline of the protesters. After shaking hands with Commander Velayudhan and speaking to him briefly, she returned to the minister.

'Sir, Commander Velayudhan thanked you for making the right decision, but he thinks this is not the right time for a public handshake. He told me that there are no winners or losers today,' the commissioner conveyed diplomatically, careful not to bruise the minister's ego. 'He has a valid point, sir.'

'Well then, I must head back to Trivandrum. My personal security team and your Cochin Police failed to control a few hundred rowdy college students. It has been a wasted day for me,' the minister said, his voice deflated. With a wave, he signalled to his driver.

The commissioner stepped back and saluted as the minister's car reversed and turned around. Alexander quickly jumped into the police jeep, which sped ahead to lead the minister's motorcade. The junior officer and policemen piled into the van, following the home minister's car as it slowly withdrew from the centre of the crowd.

As the minister's motorcade retreated, the crowd erupted into applause. The protesters, no longer needing Shibu's encouragement, took over the slogan-shouting with renewed vigour. Murali hugged Shibu. They both reached out to include Baby, Rukhsana, Geethanjali, Mallika, Sashi and Suresh in a group embrace. Around them, students danced in the street, celebrating their victory.

Ramesh Babu raised his fist up in the air and shouted, 'Lay out the lush floral carpet bedecked with *sankhupushpam* and *jamanthi* flowers!'

'Our leaders, Murali, Shibu and Rukhsana have led us to victory!' The crowd echoed his words with enthusiastic chants.

Silence fell once more as Commissioner Sreelekha, accompanied by SI Ashraf, approached Commander Velayudhan and shook his hand again. After exchanging a few words, she beckoned Murali and Shibu to join them.

'Well, young men, I am told you had a difficult day but got what you wanted,' she said. 'Your actions have upset the HM. He will likely order an internal investigation, and the Cochin Police will be tasked with carrying it out. If that happens, I intend to appoint SI Ashraf to lead it.'

'Is there anything these young men and women should be worried about, Commissioner?' asked Velayudhan.

'Commander, I am not worried about Shibu and Murali; they know their way around. However, I don't want any of the innocent students here today to get entangled in the investigation.' The commissioner noticed the puzzled looks on the young faces around her. She turned to Ashraf. 'Sub-Inspector, if any of the students gathered here is asked by police investigators where they were today, what do you think their response should be?'

Ashraf seized the moment, lowering his voice as he addressed the students gathered around him. 'Just tell the investigator—who will be one of my men—that you went straight home from college because of the strike. When you reached home, your mothers sent you to buy vegetables, milk, coconuts, palm oil or whatever. None of you came here or had prior knowledge about anything that happened here. Understood?'

'Got it!' Shibu grinned. 'We will make sure every student is aware of this.'

'Good. In that case, my job here is done,' the commissioner said. She then looked at Murali and Shibu. 'Please ask the protesters to leave. It's rush hour; we need to open the road to traffic.'

With a final handshake with Commander Velayudhan, the commissioner turned and walked back to her car, Ashraf saluting her as she departed.

As the commissioner's car departed, Sashi noticed a journalist approaching his father. True to his nature, Velayudhan, uncomfortable with taking credit or displaying emotion in public, brushed the journalist aside. His naval training set in as he quietly shook hands with each of the men and women who had held the frontline. After the last handshake, Velayudhan looked towards the hospital, clutched his walking stick and began to walk slowly towards the front entrance. The crowd quietly parted to make way for him.

Sashi glanced at Shibu and found him looking at their father. He thought he noticed, perhaps for the first time, a look of awe in Shibu's eyes. Sashi had no doubt it was their father's advice that had led to their sweet victory.

The people who had made up the frontline gathered in a circle around Murali and Shibu. A group of student protesters led by Ramesh lifted Murali and Shibu on to their shoulders. The crowd erupted into a wild frenzy of celebration, cheering and chanting for several minutes.

After Murali and Shibu were back on the ground, Sashi turned to his mother. 'Mummy, you almost gave me a heart attack. You put yourself in grave danger. What were you thinking?' he asked.

'Very true, chetta! I was going to ask Baby amma the same question,' Murali said.

'Makkalae, to be perfectly truthful, I was not thinking at all,' Baby explained calmly. 'Since none of my children were at home, I came to buy coconut oil, rice and lentils from Kamala Stores. I happened to see this huge crowd and guessed it had something to do with the plans you discussed at home a few days ago. When I reached the front of the hospital, I was shocked to see that at the centre of the protest were my boys, Shibu and Murali, confronting the police officer. Call it a mother's instinct; I just knew I had to do something.'

'Amma, today you were like Goddess Kali. You vanquished

the home minister of Kerala but without violence. Only a mother or Mahatma Gandhi could do that,' Murali said, shaking his head in disbelief.

Baby smiled. 'Enough of making fun of me. I am glad that it is over. Can someone tell me what happened to my grocery bag and umbrella? Without that, there will be no dinner for us tonight,' she said, prompting the boys to laugh.

Rukhsana stepped forward with both items. 'Your goods are safe, amma. Shibu handed them to me. Here, hold your umbrella; I will carry your bag.'

'Give the bag to Sashi and the umbrella to Suresh. They must go home now as my mother is alone. I have one more task to complete,' Baby said as she examined the bandage on Rukhsana's head. 'Molay, is it hurting you? Come, let's go inside the hospital to get your wound cleaned and bandaged.'

Rukhsana smiled. 'I am okay now, amma. Murali pulled me away just in time, so the blow was not direct. Just a small cut.'

'I read a lot about you in the newspapers. You are a very strong girl,' Baby said, holding Rukhsana's arm and examining the bloodstains on her sari. 'This white half-sari looks good on you. After this, you should come home with me and change into a fresh one.'

'Thank you, amma. I have heard so much about you from Shibu and Murali. Even though we have not met before, I feel like I know you already.'

Baby untied the hijab that served as a makeshift bandage on Rukhsana's forehead and examined the wound. 'The bleeding has stopped, but you should hold this kerchief over it. Come with me, girl. Your wound needs proper cleaning and bandaging. Dr Verghese is a good friend of Shibu's father.' As an afterthought, Baby added, 'Do you think it is possible to see Vaikom Karnan? I feel I have earned the right to see such a great man today.'

'Sure, amma, you certainly have. Today, you showed us what

a mother's courage looks like. It gave me goosebumps!' Rukhsana said.

Baby leaned closer to Rukhsana. 'Molay, I don't want to embarrass you, but I have to tell you something that has been on my mind.'

'What is it, Baby amma?'

'Molay, if you had not already been taken by Murali, I would have chosen you for my Shibu,' she whispered. 'Other than his curly hair, jeans and being a bit short-tempered, Shibu is the carbon copy of Murali. They even love the same food—'

Rukhsana interrupted, 'Yes, I know. *Kappa* and *meen* garnished with coconut chips! Right, amma?'

Baby smiled. 'Oh my God! You already know the most important thing about the boys.'

Rukhsana's face lit up in the twilight as she laughed and placed her free arm around Baby. They walked towards the hospital entrance together. As they entered the building, Rukhsana stopped, spotting Alex approaching them hastily.

'What is the matter, Alex?' she asked.

Alex, out of breath, replied, 'Karnan sir has regained consciousness! He is speaking and asking about all of you.'

'Oh my God!' Rukhsana shrieked, covering her mouth in shock.

Baby turned around and shouted, 'Murali, Shibu, come fast. Something very urgent!'

The students who had encircled Murali and Shibu parted as the two boys rushed towards Baby, Rukhsana and Alex.

'What happened?' Murali asked, trying to push his dishevelled hair back into place.

'It is about Karnan sir. He opened his eyes and spoke a few words,' Alex explained.

'What? Maamen woke up? When?' Murali asked, his mouth wide open.

'Yes. It happened during all the commotion outside. Vasu sir asked me to bring you up to the ICU. Dr Joseph is also there.'

Murali looked at Shibu, then at Rukhsana and Baby. 'Come, let's go. The lift is too slow; let's take the stairs!' he exclaimed.

As Murali and Shibu raced up the staircase, they noticed Velayudhan, walking stick in hand, slowly making his way up. Shibu asked Murali to go ahead as he slowed down to accompany his father.

~

Standing at the very spot where his mother had made her bold stand, Sashi took a moment to survey the scene. Turning around, he spotted Suresh engaged in an animated conversation with Unnikrishnan, the younger brother of Prakash. As Sashi approached the boys, he overheard them arguing over whose older brother had played the more critical role in the protest. Sashi could not help but smile as Suresh boasted about having not only two brothers but also his parents involved—a fact that Unnikrishnan could not argue against.

Sashi grabbed Suresh's arms. 'Enough of that. Both your brothers did a fine job today. Suresh, come with me; it's time for us to go.' Suresh made a sad face and asked for five more minutes with Unnikrishnan.

After a brief nod, Sashi shook hands with Jayan, Prakash, Abdul, Ramesh and the other student leaders who had gathered around him. Abdul pulled him aside to discuss calling off the protests so the students could go home before it got dark. It dawned on Sashi that with Murali and Shibu having left the scene, the mantle of leadership had fallen on him. Not used to speaking to a group of people, he looked nervously at Abdul, who raised his hand to quiet the crowd. As more protesters gathered around them, Sashi's nervousness abated slightly, bolstered by Abdul and Ramesh standing beside him.

'On behalf of our leaders, Murali and Shibu, I want to thank each of you,' Sashi began, looking into the bright eyes around him. 'Because of the steadfast courage you showed today, we sent back the home minister of Kerala. We won today, but there is more for us to do. As my father—the old man with the walking stick whom you saw threatening the deputy superintendent—would have said, this was just a skirmish; the real war lies ahead. We will need the same courage and discipline we showed today to emerge victorious.'

In a show of enthusiasm, the crowd began shouting slogans in praise of Shibu and his father. Sashi held up both hands to indicate he had not finished speaking.

'Before you go, I have some good news to share,' Sashi continued, his confidence building. 'I've come to know that a few minutes ago, Karnan sir regained consciousness. I see it as a good omen for the challenges ahead of us. So go back home and tell your parents, relatives, friends and neighbours that today you sent the home minister of Kerala and his police back to Trivandrum. Let's spread the message. Thank you!'

The crowd erupted into loud applause. Slogans in support of Vaikom Karnan, Murali, Shibu, Rukhsana, Velayudhan and Baby filled the air. Sashi turned around, took Suresh's hand and backed away from the centre of the crowd. The brothers walked hand in hand past Kamala Stores, returning the owner's friendly wave.

'Do you think the police will arrest Shibu chetta and Murali chetta?' Suresh asked nervously as they made their way home.

'I don't think so. The bad policemen who came with the minister were defeated and left for Trivandrum. The Cochin Police are under the command of Commissioner Sreelekha. You know she is an Indian Police Service (IPS) officer, right? You told me you want to become a police officer when you grow up. The IPS produces the best police officers.'

'Yes, I do. I want to be a good IPS officer like the commissioner. And also like Kiran Bedi!' Suresh exclaimed.

'You saw a lot happen today. Were you afraid?' Sashi asked his brother.

'Chetta, to tell you the truth, I was afraid when Shibu chetta was fighting with the police officer. But when mummy arrived, all my fear went away.'

'Is that right? How did you know that mummy would save Shibu?'

'Mummy may not look like a hero, but she is fearless,' Suresh said. 'Do you think she is braver than daddy and Shibu chettan?'

'I think so. That is why you and I also have no choice but to be brave. After all, as the saying goes, the coconut does not fall far from the tree,' Sashi replied, wondering if his brother would understand the metaphor.

Suresh pondered the idea for a few seconds. 'Chetta, doesn't every fruit fall close to the tree?' he asked, adding, 'Mangoes, the ripe guavas at Vimala aunty's home, even the tamarind from the big tree next to our house. Does any fruit fall far from the tree?'

Sashi laughed and playfully tousled his brother's hair. 'Yes, you are right. That is why they use the saying to explain why children grow up to be like their parents.'

~42~

A New Dawn

15 October 1981
Medical Trust Hospital, Cochin

NURSE JASMINE OPENED THE DOOR TO THE NEW ICU UNIT. Upon seeing the larger group of people, she asked them to wait and went back inside to check with Dr Joseph if it was permissible to let them all in at once. Dr Joseph agreed, provided they maintained a safe distance from the patient, as the new unit did not have enough temporary gowns and caps for so many visitors.

One by one, Murali, Shibu, Alex, Rukhsana, Mallika, Geethanjali, Baby and Commander Velayudhan removed their footwear outside the entrance and entered the ICU. In the far corner of the room lay Karnan, his head and shoulders propped up by pillows, an oxygen mask covering his nose and mouth. Vasu sat beside the bed, holding Karnan's hand, while Dr Joseph and a young doctor stood nearby.

The room fell into an awed silence as everyone took in the unlikely turn of events.

Dr Joseph was the first to speak. 'I heard that all of you were leading the protest on the street below and successfully blocked the home minister from entering the hospital. My staff and I are working hard here to save lives, and we do not have the time to entertain politicians; so thank you for what you did today. To show our gratitude for your efforts, we give back to you your hero, Vaikom Karnan.'

Dr Joseph turned around and gestured to Nurse Jasmine to remove the oxygen mask from Karnan's face. Jasmine took her time while the small group waited in anticipation. Unable to contain his excitement, Shibu began to applaud but quickly stopped when he noticed Nurse Jasmine's look of disapproval. Murali took a step forward but the nurse, worried about infecting the patient, requested him to step back.

As Dr Joseph turned around to face the group, a rare smile flickered on his face. 'Talk about timing!' he said. While you were on the street fighting the police, Vaikom Karnan regained consciousness. We don't know if the recovery is temporary or permanent, so I must warn you that his condition remains very fragile. Please keep this visit brief—no more than 30 minutes. I must step out to complete my rounds. My assistant, Dr Ravi, and Nurse Jasmine will be here.' Vasu stood up and leaned closer to Karnan. He whispered, 'Karnan chetta, look who is here to see you. They just stopped the home minister from entering the hospital. Just imagine that—a few thousand unarmed students handed the HM a sound defeat. Is there anyone here whom you do not recognize?'

Karnan slowly scanned the group, then feebly waved at them. He pointed at Commander Velayudhan standing at one end of the group.

'Do you not remember Commander Velayudhan?' Vasu asked. 'He is the young Navy sailor who came to meet us in Bombay on New Year's Day in 1946. Next to him is his wife, Baby. They have come to see you.'

Karnan spoke with a frail voice, 'Oh. Velayudhan, please forgive me; I did not recognize you. It is my honour to meet you and Baby.'

'The honour is ours, Vaikom sir,' Velayudhan said. 'Today, our boys put up a good fight. They made you proud.'

Karnan's eyes turned to Baby. 'You know, Baby, on the day of the incident, I remember telling Shibu that I would visit your home sometime soon...little did I know what was in store for me that night,' he said with a smile. 'You must be very proud of Shibu. He

A New Dawn   251

reminds me of the young Velayudhan, the handsome Navy sailor I met back in 1946.'

'Maamen, if it weren't for the advice of Velayudhan uncle and the courage that Baby amma and Shibu showed today, we would not have succeeded,' said Murali.

Velayudhan placed his hand on his heart as a sign of gratitude and respect. Overwhelmed with emotion at the mention of her son, Baby wiped tears from her eyes. Rukhsana placed a comforting arm around Baby's shoulders.

Vasu looked at the others in the room. 'Let's see who else you have not met yet. The girl in the light blue sari is Rukhsana's friend, Geethanjali, and the lady in the violet sari—'

'Mallika Sukumaran, actress, social activist and a great poet. Champion of women's liberation…a thinker far ahead of our times. Who does not know her. I have read every article and poem she has written,' Karnan said, waving at Mallika, who acknowledged the praise with a namaste.

Karnan continued, 'Geethanjali, I have heard about you. You must be the brave girl who asked me questions at my book-reading events on behalf of Rukhsana. Happy to meet you again.'

'Karnan chetta, it looks like, after the incident, your memory has improved,' Vasu quipped.

There was muffled laughter in the room.

'Vasu, where is Jalaja?'

'She went home yesterday to check on her mother and make sure that the new maid is taking care of her,' Vasu explained.

'Oh, I see. My condition has made life difficult for all of you,' Karnan said, his eyes scanning the room.

'What nonsense are you saying!' Vasu countered. 'What difficulty? Sitting in the room and eating the nice food that Baby and Alex make for us? We are doing just fine. You are the one who is going through a lot of difficulty.'

'Where is Rukhsana?' Karnan asked.

Murali and Shibu stepped aside so that Karnan could see Rukhsana. She held the handkerchief against her wound with one hand and had her hijab in the other.

'Are you trying to hide from me? Without your hijab on your head, I almost did not recognize you. I see you are wearing a white half-sari. You remind me of Bhargavi from *Bhargavi Nilayam*,' Karnan said light-heartedly. The elders in the room laughed at the reference.

'I don't think any of the children have seen the movie,' Mallika observed, adding, 'but today, Rukhsana was like the ghost Bhargavi. She sent a shiver down the spines of the police officers.'

'Is that right?' Karnan said, surprise etched on his face. 'Do you know that the story was written by my good friend Muhammad Basheer? Anyway, what is the story behind the half-sari?' he asked Rukhsana.

'Mallika aunty, our fashion adviser, told us that if we are going to get beaten up by the police, we might as well do it in *naadan* style. So we thought, what better dress for an Indian woman than a sari? But I am uncomfortable wearing one, so I borrowed Geethanjali's half-sari.'

There was a smattering of laughter in the room.

'Rukhsana, I told you to wear a full sari. You did not listen; that is why the police beat you up,' Mallika said playfully.

'Thank God I was wearing a sari today,' Baby quipped.

Karnan joined in as everyone shared a hearty laugh. The effort was too much for his frail body and caused him to cough. Just as quickly as it had begun, the laughter died down. Nurse Jasmine stepped forward, but Karnan held up an arm to indicate he was not done.

After a few seconds of silence, Karnan spoke in a soft voice. 'It is so nice to see all of you make light of the serious events that brought you together. Vasu updated me on everything that has happened since I was shot.' He paused to take a deep breath.

'I was not joking when I said that I was confident about the future of our nation.' Karnan looked around the room. 'You—each of you, and every young YDSK volunteer—are the reason for my confidence. Unlike old people like me with one foot in the grave, you are not afraid to fight the good fight, to take responsibility and to lead. That's exactly what was lacking until today.' Karnan paused as he coughed again.

Nurse Jasmine voiced her concern. 'Karnan sir, I think you should get some rest now.'

'Nurse, I am fine. I have a few matters to clarify. Who knows when I will get the next opportunity to meet all these fine people together.'

'Maamen, I don't want to miss this unexpected gift of your counsel,' Murali said. 'I learnt from MLA Shivan that Chief Minister Nayanar is considering offering him a ministerial position. The Left Front has offered to give the YDSK seven more Assembly seats to contest in the next election cycle. Don't you think such an arrangement will help us reach our goal of power-sharing?'

There was silence as Karnan pondered the question.

'Will it, Murali?' Karnan asked. 'You see, genuine power-sharing arrangements should not be forced by a crisis. They must come naturally. While a seat in the ministry looks very enticing, it is just one among about 20 Cabinet members. I fear that if MLA Shivan accepts the CM's offer, his powerful voice for change will be silenced forever. So will yours and Shibu's.'

'Maamen, don't you think getting a seat at the table gives us more power?' Murali's voice had a hint of frustration. 'You know as well as anyone that it has taken a lot of hard work for us to get to this point.'

Karnan was quick to respond. 'Yes, I do. Listen, Murali, I don't wish to minimize the sacrifices all of you have made. But I ask, gaining power to what end? Is this compromise in the long-term interests of the people of Kerala?'

There was silence in the room.

Velayudhan's deep voice cut through as he spoke up. 'Karnan sir, you have posed the right question. The CM has offered nothing more than a bribe—plain and simple. If they accept it, the YDSK will become like any other political party. It will lose the trust of the people. I don't have any political affiliations, but I ask Murali, Shibu and Rukhsana to think about another issue. Is the elevation of one of your leaders to the position of a minister what you, and the thousands of young students who braved the rain and the police lathi charge today, have been fighting for over three years? Are you not squandering this opportunity for a more impactful and systemic change that will last for a very long time?'

Silence engulfed the room again as Karnan joined his hands in a namaste as a sign of thanks directed at Velayudhan.

'May I voice my opinion?' Mallika asked.

'Of course, Mallika. We would love to hear what you think,' Velayudhan encouraged.

'If you look at the history of every significant political movement that has resulted in lasting change that benefited the masses—the French Revolution, the American Revolution, the Indian Freedom Struggle, the Civil Rights Movement in America, the Communist Movement in Kerala—each of these started with a seemingly radical idea floated by a small group of people. It was never a mass movement at the beginning. A few leaders' steadfast courage and refusal to compromise opened people's eyes. They made each of these a mass movement... Allow me to pose another question to our young leaders.' Mallika paused and looked at Murali, Shibu and Rukhsana. 'Putting aside the question of what is in the best interests of the people of Kerala, what does your heart tell you?'

'That is an excellent question, Mallika,' Baby said. She looked at Shibu and Murali. 'The question is: what does your heart—not your head—tell you?'

The tension in the room was palpable as silence returned and Karnan flashed another namaste at Mallika.

Murali spoke with a measured tone. 'Maamen, Velayudhan uncle, Mallika aunty, thank you for sharing your thoughts. You have given us a perspective that we did not have before. Shibu and I were in a quandary when MLA Shivan informed us of the CM's offer. We were unsure which path to take, and we did not have time to think about the consequences. Shibu, Rukhsana, what do you think?'

All eyes shifted to Shibu and Rukhsana. Shibu spoke first.

'I agree with Murali. We are lucky to get the advice of people we greatly admire,' Shibu said with his characteristic confidence, glancing at his father. 'Now the path forward is clear. We will forge ahead and build our political platform. Our goal is to earn the people's trust by our deeds, not by entering into opportunistic power-sharing arrangements. My mind is made up.'

'So is mine,' Rukhsana added, looking at Shibu. 'You all know I am new to politics, but I have been a keen student of history. Kerala's progress has been in fits and starts. I believe the time is ripe for a clean break from the past. Karnan sir's challenge to the youth of Kerala is etched in my mind: "The stage is set; the curtain has risen. It's our moment to step into the spotlight and play our roles." We must not let another mother go through what amma endured today.'

'Well said, Rukhsana. Are you referring to Shibu's amma?' Vasu asked.

Rukhsana smiled. 'Yes, I was referring to Shibu's amma, who saved the day for all of us today. When the police fired the tear gas, and all seemed lost, she calmly walked in with her weapons of choice—a grocery bag and an umbrella.'

'It's time all of you stopped making fun of my grocery bag and umbrella,' Baby said in mock protest as everyone laughed.

Murali chimed in, 'Maamen, I wish you had been there! It

was a sight to behold. We were all amazed, as was the home minister's security. When the police officer raised his baton to strike Baby amma, the entire crowd heard Velayudhan uncle's roar: "Don't you dare!" At that moment, I saw fear in the officer's eyes, and I knew victory was ours.'

'Sounds like I missed some exciting action today. I wish I had witnessed it!' Karnan's smile was visible across the room. His tone then turned sombre. 'Rukhsana and Murali, I like that you call Baby "amma". In our culture, "amma" is another word for courage and sacrifice,' he said, his voice strained by the effort.

After a brief pause, Karnan continued, 'Makkalae, you made an old, bedridden man very happy and proud. Very, very proud! I truly believe this is the right path to take. I am glad to hear that Velayudhan, Baby and Mallika—people I greatly admire—agree with me. Vasu has not spoken yet, but I know where his heart lies on this matter.' Karnan paused to catch his breath.

Taking a few deep breaths, Karnan continued, 'I have always maintained that this is also the longer and more difficult path. You stand at the proverbial fork in the road that the great American poet Robert Frost wrote about. One path is easy, the one most people take. But you've chosen the road less travelled. It may take years, maybe even decades, to know if you made the right choice. But I am certain it will make all the difference in your lives…and in the lives of the people of Kerala.'

He paused, looking at each of them intently. 'This is the only ethical way to earn the people's trust. Focus on building a people's movement in a just and inclusive manner. I assure you, the YDSK will one day earn that trust, resulting in a sweeping mandate for deep and systemic change. That has been the dream that Vasu and I have shared for all these years. It is the same dream you fought for today.'

Vasu nodded, his deep voice cutting through the quiet. 'Karnan chetta, I am sure they appreciate the sacrifices you have made.

Today, MLA Shivan, Murali, Shibu and Rukhsana can be bold because they have your broad shoulders to stand on.'

'Yes, that is so true, Vasu uncle,' said Shibu. 'Now the fog in our minds has lifted. Our marching orders are clear. Thank you, Karnan sir. We will inform MLA Shivan of our collective decision. I know he will agree with us.'

Nurse Jasmine stepped forward. 'That was a fascinating discussion. You all have my support. However, you have exceeded the 30 minutes Dr Joseph allowed. Karnan sir needs to take some food and medicines, and rest now.'

Karnan reached out to grab Vasu's hand. Vasu bent down as Karnan whispered something in his ear. After a few seconds, Vasu stood up and addressed the group. 'Karnan chetta would like to speak to Murali, Rukhsana, Velayudhan, Baby and Mallika. Can you come back tomorrow evening? Hopefully, he will be awake then.'

'Murali, Rukhsana and Mallika, it is late and you must be tired after everything that happened today,' Baby said. 'Come have dinner with us. You can stay at our home tonight.'

Karnan waved at the group as they filed out of the ICU. After the last person was out, Karnan closed his eyes, exhausted.

'Vasu, you have often asked me if all the sacrifices we made over the years were worth it,' Karnan said, his eyes still shut. 'Did you get the answer today?'

'Yes, I did. Loud and clear,' Vasu said with a smile. 'Now, let the young leaders worry about the future of our people.'

Karnan shifted and pulled the bed sheet over his body, then paused mid-action. 'Vasu, when I saw everyone so happy with what they accomplished today, I did not have the heart to bring up the matter of who authored the book. But it has been on my mind.'

'I know. You did the right thing. Our children made us so proud today. I will arrange the meeting tomorrow to discuss it,' Vasu gently assured his friend.

Karnan took a deep breath. 'Please make sure that all the elders are present. Murali, Rukhsana and Shibu will need good advice for the battles ahead. Who knows how long I will live.'

'There you go again!' Vasu admonished him. 'Thanks to the blessings of Lord Shiva, you are well on your way to recovery. You will be here to lead them for a very long time. Now, it is time for you to get some rest.'

PART SIX

REVELATIONS AND RESOLUTIONS

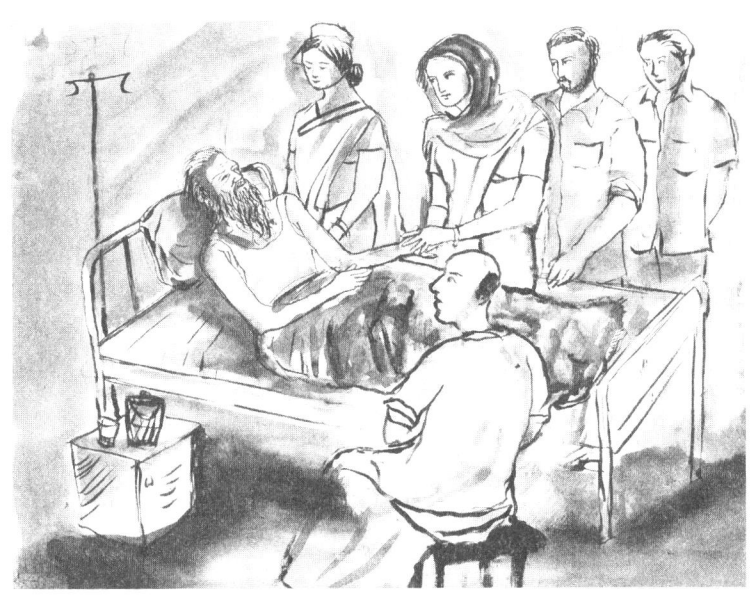

~43~

The Nurse from Kashmir

16 October 1981
Medical Trust Hospital, Cochin

MURALI WAITED NERVOUSLY NEAR THE DOOR OF THE ICU ward. Baby and Velayudhan were seated on a bench a few feet down the hallway, chatting with Rukhsana and Mallika. It was 6.30 p.m. on the day after the successful blockade—their second attempt at meeting Karnan that day. The first attempt, at 5 p.m., had failed because Karnan had been drowsy from his medication.

The day before, Vasu and Murali learnt from Nurse Jasmine that Dr Joseph had left for Madras to attend a medical conference. This allowed them to arrange the meeting Karnan had requested without the strict time limits that Dr Joseph usually insisted on. Murali had reviewed with Rukhsana the possible topics Karnan might want to discuss, and they both agreed it would probably be about the future of the YDSK.

Twenty minutes passed before the ICU door opened and Nurse Jasmine beckoned Murali inside. Velayudhan, Baby, Mallika and Rukhsana followed him. Murali noticed that Karnan, though pale and weak, was propped up in bed, talking to Vasu. He smiled as the small group gathered about 10 feet from his bed.

'Vasu told me you tried to see me earlier. I am sorry to put all of you through this…' Karnan began.

'Please don't. It's no trouble at all,' Velayudhan replied. 'Talk to us only if you are feeling up to it. We can always come back tomorrow.'

'No, today is as good a time as any,' Vasu said. 'Karnan chetta wanted to talk to all of us.'

Karnan requested everyone to come nearer his bed.

'Let me get straight to the point,' Karnan said, his tone unusually serious. 'Vasu informed me that the book *The Last Revolutionary*, supposedly written by me, was nominated by Kerala University for the 1980 Bharatiya Jnanpith Award a few months ago. I just learnt that the book has been shortlisted as one of the five finalists.'

Karnan paused and made brief eye contact with each person around him. 'I read a few chapters of *The Last Revolutionary*. I must say it is really well written. However, there is one small problem,' Karnan paused before speaking. 'I am not the book's author. I know someone in this room is. I want to know who.'

Vasu offered further clarification. 'This is a matter of Karnan chetta's personal credibility. We must know the truth and inform the selection committee before it's too late. We already had a conversation with Alex on this matter,' Vasu said, looking at Murali. 'Son, we believe you wrote the book. Is this true?'

Murali glanced nervously at Rukhsana and started to mumble, 'Maamen, I am sorry—'

Vasu interjected, 'Maamen is not asking for an apology. We understand why you did it. The question is why didn't you tell him first?'

Rukhsana stepped forward, placing her hands on the metal railing of the bed. 'It is not Murali's fault. The idea was mine…I am responsible,' she said.

A heavy silence filled the room; Karnan's eyebrows arched as he looked at Rukhsana.

Murali shifted uneasily, crossing his arms over his chest. 'Rukhsana, please let me handle this,' he pleaded.

Rukhsana's voice was firm. 'Karnan sir, I take full responsibility for *The Last Revolutionary*. I wrote it with the help of Mallika aunty. If you don't believe me, you can ask her.'

Karnan turned to Mallika, who nodded silently.

Mallika adjusted her sari and took a deep breath before

speaking. 'Yes, it is true. I edited and translated the manuscript. Rukhsana has been obsessed with this book for many years. She started writing it as a teenager. Her passion for the story drew me in, and I can vouch that she never planned to publish her work.'

Rukhsana took up where Mallika left off. 'To me, the book is the true story of a great freedom fighter and his life experiences, as accurately as Mallika aunty and I could research them. I just happened to be the one to chronicle those events. As far as I am concerned, Karnan sir remains the real owner—the original creator—of these experiences.'

Vasu stood up, clearly agitated. 'Why didn't you inform the person you were writing about, Rukhsana? You had access to him through Murali. Was that too much to expect?'

'That is a reasonable question. To explain, I will need to tell you the whole story,' Rukhsana replied calmly. 'Yes, like all of you, I admire Karnan sir, which is reason enough. But the real reason is much more complicated.'

'If so, why don't you tell us?' Vasu demanded.

Rukhsana was taken aback by the sharpness in Vasu's voice. She hesitated, her gaze shifting to Mallika, who nodded and gestured for her to continue.

The room fell silent as Rukhsana took a few moments to gather her thoughts. She then looked at Murali, tears welling up in her eyes. 'I am sorry I did not tell you everything,' she said. 'I knew I would have to eventually, but I was afraid of losing you. Today, I promise to tell the whole truth.'

'Go on. We are listening,' Vasu urged.

Rukhsana took a deep breath. 'You must be wondering why an Indian Muslim girl who grew up in the Gulf ended up in Cochin, spending years writing about a man she had never met. To explain that, I have to take you back to 1937 to meet the hero and heroine of my story.'

'1937?' a feeble voice repeated. It was Karnan.

Rukhsana spoke with resolve. 'Yes. In 1937, an idealistic young man, barely 27 years old, broke his arm in a scuffle with the British Indian police in Bombay. He was admitted to a local clinic, where a young nurse, the heroine of my story, tended to his wounds. She hailed from a well-to-do family of silk merchants originally from Kashmir, who had settled in Mumbai in the 1920s.'

Karnan groaned, shifting uncomfortably in his bed.

Sensing his discomfort, Vasu turned to Rukhsana. 'Can you get to the heart of the story? We are in an ICU—'

Velayudhan interrupted, 'Vasu, please let her finish.' He gestured to Rukhsana. 'We want to hear your story, all of it.'

With a steely look, Rukhsana resumed her tale. 'Over the next few weeks, the injured freedom fighter met the nurse twice a week at the clinic. They developed a bond, which soon turned to friendship and eventually blossomed into love, albeit a forbidden one.'

'Forbidden love! Why?' Baby asked.

'Because the hero of my story was an unemployed Hindu, and our heroine was a well-educated Muslim girl with a good job, whose father was a trustee at the Juma Masjid.'

'Aah, in those days, that would certainly be considered forbidden love,' Baby remarked, encouraging Rukhsana. 'Molay, tell us what happened next.'

Reassured by Baby's words, Rukhsana continued. 'After he was fully recovered, the young lovers started meeting outside the hospital—first at Juhu Beach and later at the cramped apartment in Mulund that the young man shared with his friends. He would tell her stories of his adventures fighting the British. The young nurse, only 23 then, was captivated by her lover's dangerous lifestyle and eagerly learnt about the Indian freedom struggle.

'One day, a relative of the nurse spotted them together at the beach and reported it to her father. The retribution was swift and severe. Her parents forced her to give up her job and locked her in her bedroom. She fell ill, and a doctor was called in. That was when they discovered she was pregnant. Meanwhile, our hero—the freedom fighter—unaware that his lover was carrying his child, had left Bombay on a secret mission to Calcutta. He did not have a chance to say goodbye.'

'Oh my God. Did her parents allow her to carry the baby?' Baby asked.

Rukhsana reached out and held Baby's hand. 'If her parents thought they had everything under control, they were mistaken. Despite the severe pressure, our heroine refused to get an abortion and insisted on carrying her love child. To avoid burdening her parents or her lover, she agreed to her parents' demands to marry Javed, a much older, thrice-married Islamic cleric, and relocated with him to Dubai.'

Rukhsana paused, expecting questions, but the room remained silent. She continued.

'In 1938, she gave birth to a baby girl, Zainaba. Our heroine settled into the role of a dutiful mother. A year later, Javed married again—his fifth time—and left his fourth wife and daughter to fend for themselves. Our heroine found a job in a hospital but, without the support of a father, Zainaba grew up rebellious and dropped out of high school.

'In 1957, at the age of 19, in an attempt to spite her father, Zainaba eloped with Faisal, a former employee of her father's. Faisal, who came from a poor family in Malappuram, had little education and worked odd jobs. The following year, Zainaba had her first child, a girl. This little girl, born to parents of mixed heritage, fell through the cracks as her parents' marriage deteriorated. Her mother was too young to fully embrace motherhood, and her father had hoped for a male child. Her only true friend was her grandmother.' Rukhsana paused and nervously glanced around the room.

'The Kashmiri nurse?' Baby asked softly, piecing together the story.

'Yes, Baby amma. The heroine of my story—the brave nurse from Kashmir—became the caretaker of the little girl, so her parents could go to work.'

'When the little girl was 12, her parents died in a car accident. By Allah's mercy, she still had her grandmother. Her grandmother became her mother, her father and her best friend. She taught the little girl Hindi, Urdu and Malayalam, and introduced her to Bollywood movies.'

A knock on the door interrupted Rukhsana's story. The nurse was about to open it, but Velayudhan stopped her.

'Let it be. Keep talking, Rukhsana,' Velayudhan urged.

Rukhsana continued, her pace quickening. 'Her grandmother legally changed her granddaughter's last name to Mirza—the original Kashmiri family name. As the little girl learnt more about her grandmother's past and about her grandfather, the Indian freedom fighter, her desire to meet him grew stronger.'

Baby stepped forward and gently caressed Rukhsana's face. 'Molay, I did not attend college, but even before you mentioned the last name, I figured out that you are Zainaba's daughter,' she said. 'But I would like to know who the heroine of your story is—the brave Kashmiri nurse who bore the child of her forbidden love affair.'

Silence fell in the room as everyone waited to hear Rukhsana's response. She nervously fidgeted with her hijab and looked at Karnan.

The knocking on the door grew louder. The nurse opened it and Shibu burst into the room.

'I have important news to share,' Shibu announced, ignoring Nurse Jasmine, who was gesturing at him to lower his voice. 'The LDF government is on the brink of collapse. But that is not all...' He paused and looked around the room.

The mood in the room brightened, though the reaction was more subdued than Shibu had hoped.

'What happened? Is everything okay?' Shibu asked.

'Rukhsana was in the middle of telling us her story,' Baby explained. 'But with the good news that you bring, I think it is best to take a break and return to it later.' Murali walked towards Shibu. 'Did you say you have more good news to share?' he asked.

Shibu grinned and pumped both fists in the air. 'Yes, Murali. I have news you won't believe. The home minister has resigned!' he announced triumphantly. 'I heard it on the radio.'

'What?' Murali exclaimed as he grabbed Shibu's shoulders. 'I hope you are not joking.'

'The news was on All India Radio. There is a big celebration on the streets. Let's go down. It is a huge victory for us,' Shibu said.

'Oh my God!' Baby exclaimed. 'Our children were right about the blockade of the minister. This happened within 20 hours of our victory yesterday.' She turned to Mallika. 'I am going down with the children. After all, I played a small part too. Would you like to come?'

'Small part?' Mallika asked. 'Baby *chechi*, you were the heroine. Yes, I would love to accompany you to the street. As you are a celebrity now, you will need a bodyguard.'

Everyone joined in the light-hearted laughter.

Nurse Jasmine opened the ICU doors to let in three attendants and a young doctor. The hospital staff encircled Karnan's bed to perform routine feeding and cleaning tasks. One by one, everyone in the room said goodbye to Karnan and followed Shibu outside the ICU. They took the elevator to the ground floor. After everyone stepped into the lobby, Shibu was bombarded with questions about the HM's resignation. Shibu began sharing what he had learnt from the various sources.

~44~

The Home Minister's Waterloo

16 October 1981
Kerala, India

THE MORNING AFTER THE BLOCKADE, THERE WAS A SWIFT and severe backlash against the home minister's actions. The leading newspaper in Kerala, *Malayala Manorama*, featured the story on its front page with the headline: 'Kerala HM's Security Unleashes Violent Attack on Student Protesters'. The accompanying photograph showed the deputy superintendent firing tear gas at the protesters while the home minister watched from the safety of his car, reinforcing the YDSK claim that the attack had been premeditated by the police.

Mathrubhumi, another prominent Malayalam newspaper, added a historical context to its coverage with the headline: 'Kerala's Napoleon Meets His Waterloo'. They likened the home minister's retreat to Napoleon's defeat in the Battle of Waterloo, hinting that this incident could spell the end of his political career. The photograph of the short-statured home minister alongside the headline emphasized his uncanny resemblance to the infamous French dictator.

Even the typically supportive *Deshabhimani*, a left-leaning daily closely allied with the ruling Communist Party, did not hold back. Its blistering full-page editorial criticized the home minister's callousness in handling a situation involving a man who remained an icon of the socialist movement. The report featured a photo of Deputy Superintendent Alexander raising his baton to strike Baby Velayudhan, who was clutching the YDSK flag close to her chest, flanked by Murali, Shibu and Rukhsana. The caption read: 'Home Minister's New Law Enforcement Strategy: Attacking Innocent Mothers'.

At 10.30 a.m., leaders of the ruling LDF's two major coalition partners, the Congress (U) and the Kerala Congress (Mani), realized that staying in power could irreparably damage their credibility and announced their withdrawal of support for the government. In a joint statement, Mr A.K. Antony of the Congress (U) and Mr K.M. Mani of the Kerala Congress (Mani) cited the home minister's poor judgement and lapses of integrity as key reasons for their decision, signalling the collapse of the LDF's governing majority.

Adding to the government's woes, the Communist Party leader Mr V.S. Achuthanandan, known for his grassroots appeal like Vaikom Karnan, was overheard on a hot mic describing the home minister's actions with a biting Malayalam folk saying: 'The HM took a snake that was peacefully sitting on the fence, basking in the sun, and placed it in his underwear. Obviously, there can only be one outcome.'

Caught off guard by the rapid turn of events, Kerala's chief minister, Mr E.K. Nayanar, urged the Congress (U) and the Kerala Congress (Mani) leaders not to make any hasty decisions that could plunge the state into political turmoil. A seasoned politician, Mr Nayanar refrained from defending his home minister. Instead, he expressed regret over the incident and relief at the news of Vaikom Karnan's recovery, reminding reporters of their shared history as freedom fighters against British rule. Facing mounting pressure from all sides, the chief minister convened an emergency Cabinet meeting at noon in Trivandrum. During the heated session, senior Cabinet Ministers K.R. Gouri Amma and Lonappan Nambadan condemned the home minister's actions and called for his censure.

The Cabinet passed two key resolutions. The first demanded the immediate suspension of Deputy Superintendent Thomas Alexander and called for an internal investigation of the incident. The second instructed the DGP to immediately transfer the investigation of the shooting of Mr. T.K. Karunakaran to the CBI. The home minister and his supporters resisted the resolutions, arguing that it would weaken law and order in the state. Unable to reach a consensus, the chief minister adjourned the meeting.

Immediately after the Cabinet meeting, a group of five MLAs from the ruling Left Front, all under 35, met privately with the chief minister along with seven YDSK MLAs led by Shivan. They denounced the home minister's actions and warned the chief minister that the coalition government could lose majority support if corrective action was delayed. They went beyond the Cabinet resolution and called for the minister's immediate resignation.

Within an hour, the chief minister's principal secretary circulated an official memo to the Cabinet—which was leaked to the press—announcing the CM's decision to hand over the investigation to the CBI. Shortly afterwards, the CBI director appointed Mr Narasimha Iyer, a respected IPS officer, to lead the investigation. Within one hour of the news of this appointment, the home minister of Kerala submitted his resignation to the chief minister.

∞

The home minister's abrupt resignation and the imminent collapse of the ruling government were broadcast over the radio at 5 p.m., sparking wild celebrations among the student protesters gathered outside Medical Trust Hospital. To mark the occasion, the owner of Kamala Stores supplied leftover firecrackers from Diwali, which were promptly set off by the jubilant crowd.

When Murali, Shibu, Rukhsana, Baby and Mallika joined the celebrations on the street outside the hospital, they were mobbed by the cheering students. Flower garlands were placed on their necks as the YDSK volunteers lined up behind them to form an impromptu procession, with Sashi Kumar and Ramesh Babu leading the excited crowd.

Ramesh waved at Shibu and Murali. He took a deep breath and adjusted his usual slogans to suit the occasion.

'Lay out the lush floral carpet bedecked with sankhupushpam and jamanthi flowers!'

'Our leaders have led us to a resounding victory!'

'The home minister has met his Waterloo!'

'Rejoice, people of Kerala. Change is coming!'

The crowd roared back each line with enthusiasm. Onlookers joined the procession, swelling the ranks until M.G. Road was filled, bringing traffic to a standstill. Passengers on buses waved and cheered from their windows.

Amidst the celebrations, neither Sashi nor Shibu noticed that Suresh had joined the procession with his friend Unnikrishnan. Though the boys did not understand the reference to Waterloo, they loved how the word rolled off their tongues, shouting the slogans until they were hoarse.

~45~

Secrets Revealed

16 October 1981
Medical Trust Hospital, Cochin

RETURNING FROM THE STREET CELEBRATIONS, BABY, Velayudhan and Mallika headed to the room that had been allotted to Vasu and his family to rest and discuss the events they had witnessed. Meanwhile, Murali, Shibu and Rukhsana went to fetch food from a nearby restaurant. After delivering the food to the elders, the three friends found a quiet corner of the hospital to discuss their plans. Shibu noticed a tension between Murali and Rukhsana, which he assumed stemmed from their earlier meeting without him. He chose to focus on pressing issues related to the expanding YDSK membership, driven by favourable media coverage and defections from the SFI.

At 8.45 p.m., Mallika came to call them back to the ICU. She explained that Vasu wanted to finish the discussion before Karnan took his medication and went to sleep. Shibu offered to stay outside but Murali and Rukhsana insisted he join them. A new duty nurse, Marykutty, ushered them in, reminding them that Dr Joseph's time limit for ICU patient visits was 30 minutes.

Karnan looked relaxed as he talked to Baby and Velayudhan. Vasu updated him on the celebrations that had taken place outside. Karnan gestured to Murali, Shibu and Rukhsana to come closer and hold his hand.

'I am so proud of the student movement the three of you started years ago. It has begun bearing fruit today. I commend you for sticking together through a long period of personal trial. That is not easy,' Karnan said. Murali, Rukhsana and Shibu exchanged nervous glances.

After a brief pause, Karnan added, 'An even bigger test lies ahead. You must figure out how to stay together and protect each other when the sharp arrows start raining down from all sides. For that, you need the counsel and wisdom of elders. I may not be here for longer, but look around—you have so many mentors you can learn from and depend on. Always remember that.' The room fell silent as Karnan took a deep breath.

'That is why I want to clear the air about Rukhsana's past tonight,' Karnan continued. 'I want all of you to fully understand who she is—her motivations and what is in her heart.' Karnan's eyes settled on Rukhsana. 'Please continue your story.'

While Rukhsana collected her thoughts, Baby filled Shibu in on what had happened before.

'After my parents passed away, my grandmother, my ummama, saved me. There was nothing left for us in the Gulf. She planned for us to relocate to Kerala—the land my father was from—so I could pursue my higher education. Sadly, in 1976, my ummama passed away due to a stroke...' Rukhsana's voice faltered.

Murali felt his heart race, sensing Rukhsana's pain. Mallika handed him a handkerchief, which he passed to Rukhsana. After a few seconds, Rukhsana resumed her story.

'Losing my ummama was the most painful event in my life. For the first time, I felt completely alone. A few months later, when I learnt that Geethanjali was returning to Kerala to study at Maharaja's College, I saw it as a sign from the Almighty to fulfil my grandmother's wishes.'

'You made the right decision,' Baby said.

Velayudhan shifted the focus back. 'Rukhsana, tell us what happened after you arrived in Cochin. When did you start writing the book?'

Rukhsana nodded and continued, 'I moved in with Geethanjali

at Mallika aunty's home. I began researching Karnan sir's past. I visited the Ernakulam Public Library frequently and attended many public events where he spoke. To avoid attention, Geethanjali acted as my public face while I worked quietly behind the scenes.

'As my research progressed, what emerged was a portrait of a fascinating man—a true "Renaissance Man", as Pottekkatt sir described him. I initially made my notes in English, and Mallika aunty helped translate them into Malayalam. Fortunately, she had extensive knowledge of Karnan sir's past and helped reorganize my notes into a memoir written from his point of view, using a third-person narrative.'

'Aha, it did cross my mind…the use of the third person is unusual for a memoir. Karnan chetta would have written it in first person,' Vasu remarked.

'What about Murali? Did you know who he was when you first met?' Baby asked.

'Baby amma, everything I have said till now happened before I met Murali,' Rukhsana said, glancing nervously at Murali. 'But I would be lying if I said I did not know who he was. I can honestly tell you that my feelings for him developed later.'

'Yes, I know,' Baby said. 'Shibu had told me about the first time that you met Murali.'

'Murali showed me a different side of Karnan sir, one I would never have found through research,' Rukhsana said. 'I learnt that he was a loving uncle and a loyal friend. Murali provided me with the richest treasure trove when he shared the personal diaries that Karnan sir gifted Vasu sir. From those, I learnt about his innermost thoughts and feelings—from the day he left home to his days with the Azad Dasta and his return to Kerala. The portrait of Karnan sir was nearly complete.'

Rukhsana's thoughts raced back to her 19th birthday, when Murali had gifted her the old handwritten diaries of his uncle. *I hope Murali realizes how valuable the diaries were for me. Without those, this book would not have been possible.* She continued, 'All the work I did was for my own pleasure. I had no plans to publish it. Then, when I met Karnan sir for the first time on the day of the incident, he confided his desire to write a book that would inspire the people of Kerala to organize and reclaim their freedom. Later that night, sitting in the hospital, I realized that what could better inspire the people of Kerala than the true story of his own life?'

Vasu shook his head in disbelief but felt a sense of relief as Rukhsana's story seemed credible. 'From what you have said, you and Mallika had been working on the book. When did you tell Murali about your project?'

Rukhsana's response was quick. 'The day after the incident, when Murali asked me to accompany him to visit your home and Karnan sir's. I felt it was a sign from God to place the manuscript where it belonged. During a break on our journey, I shared my thoughts with Murali.' She glanced at Murali, who recalled Rukhsana's surprise revelation about the book. At that time, her plan seemed both logical and appropriate.

'Yes, that is correct,' Murali confirmed.

'Given the uncertainties we faced that day, Murali agreed that a memoir would be a fitting tribute to Karnan sir. Later that night, when we reached Vaikom, I left the manuscript on Karnan sir's writing desk. Murali asked Alex to take it to the hospital and hand it over to Vasu sir.'

The room fell silent again. Baby spoke up. 'Molay, I still do not fully understand why you did all this. What was your motivation?'

'Why did I do this?' Rukhsana repeated slowly. 'There is one reason, Baby amma... I believe you will agree it is good enough.'

Karnan coughed. With a heavy voice, he said, 'Molay, I think I know, but I want to hear it from you.'

'Go on, tell us,' Velayudhan urged. 'Nothing to be nervous about.'

Rukhsana glanced at Velayudhan and then at Baby. 'I am related to Karnan sir by blood,' she said.

Gasps of surprise filled the room.

'Related by blood! Did I hear you right?' an astonished Baby asked.

Vasu stood up, livid. 'What do you mean? How?' he asked, turning his gaze to Murali. 'Were you aware of this?'

Caught off guard, Murali stammered, 'Acha, I knew…I mean, I got to know Rukhsana had written the book after maamen's incident. But the blood relationship is news to me.'

Rukhsana chimed in, 'I know my story may sound like a plot from a Hindi movie. But I swear on the memory of my beloved grandmother that everything I have said is true.'

Baby reached out to embrace Rukhsana. 'Molay, I believe you are telling the truth,' she said. 'But you have not yet told us who the heroine of your story is.'

Before Rukhsana could reply, Karnan spoke, his voice choked with emotion. 'Nafeesa. That was her name. Nafeesa Mirza. The only woman I have ever truly loved.'

Baby gasped, '*Eashwara!* The young man you mentioned at the beginning of your story was our Karnan chettan!' she said. 'So you really are grandfather and granddaughter!'

'Yes, Baby amma, I am the grandchild of Vaikom Karnan and Nafeesa Mirza. They are my grandparents—my *uppapa* and ummama,' Rukhsana confirmed.

The room fell into a stunned silence for a full minute.

'Rukhsana, everything you said makes sense. Now I understand your determination to tell your uppapa's story,' Velayudhan said.

Karnan shifted in bed. 'I am so sorry I let her down…'

'You did not let anyone down,' Velayudhan said firmly. 'You were not even aware that Nafeesa was pregnant or that she was sent to the Gulf. If there's blame to be placed, it's on her parents. But those were different times.'

'Velayudhan, that is why my respect for Nafeesa has grown immeasurably,' Karnan said. 'Even though I couldn't give her anything, she left me the most precious gift I have ever received—our granddaughter.'

As the room fell silent once more, Nurse Marykutty stepped forward, an apologetic look on her face. Karnan tried to buy more time, but the nurse would have none of it. Instead, she informed them that she would be on duty until noon the next day and suggested they could meet again in the morning, provided Karnan was feeling up to it.

~46~

Scarlet Bonds

17 October 1981
Medical Trust Hospital, Cochin

AT 8.15 A.M. THE NEXT MORNING, VELAYUDHAN, FLANKED BY Baby and Shibu, walked into the hospital lobby, where they were greeted by Murali, Rukhsana and Mallika, who had spent the night at the hospital. Due to a power cut, the elevators were not working, forcing them to take the stairs to the ICU.

As they slowly climbed the stairs, the conversation shifted to the surprising news that they had learnt last night.

'Nafeesa is indeed a heroine. What a strong heart she had,' Mallika remarked.

'And her love for Karnan chetta transcended time,' Baby added.

Murali, still regretting his harsh words from the day before, gently reached out to hold Rukhsana's hand, hoping to offer some comfort.

Nurse Marykuttuy, weary from lack of sleep, led them into the ICU, gently reminding them of the 30-minute time limit. They took the same positions by the bedside as the night before, watching as Vasu fed Karnan a liquid meal from a bowl.

Pushing Vasu's hand aside, Karnan looked around at those gathered. 'I hope you all have had something to eat. We still have some loose ends to tie up.' He turned his gaze to Rukhsana and addressed the others. 'Now that you have heard Rukhsana's story, does anyone have any questions for her?'

Sensing Rukhsana's nervousness, Baby placed a comforting arm around her.

'Molay, I am glad that sharing your story has lifted a heavy burden off your heart. I have been thinking all night about what you told us, and am curious—what did Nafeesa think about your hijab?' Baby asked.

'It was her idea. She believed it would protect me.'

Karnan held up a hand, and silence followed. 'I remember you mentioning that the scarlet colour was your grandmother's choice.'

'Yes. Ummama loved the colour, but her parents were very traditional, so she never got a chance to wear it herself,' Rukhsana said. 'On my 17th birthday, she picked out five hijabs for me—all in slightly different shades of scarlet.'

'Why scarlet?' Baby asked.

'Ummama explained that scarlet stands for strength and love. She said it would protect me and help me find love.'

'Aha, how far-sighted your ummama was!' Baby exclaimed. 'The scarlet hijab has indeed fulfilled her beliefs.'

Rukhsana turned to Karnan. 'On the day of the incident, you reminded me that scarlet is the colour of blood and represents courage, sacrifice and revolution—perhaps that is why I was unconsciously drawn to it. Now, I have grown to love the colour as much as my ummama did.'

Mallika placed a hand over her mouth. 'Rukhsana, I just realized that both your grandparents—each for their own reasons—were drawn to scarlet. That cannot be a coincidence.'

Rukhsana placed a hand over her heart. 'No, Mallika aunty, it cannot be. I am convinced that ummama knew that uppapa also liked the colour. Maybe she gave me the scarlet hijab as a talisman—a good luck charm—to help me find him.'

Karnan stirred, drawing the attention of everyone. 'Nafeesa knew,' he said in a feeble voice, barely audible.

Gasps of astonishment echoed around the room.

After a few minutes of silence, Karnan asked for a drink of water. With Vasu's help, he sat up and spoke directly to Rukhsana, his voice louder. 'My dearest child, I am sorry for the doubts Vasu and I had. After hearing your story, I am absolutely certain that you have told the truth. It seems to me that your ummama's hands guided you to Maharaja's College for a reason.'

Rukhsana wiped a tear with the corner of her hijab. 'Yes, uppapa, now that you mention it, I think that indeed was the case. I did not think much about it then, but I recall it was ummama who convinced Geethanjali and me to travel to Cochin and join the college. She insisted that I enrol in History and Political Science courses.'

'She must have known that Karnan chetta is a frequent guest speaker there and would cross paths with you some day,' Vasu suggested.

Karnan nodded and continued, 'Yes, this is certainly Nafeesa's doing,' he said. He looked at Rukhsana. 'Just as our shared love for the colour scarlet, we also had a shared love for literature and history. I am glad that you do too.'

A faint smile came upon Karnan's face as he looked at the faces around him. 'One thing is clear as daylight—my granddaughter is a much better writer than I ever was. I want the world to know that age, gender or religion are no barriers for talent,' he said.

'She gets her talents from you, Karnan chetta,' Vasu said.

Karnan dismissed Vasu's remark with a wave and resumed talking to Rukhsana. 'A member of the Jnanpith Award committee is coming to meet me in a few days. I intend to tell the truth about who wrote the book. It will most certainly disqualify me from the award, which was not mine anyway. But a new literary star will be born. That will be my greatest legacy.'

Rukhsana looked down. 'I am so sorry for the trouble my actions have caused you—'

Karnan held up his hand to stop her. 'No. No. Molay, you have nothing to be sorry about. You and Murali had good intentions. I value that. There is one more important matter. My guru

Jayaprakash Narayan used to remind me: "The revolutionary will die some day"...'

'But the revolution must live on,' Rukhsana completed.

Karnan laughed. 'I am glad you remember,' he said, adding, 'To make this possible, I have a personal request for you and for Murali.'

'What is it?' Rukhsana asked.

'If S.K. Pottekkatt is selected as the winner of the 1980 Jnanpith Award—and there is a very good chance he will be—I want you and Murali to accompany him as his guests when he travels to New Delhi to receive the award from the president of India. That should be a good introduction for you and the YDSK to the rest of India. Can you do that for me, my children?'

Rukhsana, overwhelmed with emotion, covered her mouth with her hand. 'Yes, uppapa, representing you will be the highest honour of my life.'

'Murali?'

Murali hesitated. 'Maamen, how can I leave when you are in this condition?'

Before Karnan could respond, Velayudhan stepped in. 'Murali, you will be gone just for a few days. We are all here with your maamen. You should go with Rukhsana to Delhi.'

Baby and Mallika also urged Murali, and he relented. Relieved, Karnan leaned back on his bed. 'Thank you both. If he wins, I will request Pottekkatt to plan your travel and stay. He will do that for me,' he said. 'What do you think, Vasu?'

Vasu's face showed concern as he spoke haltingly. 'Karnan chetta, don't you think it would be wiser for an elder to accompany them? ...You know Jalaja, she will be unhappy...'

'Yes, you are right, Vasu. They are both unmarried. I did not think of that,' Karnan responded. He looked at Mallika. 'You know Delhi better than any of us. Would you mind chaperoning them?'

Mallika smiled mischievously and nodded. 'I will do so

gladly, provided you can get me admission to the Jnanpith Award ceremony. I am a big fan of Pottekkatt sir and would love to see him receive the award.'

Karnan smiled. 'Thank you, Mallika. I am sure we can organize that.' He let out a long sigh and turned his attention to Rukhsana. 'Molay, you have given a new meaning to my life. Things I could never have foreseen have happened. Unlike Vasu, I never believed in God, but if this is not His hand at play, I don't know what is.'

Vasu looked at Rukhsana. 'Molay, everything you've said makes sense, but tell me one thing. Why did you try to visit the ICU alone one night?'

'Acha, what are you saying?' Murali asked sharply.

Rukhsana calmly replied, 'Yes, it's true... Uppapa had been in a coma for nearly a year, and I feared he'd never know that I'm his granddaughter.' Wiping away her tears, she continued, 'That day, Murali wasn't at the hospital, and it was my only chance... But when I saw SI Ashraf outside the ICU, I panicked and left. It was foolish.'

Vasu felt a pang of guilt for doubting Rukhsana's motives. Clasping his palms in prayer, he looked up, silently thanking the Almighty for guiding her through this time of trial. As he started chanting 'Om Namaha Shivaya. Shivaya Namaha Om,' Baby and Mallika joined him, repeating the prayer softly, their voices filled with reverence.

As soon as the prayer was over, Nurse Marykutty walked up to Karnan's bedside. Without needing to say a word, everyone understood that their time was up. They all said goodbye to Karnan and Vasu, and silently exited the ICU ward.

∞

As the door closed behind them, Karnan asked, 'Vasu, my hearing isn't what it used to be, so I may have misheard. Did Rukhsana call me "uppapa"?'

'Yes. She certainly did,' Vasu said, grinning. 'My heart skipped a beat every time I heard it. You are lucky to be promoted to a grandfather without the punishing role of a father.'

Karnan smiled and raised his head from the mattress. 'I must confess, having a brave girl like Rukhsana as a granddaughter is a dream come true.' He paused and then added, 'Vasu, does this mean that after Murali and Rukhsana get married, you and I will be legally related?'

Vasu laughed. 'Oh yes. That is very true. As all in-laws do, we can start complaining about each other through official channels.'

Karnan joined in the laughter. 'Vasu, I see another benefit to this development. Now that I know that Rukhsana is my granddaughter, Jalaja has no more cards to play to delay the union.'

'Don't count on that!' Vasu replied with a knowing smile. 'Believe me, Jalaja will come up with some other excuse, like Rukhsana not knowing how to recite the *Gayatri Mantra* or who won the battle of Kurukshetra.'

Karnan laughed. 'Or not knowing how to prepare *avalose undas* with the right firmness!' he added, knowing Jalaja's expertise in making the snack.

Nurse Marykutty, who had been standing nearby with Karnan's medication, gently tapped Karnan on his shoulder. Karnan took the medication and looked at the nurse with a twinkle in his eye. 'Marykutty, do you know that facts are sometimes stranger than fiction?'

The nurse looked at Karnan with disbelief. 'Sir, you are a well-educated man, but I must confess that this is the most ridiculous statement I have heard,' she said. 'I prefer fiction. Facts are always boring—just like the man I have been married to for 27 years.'

Karnan and Vasu burst into laughter, causing a concerned look to cross the nurse's face.

Vasu said, chuckling, 'No, Marykutty! Not if your name is Vaikom Karnan.'

'Or, for that matter, Vasudev Panicker,' Karnan added.

Nurse Marykutty shook her head, then looked up and made the sign of the holy cross in the air. Karnan and Vasu giggled like little children as they unsuccessfully tried to muffle their laughter, which grew louder, feeding off each other's and echoing within the bare walls of the ICU ward.

~47~
A Night to Remember

12 November 1981
New Delhi, India

THE SOOTHING NOTES OF HINDUSTANI CLASSICAL MUSIC filled the air at the Vigyan Bhawan auditorium in New Delhi, which was packed to capacity for the Jnanpith Award ceremony—India's highest honour in literature. As the guests stood up and applauded, the president of India, Mr Neelam Sanjiva Reddy, was ushered on to the stage, flanked by a dozen officials and security personnel. The president, in his signature all-white attire—a Nehru jacket, trousers, a Gandhi cap and thick black-rimmed glasses—greeted the audience with a warm smile and a namaste before taking his seat on the oversized red chair at the centre of the stage.

Mrs Sheila Kaul, the Union Minister of State for Culture, Education and Social Welfare, elegantly dressed in a blue sari, was seated beside the President. To her left was S.K. Pottekkatt, the newly announced recipient of the award, making him the second person from Kerala to win this prestigious honour. Beside Pottekkatt sat Harivansh Rai Bachchan, a member of the board of trustees of the Bharatiya Jnanpith organization. Senior government officials and selection committee members occupied seats on either side of the president.

Murali, seated towards the back of the auditorium next to Rukhsana, could sense her awe at the grandeur of the event—a sentiment he shared. During their journey, they had debated whether she should wear a more subdued hijab for the occasion. Murali was pleased that Rukhsana had stuck with her scarlet hijab.

Neither had ever attended an event of such significance before. Murali felt a little uneasy wearing the ready-made shirt and trousers that Rukhsana had selected for him, a departure from his usual practice of getting clothes tailored locally. He noticed that Rukhsana was perched on the edge of her seat, captivated by the Indian literary giants she had long admired.

Murali's thoughts drifted back to the whirlwind of events that had unfolded in the past few weeks, following the home minister's resignation. He remembered being in the ICU when a member of the Jnanpith Award selection committee, Aditya Jha, had visited Karnan. Taking Vasu and Murali into confidence, Mr Jha revealed that the committee was evenly split between awarding the honour to Karnan and Pottekkatt. While one half of the committee was moved by the emotional appeal of the story of a freedom fighter battling for his life, the other half believed that Pottekkatt's extensive body of work made him more deserving of the award.

Karnan had shocked Mr Jha by revealing that *The Last Revolutionary* had not been authored by him but by his granddaughter, and was published under his name when he had been in a coma. After grasping the situation, Mr Jha asked to meet Rukhsana. Following several phone calls with his colleagues in New Delhi, Mr Jha expressed regret that the nomination had to be revoked due to the unusual circumstances surrounding the book, a decision he agreed to make without prejudice. In recognition of Rukhsana's undisputable literacy talent, he accepted Karnan's request that she and Murali be invited to attend the Jnanpith Award ceremony in Delhi if Pottekkatt won.

The following day, Mr Jha updated the Jnanpith Award jury on the developments, and they unanimously voted Pottekkatt as the 1980 award winner. The news was first announced by the chairman of the Bharatiya Jnanpith organization in Delhi. Although there was some disappointment among Karnan's fans and political followers, the decision was warmly received by the Kerala literary community.

Murali had been tasked with releasing a statement from Karnan, congratulating his friend, whom he called 'one of the literary giants of Kerala'. The next day, Pottekkatt visited the hospital to personally wish Karnan a speedy recovery. To the press gathered outside the hospital, an emotional Pottekkatt remarked that no award could ever capture the essence of Vaikom Karnan's heroism. He reiterated the title of 'Renaissance Man' that he had previously bestowed on his friend, adding that Karnan's legacy would continue to inspire millions across India.

Murali also recalled the unexpected withdrawal of support by key coalition partners, which had sealed the fate of the LDF government. With the loss of the majority support among elected MLAs, Chief Minister E.K. Nayanar resigned on 20 October, prompting the governor to declare president's rule in Kerala. *Truth be told, the events have gone far beyond my wildest dreams. Maamen is right; truth is often stranger than fiction*, thought Murali.

These cascading events set the stage for Murali and Rukhsana as they embarked on the over two-day train ride from Cochin to Delhi via the Kerala Express. Unfortunately, Mallika had to cancel her plan to accompany them due to a sudden illness that the doctor suspected to be yellow fever, leaving the young couple to travel alone. Despite Murali's lingering concerns about leaving Cochin while his uncle was still bedridden and with the YDSK protests gaining momentum, he found reassurance in the words of Shibu and Geethanjali, who came to see them off at the train station, promising to take care of everything in their absence.

∽

Murali was jolted from his thoughts by Rukhsana's gentle tap on his arm, signalling that the ceremony was about to begin. The master of ceremonies welcomed the audience, promising that this would be the most exciting Jnanpith Award event ever. Minister Sheila Kaul spoke next, emphasizing the richness of Indian arts and literature and commending the selection committee for their diligent review of thousands of literary works in over 20 Indian languages to choose the finalists.

Murali listened attentively as Mr Jha introduced President Reddy. He learnt that the president had been imprisoned during the Quit India movement from 1940 to 1945. In response to Jayaprakash Narayan's call for a 'total revolution', President Reddy had emerged from political exile in 1975. Elected as a member of Parliament in March 1977, Reddy had served as Speaker of the Lok Sabha before being elected to the highest office in July 1977. As Mr Jha recounted these milestones, the audience applauded, and Murali couldn't help but notice the parallels between President Reddy's life and his uncle's. *With a bit of luck and providence, this could have been maamen's story.*

Known for his love for Indian literature, President Reddy received warm applause when he mentioned that he had read all five finalists' books. He joked that he was glad not to be on the selection board, as choosing the best work from among so many outstanding pieces would have been an impossible task. He expressed his gratitude to all the nominees, the organizers, and the Indian press, urging them to spread the message of the shortlisted books to the people in the Indian villages.

As the president was handed the award citation, he read aloud the document, officially crowning Mr Sankarankutty Kunjiraman Pottekkatt as the winner of the 1980 Jnanpith Award for his outstanding travelogue *Oru Desathinte Katha*. The president highlighted Pottekkatt's impressive track record as a writer, novelist, teacher, poet, politician and author of over 60 books. Upon the president's request, Pottekkatt stepped on to the stage to accept the award, which comprised a citation, a bronze replica of Goddess Saraswati and an envelope containing the cash prize. After presenting the award and shaking Pottekkatt's hand, the president stepped aside and gestured to him to address the gathering.

Pottekkatt expressed his gratitude for the recognition and shared his desire to dedicate the honour to his dear friend, freedom fighter Vaikom Karnan. Quoting the American writer R.G. Ingersoll, he described Karnan's heroism: 'When the will defies fear, when duty throws the gauntlet down to fate, when honour scorns to compromise with death—that is heroism.' Issuing a challenge to all writers to write with courage, Pottekkatt noted that *The Last Revolutionary*, based on Karnan's true story, had sold nearly 5,00,000 copies across India—more than any other book in the country since independence. He acknowledged the presence of Karnan's nephew, Murali Vasudev, whom he called the 'courageous leader of Kerala's new youth-led political movement', and granddaughter, Rukhsana Mirza, who he predicted would be a future winner of the Jnanpith Award. Pottekkatt concluded his speech by committing himself to mentoring the next generation of Indian writers.

After the ceremony concluded, an official approached Murali and Rukhsana, informing them that the president wished to meet them backstage. Greeting them warmly, President Reddy mentioned that he was closely following the political developments in Kerala and was praying for Vaikom Karnan's health. He praised Murali's and Rukhsana's efforts to mobilize the youth, advising them to maintain peace in their movement. Speaking off the record, he offered to arrange a meeting with the governor of Kerala, Jothi Venkatachalam, whom he knew well.

To Rukhsana's surprise, the president asked one of his aides to bring a copy of *The Last Revolutionary* and requested her to sign it with a message for his granddaughter, whose birthday was coming up next week. Murali watched as Rukhsana wrote: 'The revolutionary will die some day, but the revolution must live on.' She looked up at Murali with a mischievous smile and then scribbled the name 'Vaikom Karnan' below her message.

In a final act of kindness, the president summoned the press photographers and publicly posed for photos—signed book in hand—with Murali and Rukhsana standing on either side. Murali sensed that with his vast experience in politics and the media, the president was making a deliberate move. He knew that the press would publish stories about the people the president posed with at events, and perhaps the president was sending a subtle message through the media that he could not convey directly as the head of state.

Since Pottekkatt was still busy answering questions from the media, Murali and Rukhsana decided to walk back to Kerala House, the government guest house in New Delhi where they were staying along with Pottekkatt and his guests.

As they strolled under the cool, moonlit night, Rukhsana held Murali's arm tightly. 'Murali, this evening has been magical for me,' she said softly. 'There is no one else I would rather share it with. Thank you for believing in me and bringing out the best in me.'

Murali gently caressed her face. 'Rukhsana, there is no place I would rather be right now than walking beside you, holding your hand. I love you for who you are. Your passion to uncover your past has earned you the right to be here among some of India's greatest writers.'

They kept talking as they strolled hand in hand, occasionally stopping to ask for directions. Tired after an hour of walking, they hailed an autorickshaw to take them to Kerala House. During the ride, Murali shared with Rukhsana how magical the night had been for him as well. Before they retired to their separate rooms, he spoke with awe about the special feeling invoked by meeting President Sanjiva Reddy. Though he could not describe it, Murali knew it was the same feeling he had had when he was with the man he admired the most—his maamen—that inexplicable sense of being in the presence of greatness.

~48~

Kiss on the Kerala Express

13–15 November 1981

DESPITE THE WORRIES THEY KNEW AWAITED THEM BACK home, Rukhsana and Murali found their time away refreshingly peaceful. Both had kept the promise they made to each other to leave their concerns for Kerala behind until they returned to Cochin. Early the next day, they joined S.K. Pottekkatt for a leisurely tour of Delhi's attractions, including the Parliament House, the Amar Jawan Jyoti memorial and the Red Fort. They returned just in time to freshen up and pack their bags to catch the evening Kerala Express train back to Cochin.

The train journey from Delhi to Cochin took almost three days. Despite the underlying tensions about the situation in Kerala, they found moments of youthful joy. When the train stopped at Jhansi, a group of college students from Kerala joined them. Some immediately recognized Murali and Rukhsana from the press reports. Seizing the moment, Rukhsana put Murali on the spot by requesting him to sing a song for the students, which resulted in an avalanche of requests that kept Murali busy for hours.

On the second day of the journey, Murali stepped off the train at Nagpur station to get tea for Rukhsana. As part of a prank planned with the students, he climbed back into a different compartment at the rear of the train. Rukhsana, worried about his sudden disappearance, had to be restrained by the students from pulling the emergency stop chain. When the train stopped at the next station, almost one hour later, Murali shocked Rukhsana by quietly coming back to sit beside her, pretending he had just gone to the toilet. When the students burst out in laughter, Rukhsana realized the joke was at her expense.

By the third morning, the train crossed from Tamil Nadu into Kerala through a gap in the Western Ghats, which Murali described as the 'Palakkad Gap'. To Rukhsana's surprise, she found that the scenery outside had shifted from dry landscapes to lush green forests interspersed with paddy fields. Murali used his rudimentary knowledge of geography to explain that the Western Ghats ran like a spine along the eastern border of Kerala and blocked the winds travelling across the Arabian Sea, resulting in plenty of rain along the Kerala coast.

As the train neared Palghat station and began crossing the majestic Bharathapuzha River, Murali and Rukhsana walked to the end of the compartment, towards the large doors. They had the area all to themselves. The cool morning breeze swept in, and Murali, standing behind Rukhsana, wrapped his arms around her. The invigorating gusts of wind heightened the moment, and with the serene river below them, Murali gently kissed her on the lips. Holding each other tightly, they stood there, enjoying the fresh air and quiet beauty of Kerala's landscape.

Murali broke the silence. 'I have been wondering when to ask you, but this moment feels perfect,' he whispered. 'Rukhsana, will you be my wife?'

Rukhsana turned to face him, looking deeply into his eyes. 'Do I have a choice?' she asked with a teasing smile.

'Not really!' Murali grinned. 'It was not so much a question. It was a statement of what should logically be the next step in our relationship. Marriage…a home…children.'

'Is that right?' Rukhsana asked, her gaze steady. 'What about our immediate responsibilities and all the challenges we have taken up?'

'Well, we cannot walk away from any of it. But that does not mean we must put our personal lives on hold forever. My desire is to marry you while maamen is still alive. I want to seek his blessings.'

'Not forever, no,' Rukhsana said. 'But now is not the right time for us to get married. Let your maamen recover fully and come home. We also need more time to convince your mother. With Baby amma and Velayudhan uncle's help, I know we can do that. In the meantime, let's put all our energies into the movement we have started. What do you think?'

Murali was quiet for a few seconds. He knew that Rukhsana was right about the need to focus on the YDSK's political future. That would also be what his maamen would want them to do. He found himself marvelling at the clarity in Rukhsana's thoughts and her sense of purpose. He pulled her closer and whispered, 'You are right, as always. That is why I love you.'

Rukhsana smiled, stood on her toes and kissed him on the lips.

'And just for the record, Murali, I want three children—one boy and two girls. I have already picked out their names.'

'Really? Seems to me you have thought about this quite extensively. Three sounds about right. What are the names you have selected?'

'Are you ready for it?' Rukhsana asked. 'The name for the boy, of course, must be Karnan. The girls—Nafeesa and Uthara. What do you think?'

Murali's face lit up with a grin. 'I love all three names just as much as I love you,' he said.

Rukhsana pulled away from Murali's arms when they heard footsteps approaching. A man in a black jacket and white trousers appeared in the doorway. Murali asked him if he wanted to see their tickets, but the ticket collector waved the question off with a smile. 'Your friends told me who you are. I pray that Vaikom Karnan recovers soon. Kerala needs him now more than ever,' he said, before moving on through the narrow pathway to the next compartment.

Moments later, the train came to a halt at Palghat station. Less than three hours later, they crossed the twin bridges spanning the two branches of the Periyar River as they approached Alwaye, a town near Cochin. Twenty-five minutes later, the train finally pulled into Ernakulam North station.

As they gathered their belongings to disembark, Rukhsana grabbed Murali's arm. 'Murali, Murali, did you hear that? Someone called your name. It sounded like Alex.'

'Alex? I wonder why he is here.'

'Maybe your father sent him. Come, let's find out.'

As they stepped on to the platform, Alex came running, out of breath.

'Murali, thank God you're back.'

'What's the matter, Alex?'

'I hate to be the bearer of bad news…but Karnan sir…'

Murali grabbed Alex by the shoulders, shaking him. 'What do you mean, Alex? Is his condition serious again?'

Tears streamed down Alex's face. 'He's gone!' Alex cried. 'Karnan sir's soul left his body yesterday evening.'

'Oh my God!' Rukhsana gasped, her eyes wide.

As Murali staggered back, Rukhsana held his hand and helped him sit on top of his luggage.

'He was getting better when we left,' Rukhsana murmured. 'Alex, tell us what happened.'

'Shibu and I were by his side when he asked me to call Vasu sir,' Alex began. 'They spoke about their days as freedom fighters for over an hour. Karnan sir revealed that attending the Jnanpith Award was his dream and that he was happy he could realize it through you both. He was eager to hear about your trip to New Delhi. He even asked Nurse Jasmine if he could join me at the train station to receive you.'

Rukhsana pulled her hijab over her face, her body wracked with sobs. Murali placed an arm around her to comfort her.

'Karnan sir was very happy. He enjoyed Shibu's jokes about the minister getting stuck in his car due to our blockade. He even joked with Shibu that he had not had a drink for almost a year—the longest stretch of his life without alcohol. He laughed when Shibu promised to have an extra peg of rum on his behalf,' Alex said as he managed an awkward half-smile.

'I am so glad to hear that. Maamen was surrounded by people who were dear to him,' Murali said.

'He was the happiest I have seen him in a long time. He asked me to book a big boat for all of us to take a backwaters trip this Christmas.' After a brief pause, Alex added, 'The one regret Karnan sir mentioned was not taking the leadership of the Communist Party when he had the opportunity. He instructed Vasu sir to ensure that this mistake is not repeated.'

Murali exchanged a glance with Rukhsana. 'For maamen to admit that…it shows such humility. This is what made him a great man. Alex, we will certainly not repeat the mistake,' Murali exclaimed.

Rukhsana reached out and held Murali's arm. 'But Murali, what if your maamen was right?'

'What do you mean?'

'I am referring to the advice he gave us at the hospital. What if his principled stand of not sharing power with those who do not share his values *was* the right approach? If he had compromised, would the YDSK even exist today?'

'I don't know, Rukhsana. That is a question we may never find an answer to. But I agree that we need to consider this decision very carefully,' Murali said. He then turned his attention back to Alex. 'At what time did maamen pass?'

'Around 6.45 p.m. After having dinner, Karnan sir complained of chest pain. By the time the attending doctor arrived, it was too late. Just like that, holding the hand of his best friend, he was gone. I wailed like an orphan,' Alex's voice choked. 'Dr Joseph told us it was a massive heart attack.'

Murali stood up. 'In that case, we have to get there as soon as possible.' Seeing the puzzled looks from Alex and Rukhsana, he explained, 'I know it is important for achan that we follow the Hindu tradition of cremation before sunset on the day after the passing of the soul.'

Alex wiped his tears with his shirt sleeve. 'Vasu sir has already arranged the last rites. He sent me to take you to the crematorium.'

As they walked towards the exit, Murali turned to Rukhsana and quietly said, 'I think we made a mistake going to Delhi. I should have trusted my instincts and stayed.'

Rukhsana's voice had an edge to it. 'Well, Murali, we had no way of knowing,' she said. 'And besides, this was *his* idea. He wanted us to live his dream, to attend the award in Delhi—'

Alex interjected, 'Oh, I forgot to tell you something...'

'What is it, Alex?' Rukhsana asked.

'While you were away, Baby amma, Commander Velayudhan and Mallika chechi visited the hospital daily. They took turns reading the book to Karnan sir and they finished it the night before he passed...' Alex paused as Rukhsana let out a sob. Murali placed a hand over Rukhsana's shoulder and nodded for Alex to continue.

'Karnan sir enjoyed the book so much that he repeatedly asked Baby amma and Mallika chechi to read certain scenes again. I even saw him tearing up a few times. I guess it was very emotional for him to hear his life story.'

'I am happy to hear that, Alex. At least maamen got the chance to relive his own illustrious past before he left us. We can take some comfort that God called him after the last page of his story was read,' Murali said softly.

PART SEVEN

THE REVOLUTION MUST LIVE ON

~49~

Last Rites

15 November 1981
Cochin, Kerala

IT WAS HALF PAST TWO IN THE AFTERNOON WHEN THE TAXI arrived at the crematorium. Dark clouds had gathered overhead, and a light rainfall had begun. As Murali stepped out, Shibu came running and embraced him. Alex opened the car door for Rukhsana, and the four of them walked briskly towards the large crowd that had gathered at the centre of the crematorium. There was a heavy presence of policemen, with several cars bearing government tags.

Murali went to his father, who was standing with Velayudhan, Ashraf, MLA Shivan, Abdul, Sashi, Ramesh and a group of local elected officials. Baby quietly approached Rukhsana, taking her hand and leading her to where a group of women stood under a tree. Among them were Jalaja, Geethanjali, Mallika and Vijayalakshmi. As Murali approached, a murmur arose among a few hundred college students who had gathered. A student started to shout a slogan but was hushed by the crowd.

In the distance, Murali's eyes fixed on a raised cement platform. Atop it lay the pyre made of large piles of firewood, and upon it, Karnan's body, wrapped in a pristine white cloth, his feet pointed south as per tradition. His toes were tied with a string, and a red tilak marked his forehead.

Murali could smell the scent of sandalwood and turmeric paste from the pyre and knew that the Hindu rites were being meticulously followed. *Maamen was an atheist, so it is evident that achan has taken full responsibility for the last rites.*

As Murali walked closer to the pyre, an overwhelming wave of emotion surged through him. The sight, the smell, the weight of the moment—it all became too much. His heart felt like it had been struck by a heavy hammer, the ache growing unbearable. He could feel his pulse racing, his chest tightening with grief. Finally, unable to hold back the flood of sorrow, he broke down, sobbing uncontrollably. 'Please forgive me, maamen,' Murali cried. 'I was not by your side when you needed me.'

Vasu rushed to hold his son. 'Son, you've always been in his heart,' Vasu whispered. 'You're the son he never had. For Hindus to attain *moksha*, the funeral pyre must be lit by the son.'

Jalaja walked up from behind and caressed Murali's hair. 'Go, son, it's time,' she urged.

The priest glanced at his watch and asked Vasu, 'Is he the person we have been waiting for?'

'Yes, panditji. This is my son, Murali. He was like a son to Karnan chetta.'

'Good, let's get started.'

Murali followed the priest's instructions meticulously. He circled the pyre, reciting a hymn and placing sesame seeds on Karnan's chest, hands and legs. The priest sprinkled the body and pyre with ghee and drew three lines on the ground. Murali, holding an earthen pot filled with water, circled the pyre and threw the pot over his shoulder, letting it land and break near the head of the body.

The priest handed Murali a burning torch made from dry coconut leaves to set the pyre ablaze. As Murali approached the pyre, memories of his uncle filled his mind—the loud laughter, the crude jokes and the unwavering belief Karnan had in him. Murali directed the flame to the base of the pile of firewood. The crackling sound drowned out his thoughts as the scent of burning sandalwood filled the air. As the final step of the ceremony, Murali proceeded to circle the burning pyre three times. As the mournful wailing and sobs overwhelmed him, Murali could hear the distinctive sound of Rukhsana weeping and Baby consoling her. A few onlookers shouted slogans in praise of Karnan.

Suddenly, the sound of car doors opening and shutting interrupted Murali's walk around the burning pyre. There was a flurry of steps, and a man wearing a grey Nehru jacket appeared, carrying a large wreath, followed by two aides. The message on the wreath read: 'Prayers for a Great Soul—Governor of Kerala'. The man placed the wreath beside the burning pyre and folded his hands in prayer. He then walked over to MLA Shivan, who greeted him. After a brief exchange, MLA Shivan introduced him to Vasu and Murali.

'This is an unbearable loss for the people,' the man said. 'I am Anand Dixit, principal secretary to Governor Jothi Venkatachalam. She wanted to come, but fell ill this morning. She sends her heartfelt condolences.'

Vasu thanked him and the governor for the thoughtful gesture.

Mr Dixit took Murali aside and spoke quietly. 'She wanted me to invite a group of the YDSK leaders, including you, MLA Shivan, Shibu and Rukhsana, to meet her as soon as possible.'

'Sorry, Mr Dixit. I do not understand. What is this about?'

'The governor wants to end the president's rule in Kerala, and is exploring all options to form a new government. Although the YDSK is a small party, she feels that it should also have a seat at the table for the discussions or at least be heard. When can you travel to Trivandrum?'

'Oh! I thank Governor Venkatachalam for the invitation. I must travel with my father to take maamen's ashes to North India. But you can coordinate with MLA Shivan to set up a time to meet the governor.'

Overhearing the conversation, Vasu stepped forward. 'Murali, this is an important meeting. Karnan would have wanted you to attend. I will travel to North India by myself.'

Last Rites

'In that case, I want you to take Alex with you,' Murali told his father. He looked at Mr Dixit and said, 'Please inform the governor that we will meet her on Wednesday, 18 November, around 11 a.m.'

'Thank you, Mr Murali. I will inform the governor. Her personal secretary will arrange to pick you up from the train station. I will take my leave now.' Dixit folded his palms in farewell and walked out.

About two hours later, the fire in the pyre died down, leaving only white ashes. The priest summoned Vasu and Murali and informed them of the final ritual—the ashes should be immersed in a holy river. Vasu informed the priest that Karnan had left explicit instructions that his ashes be divided into three equal parts and immersed in the Periyar River and the Vembanad Lake in Kerala, and the Kosi River in North India. Vasu added that he would also like to immerse a handful of Karnan's ashes in the Ganges River in Kashi, North India.

The priest admired Karnan's foresight and the clarity of his instructions, noting how rare it was for someone facing death to leave such detailed directives. He praised Karnan as a wise man who wished for his remains to support new life through the cycle of nature.

~50~
The Governor's Offer

18 November 1981
Trivandrum, Kerala

SITTING IN THE RECEPTION AREA OF THE RAJ BHAVAN, THE governor's official residence, Rukhsana felt an unusual sense of calm. She glanced around the palatial residence, a remnant of British India designed as a guest house to accommodate state guests and dignitaries. Perched on a breezy hillock and showcasing traditional Kerala architectural style, the mansion was surrounded by expansive flower-filled gardens. Rukhsana's eyes were drawn to a fountain in the centre of the lawn facing the governor's office room, and she wondered what the view would be like from the inside.

Reflecting on the events in her life since arriving in Cochin, Rukhsana realized how starkly different her current situation was from the lonely days of her youth in Abu Dhabi. Five years ago, she had taken a chance and travelled to a new land, seeking answers to deeply personal questions. Although she did not recall her grandmother ever expressing any grudge, Rukhsana had always harboured a distinct curiosity about her grandfather, a man who seemingly had not taken responsibility for the outcome of his actions.

The decision to travel to Kerala using the meagre savings her grandmother had left her was not a particularly difficult one. After all, she was a citizen of India, and she was following her best friend to a land where her only known relative lived. What she hadn't anticipated was her unplanned involvement in the students' political movement at Maharaja's College after meeting Murali. Initially, she was content supporting Murali and Shibu in their activism while secretly pursuing her passion project of documenting her grandfather's life. However, the shooting incident had completely changed the trajectory of her life, leading to Murali, Shibu and herself becoming household names across Kerala.

Rukhsana's mind wandered to the whirlwind of significant events that followed the shooting: the visit to Murali's home, the student-led uprisings all over Kerala, the adrenaline rush during the blockade against the home minister's hospital visit, the relief of revealing her identity to the people she cared about, the joy of attending the Jnanpith Award ceremony and meeting with President Sanjiva Reddy, Murali's proposal on the train and, finally, the pall of gloom cast by the passing of her grandfather. It seemed too much to handle. Despite the overwhelming nature of these experiences, she was happy to be in the company of three men she respected, and who, in turn, respected her. In a short while, she would be sitting across the table from the governor of Kerala. *Everything happens for a reason; I have to learn to live with the good and the bad.*

When she first arrived in Kerala, she had been plagued by questions about her grandfather. After the love of his life suddenly disappeared, what attempts had he made to find her? Had he gone seeking his lover in the neighbourhood she lived in? Had he confronted her parents for answers? Had he been aware that his beloved was pregnant with his child? Many of these questions were answered in her grandfather's diaries. *His notes showed that he cared very deeply for ummama, the only woman he had ever loved. Yes, he cared a little more for his country. What is so wrong with that?* Rukhsana wondered how she would handle such a dilemma and felt grateful not to have to face such a test herself.

Rukhsana reflected on how her chance encounter with Murali at Maharaja's College on 15 August 1977 had dramatically changed the course of her life. A smile touched her lips as she admitted the melodrama in meeting someone who was like a son to the man she had come to confront. But Rukhsana dismissed the thought that the allure alone would have been enough for their friendship to take root and blossom into love. She had been drawn to Murali's charisma and dedication to public service. *Of course, it helped that he's good-looking... His golden voice did not hurt either.*

Rukhsana glanced at Murali and found he was looking at her quizzically, perhaps wondering why she was smiling. The timing of their first meeting had been impeccable. Rukhsana wondered what would have happened if Murali had already been in a romantic relationship with someone else. *Considering his popularity on the college campus, especially among the girls, it was a miracle that he did not have a girlfriend. Ummama would be pleased that the scarlet hijab not only led me to my grandfather, the love of her life, but also to the love of mine. But I wonder how she would have reacted to my relationship with Murali. Would she have approved of me following in her footsteps and falling in love with a Hindu man from Kerala?*

Adjusting her hijab, Rukhsana let the cool breeze from the Arabian Sea flow through her hair. She recalled asking Murali if she should choose a less conspicuous hijab for the Jnanpith Award ceremony. Murali had encouraged her to wear the scarlet hijab, saying it represented an essential part of her heritage and identity. She loved his argument that a person's identity was like the foundation of a building—the stronger it was, the taller it could be built and the more resilient it would be against challenges.

Inspired by Murali's words, Rukhsana had chosen the darkest shade of scarlet for her hijab, which her grandmother had gifted her, for the meeting with the governor. She felt confident wearing it, though she preferred draping it loosely over her shoulders like a dupatta, rather than wrapping it tightly as was customary in the Middle East.

The intercom by the reception desk buzzed loudly, jolting Rukhsana out of her thoughts. The receptionist picked up the phone and spoke briefly in Malayalam before approaching the group.

He addressed MLA Shivan. 'Sir, the governor is ready to meet you now.'

Murali, Rukhsana and Shibu followed MLA Shivan into an office through the large double doors. Governor Jothi Venkatachalam sat behind her work desk, dressed in a light blue sari paired with a dark blue blouse. Her grey hair was neatly arranged in a bun.

'Namaskaram, welcome to Raj Bhavan,' she greeted warmly, rising from the desk and walking towards them with her hands clasped together. Rukhsana noticed the soft musical chime of the governor's large golden bangles as they moved up and down her hands. 'You are all so young…I feel old,' she added with a smile.

MLA Shivan returned the greeting and introduced Murali, Shibu and Rukhsana. The governor extended her condolences over Vaikom Karnan's passing, acknowledging his role as a moral force in Kerala politics. She noted that Karnan's shooting had been the catalyst for their meeting and had profoundly shaken the state's peaceful political climate.

Shivan agreed, mentioning that the turmoil in Kerala might not have been so severe had Karnan not been shot. After securing a promise of confidentiality regarding the day's discussions, Governor Venkatachalam explained the purpose of the meeting.

'Since all of you are immersed in Kerala politics, you are aware that given the current loss of confidence in the Left Front government, I recommended the imposition of president's rule in Kerala,' the governor said. 'As per the Indian constitution, this is a temporary state of affairs. My role as governor is to facilitate the formation of a new government led by someone who commands majority support from the MLAs.'

'Yes, madam. That is also our understanding,' MLA Shivan responded.

The governor continued, 'I have begun preliminary discussions with leaders from various political parties but wish to expand my outreach beyond the traditional Left and Right coalitions that have long dominated the state. This is where the YDSK comes into the picture.'

'Madam, the YDSK has big plans, but we are still a small player in Kerala politics. What role do you see us playing?' Murali enquired.

Governor Venkatachalam stood up, pushing her chair back. 'Murali, don't underestimate yourself,' she said firmly. 'Seven MLAs may seem modest in a large state like Tamil Nadu, but as you have seen, in Kerala, it is a significant number—it can make or break a coalition government. The most important thing is that the YDSK has harnessed the political momentum by mobilizing the youth. You will see the result in the next elections. I have no doubt you will have more seats at the table,' she said.

She placed her hands on the desk, her golden bangles jingling softly, and lowered her voice. 'I am not alone in this assessment. President Sanjiva Reddy also shares my view.' She stood up straight again. 'But to be clear, my role as governor is to be an impartial judge. The Indian constitution requires me to invite any party or coalition that can prove they can secure a simple majority of the elected MLAs.'

'Forgive me, Governor, but that will require us to make many compromises,' Shibu said.

'Shibu, that is for all of you to decide,' the governor replied. Her voice took on a sharp edge. 'All I can say is that I have been keeping my finger on the pulse of the people of Kerala. I believe that they are ready for change.' Her eyes fixed on Rukhsana. 'What do you think?'

Rukhsana, who had been silently following the conversation, leaned forward and adjusted her hijab to cover her hair partially. 'Madam, Karnan sir, our mentor, instilled in us an optimistic view of public service,' Rukhsana began. 'To be honest, I had my doubts at times. But he convinced me that change is inevitable and that it will happen in my lifetime. I have seen it begin to happen. As you said, President Sanjiva Reddy also believes change is coming. So now, I am a believer.'

Governor Venkatachalam clasped her hands and sat down. 'Both Vaikom Karnan and President Reddy are absolutely correct!' she exclaimed. 'Rukhsana, why do you think your remarkable book, *The Last Revolutionary*, is the bestselling book in India today?'

'Hope, madam. It gives us hope for a better tomorrow,' Rukhsana responded.

'Exactly. And hope is in short supply in Kerala these days,' the governor said, leaning back in her chair.

'Hope, enabled by a just social and economic order, is what we have been fighting for,' Shibu added.

Governor Venkatachalam smiled. 'Well, in that case, this is your opportunity. I can give you two weeks to prove that the YDSK can be part of a coalition with a majority vote in the Kerala Assembly. I advise you to stay back in Trivandrum for a few days and get to work. What do you think?'

'Excuse me, Governor, but may we have a few minutes to discuss?' Rukhsana requested, much to the surprise of the others.

'Of course. You can stay here. I will be back in 10 minutes.' The governor stood up and walked out of the room.

MLA Shivan, Murali and Shibu gathered around Rukhsana to discuss the offer. Rukhsana asked each of them to express their heartfelt feelings, keeping Karnan's legacy and memory in mind. She listened attentively and pushed back on each person's response until she had secured their full agreement.

Twelve minutes later, Governor Venkatachalam returned to the room. 'Tell me what you have decided,' she said, sitting down.

'Madam, we have agreed on a plan of action. Rukhsana will speak on behalf of all of us,' MLA Shivan said.

The governor turned to Rukhsana, who spoke with measured calm. 'Madam, we deeply appreciate your confidence in us. It has lifted our sagging spirits. Our decision is guided by the legacy that Karnan sir has left us. His advice was to strive for systemic changes that benefit the common man and can last for a long time. He cautioned us against forming short-term opportunistic alliances with those who don't share our values and vision for Kerala.'

'I understand,' the governor said, pursing her lips. 'Does this mean the YDSK is unwilling to accept a seat at the table?'

'We do want a seat, madam,' Rukhsana replied. 'But not today. Karnan sir advised us to earn the trust of the people first. We believe we have not yet completed this important task. Once we have, we will claim our rightful place at the table.' She paused and glanced at Murali and Shibu.

Shibu leaned forward and placed his hand on the table. 'Governor, our goals have become more than just securing a seat at the table. With the help of the people of Kerala, our aim is to reset the table itself.'

Governor Venkatachalam smiled. 'Very well. I must say I did not anticipate this response,' she said, pausing briefly before continuing. 'But I respect your decision and your complete dedication to Vaikom Karnan's vision and legacy. It speaks to your character and gives me hope that the future of Kerala is in good hands. I wish you the very best.'

The governor rose and shook hands with each of them, thanking them and wishing them luck before walking them to the door.

As they moved down the hall, the receptionist came running after them. 'The governor would like to have a word with Rukhsana madam,' he said.

Rukhsana looked at the others and then followed the receptionist.

On seeing Rukhsana re-enter her office, the governor stepped forward and reached out to hold Rukhsana's hands. Noticing the henna tattoos on Rukhsana's palm, the governor smiled.

'I loved wearing henna on my hands when I was a little girl,' the governor reminisced, examining the intricate design. 'They look lovely on you. I wish I could have them too,' she added with a wistful smile.

'You certainly can if you want. May I remind you that you are the governor; no one would object,' Rukhsana said with a smile.

The governor chuckled. 'Except it would be on the front page of every newspaper,' she said. 'Anyway Rukhsana, I could not let you leave without telling you how much I loved reading *The Last Revolutionary*. Congratulations on the nomination for the Jnanpith Award. That is a victory in itself.'

'Thank you, madam. Every word I wrote came from my grandfather's mouth—pen or deeds. I just chronicled them. Mallika Sukumaran brought them to life in the form of a memoir. Without my grandfather, there would have been no book.'

Governor Venkatachalam stepped closer. 'Yes, I am aware that you have given all the credit to your grandfather for inspiration, but you are the one who wrote the book,' she said. 'I have a question about the title. Why did you refer to Vaikom Karnan as "the last revolutionary"?'

'That is what I believed when I was writing the book. But my perspective has evolved over the past year since my grandfather was shot.'

'How so?'

'Well, madam, the idea of the "last revolutionary" carries a certain allure, much like something fleeting yet significant. From his diaries, I learnt that my grandfather viewed his mentor, Jayaprakash Narayan, as the last revolutionary. But after independence, the mantle seemed to fall on my grandfather's shoulders. Due to his independent thinking, my grandfather also had many enemies. After he was shot, the mantle was picked up by Murali, Shibu and MLA—'

'And by you, Rukhsana,' Governor Venkatachalam interjected softly. 'I have been following your story in the press. You are no longer just the "girl in scarlet hijab", as the media once labelled you. You have followed your grandfather's footsteps and become a revolutionary yourself!'

Rukhsana fidgeted with her hijab, her cheeks turning red. 'You are too kind, madam. Please don't believe everything you read in the press. I am just an ordinary Indian girl caught up in extraordinary times,' she said.

'Ordinary girl?' The governor smiled warmly. 'Granddaughter of a famous freedom fighter, and a student leader, acclaimed writer…maybe even a future chief minister? No, Rukhsana, I don't see anything ordinary in you.'

Rukhsana smiled shyly. 'I understand that my mixed background is a little unusual. It is also true that the people of Kerala know me as the girl in scarlet hijab, but that does not fully define who I am. My heritage is from Kashmir as much as it is from Kerala. I am a writer as much as I am a political activist. My religion is Islam because of my grandmother as much as it is Hinduism due to my grandfather.'

'Well said, Rukhsana. Not many girls in India can claim such a rich heritage, much less your steadfast courage. And that's why young girls all over Kerala love you,' Governor Venkatachalam exclaimed. After a brief pause, she added, '"The last revolutionary" somehow sounds quite ominous.'

Rukhsana smiled. 'Madam, I must admit that the title sounds ominous, but I love the romantic idea of the lone hero, the last revolutionary. And since the book has been received so well by readers all over India, I don't want to tamper with the title.'

'I see your point. But how would you convince ordinary people to keep faith in the political system and believe a revolution never ends?'

'My grandfather often reminded his trusted followers—few

as they may be—that the revolutionary will die some day, but the revolution should live on,' Rukhsana said. 'He believed that the nature of social change requires that when one revolutionary exits the stage, one or more conscientious followers step forward to pick up the mantle. That is the only way to ensure a revolution never dies.'

Governor Venkatachalam nodded. 'I see that your grandfather's hopes and dreams now live on with you, along with Murali and Shibu,' she said. 'It was so nice to meet you in person. Please come back and stay with me whenever you want. I may need your help with my book idea about my father.'

'Absolutely, madam. I am a big fan of your work supporting women's causes all over India. I would love to return and spend time with you in this lovely place,' Rukhsana said. 'May I take your leave now? We must catch the 3.30 p.m. train for Cochin.'

Governor Venkatachalam and Rukhsana walked out to rejoin the others. At the reception desk, the governor instructed her staff to arrange a car to take Rukhsana, Murali and Shibu to the train station and another to drop off MLA Shivan at the Kerala Legislative Assembly. The governor bid them farewell and walked out to the lawn, where a group of khadi-clad political power brokers were anxiously waiting to meet her.

~51~

Young Revolutionaries

18 November 1981
Ernakulam South Train Station, Cochin

THE RETURN JOURNEY TO COCHIN PASSED BY QUICKLY. Murali, Shibu and Rukhsana discussed the meeting with the governor in detail. Rukhsana also told them about her private chat with the governor. Both men complimented Rukhsana for the confident way she had dealt with the situation. Murali and Shibu agreed to recommend her as the official spokesperson for the YDSK to the executive committee. Halfway through the journey, Shibu surprised Murali and Rukhsana by confiding that when they had been away in New Delhi, he had met Geethanjali twice in private. With uncharacteristic shyness, Shibu confessed that he liked Geethanjali and sought Rukhsana's help to arrange a casual group picnic to Bolgatty Island. Rukhsana teased Shibu that she would charge a fee for her matchmaking service. She also used the opportunity to extract a promise from him that he would give up alcohol. Rukhsana did not hide her delight at this new development, something she and Geethanjali had not had the chance to discuss given the recent busy weeks.

They were surprised to see SI Ashraf waiting for them at the Ernakulam Junction train station. Dressed in plain clothes and carrying a box, Ashraf explained that he had learnt about their plans from Sashi and had come to deliver something valuable to Murali.

Ashraf handed the box to Murali and asked him to peek inside. Curious, Murali grabbed the box and opened the top. Inside was a gleaming chunk of metal. Murali could not believe his eyes. *Oh my God, it is Kali!* After a few seconds of silence, Murali looked at Ashraf, then smiled and hugged him.

'Ashraf, this is the most valuable gift I have ever received,' Murali said, his voice cracking. He showed Rukhsana and Shibu what was inside. 'This revolver, Kali, once belonged to General Mohan Singh, the founder of the Azad Hind Fauj. He gifted it to achan in 1942. It is my father's most prized possession. How did you find her?'

'Truthfully, on the day of the incident, I was unaware of the revolver's history. I came to learn all about Kali from Vasu sir later,' Ashraf explained. 'He told me that he had gifted Kali to you.'

'Well, it was more of a demand from me,' Murali said with a smile.

Ashraf nodded and continued. 'That is why I went back five times to search for it but was unsuccessful. As a final attempt, I hired two local fishermen yesterday, and they found it in 10 minutes. I was so relieved that I took the revolver home and gave her a thorough cleaning.'

Murali, clearly moved, responded, 'I don't know how to thank you, Ashraf. This is a splendid omen and will make achan very happy,' Murali said, before adding, 'and me too.'

'You are a good man, Ashraf,' Shibu said. 'I never got a chance to thank you for all you have done for us. You are like family now.'

'Yes, thank you so much, Ashraf... Are you off duty today?' Rukhsana asked.

'Well, there have been many developments...'

'Like what? Tell us.'

'I quit my job. The department transferred me and Commissioner Sreelekha. We learnt that the HM issued the orders before he resigned, as revenge against us for not taking action against the students who organized the blockade. Anyway, the political interference was becoming too much. I could not take this nonsense any more.'

'Well, the loss is for the Kerala Police force... What are your plans now?' Rukhsana asked.

'Well, I don't have any yet. I will figure something out...'

'Why don't you join us?' Shibu urged. 'With the possibility of an election looming, the YDSK can use the services of a security professional like you.'

'It sure sounds interesting,' Ashraf replied, intrigued.

Rukhsana stepped forward. 'Hold on. I think there is a better opportunity for Ashraf,' she said. 'With his exceptional track record of solving high-profile crime cases and as the man who took down Vaikom Karnan's assailant—'

Murali interjected playfully, 'I have something to say about that...'

Rukhsana placed a hand on Murali's arm. 'Officially, Ashraf fired all three bullets,' she said with a smile. 'The point I want to make is that Ashraf would be an unbeatable political candidate anywhere in Kerala. A tough, no-nonsense crime fighter personally mentored by "the last revolutionary". If the Muslim League dares to run a candidate against Ashraf in North Kerala, I can guarantee they will lose their security deposit. Just imagine that!'

Murali and Shibu laughed and nodded in agreement.

'Now that sounds even better,' Ashraf said with a grin. 'You have promoted me from a security officer to an MLA in five minutes. If we talk some more, maybe the offer will rise from an MLA to the role of the home minister of Kerala.'

Shibu laughed and gave Ashraf a playful slap on the back. 'The position is yours, Ashraf, provided you promise to fire Thomas Alexander on day one,' he quipped.

'I accept. If not day one, maybe day two,' Ashraf said with mock seriousness. Then his face grew serious. 'Seriously, I would rather be part of something bigger than myself, working with a group of people who, like me, have been shaped by the ideas and values of Professor Karnan.'

Murali reached out to shake hands with Ashraf. 'Welcome to the team, Ashraf.'

Shibu addressed everyone with a thoughtful expression. 'I see our movement as a continuation of the historic freedom struggle that Karnan sir and millions of men and women fought for. It will be a long struggle and may take decades—maybe even 50 years—to break the stranglehold that the Congress and the Communist Party have over the people of Kerala. But it is bound to happen one day.'

'If it takes 50 years, so be it. It's a privilege to be on the right side of history,' Rukhsana said.

'Fifty years? That will be 2031. I am not sure whether I will be alive then, but if it means a better future for our children, count me in,' Ashraf quipped. Then he said in a serious tone, 'By the way, you should also talk to Commissioner Sreelekha before we leave. She will be here for another week.'

'That is a good idea, Ashraf. I will ask my father to meet her,' Shibu said. He glanced at his watch and looked at Murali and Rukhsana. 'It's almost 8.30 p.m. Why don't you both stay at my home tonight? My parents would love to hear about our meeting with the governor. They will not believe me if I tell them what happened.'

'Yes, I would love to see how Baby amma reacts to the story,' Murali said. He hesitated and glanced at Rukhsana. 'Also, there is another reason why Rukhsana and I want to stay back in Cochin tonight...'

'Tell them, Murali,' Rukhsana encouraged.

'Tomorrow is Rukhsana's birthday. We are not planning a formal celebration as we are mourning maamen's passing, but we both want to visit the bamboo grove at Subhash Bose Park, where we first met alone.'

Shibu and Ashraf wished Rukhsana a happy birthday. Shibu invited everyone for lunch at his home the next day and Rukhsana teased Shibu that she would come only if Geethanjali was invited. Shibu readily extended the invitation to Geethanjali.

Ashraf accepted the invitation on the condition that a bottle of Velayudhan's Hercules 3X rum from his Navy quota would be served to celebrate their victories.

After Ashraf departed, Murali, Shibu and Rukhsana walked outside the train station towards the autorickshaw stand. One of the drivers, Hari, recognized Shibu and greeted him.

'Where to, Shibu sir?' Hari asked as he unfolded his mundu.

'Ah, Hari, how are you? We are headed to my home on Mills Lane.'

'Shivakadaksha Bhavan, right?' Hari said. He turned around and shouted to his friends, who were resting under a tree listening to music on the radio. 'Everyone, come and meet the YDSK leaders Shibu, Murali and Rukhsana.'

The radio stopped playing. About two dozen autorickshaw drivers emerged from the shadows. Hari introduced one of them—a bearded man wearing a khaki shirt and a black lungi—as Johnson, president of the Cochin City Autorickshaw Drivers Union.

Johnson stepped forward to shake hands with Shibu. 'Most of us are good friends with your elder brother, Sashi. Because of him, about 50 auto drivers were in the crowd when you fought the deputy superintendent in front of Medical Trust Hospital. You fought very bravely and did not need us. We respect that.'

'What did you expect? He is the son of an officer of the Indian Navy,' Hari said.

'Believe me, Johnson, I was just getting started. Alexander escaped only because my mother came in the way,' Shibu said.

'It sure was an epic battle!' Johnson exclaimed as he extended his hand to Shibu. 'We were all mesmerized watching you, your father, mother and brothers all in action at the same time.' He reached down to fold his lungi loosely around his knees. 'I can tell you this much—if the police officer had dared to hurt your mother, we would have all stepped into the arena and broken his backbone.' Johnson spat on the ground, cursing, '*Polayadi mon!*'

After a brief silence, Rukhsana spoke up. 'Johnson, which party is your union affiliated with?'

'The Communist Marxist party. But we are unhappy with how the Left Front government has treated us. We are reviewing our political alliances,' Johnson replied.

'We need to talk, Johnson,' Murali said. 'The Kerala Taxi Drivers' Union led by Abdul Navaz is now aligned with the YDSK. We would like to get your support too.'

Johnson nodded his consent. 'Abdul is my mentor and friend. If he is in, so are we.'

Shibu placed an arm on Johnson's shoulder. 'Thank you, Johnson. We want your support, but we also want to earn it. Before you decide, we would like to know what problems auto drivers face and have an honest discussion about what we can help with and what we cannot.'

'See, Johnson. I told you. This is honesty!' Hari exclaimed. 'We have not heard these words from any party leaders before. I support the YDSK.'

'Yes, we are very much open to that discussion. I was thinking of talking to Sashi about it,' Johnson said. 'By the way, how did your meeting with the governor go?'

'How did you know about that?' Rukhsana asked.

'It must have been the Congress MLAs who came after us,' Shibu whispered to Rukhsana.

'Well, the news is all over the radio. The three of you are young revolutionaries, but you have already sacrificed a lot,' Hari said.

Her grandfather's diary notes of the extreme hardships he faced as a young freedom fighter flashed through Rukhsana's mind. *Leaving home at a young age...hunted, arrested, beaten, repeatedly jailed, and forced to sacrifice the love of his life... Compared to that, what we have done is nothing,* she thought. Still, she decided to keep the conversation going.

'That's good to know, but remember, we are young

revolutionaries without money in our pockets,' Rukhsana said. 'Please don't charge us more for the auto ride just because we are in the news.'

The auto drivers assembled around them erupted in laughter. Shibu shook hands with Johnson and promised that his brother would set up a meeting with him the following week.

Shibu followed Murali and Rukhsana into Hari's autorickshaw. Hari sat in the driver's seat and bent down to pull the lever to crank the engine. The engine roared to life on the third attempt. Hari half-turned around in his seat.

'This ride is on me,' he said. 'After this trip, I can go home and tell my two daughters that their father gave a ride to three young revolutionaries today, and one of them was the girl in scarlet hijab.' He hesitated and added, 'Rukhsana madam, my younger daughter, Lakshmi, wanted to know the reason you chose scarlet. It is her favourite colour.'

Shibu exchanged glances with Rukhsana and Murali. 'She will tell you, but only if you and Lakshmi agree to become life members of the YDSK,' he said with a serious look.

As Murali and Rukhsana burst out laughing, Hari also joined in the merriment.

Acknowledgements

I WAS WARNED THAT THE JOURNEY OF A FIRST-TIME AUTHOR is difficult, lonely and often bewildering. This was not a lie. While most authors practise their craft in solitude, I quickly realized that no creative work is accomplished in isolation. No author can solely claim all the credit for their work. Writing is almost always influenced by people, past events in the authors' lives and the materials they may have read, seen, heard or experienced.

The constant encouragement and tough love of my first fan, my late mother, Baby Velayudhan, remain the wind beneath my wings. She celebrated even the most trivial articles I wrote in high school and her support will forever inspire me.

When I encountered obstacles in the storytelling process, which happened often, memories from my childhood in Kochi came to my rescue. I would let my mind drift to those bygone days—walking to the Ernakulam Shiva Temple with my grandparents, listening to stories of their younger days in British India or about Mahatma Gandhi's visit to Kerala; the excitement of being a student political leader in college; the tales my brothers shared during the dark days of the national Emergency in India about the exploits of Jayaprakash Narayan; and the long nights spent with relatives and friends watching plays and storytelling events at temple festivals. I am forever indebted to them.

Creating something original and staying the course long enough often brings unexpected gifts in the form of angels who appear to help along the way. For me, one such individual was Pradnya Desai, my former student, a thoughtful reader of fiction with magical editorial skills far beyond her young years. She was my first reader and dedicated hours to editing and providing feedback that significantly improved this story. I cannot thank her enough and am confident that she will become a great author in the future.

I am deeply grateful to my wife, Neerja, and son, Yuvraaj, for giving me the time and space to undertake and complete this project. Additionally, my sister Shashikala, aunt Geetha and nieces Vandana and Sreevidya were vital members of my early readers' circle. Experts who provided encouragement, advice and guidance include noted Malayalam writer and IAS officer K. Jayakumar, the well-known historian and writer Manu S. Pillai, Malayalam film and TV actress Mallika Sukumaran, my mentor Dr Madhavan Pillai, former editor of *The Indian Express* and *Outlook* magazine S.B. Easwaran and literary consultant Aiswarya Thara Bhai. I also appreciate the feedback from my friends Dr C.V. Sreenivasan, Chitra Suresh, P.M. Carriappa, Lata Setty, Neetha Raman, Dinesh Gurpur, Sandeep and Soma Vyas, Anu Raina and Jayamohan Pillai. Each of them played an important part in helping me take a small but critical step towards completing my over-two-year journey from an idea to a book.

I am indebted to my friends Bhaskar Majumdar and M.K. Srinivasan for introducing me to Mr Dibakar Ghosh, Editorial Director at Rupa Publications, helping me bypass the dreaded 'slush piles' of overworked literary agents. Amid the long delays inherent in the traditional book submission process, the speed and professionalism of Rupa Publications was a breath of fresh air. I am grateful to Mr Ghosh for believing in me and the potential of my story. His excellent suggestions enhanced the intrigue and deepened the connection between the plot and the title. He did me a great favour by introducing me to Anupama Roy, my editor at Rupa. She balanced speed with precision and attention to detail in ways that greatly enhanced the readability of my story. I cannot thank her enough.

I am also thankful to my pre-publication developmental editors—Laurie Chittenden, Jordan Mulligan and Susan DeFreitas—for challenging me to improve my story by adding conflict. I am grateful to my sensitivity reader, Eman El-Badawi, who, despite her busy role as mayor of Cranbury, New Jersey, took the time to offer many excellent suggestions. Special thanks go to Ramesh Babu for doing an outstanding job with the Malayalam translation and to Vandana for her proofreading support.

Furthermore, I sincerely appreciate every member of my advanced copy review and book launch teams for their invaluable contributions. I gained extensive knowledge about writing, publishing and marketing thanks to the organizers of literary conferences such as the Jaipur Literature Festival, Writer's Digest, the Kauai Writers Conference and Bound India.

As this story is about heroism, with a woman as the protagonist, and is set in Kerala, it would be remiss not to acknowledge the brave women of the Kerala film industry, whose steadfast courage has exposed cowardly criminals and ignited the MeToo movement in the state. These women are fighting for their freedom and deserve our support. I stand with them.

Finally, I am most grateful to you, dear readers, for taking a chance on an unknown author.

Thank you!

Glossary

Acha/Achan	Malayalam word for 'father' (Hindus in Kerala address their fathers this way.)
Alvida	Hindi term for 'goodbye'
Amma	Malayalam word for 'mother' (Hindus in Kerala address their mothers this way.)
Ammachi	Malayalam word for 'mother' (Christians in Kerala address their mothers this way.)
Amumma	Malayalam word that means 'mother's mother' or 'grandmother'
Appachan	Malayalam word for 'father' (Christians in Kerala address their fathers this way.)
Arjuna	One of the five Pandava brothers and the central protagonist of the Hindu epic *Mahabharata*.
Avalose unda	Also spelled Avaloseunda, it refers to a traditional snack made of roasted rice flour balls flavoured with cardamom, sweetened with jaggery and mixed with freshly grated coconut.
Bidi	A type of cheap cigarette made of unprocessed tobacco wrapped in leaves.
Beta	Originally means 'son' but people may also affectionately address their daughters this way.
Bhai	Hindi word for 'brother'
Bharathapuzha	'River of Bharata', also known as the Nila or Ponnani River; it is the second-longest river in Kerala.
Bharatiya	Hindi word for 'Indian'
Bhargavi Nilayam	Translates to 'House of Bhargavi'; this was a 1960s hit movie that featured the ghost of a woman wearing a white sari that haunted the home she was killed in.
Brahmastra	Divine weapon that is capable of destroying the universe.
Charkha	Spinning wheel that was used to make cotton in India.
Charminar	A cigarette brand named after the Charminar monument in Telangana, India.
Charu kasera	Traditional easy chair

Chechi	Malayalam word for 'older sister'
Chetta/chettan	Malayalam word for 'elder brother'
Dupatta	A garment worn by Indian women; it is similar to a scarf and can be worn in different ways.
Durga Maa	Hindi for 'Mother Durga'; it is a term of address for Goddess Durga, another name for the Hindu goddess Kali.
Ekalavya	A skilled self-taught archer from the *Mahabharata*, an Indian epic.
Gayatri Mantra	A Sanskrit mantra (chant) written during the Vedic period (1500-500 BC).
Gunda	A hired criminal
Idukki	The name of a district in the state of Kerala known for its hilly terrain.
Inquilab zindabad	Literal translation: 'Long live revolution'.
Inshallah	An expression which means 'if God wills'—commonly used by Muslims.
Jai Hind	A patriotic greeting in Hindi that means 'Victory to India' (Hindustan).
Jamanthi	A holy flower often used in Indian rituals
Kalaripayattu	A form of martial arts practised in Kerala
Kali	Another form of Goddess Durga
Kappa and meen	A popular traditional dish of Kerala comprising boiled tapioca and fish curry
Karimeen	A variety of fish beloved by the people of Kerala
Kavach	Body armour
Kerala People's Arts Club	Abbreviated as KPAC, is a famous theatrical organization in the state of Kerala formed in 1950 that was influential in popularizing the communist movement.
Khadi	A cloth woven by hand in India during the Indian freedom struggle.
Kurukshetra War	Described in the ancient epic *Mahabharata*, this event serves as the foundation of the sacred Hindu text, the Bhagavad Gita (the 'Song by God').
Lakh	Is equal to one hundred thousand
Lathi	A stick carried by Indian police officers as a weapon
Maamen/Ammavan	Malayalam word for 'uncle'

Mahabali	A revered king of ancient Kerala
Makkalae	Malayalam word for 'children'; often used by parents as a term of endearment.
Masala dosa	A popular South Indian breakfast where a crispy crepe made of fermented rice and lentil batter is served with flavourful spiced potato filling.
Mathrubhumi	Motherland
Molay (or Mol)	'Daughter' in Malayalam; a term of endearment used by elders to address young girls.
Mone (or Mon)	'Son' in Malayalam
Mundu	A sarong-like cotton garment that is worn around the waist in the Indian states of Kerala, Tamil Nadu, the Lakshadweep archipelago and the Maldives.
Murappennu	Maternal uncle's daughter
Muthachan	'Grandfather' in Malayalam
Mutton biryani	It is a popular one-pot meal made using long-grain basmati rice layered with a spicy mutton (goat meat) layer, fried onions, fried cashew nuts, fried raisins and saffron milk.
Naadan	Doing things the local (Kerala) way
Nadaga gananal	Songs found in the dramas usually performed at temple festivals
Nair, Namboodiri	Affluent upper-caste families in Kerala
Namaskaram	Malayalam version of namaste, an Indian greeting used when people meet.
Onam	The annual harvest festival celebrated by Malayalis in Kerala or in any other part of the world to mark the homecoming of the Great King Mahabali.
Oru Desathinte Katha	Malayalam for 'The Story of a Country'
Pappadum	Traditional crispy flatbread made from lentil flour and deep fried
Pazham pori	Banana fritters
Polayadi mon	Curse word in Malayalam that translates to 'bastard'.
Red Fort trials	Also known as the INA trials, it was the British Indian trial by court-martial of several officers of the Indian National Army between November 1945 and May 1946 on charges of treason.
Saab	Hindi word for sir; a term used to convey respect.

Salwar kameez	A garment worn by Indian women, consisting of loosely pleated trousers, a long kurta extending below the knees, and a dupatta.
Sankhupushpam	A holy flower often used in Indian rituals
Sari	A garment worn by Indian women
Satyagraha	Hindi term that means 'search for truth' and stands for a form of non-violent resistance or protest advocated by Mahatma Gandhi.
Swayamvaram	Sanskrit word for the ceremony held in ancient India where a girl of marriageable age chooses a husband from a group of suitors by placing a garland around his neck.
Talwar	HMIS (His Majesty's Indian Ship) Talwar (meaning 'sword' in Hindi) was a British Royal Indian Navy warship that was located at Colaba, Bombay Harbour, during the Second World War.
Thulam	A Malayalam month roughly coinciding with October
Tulsi	A medicinal plant, which has religious importance; also known as 'Indian basil'
Umma	Malayalam word for 'mother', used by Muslims in Kerala
Ummama	Malayalam word for 'grandmother' (mother's mother), used by Muslims in Kerala
Uppa	Malayalam word for 'father', used by Muslims in Kerala
Uppapa	Malayalam word for 'grandfather', used by Muslims in Kerala
Uthara	A princess in the Hindu epic *Mahabharata*, known for her beauty and dancing skills
Vaikom Satyagraha	A non-violent, anti-untouchability movement in Travancore from 1924 to 1925 led by Congress leaders T.K. Madhavan, E.V. Ramaswamy, Sree Narayana Guru, and Mahatma Gandhi.
Vigyan Bhavan	A premier conference venue of the Government of India in New Delhi

Author's Note

Dear Reader,

This novel will forever remain close to my heart—not only because it is my first book but also because it explores the qualities of the human heart that I most admire: courage, love and sacrifice. Written during a time when I faced the first major health crisis of my life, which coincidentally, was related to my heart, this book became an extremely personal journey. The experience of unearthing my past to write this story helped me rediscover myself, realign my priorities and reconnect with my roots.

Another reason this book is so special is that many of the characters are inspired by people dear to me. They include my parents, Baby and Velayudhan; my grandparents, Kalyani and Kandappi; my brothers, Sashi and Shibu; my sister, Shashikala; my uncle, Sivadas; and my aunts, Joy, Chandrika and Geetha. Had they been confronted by the fictional events I have imagined for this story, I have no doubt that their actions would have been along the lines I have depicted. I also loved setting this story against the backdrop of one of my favourite places on earth—the city of Kochi (formerly Cochin), Kerala, India—a place so unique that ancient mariners referred to it as the 'Queen of the Arabian Sea'.

The idea of a small group of people standing up to enemies far more powerful than themselves, willing to fight and die for their values, has always sparked my imagination—whether it's the Spartans' heroic stand against the mighty Persian Empire at Thermopylae, the Indian revolutionary Chandrashekhar Azad taking his own life to keep his promise of never being captured alive by the British, the young Allied soldiers being showered with bullets on the distant shores of Normandy, France, in 1944, the Azad Hind Fauj's dream of freeing their motherland, or the modern-day Ukrainians facing overwhelming odds.

Even more fascinating to me is the figure of the lone revolutionary—

the one person who fights on, knowing it's a losing battle but finding meaning in the struggle itself. This idea forms the heart of my novel, which had been brewing in my mind for a long time.

The seed of this story was planted on a hot summer day when I was in the eighth grade. I followed my older brother, Sashi Kumar, to a literary event in Kochi, featuring the renowned Malayalam writer Sukumar Azhikode. After the event, we noticed a young girl standing in line to meet the writer. Her head covering and focused demeanour left a lasting impression on me. For reasons I cannot comprehend or explain, that fuzzy image—an ageing writer at the pinnacle of his fame and a young female fan hoping to have a word with him—persisted in my mind.

Over the years, I imagined countless stories around these two characters. How did the author develop the ability to speak and write with such eloquence? Could he have been a freedom fighter…or maybe a future chief minister? Was the girl just a reader or a die-hard fan? Was she somehow related to him… A secret admirer? Decades passed but my questions remained unresolved. I secretly tucked away these little nuggets of creative thoughts in my mind and whenever time permitted I revived them and nurtured the storyline.

In 2022, I finally embarked on the exciting journey of putting pencil to paper (yes, I hand-wrote the first and second drafts). It took me over two years of writing, revising, editing, embellishing and rewriting to get this story where it is today. What started as a hobby soon became an obsession. I wrote late into the night after my family went to bed. Into the wee hours of the morning, my thoughts would often drift to the conversations I had with my father long back—his experience as a young sailor hired to support the war efforts of the Royal Indian Navy, working on the deck of the ships docked at Bombay Harbour and dreaming of serving a free nation. These stories, along with the countless conversations with my grandfather, mother and brothers about politics, freedom fighters and heroism became central to my novel.

As my story unfolded, fascinating characters emerged, a composite of multiple real-life people I knew or had read about. I especially loved incorporating larger-than-life historical figures such as Mahatma

Gandhi, Jayaprakash Narayan, Ram Manohar Lohia, T.K. Madhavan, E.K. Nayanar and President Sanjiva Reddy into my story. Often, when I reread the chapters that I had written, the raw emotions of the story gripped me by the throat (and heart) and forced me to do better. More research, more character development, more conflict and countless revisions. I wrote parts of this novel in 13 countries and in various locations—my study, cafés, airports, trains and even in my car while waiting for my son at the swimming school. When I got stuck, I travelled to new places to refresh my mind.

Throughout the writing process, I sought inspiration from authors whose work I admire, including President Barack Obama, Senator John McCain, Alex Haley, Delia Owens, Amish Tripathi, Arundhati Roy, M.T. Vasudevan Nair, K.R. Meera, Thakazhi S. Pillai, Dr Shashi Tharoor, Dr Abraham Verghese, Jhumpa Lahiri, Chitra Banerjee Divakaruni, Khaled Hosseini, Mark Sullivan, Kate Quinn, Anthony Doerr, Taylor Jenkins Reid and Mark Zusak. While they are in a league of their own, I carry a quiet hope that their writing magic may somehow rub off on me.

Though this book is fictional, I have strived to remain true to the major real-world events of that time. Key historical events woven into my story include Mahatma Gandhi's visit to Vaikom, Kerala, in 1925, Jayaprakash Narayan's escape from Hazaribagh Jail in 1942, the establishment of the Azad Dasta, the mutiny of the Royal India Navy in 1946 and the fall of the Nayanar government in 1981. Some incidents and dialogues I imagined for this story are inspired by quotes from books, movies and plays I encountered growing up. Fans of the Kerala People's Arts Club (KPAC) will recognize the incident where Baby asks her son Shibu to hand her the flag to challenge the police, as being inspired by the popular 1950s' Malayalam drama *Ningalenne Communistakki* ('You Made Me a Communist'), which I first watched as a young boy growing up in Cochin in the 1970s. The scene where Shibu taunts the police officer with the line 'Want this flag? Come get it' was inspired by Steven Pressfield's spectacular novel *Gates of Fire* (1998). These, mixed with personal reflections, brought my characters to life and, in turn, resurrected my spirits and recharged my creative zeal.

For information on historical events, politics, culture and freedom fighters of India, I relied on various sources ranging from the treasure trove of Amar Chitra Katha's comic collections to online news articles, Government of India websites and Wikipedia reports. Additionally, I referenced works of esteemed Indian historians such as Dr Bimal Prasad and Sujata Prasad, Professor A. Sreedhara Menon, Mr Sukumar Azhikode and Professor K.N. Panikkar, who have diligently chronicled the activities of leaders and events that have shaped modern India.

My goal with this book is to bring to light the unknown heroes of India's freedom struggle and tell their stories in a way that compels readers, especially the younger ones, to ask: did such events really happen? Did people like these really exist? I hope some readers will dig deeper and realize, as I did, that history is often as much about what is unsaid as what is recorded—and sometimes, facts can be stranger than fiction.

Ultimately, this novel is a labour of love—love for the land of my birth, India, her brave sons and daughters, and the incredible diversity that makes her the nation she is today. I hope to have captured but a tiny fraction of that uniqueness.

I hope you enjoyed reading this book as much as I did writing it. I invite you to visit my website https://authorsureshkumar.com/books/ and sign up for my newsletter so we can stay connected. Your support means the world to me, and I hope to bring you more stories in the future. Thank you for your patronage.

∞

Book Review Request

Thank you for reading this book!

If you enjoyed it, I would greatly appreciate it if you could write an honest review on Amazon, Goodreads or any other platform of your choice. I read every review, and your feedback will help new readers discover my book.

Sincerely,
Suresh U. Kumar